LILAC
COTTAGE

LILAC COTTAGE

By
CARRIE FANCETT PAGELS

Hearts Overcoming Press

Mackinac Cottages Series
Book 2

ISBN: 978-1-7366875-6-7

Cover Design by: Ampersand Book Design

Hearts Overcoming Press

Published in the USA

DEDICATION

To:
Tamara Tomac

One of the sweetest ladies I have ever known,
and a true blessing to me and my writing ministry!

MACKINAC COTTAGES SERIES:

Book 1: Butterfly Cottage

Book 2: Lilac Cottage

Associated book: Behind Love's Wall—Contemporary Section of the Dual Timeline

*Author's Notes, Acknowledgements, Bio
and Social Media information
are at the back of this novel.*

Characters List

Heroine: Sadie "Rachel" Dunmara, 25
    (Gram Margaret Dunmara - heroine's grandmother)
    (Judge Raymond Dunmara - federal judge in Chicago, deceased 12 years)
    Selma Dunmara - Rachel's mother
    [Sadie Duvall Swaine & Robert Swaine – Margaret's grandparents, Rachel's great-grandparents]

Hero: Jack Welling, turning 30
    (Olivia Welling - Jack's younger sister)
    [Jack is the great-great-nephew of Jack Welling, Sr., his namesake]

Second heroine: Kareen Parker, mid 70s, (deceased husband is Hampy Parker)
    Gianni Franchetti, late 60's - Kareen's secret new husband
    (Sylvia - Gianni's deceased wife)
    Maria Parker - Kareen's daughter-in-law, mid 50s
    Hamp Parker – Kareen's son, mid 50s
    Carter Parker, 22 - Kareen's grandson
    Hampton Parker III "Parker", 26 – Kareen's grandson, Carter's brother
    Maria's grandsons: RJ, Sean, and Austin

Andrette Brown Herron - manager of Lucky Bean
    Carolyn May – Owner of Lucky Bean
    Juan Pablo Gomez – barista
    Starr Bourne – barista

Dawn & Jim Charbonneau, family friends of the Dunmaras, and owners of Butterfly Cottage
    Jaycie Charbonneau Parker, Dawn & Jim's daughter, Hampton ("Parker") Parker III's wife
    [Dawn is the granddaughter of Jack Welling, Sr., daughter of Jack Welling, Jr.]

Linda Sorensen – Police Department Administrator
Joy Ellis – Bank Manager

Prologue

Chicago, January 2022

*S*he's stopped speaking." Not the words Rachel wanted to hear from the nightshift nurse, who always gave Rachel the straight scoop on her grandmother. The RN's words slit Rachel's heart like a surgical scalpel.

Talking with Gram had kept Rachel going. *Oh God, now that I've found You, Abba Father, don't take her away from me.*

"Are you alright?" Nurse Nancee gently touched Rachel's shoulder.

Rachel compressed her lips. If Gram never spoke again then how could her world be all right? This failing woman had been her best friend and a better mother than her own mom. Gram had been her rock. Rachel drew in a slow, shuddering breath.

"Why don't you come sit down by her and hold her hand?" Nancee pointed to the upholstered chair adjacent to the bed, at a spot Rachel knew well.

She dipped her chin. The confusion and loneliness swirling in her head were worse than when the Admiral had left her and Mom. Her third stepfather, the Admiral, as she called him, had been her favorite. Then he'd left them, promising Rachel he'd keep in touch—but he hadn't. She sniffed.

How can I do this? How could she manage without Gram's practical advice? Without the kindly woman's laughter that grounded her to the moment, keeping her from trailing off into her frequent reviews of choices and outcomes that left her feeling helpless and confused?

"Gram? It's Rachel. I'm here."

No response. Gram lay curled on her side, away from her. Her grandmother normally woke when Rachel visited, almost daily, depending on her work and online college schedules.

No. This can't be happening. Not now. "I need you, Gram." Rachel scooched the chair closer to the bed.

Still nothing.

What would she do if Gram never came back? Never spoke again? She'd been warned when Gram stopped eating, that would be the end.

She clasped her hands together hard. Still, she should be grateful Gram was being well cared for in a beautiful facility. She had to take comfort in that fact.

Rachel bowed her head. *Lord, help Gram and her caretakers. Be with the nurses and doctors and guide them. Amen.* The scent of roses and gardenias carried from the nearby table. Rachel had splurged with her bonus from work. At least Gram had her favorite flowers nearby.

The door creaked open, allowing soft laughter and voices in conversation to carry through.

"Hi again." Nurse Nancee moved toward the bed. "I wanted to ask you about something."

Nancee's serious tone put her on notice.

"Sure." Rachel straightened.

"I was wondering about your mother." She gave a little shrug. "I've never met her."

"Yeah, I don't think she's ever visited." *No surprise there.*

"That's what the records show." Nancee's soft features bunched together.

"She'd only be here if it benefited her in some way." *Like monetarily.*

"Your grandmother said your mom was a complete narcissist— sorry I don't mean to offend you, but that's what she said."

"Right. I understand." Rachel pushed a lock of hair from her forehead. *Which is why I've lived with Gram since I was sixteen.*

"Your grandmother said she didn't know what she'd done wrong with your mom. I assured her that you can do everything right and still get a child who goes off the rails." Nancee shook her head slowly. "I've been through that with my son."

"I'm not sure if my mom ever got *on* the rails to begin with." Rachel raised her eyebrows. "I'm sorry Gram feels bad about it, though."

Nancee slacked her hip, her expression serious. "I wondered if your grandmother had ever done power of attorney for you. Did she?"

"We were just talking about that." Did Gram realize she was near the end? "Gram was supposed to call Sharon Dardanes from the Lyonis law firm." The petite attorney was Gram's lawyer and Mr. Lyonis had been her grandfather's longtime legal consultant and lawyer.

Nancee drew in a deep breath. "Because *if* your mother is next of kin—which I understand she is and an only child—then she could end up making decisions from here on out."

Her breath left her. Rachel forced herself to inhale slowly. "I'll call Mrs. Dardanes and see if Gram did that."

The nurse's blue eyes filled with compassion. "I just wanted to let you know. Because if there are any decisions we need to make, then you've got to have that power of attorney. Okay?"

"Yes. Thank you for telling me." Her hands began to shake, and she clasped them in her lap. She and Gram had never thought this day would come so quickly—when Gram couldn't communicate her wishes.

"I'll be praying for you, Rachel."

"Thanks, Nancee." The sweet nurse had become a friend.

"And don't forget to email me about my alma mater in Michigan. They've expanded their nursing program."

"Will do."

Nancee had been a blessing. She'd advised Rachel about nursing training programs and shared her own experiences. When Gram was gone, Rachel would miss her time with Nancee, too.

When the door closed behind the nurse, Rachel put her head down on the bed and stretched a hand for her grandmother's back. *Don't go yet, Gram.*

Alone. Rachel would be fully alone.

Never will I leave you nor forsake you. Rachel swiped at her eyes. Pastor's words—from the Bible—needed to be true.

They had to be.

Chapter One

Outside Chicago, April 2022

*M*aybe it was the double shift of waitressing the day before, or maybe it was having to wait a half hour while her roomie finished her long bath, or maybe the lack of caffeine—but Rachel's head threatened to explode. She knocked on the rickety wooden bathroom door. Although the building was rundown, at least the apartment was in one of suburban Chicago's safer neighborhoods.

"I'll be out in two minutes," Leesa called, a mix of forced humor and annoyance in her voice.

Two minutes meant five. The scent of French roast carried down the hallway. At least someone had brewed coffee that morning. She exited the hall to the kitchen, which was a wreck. Stray spaghetti noodles clung to the side of a pan. A glob of tomato sauce lingered at the bottom of the sink which was littered with salad remnants. A quarter of a baguette, smeared with garlic spread, sat atop a crumb-dotted plate. Rachel had just bought the makings for a spaghetti dinner the day before when she'd shopped for the week—and Leesa and her date had used them. She clenched her fists so hard that her fingernails bit into her palms.

At least the coffee, that blessed fluid, was indeed brewed. She poured herself a cup and added some French vanilla creamer to sweeten it. She grabbed the bakery box from the dining room table. Only one of the Boston creams was left. They'd been a rare treat that she'd bought for herself. She grabbed the last one and downed it with her coffee. She'd lost eighty pounds in the past year—not on purpose—and was told she couldn't afford to lose more. Her limited wardrobe certainly screamed that fact, too.

When Rachel returned to the hallway by the bath, Leesa stood there, wrapped in a towel and wearing a sheepish look.

"Morning." Rachel's voice came out halfway between a grumble and forced cheerfulness. She'd taken Leesa's shift at the diner yesterday because her roomie was out "sick" but was actually on a day trip with her boyfriend.

Leesa grinned. "It's a great day."

Rachel bit back a retort. The thing getting her through, was looking forward to the wonderful Easter services that her church was planning. This would be her first year fully embracing her faith, and she couldn't wait to participate in all they were offering.

"Hey, I need a favor."

Not another. Rachel lowered her head. She was about bankrupt in favors doled out to her roomie.

When she didn't respond, Leesa continued, "My new squeeze wants to stay over tonight and it might be kinda awkward, well. . ."

And where was Rachel supposed to go? Sleep in her car again? She swallowed hard. The church parking lot had worked out pretty well the last time. "Do I have an option?" *Like no—he can't stay here?*

"Well, not really. I do have the lease after all."

Rachel sucked in a breath and met Leesa's smug look. It was true. But Rachel was paying half the rent now. They'd have to have a convo about this tomorrow. It was time to confront her. Rachel's safety was at risk.

"Great. I appreciate it." Leesa's tone said otherwise.

"You're coming to work, though, right?" Another double shift was out of the question.

"Yeah, but I need to swap you. I'll do early and you do late. Okay?"

"Sure." Work the afternoon shift and then sleep in the back of Gram's sedan in the church parking lot. *What could be better than that?*

A few hours later, at two o'clock, Rachel entered Pop's Diner, as chill air swept into the place with her. They didn't call Chicago the Windy City for nothing.

"Leesa just left." Her boss, Jeremy, jerked a thumb over his shoulder.

Waitresses were supposed to overlap by fifteen minutes so they could communicate any needs about the tables. Rachel shook her head.

"She said to tell you all the regulars have been topped off with coffee and there's just one order outstanding. That's for table two."

"Thanks." She put her belongings away just as Cook dinged the bell.

"Two is up," Cook called out.

Rachel turned and spotted two full ham dinners. She whisked the plates to her tray and delivered them to table two.

The couple were regulars, Smitty a retired accountant, and his wife who ran a nonprofit in downtown Chicago.

"Hey, doll, good to see ya." Smitty beamed up at her, his blue eyes flashing.

"Good to see you both, too." Rachel slid his wife's plate in front of her.

"That other waitress, the smart-alecky one, tried to get Smitty to pay before she left but I wouldn't let him."

"No?" Rachel placed the elderly gentleman's food before him.

"She was right." Smitty crinkled his nose. "I think she wanted her tip before she left."

"But you're doing the work." His wife tapped her hand on the table.

Once again Leesa was trying to take advantage of Rachel's goodwill. The couple's coffee cups were empty, despite what her roommate had told Cook. "Let me get a refill on that coffee. And I don't see your water glasses." Rachel frowned.

"Oh, you're such a dear. Yes, we didn't want to bother that Leesa. She seemed so distracted."

The sweet couple always had water with their meal, though. "I'll take care of it."

"Thanks, doll."

Rachel would definitely have a conversation with Leesa later. *Well past time.*

The afternoon shift was busy. With the day so drizzly and cold, more customers streamed in all evening long. But now, they were ready to close. A headache pulsed at her temples.

Jeremy cocked his head. "You okay, Rachel?"

She forced a smile. She should be happy, she'd earned enough tips that night to fill the gas tank many times over plus contribute to the Easter collection at church. Leesa sure had the good shift when it came to better-tipping customers. The better earnings from the previous night hadn't been a fluke. She'd earned four times as much in tips as she normally did on both later shifts.

"No, I'm fine." Except she was drop-dead tired and dreaded camping out again like a homeless person. She'd paid hard-earned money for her rent.

"Good. I'm gonna lock up in a minute and then let's talk." He scratched beneath his nose.

"Talk?" That didn't bode well. Her gut clenched.

"Yeah. The last customer is leaving now."

Jeremy followed the man to the swinging glass door. "Goodnight, Mr. Johnson. See you tomorrow?"

"Sure thing." The elderly man stepped out into the night air and hunched his shoulders forward.

Rachel went to the table where sweet Mr. Johnson had been seated. It was nearly spotless. She wiped a few crumbs and cleared the remaining water glass. He'd left a dollar. Maybe that was all he could afford. Leesa would have complained if someone had only tipped her a buck, but Rachel had come to realize the value of money. And how sometimes someone couldn't tip much. One reason she never ate out. That and being broke. She wanted to be generous, but she couldn't be. *Not right now and maybe never again. Don't say that—you'll get to be a nurse one day. It will happen. And things will be all right.*

Their cook, bus boy, cashier, and the other waitress left, one after the other until only Rachel and Jeremy remained.

Her boss pointed to a booth. His red face and averted gaze left no doubt in her mind this was not good. She needed all of her hours.

She didn't sit. "If this is bad news I'd like to be standing."

He nodded. "All right. I hate to do this, but I have to let you go."

What? Rachel's jaw spasmed. She couldn't respond.

"It's not your work. You've done a great job. I'll give you a good reference."

They had steady customers and not enough wait staff. "How will you keep up?"

He ran his tongue over his upper lip. "My wife's niece needs a job."

Her breath caught. This was so unfair. She wanted so badly to tell him that Leesa, who was a frequent no show at work, was the one who should be fired. But she suspected her roommate might be sleeping with the manager on occasion. She wouldn't put it past either Leesa or Jeremy.

"What about my pay?" She'd just worked three shifts in the last thirty-two hours. Rachel needed that check.

"Come by in the morning and I'll have it ready." He puffed out a breath. "I'm sorry. But if I don't do this then my wife is gonna make my life—"

Rachel raised her hand. "It's all right. God provides." Wow, where did those last two words come from? She was a newbie when it came to this God-thing.

Jeremy rocked back on his heels. "Well, yeah."

"See you tomorrow."

"Yeah, yeah."

She gathered her belongings, unlocked the restaurant door, and departed as Jeremy clicked the lock shut. Something about the sound made her think of a grinding to an end but with something bigger than her job. Tears filled her eyes.

Head down, she headed toward her car, and her sleeping place for the night.

An old federal-era light on the corner, quaint but useless since it never lit, suddenly sputtered. Rachel straightened. Fireworks seemed to go off in the thing. Was it going to explode? Fear clutched her heart. Then a soft warm glow filled the white globe at the top. A pure white light glowed on the street, casting a path to her car.

Chills shot up and down her arms as she stared in disbelief.

Jeremy had cursed that light regularly. Leesa called it useless. Yet here it was giving her light as she crossed the street to the car.

She unlocked the car, got in and relocked the door. Soft light illuminated the contents of her grandmother's sedan. She'd placed several blankets on top of her sleeping bag and pillow in the back. Would she be safe tonight? Somehow that renewed light seemed a message that she would be.

As she started the car and then pulled into the street, she looked in her rearview mirror. The light went out again. Her hands trembled on the steering wheel. Was God trying to tell her something?

He was with her. *Absolutely.*

This car was the one thing in the world that she had. She still thought of it as Gram's though.

There's more. That thought came from out of nowhere.

Gram's cottage was there. *Unoccupied.*

But I'd be trespassing. No. Not an option.

She drove on to the church's large and secluded parking lot. A safe area. She had no other options. Too bad the couture shop where she'd worked had closed. That upstairs apartment had been a godsend.

There's more.

That was a silly thought, because she'd exhausted favors sleeping over on her handful of friends' couches.

Her apartment was paid through the month. She'd have to stand up to Leesa and tell her she was not going to sleep in her car again.

Rachel parked, cut the engine, and went to the back. Strange to think that in a couple of weeks, this lot would be filled with a menagerie of animals for the children's Easter service. She had really looked forward to participating whenever she was off from work. She'd imagined herself basking in the joy and reverence of what the Lord had done for them. *For me.* Pastor Michael's preached that Jesus would have gone to the cross even for only one of them. She drew in a deep breath, humbled by that thought. She settled into the backseat, then covered herself as fully as she could. How did homeless people manage to do this every night? *God, keep me and everyone in a situation like mine safe, too.*

She slept fitfully. Images of Gram's cottage, of her friends at Mackinac, of her neighbor and best friend who'd suddenly stopped writing to Rachel, all mixed together like a slideshow of turquoise-colored water, lighthouses, bicycling, fudge shops and carriage rides.

Rapping on the window and woke her. Had someone seen her there? She opened her eyes. Light filtered through the gaps in her blankets. It was later than she should be leaving. *Oh no.*

She pulled back her coverings.

Reverend Michaels gazed at her through the window.

"Rachel? What are you doing here?" he called.

An hour later, after cleaning up inside the church restroom and changing clothes, Rachel thanked her pastor and headed to the restaurant.

Cook tapped an empty spot at the counter. "Come on I'll make you the morning special."

Her stomach growled in agreement. "Thanks." She hung her coat and took a seat on the red vinyl covered stool.

Someone giggled in a corner booth. Rachel swiveled to spot a slim girl, with two poufs of pink and blue hair, taking an order.

"That's your replacement." Cook rolled his eyes.

The lady seated to Rachel's left shook her head slightly.

Rachel pulled her phone from her purse and checked her messages. One caught her eye. It was from Gram's friends, the Charbonneaus.

Heading to Mackinac next month. Will you be there?

Would she? Rachel rubbed the side of her head.

Cook slid a cup of coffee and a short glass of orange juice in front of her.

"Thanks."

The lady adjacent to her passed the cream and sugar containers.

"Thank you."

The scent of the fresh coffee tickled Rachel's nose. She loved coffee. Always had, since she was a little girl. Gram and Grampa had let her have it when she visited their high-rise in the city. She'd felt special having that secret treat mixed with a generous amount of cream and sugar. Mom bought every expensive type of coffee known to man and would opine on the quality of the coffee beans. Of course Mom's were always ground fresh. She'd have Rachel refill her cup for her, bring her creamer and specialty sugars—and never allow her a sip.

If only Mom's issues were limited to coffee.

Lilac Cottage

Mom was a toxic narcissist. Just knowing and finally realizing it had finally set Rachel free from her guilt over being 'not enough.' That and years of therapy with Dr. Svendsen that Gram had paid for after Rachel had moved in with her. *And now getting refined by God's grace.*

Cook slid a plate of fried eggs, hashbrowns, bacon, and toast in front of her.

"That looks good." The man to her right waggled his bushy white eyebrows. "I had the Denver omelette but I'm gettin' the special next time."

She didn't recognize him, attired in a red-and-black checkered wool jacket, faded old-style jeans, and well-worn leather work boots.

She smiled at the stranger, then looked up at Cook. "Thanks so much."

"Hey, if I could change anything. . ." Cook glanced between her and the new waitress, "I would."

"I appreciate that," her words came out in a whisper.

Her now former co-worker went back to cooking and Rachel bent her head. *Thank you, God. I need Your help. I need a new job and fast! Amen.*

As she tucked into her food, the lady to her left passed her a small bowl of jams and jellies and butter.

"Thanks."

"Did you hear about that?" The older man to her right pointed to the big TV mounted overhead in the front corner near them.

Footage of men and women appeared on the screen, attired in winter gear, stepping onto docks. *Mackinac Island docks.* She recognized them immediately despite snow topping the buildings. She strained to hear the announcer's voice, over the chatter in the restaurant.

"These passengers were stranded in the Straits of Mackinac aboard Star Line ferries when. . ."

"Ain't that somethin'?" the stranger asked.

"Icy conditions unusual for this time of year," the newscaster continued.

"Snowed up there, too." The customer leaned in as though it was a huge secret.

The television news cut to other images. Rachel took a tentative bite of her eggs.

"Don't usually get new snow this time of year on the island." The silver-haired man took a sip of his coffee.

Snow. On Mackinac. *Lilac Cottage's lawn on the West Bluff would be covered.* It would be cold. This guy seemed pretty familiar

Carrie Fancett Pagels

with the island. Had she ever run into him when she'd been up there? Doubtful. There were tens of thousands of people who came onto and off of that island daily in high season.

"Lots of those people were goin' over to start their jobs for the season." He sipped his coffee. "Lots of work up there."

Chills worked their way up her arms. She looked hard at the man next to her. He appeared to be in his fifties or sixties. Maybe Hispanic but with a distinct Yooper accent. Faded dark eyes. A kind voice. He had a weathered face that suggested he worked outdoors, and he had the clothing to match. Maybe in the logging industry which was big in Michigan's Upper Peninsula.

Rachel ate more of her eggs and considered. Most children of owners on the bluff, an area of affluent seasonal residents, did at least one summer's worth of work on the island. Not Rachel, though, unless she counted taking care of Gram. Even snotty Jack Welling, next door, had worked as a dock porter one season. That was when Rachel had first gotten to know and befriend his sister, Olivia. They'd become best friends. But Olivia had stopped responding to Rachel's letters years ago. They'd both been thirteen that last summer they were together.

She focused on the man beside her. "It seems early to be moving onto the island. The season hasn't started yet."

"Oh—but *hiring* has." He raised his dark eyebrows. "And as you saw on that news clip, the workers are already heading there."

She'd gone up only briefly the previous summer. Gram had been so sick she couldn't come with her. Rachel had flown in, taken a shuttle to Sheplers' dock in Mackinaw City, and then ferried over to the island. How many people had to take care of Gram's cottage? Rachel had met with a half dozen while she was there. Was her mother dealing with those ongoing needs for the cottage now? Rachel couldn't picture it. She tugged at the gold cross on her necklace. Gram had always told Rachel it was up to her to make sure Lilac Cottage was kept up. This was the time of year Doud's Market usually sent Gram a message asking for her order for canned goods and the like. Was Mom receiving those requests?

"You look deep in thought, miss." The man sipped his coffee. As he did so, Rachel could have sworn he looked much younger, for just a moment. His skin seemed smoother, more youthful.

She blinked hard. Perhaps it was the steam rising from the coffee and the man's enjoyment of the brew. "I, um, I imagine there are a lot of people who have to get things ready for property owners."

"Yes. That's true. And some of those folks need to get there early this year, too." The gravity in his voice, and the way he seemed to be reading her mind unnerved Rachel. "Best eat up, miss, you've got a *long day* ahead of you." He winked, set a cash tip on the counter, and departed.

Rachel stared at her food. Her empty stomach agreed that she should eat. She took some bites of the hash browns and toast. Soon her plate was almost empty.

Cook stopped in front of her again. "I've got your check. Jeremy left it for you."

What a chicken. He didn't have the courage to face her.

"Oh, and was that guy an old friend of yours?"

"No." She frowned. "I have never seen him before." Although he reminded her of someone.

"You sure?"

"Positive."

"Well, he left something for you. Said not to give it to you until he left."

Weirder and weirder. "Um, okay." She laughed nervously. What was up with this?

The lady to her left shrugged. "Hey, don't look a gift horse in the mouth they say."

Cook shook his head. "What's that supposed to mean, anyways? I've always wondered. I mean what kind of horse is a gift horse?" He grabbed the five-dollar bill that the stranger had left on the counter.

"I guess be grateful for anything you get. Any surprise gift." Rachel forked the last of the hashbrowns into her mouth. *So good.* No wonder this place kept busy despite Covid sputtering outbreaks of new variants. *Ugh. We need to get to the end of this pandemic.*

Cook bent over and when he straightened, he handed her a children's lunch box and an old red-and-black plaid tote that matched the stranger's flannel shirt. She vaguely recognized the items. A memory surged forward. Gram had given them to her at a visit. When Rachel came back to her own home after an extended visit with her grandparents, she'd brought the gift items with her. Mom had made her throw them out. Mom had screamed that Gram could afford far more than a tote and a lunch box and that she should have sent Rachel home with a check for a few thousand dollars to pay for their expenses. Mom's third husband had just left them, and he'd been footing their bills. Mom wasn't good about keeping a steady job. She'd made Rachel toss both gifts in the bin and then had her pull the trash can to the street for pickup.

Rachel had thrown the cute lunch box and the tote away, as directed. But on her way to the street, struggling with the heavy trash can, a man stepped toward her and offered to help. A Hispanic man of about forty with dark eyes and a kind voice. Rachel drew in a quick breath at the memory. But how had he found her after all these years?

"These are mine," she whispered.

"Looks like that gentleman returned them to you, hon." The lady patted Rachel's shoulder.

Maybe this was all a dream. Maybe she'd wake up in her bed in the apartment and be grateful she had a job, a place to sleep, and a car that ran well. She held the two items, which had a bit of heft to them.

"I wonder what's in them?" The older blond lady had a twinkle in her eyes.

"Let's peek inside." Rachel set the tote on her lap and opened it. The two of them looked in.

"I see a map." Cook pointed to the folded old-school paper map.

"A Michigan map." The lady grinned. "I've got friends there."

"And is that a can of cheese spray?" Cook cringed. He was a fan of genuine real cheese.

She laughed. "I used to love that stuff." She used to spray it all over Ritz crackers when she and Gram and Grampa were on their drives up to the island.

"And I see my favorite crackers." The lady pressed her hands together.

Sure enough—Ritz crackers. Rachel closed the tote, suddenly afraid to see what else might be in there. Something strange was going on. Or was the universe trying to tell her something?

"You all right, hon?"

"Yeah, I'm fine." She would be. *God has my back, right?* Now to take action. But she was exhausted.

The lady sipped her coffee and Cook refilled another customer's coffee mug.

Rachel closed her eyes for a moment. From here, she'd go to her apartment. She'd tell her roommate that there were no more sleeping in her car plans—that wasn't happening again. And she was going to get a good long nap. Then she'd get up and find another job.

Behind her, customers laughed in the booths that lined the wall. The scents of pancakes, coffee, and sizzling sausages filled the air. She opened her eyes, taking in the quaint Mom and Pop feel to the restaurant. She'd enjoyed working in this place.

Cook pointed at the items left by the stranger. "You want me to toss that old stuff that guy left?"

"No!"

He raised his eyebrows.

"Sorry, I didn't mean to snap at you. I'm just beat."

"Hey, you got a lot going on and Jeremy did you dirty. Dumb crumb bum."

Rachel pulled out her wallet and passed Cook a ten-dollar bill for the breakfast special.

He raised his hands. "On the house."

"At least let me give you a tip." She cocked her head.

"Nope. Not today, sunshine."

Moisture surged in her eyes. "I'm gonna miss you."

"We're going to miss you, too." He cast the new waitress a quick glance. "Check back with me in a couple of weeks. I wouldn't be surprised if she's gone by then."

Rachel rose. "All right. God bless you."

"And you, too." His blue eyes glistened, and he turned around.

The lady to her left patted her hand. "God go with you, miss."

She nodded. He always did. That's what Pastor said.

Rachel stole a glance back at Pop's Diner as she carried the tote and lunch box out to the car and started the motor. In her spirit, she sensed she'd never be back there. Strange how since she'd committed her life to the Lord, she had these *knowings*. She shivered, though not from the cold then drove to the apartment, determined to state her case firmly. But if Leesa already knew Rachel had been fired, then would she have any bargaining power with her roommate?

She pulled into the apartment parking lot, but her spot was taken by someone in a sky-blue Camaro with a rusty scratch down the side. *Ack!* Someone had stolen her place. She drove around until she found a designated visitor's parking spot near the dumpster and parked.

She hurried into the two-story brick building and went upstairs to their apartment, holding her breath a little because of the dank odors that lingered there. The door suddenly opened.

Leesa, wearing a silky pink nightgown, stepped out into the hallway, Rachel's suitcase in her hand. "Hey Rach. I was just going to text you."

Rachel hated being called Rach. "What's going on?" Of more concern was her belongings being shoved at her.

"My new guy is moving in and he doesn't want, ya know," she rolled her eyes, "roomies being around."

Rachel gaped at her. Her knees began to tremble.

Her roommate shoved a wad of bills at her. "That's the rest of your rent back for the month."

"What?" She was kicking her out into the street?

"Maybe ask someone at work if they can rent you a room."

That was how they'd met, when Rachel had lost her job at Gram's couture designer's shop and had applied at the restaurant around the corner.

"They let me go," Rachel croaked.

Leesa's eyes widened. "Oh, I'm sorry."

"Hey, babe, are you comin' back to bed or what?" A guy's gravelly voice called from inside.

Leesa shook her head. "Gotta go." She closed the door in Rachel's face.

Gotta go.

Where did Rachel have to go?

Chapter Two

Lower Michigan

*A*m *I really planning to break the law and trespass at Lilac Cottage?* The highway's white lines flashed past as she drove north. The keys to the Mackinac Island house cowered in the bottom of her old Michael Kors purse—a hand-me-down from Mom. So, would using those keys make her a squatter? But wasn't squatter just another word for trespasser? Rachel blew out a puff of air as she clutched the steering wheel tighter.

The locksmith had warned her last year that they'd need to replace the worn locks. What if they had finally given out? What if Mom had already had new ones put on?

How many years in jail for breaking and entering?

Gas tank now below a quarter, she took the exit off the interstate and drove to a station at the edge of an open field—its sign flickering light in the dusk. She could pay for this gas but what was she going to do for money up North? Rachel had an account in her name on the island. A very old one. But she could cash her last paycheck from Jeremy there—*if* the bank was open this early in the season. Surely, they had to be for the locals. About four hundred people lived there year-round.

"Yeah, the bank must have some hours."

Yikes, now she was talking out loud to herself. Rachel parked by a fuel pump and rubbed the side of her head. Exhaustion loomed large, brought on from the last forty-eight hours of working, sleeping in her car, and being kicked out of an apartment for which she'd paid good money. Not only that, but Leesa had kept all the groceries Rachel had just purchased. Her stomach rumbled as she pulled into the gas station's entrance.

One hundred fifty miles and almost three hours ago Rachel had sat in her car by the apartment's dumpster, wondering if she should jump in there, too. But she'd opened the checkered tote again and found a copy of the latest Mackinac Island *Town Crier*. In the Help Wanted section were two columns of jobs listings ranging from highly technical to service industry employees. Several had caught her eye.

Her favorite coffee shop, Lucky Bean, was looking for a cashier and baristas. She didn't have the barista experience, but she could ring someone up at a register with the best of them. And Mom's coffee snobbery had made Rachel somewhat of a pro in understanding what made a good cup of Joe, as Cook called it.

Also, in the ads, someone needed an assistant manager for a construction project and the pay was *sick*. So good it probably wasn't a genuine offer. She might not have all those skills, but she was a quick learner, and she needed the insane pay the project was offering. But at this rate, if she kept working these service jobs, how would she ever finish her nursing degree? She had a handful of years before she turned thirty. She prayed she could call herself Rachel Dunmara, RN, by then.

Rachel got out of the car. She shivered as she pumped the gas and then went inside to pay. She got a ten cent a gallon discount if she paid cash instead of using a card and every little bit would help. Was she shaking because of the cold or was it because of her crazy idea of becoming a squatter? Or from anger—an unwanted beast best kept at bay?

When she'd counted the money that Leesa had given her, Rachel had found that her roomie had the nerve to stiff Rachel the full amount that she owed her for the refund of the rent. Not enough cash in that wad of bills for a hotel room. And it was going to be even colder up North than it was here.

She strode into the country gas station. Her phone dinged with a text message. She pulled her old iPhone out of her coat pocket.

Gram's friend, Dawn Charbonneau, had replied. Dawn was the bomb. So sweet.

Yes, of course you can stay at Butterfly Cottage. We won't be up North until well into June. You're welcome to leave your car parked in the first spot out front while you're on the island. Help yourself to the pantry items. We'll replace all that once we get there.

It was cute how she didn't abbreviate anything in the text message. *Old School.*

TY, Rachel replied but then erased the message and retyped, *Thank you so much!* Gram had taken years to get used to the abbreviations in texting.

Oh Gram, how I miss you.

Mrs. Charbonneau texted her the code for the lock.

Maybe I should be honest and tell Gram's friend that I'm now officially homeless.

Rachel puffed out a hard breath. She'd not summoned up the nerve to tell Dawn that Gram had died. It didn't seem right texting it. Rachel hadn't worked up the courage for a phone call. And she'd kept hoping all winter that somehow she'd see Dawn and her husband, Jim, in Chicago at some point. But the couple had not returned yet from their winter home.

Inside the station, florescent lights buzzed and glared overhead but the place was warm and smelled faintly of sugar and burnt coffee.

An older woman with tinted red hair and a University of Michigan blue face mask called out, "Hi!"

"Hello." Every item that crowded on the battered wooden counter cost more than she was willing to pay. The mark-up was triple price of a regular convenience store.

Rachel handed the cashier the money for the purchase. "Pump Two."

"Here ya go, sweetie." The stranger passed her back her change. The kindness in her voice touched Rachel.

"Thanks. Have a good evening."

"You, too, dear. Be safe out there." The woman waved goodbye to her and Rachel smiled.

She returned to Gram's car—or maybe it was Rachel's car now—and got on the road again. Gram had put Rachel's name on the registration. She'd said that was so if something happened, then it would be Rachel's property and not part of the estate. Thank God Gram had done that, or Rachel would have nothing to call her own—and to sleep in if need be.

She glanced at the tote and the lunch box on the passenger's seat. There was a thermos filled with a hearty soup that smelled heavenly. Maybe she'd be stupid to eat it, but it had been a long time since Cook's yummy breakfast. The box also contained a thick turkey sandwich that smelled fresh, her favorite sandwich. How had he known that? An orange, an apple, and carrots crowded in there, too. The tote held a bill from Doud's, the grocery store on Mackinac Island. How the stranger had gotten that, she didn't know. It showed that a delivery had recently been made to Gram's cottage.

Seriously—the weirdest stuff going on.

How did that stranger know her and her family? She probably should be scared, he might be a stalker, but she felt a strange sense of peace about receiving those personal items of hers back again.

Her stomach growled. Maybe just a few bites of the sandwich wouldn't kill her.

Carrie Fancett Pagels

Lord, please bless this food, and if it's poisoned or something please don't let me harm anyone else if I die from it while I'm driving. That would be a real bummer. Amen.

Carefully, she pulled the sandwich from the pack and removed the covering. She took a tentative bite. It couldn't possibly be fresher, despite having sat in there all day. She turned the radio on.

"New life begins and the old is redeemed. Oh, I believe." That was Jeremy Camp—she recognized it from Pastor Michaels' radio—set to the Christian music channel. "To everyone who's lost their way. . ."

That's me.

"I believe you're only getting started," the singer belted out in his beautiful voice.

She was really doing this. She was going to Mackinaw City and then over to the island as if she owned that cottage. What if Mom had already sold it? But Rachel had searched the internet before she'd left and had found no listing for the property. Since Mom was supposed to inherit everything, would she and her latest boyfriend have Rachel arrested if they found her squatting there?

Rachel reached for the apple and took a bite. *Delicious.*

She may be crazy in everything she was doing right now, but God help her—she'd run out of options.

They served three square meals at the Mackinac Island jail, right?

Maybe there'd even be an Easter service for them. One could always hope.

Mackinac Island, April 2022

The thought of returning to his family's summer home on the island when Jack had been out to sea had felt like contemplating stabbing himself in the heart. But being here, a quelling peace had set in. Jack Welling crossed the snow-covered yard to the neighbors' cottage on the West Bluff. Dad had asked him to, "Take a good look around and make sure things are all right." Since when had it become Dad's job to watch over the Dunmara's property? How was that Dad's concern?

One finger pointed at Dad, and four pointed back at himself. Jack had always watched over the Dunmara's granddaughter when she'd visited with them. The kid, his sister's buddy, was a basket case. All that money in their family and she'd seemed as stupidly overlooked as the captain ignoring an impending cyclone out on the high seas. Jack hadn't been able do anything to save Olivia from her illness, so he'd given Rachel suggestions, *well okay, maybe criticisms*, to help the kid out. At least that had been his reasoning for his unasked advice to Rachel. He expelled a hard breath. Where was that girl now? He'd not seen the occupants in that cottage for over a decade. Not since before he went off to the Merchant Marine Academy in New York on Long Island. Then he'd gone on to sail after he'd finished his engineering degree.

Until this past couple of years of Covid and getting stuck for months on end aboard ship, he'd not considered *ever* coming back. Then he'd been stuck in the harbor at Los Angeles for an eternity. And he'd had his *Come to Jesus* moment.

He'd finally returned to his condo in Singapore to find that his long-time girlfriend, Mei, had cleaned him out. At least he assumed she'd done it. The police found no signs of forcible entry and neighbors reported that they saw her hauling electronics, furniture, and other stuff away. Worst of all, she'd taken family mementoes and jewelry that was special to him. His mother had been livid as had Dad. At least Jack had the good sense to not put Mei's name on his bank accounts as she'd once suggested.

Mei was the past. He was moving on. He had to. How had he ever thought that they might marry? *Stupid, stupid, stupid.*

He walked around to the back of the property next door. Boot marks with heavy tread led up to the back entrance. He tried the door. *Locked.* He peered inside and made out a Doud's Market placard hanging on the inside doorknob.

Ah, so they'd delivered here recently. Probably a yearly thing. But why had Dad gotten so concerned? When Jack had asked, Dad said, "Just being neighborly." And what kind of surveillance guy was Jack? He'd never even noticed the Doud's delivery guy had been there.

Jack pulled his iPhone from his jean's pocket. He texted his dad a quick message. *All ok at Dunmara's. Recent Doud's delivery.*

Maybe the cameras on their cottage had picked up the grocery worker's arrival. Jack had noticed the new cameras straight away when he'd arrived at their family's cottage a few weeks earlier. He'd had them on his condos, too—lot of good that did him. He snorted. Mei had turned the cameras off. He'd have a conversation with Dad soon about why he'd thought electronic surveillance was necessary on such a safe island.

Maybe things have changed.

He'd keep his eyes open.

His phone dinged. Instead of Dad, it was Andrette.

She'd texted, *Dinner tonight? Chicken n dumplings n apple pie.*

Whoa—my favorites. He grinned and texted back. *How can I refuse?*

She sent back a smiley face emoticon.

This return to Mackinac was already paying big dividends.

He was loved.

You are always loved.

He tipped back his head and gazed up at the brilliant blue skies overhead and the cumulus clouds floating by.

Thank you, God. I know.

At least he knew it now.

Chapter Three

Mackinaw City

*F*unny how performing "favors" for Mrs. Charbonneau had blessed Rachel this past week. When Dawn had asked her to stay in Mackinaw City to complete some overdue tasks for her, Rachel had almost refused. She'd wanted to get to the island. But instead of chores, these errands had become opportunities to reconnect with family friends. For the first time in a long while, a sense of normalcy seemed almost within reach. From delivering the Vacation Bible School supplies left over from the previous year to Judy at Church of the Straits and a crocheted afghan for Pastor Dave, to returning a half dozen mugs to Lorinda at the Mackinaw Bakery, Rachel had been encouraged by all these positive people. On Tuesday, Lorinda had sent her home with a box of yummy doughnuts, Long Johns, and cinnamon rolls for her and Judy and Pastor Dave.

Pastor Dave had prayed with her, too, when she'd shared that she had some big decisions to make. The Palm Sunday service had been beautiful. She looked forward to the upcoming Easter service and her heart had thrilled at the thought of celebrating in community. Despite the upheaval in her life, this celebration, which many considered the most important in the Christian calendar year, called to her as nothing else had. This Holy Week wasn't what she'd anticipated in Chicago, but she was so grateful that the members at the Church of the Straits had welcomed her.

As she'd walked back to the Charbonneau's cottage, she'd received a text from the management company about Lilac Cottage. All preparations for early season had been made. She bowed her head. *Thank you, Lord.* If she'd gone over any earlier, the utilities wouldn't have been ready. Since they were still sending her notifications, the estate must not have changed that yet.

Yesterday and today, Rachel got the house spic-and-span from top to bottom, for the Charbonneau's upcoming arrival. Dawn wouldn't tolerate Butterfly Cottage being messy. She entered the house and walked through, checking for dust bunnies. *None.*

The doorbell rang. That was a first since she'd been there.

Rachel stepped to the entryway. Through the semi-sheer curtains, she spotted a petite white-haired woman she didn't recognize attired in a blaze of purple, mustard, and lime. A black SUV with Florida plates was parked behind Rachel's. A middle-aged woman removed large pieces of luggage from the trunk. *What's that about?*

Rachel opened the door. "May I help you?"

"Who are you?" The woman scowled up at her, making her wrinkled face even more leathery, if that was possible.

Rachel gaped at the stranger. "I'm a guest here. And who might you be?" She was tempted to slam the door on the rude woman despite her being elderly.

"Irene! Dawn Charbonneau is my sister, and she said we could stay here *any time we wished.*"

Rachel clamped her lips shut. This had to be *Hurricane Irene* as Dawn's granddaughter, Jaycie, had characterized her to Rachel. Five years ago, Jaycie's Great Aunt Irene had locked her out of their accommodations at the Grand Hotel. Poor Jaycie had to be rescued by friends. Dawn had told Gram that her sister was in cognitive decline but on medication. *Maybe it's no longer working.*

The younger woman bore the weariness of the world on her face as she glanced in their direction. She set luggage on the curb.

"I've got to use the can." The geriatric woman pushed past her and headed down the hall before Rachel could stop her.

She needed to contact Dawn. Rachel quickly texted her. *Dawn 2 people here. Says she's your sis n plans to stay.*

The other stranger, attired in the Coastal Grandma style of neutral blues and tan, carried two suitcases inside the foyer. "Hi. I'm Susan. Is my Aunt Dawn not here yet?"

"No. Not for a few weeks."

Rachel's phone pinged.

No! I knew nothing of this. Argh! Sorry. Dawn must be as shocked as Rachel was.

"Did my mom *not* set this up with Aunt Dawn?" Susan huffed a sigh.

Rachel shook her head.

"I should have called her myself. My mom's been making some pretty messed-up decisions for a while now."

That would have been nice. Too late now. "I'm Rachel and I understand about parents making bad choices."

"How do you know Aunt Dawn?"

"My Gram Margaret and Dawn are. . ." *were* not *are*—but she couldn't say it.

"Best friends!" Susan brightened. "Aunt Dawn has told so many stories about her friend Mags and all the stuff they got up to over the years. Oh, my heavens, those two together!"

"Yeah?" Rachel gave a short laugh. "Were they pretty wild when they were younger? Because I've only seen the more, um, sedate side of them."

"Me oh my, yes, those two were party goers and the style icons of these parts—at least in the summers."

Gram at one time had a real penchant for designer clothing and couture outfits. "I worked for one of their designers for a bit this past year." After Gram died.

"Did you really? In Chicago?"

"Yes. Sandi Browne."

"Wow! Sandi Browne? Seriously?"

"Yes."

"I bet that renowned designer had some tales to tell, too." Susan shook her head slowly. "Auntie Dawn and Mags attended all the best parties on the island and off. The flashy stuff. And Sandi Browne got her start designing for them before she got famous."

"Really?"

"Yes, she was just a young thing back then." Susan raised her eyebrows. "And she knew how to style up two raring-to-go friends who knew how to burn the midnight oil!"

Rachel frowned. She didn't know anything about that. Gram had always just been Gram, a sedate lady who kept to herself. Maybe that was because of her condition, though.

"Didn't her daughter, Cassie Browne, take over her business, though? I read that in one of my women's magazines."

"Yes, and Cassie took the brand to North Carolina. No more Chicago for them and her mom has retired." And the plan Gram had for Rachel to work for her friend and live in the apartment had vanished like this situation was about to do. But Rachel had completed her favors for Dawn. It was time to go. Thank God Rachel had gotten the house clean.

Dawn's sister, despite being tiny, stomped down the hall toward them sounding like an elephant. "My room's already taken!" the elderly woman called out.

"Ma, that's not your room. This is Auntie Dawn's house, and I imagine Rachel is using the guest room." Susan turned to face Rachel.

Carrie Fancett Pagels

She nodded. "Right. I was on my way to Mackinac Island to stay at my family's place, but Mrs. Charbonneau asked if I could do her a few favors." She lifted her hands and turned her palms over. "And I was happy to oblige. But now I've finished those."

"Perfect timing!" Irene clapped her hands together.

The Jeremy Camp song Rachel had been playing over and over sounded in her head. "*You're only getting started. . .*" The lyrics had really appealed to Rachel and her situation. This was just step one.

Yes, she was broken-hearted over Gram, but it was time to keep going. Time to stop running around in circles.

She locked gazes with Susan, who seemed like a really nice person. "Let me pack." Rachel's *way* was on the island. She needed to get started. She needed to follow God's direction and go ahead— come what may. Trespassing or not.

"Oh, no, we can't chase you off." Susan touched her arm gently.

"It's all right. Really." Maybe God had wanted Rachel there for a chance to regroup and rest. She shrugged. "I'm done here."

Time to get started.

Jack set the remodeling plans for the kitchen onto the old-fashioned counter and tried to imagine what it was going to look like in there.

Goldie glanced up dolefully at him from her overstuffed dog bed.

"I'll feed you soon, old girl." Thankfully, Doud's had her favorite brand in stock.

His phone announced a text message.

Pls chk on DC ty

Jack exhaled sharply. Dad abbreviated Lilac Cottage as DC. There'd been no movement over there whatsoever. He'd do it in a bit after he reviewed what the designer had suggested. She'd reminded him too much of Mei, with her flashy wardrobe and sing-songy voice. Mom needed to look over this stuff, too, when she came up. But who knew when that would be.

With April almost gone, soon there would be lots of folks, including Mom and Dad, who would make some early visits up here.

Maybe then he wouldn't be alone with the ghosts of his past.

Birds chirped from the bushes, chorusing in the chilly snowflake-filled air, as though the feathered friends welcomed Rachel back. She moved forward, behind the beautiful Queen Anne style cottage. She stopped and stood still in the large backyard. *I am about to commit a crime.* A gust of wind from the Straits of Mackinac stirred the snowy air—causing the branches of the nearby bare lilac trees to tremble and her knees followed suit.

Trespassing wasn't nearly as serious as breaking and entering. Was it?

Rachel drew in a steadying breath as she took the steps to the back entrance and peered through the window's wavy frosted glass. The cottage was over one-hundred-twenty-five years old.

She drew Gram's keys from her purse, her chilly hands stiff as she inserted her grandmother's ancient key into the lock.

She turned the key but met immediate resistance.

Oh no. No Plan B.

Pray. The single word, sounded almost audibly within her heart.

Really, God? Pray about opening a lock and becoming a squatter here?

Recently, with her return to the church, the Lord had been opening all kinds of doors. Made sense that He could handle this one.

God, I want to hang out with You every day. I know You brought me here. Please help me.

She shivered. She'd never been on the island in such cold weather. She turned from facing the glassed-in sunroom, to view the garden budding with hundreds, no thousands, of yellow and white flowers poking up through the snow. They carpeted the naturalized lawn, more from Rachel's neglect in advising the gardening workers than from any landscaping plan. Still, they'd be glorious when they fully bloomed. She helped plant many of those daffodils years earlier.

Jack Welling had mocked her as she'd planted the bulbs. "You won't even be here to see them blooming," he'd taunted. "But I'll *know*," she'd told him. She'd patted over her heart, and he'd just shook his head.

Now, not only would she know in her heart that the daffodils she'd planted had bloomed but she'd actually see them. A sense of warmth, despite the chill, coursed through her. The Great and Holy Thursday, to love others as Christ had loved them.

A text message sounded on her phone.

Pastor Michaels sent a message. *I know you were looking forward to the Maundy Thursday service and we're praying for you. Sorry you couldn't be here. Next year, maybe? Blessings!*

Tears pricked Rachel's eyes. She'd wanted to participate in the foot washing part of the service to both volunteer and allow herself to be ministered to in that act of humility and reverence. The Great and Holy Thursday, to love others as Christ had loved them.

She swiveled back toward the door and then inserted and turned the key. It turned.

Success. Thank you, Lord.

Relief flowed through her as warm as Gram's hot marshmallowy cocoa on a blizzardy Chicago day. Too bad the baseboards barely sputtered out any heat. At least the electric was on.

She stepped inside and dropped her heavy backpack with a thud. She closed the door behind her, sat and texted a thank you message back to her Chicago pastor. Then she stood and pulled the sheet from the couch and collapsed onto it. The crazy cleaning sessions yesterday and today, combined with being sent on her way yet again, had sapped the last of her emotional reserves. That and the walk from the dock, slogging uphill and sneaking down the backway to get here.

No cars were allowed on Mackinac Island, other than emergency vehicles, so options were to either walk, ride a bike, or get a taxi—the latter being a carriage pulled by horses. She'd brought no bike and couldn't afford to shell out for a taxi, so she'd trekked up to West Bluff, toting her belongings. That had been a good workout.

Rachel tried to keep her eyes open as she blinked up at the paneled porch ceiling. Sleep urgently claimed her—almost like Olivia's dog Goldie jumping on her and pinning Rachel there to that couch.

This will soon be empty. Jack wiped perspiration from his forehead as he mentally removed the last vestiges of his sister's presence from her former third-floor room. Empty it would be and that was how he felt, too.

Mom had photographed Olivia's room before they'd closed up the cottage last season. She'd sent him the photo in a text and said that she and Dad intended to remodel this year. When he'd agreed to take on management of the cottage's projects, she'd instructed him to have every indicator of Olivia's presence removed. Finally. This would be the first room that he and the new crew would tackle. No more cotton-candy pink walls. No raspberry-colored carpet. The white eyelet curtains would be gone.

But Goldie still remained with the family. His sister's beloved dog lay nestled atop a small pastel rag rug that Jack's great-grandmother had made for Olivia. The goldendoodle cast a doleful glance at him in accusation.

"Sorry, old girl, but she's not coming back."

One day he'd see his sister again. *In heaven.* "Tell you what. I'll save that old rug just for you."

Was it his imagination or did the pup's ears perk up? He stepped to the window, sun faintly filtering through as the sun lowered in the afternoon sky, and then lifted the sash.

Movement at the Dunmara's place caught his attention. *Oh crud. Forgot to check for Dad.*

Someone in a gray hoodie and loose black sweatpants jogged around in the backyard of the white cottage.

Just what he *didn't* need. Crime on Mackinac Island, other than domestic disputes from tourists, was fairly nonexistent. Maybe Dad was right to be concerned. He gave a curt laugh. His condos in Panama and Singapore were in the heart of those cities, and he'd never witnessed a B&E other than his spiteful ex-girlfriend. Yet here he was, back home, privy almost immediately to criminal activity.

He stretched his neck, as tension built there.

Whoever was messing around at the Dunmaras' place had disappeared behind the house. He drew in a slow breath. Maybe it was just an island kid messing around and snooping. Heck, he and his buddies had scoped out plenty of other houses on the West Bluff unbeknownst to their parents.

Whatever. He was going over. He didn't carry a pistol with him, though, as he did in foreign ports.

The season hadn't yet begun, so it was unlikely to be anyone other than an islander. It was so dang cold most of them were bundled up and inside. But, with the pandemic, there were more cottagers arriving before the big summer season kicked off.

He hurried down the stairs, making an echoing racket as he went. No ancestral pictures of the Cadottes, Swaines, and Wellings on the walls. All of the antique furniture moved to the back half of the house and covered. The place felt like a void. Like he had, inside, these past few years.

Outside, his buddy Mitch, a dray driver, waved from his seat as the conveyance drove past. The vehicle bed was empty, so presumably Mitch had delivered his goods for the day. The Percheron horses plodded along, puffs billowing from their nostrils in the cold air.

Whoever was sneaking around at the Dunmara's was really taking a chance. West Bluff residents could have a fair amount of traffic from townies and tourists. On the other hand, a lot of the cottage owners were absent most of the time. There wasn't a Neighborhood Watch like his folks had in Grand Rapids, where they lived during the school year.

Jack ran alongside the cottage. He paused when he reached the cottage's back corner. What if this kid was armed? At almost six foot

Carrie Fancett Pagels

three and in the best shape of his life, Jack was still no match for a gun. But he'd left his in the drawer. He'd do what other islanders had done when they'd caught people encroaching on their property—he'd fake a jovial tone and direct them back to the street.

He shoved his hands into his coat's pockets and inhaled a deep breath. No one was breaking into the Dunmaras' place on his watch. Not that he was *on watch*. Although Dad seemed to think so. He marched around to the rear.

No one there.

His heartbeat ticked up a bit, always a sign to him to be attentive. He instinctively longed to wrap his hands around his absent gun. His cell phone was in his pocket. He could call the police and have them check this out instead of taking chances. His folks needed him to complete this job. And he'd needed time to decompress. He didn't need anything disturbing the peace he craved.

He approached the rear entrance to the Dunmara's sunporch and took two steps up. When he pushed on the door handle it didn't give.

Then he saw *her*.

A young woman lay on a cushioned white wicker couch, mouth open, dark hair splayed against her gray hoodie. She had the face of an angel in repose. The profile of a Greek goddess. Long dark eyelashes contrasted against her perfect creamy complexion. Elegant slim hands lay splayed across the intruder's flat abdomen.

Emotion stirred within him.

He pulled away, searching his memories. There was resemblance to pictures he'd seen of Selma Dunmara during her brief career as a model. The intruder looked like that younger version of her—maybe could be her daughter. Which meant. . . Rachel. The fatherless girl whose grandparents were more like parents to her.

Rachel Dunmara?

The girl who'd been the bane of his teenaged existence?

The girl who he'd insulted, by accident of course, when he asked why her mother hadn't taken care of certain things for her.

That had been a girl with thick eyeglasses, terrible acne, chubby, and who'd arrive dressed in the ugliest clothing he'd ever seen. Then her grandmother, Margaret, would buy her new outfits that looked more like what Jack's sister wore. Jack had truly felt sorry for the poor kid—except that she was a huge pain.

What was Rachel—if indeed that was her—doing sleeping on the back porch in these frigid temperatures? And how had she transformed into someone who looked like *that*?

Images flashed through his mind. Olivia and Rachel cutting lilacs. Olivia and Rachel playing with their dolls at a pretend tea party.

Olivia getting so sick with her leukemia but demanding her secret be kept from Rachel. Mom ordering Olivia not to be overly taxed by Rachel's visits.

Olivia. Gone.

Remorse surged through him like a roaring wall of waves on the high seas. He almost stumbled as he took two steps backwards down the stairs.

Rachel was here.

Olivia was not—never would be again.

He sent up a one-word prayer. *God.*

But he couldn't let Rachel, or anyone, freeze out there on the glassed-in porch.

Jack stepped up the stairs again and rapped on the window.

Sleeping Beauty didn't stir.

He scowled as again, he pulled on the knob. It opened. He stepped inside, hoping she'd wake. If he saw those unusually light blue-gray eyes of hers, then he'd know for sure it was little Rachel. Well, not-so-little Rachel anymore.

She didn't move.

A ring of keys hung in the interior back door that opened the main house from the sun porch. Maybe she'd not been able to get it to turn open to go inside.

Jack wiggled the key in the lock and got a satisfying click as it turned. He stomped off his feet on the mat. Still no movement from the sleeping angel.

He stepped inside the Dunmara's cottage and flipped a switch. There was electricity. It was also warmish in the house. Maybe fifty or so. Someone had already turned the heat on. Probably their property manager. Jack stepped down the hall and adjusted the thermostat marked for the first floor. He set it up to sixty-five degrees. Then he went to the living room. He lifted the furniture coverings and looked for blankets or throws on any of the furniture. Nothing there. He went to the back of the nearby kitchen, where a maid's room used to be. He opened the old-fashioned armoire, an exact replica of one in his family's cottage, and found several old wool blankets. He pulled them down and brought them to the porch.

He looked down at her. How had that girl grown into such a beauty? His heartbeat ticked upwards. He gently laid the covers over her. She stretched and rolled on her side, tugging on the blanket and pulling it under her chin. He spread the other two blankets over her, too, then stepped back. Some of the heat, from the open door, was leaching onto the porch. He checked by the baseboards and found heat vents. He opened them fully and warm air flowed through.

Jack lowered the blinds over the windows, not making any effort to be quiet. If only the noise *would* wake Rachel—but she barely stirred.

"Oh, little Rach, what are you doing here now?"

As he slipped out the sunroom door, he locked it. Nothing was happening to her on his watch.

He was starting to sound like his old man.

Scritch, scritch, scritch. Mittens must be trying to get into her bedroom at Gram and Gramps' place. She stretched. Mittens was long gone, though. And now Gram and Gramps both gone. Rachel tried to force her eyes open.

Her face felt cold. But the rest of her was toasty warm. She blinked. Lacy frosted windows enclosed Gram's sunroom. The bottom section of some of the windows beneath the vents were clear but the tops were covered in icy etchings. She tossed off the wool blankets, as dread shot through her.

What if whoever now owned this place had found her, and covered her up, while the police came?

"Hello?" she called out.

Her keys hung in the inner door, which was now open.

Whoever now occupied this place must surely have realized Rachel wasn't simply an intruder. A trespasser wouldn't possess keys, right?

"Hi there! I'm Rachel! Rachel Dunmara."

No one answered. Wet marks on the rug suggested that a man, wearing boots, had come in the back. Who all had a key? Douds' employees did. Had they returned with something they'd forgotten? Or, as she feared, had the managers for the new owners found her there?

Rachel rose and slipped into her low boots and her jacket. She exited the cottage and inhaled the piney scent of the tall boxwoods that formed a thick hedge between Lilac Cottage and their neighbor's home.

She craned her neck to peer above the tall hedge at the Wellings' cottage. No lights glowed from the third-floor windows.

Loneliness coursed through her, and she rubbed her arms.

Would this year be like Rachel's last few hasty trips to Mackinac Island? Would the Wellings' neighboring cottage remain empty? Where had Olivia and Jack and their parents gone for all these years? Rachel had been too busy caretaking Gram and taking care of things at the cottage on the last couple of trips up North to find out why her summer friend and her parents weren't there. For some reason, Olivia had stopped responding to Rachel's text messages long ago.

That had stung. Maybe her brother, Jack, had something to do with that. *Busybody.*

She'd not been allowed to be on social media—mostly because of Gramps' job as a judge. After he'd died, Gram had packed her off to private school in Virginia, insisting that Gramps wanted to do that for her. Gram came regularly to the school along the Potomac River. Mom not at all that year, her freshman year of high school. Rachel returned home for her sophomore year, enrolled in a small private school under her last stepfather's name. She shook her head at the memory of why she'd left Mom's home and moved in with Gram at sixteen.

After that, when Rachel had returned to the island with Gram, neither Olivia nor her family were there when they'd stayed. Jack was off at college and no doubt Olivia was wrapped up in "normal" high school activities and busy with friends. In the off-season both the Wellings' house, or the Canary as they called the yellow Queen Anne structure, and Lilac Cottage stood unoccupied.

As a gust of wind stirred empty branches, she pulled her coat tighter.

She recalled the evening when her mother had informed her that Rachel was booted out of Gram's high-rise. Hard to believe that was barely over a year earlier. Rachel had been living with Gram for over eight years.

Rachel's cell phone had rung that night.

She hadn't recognized the number. "Hello?"

"Rachel? This is your mom."

"Oh." That was the best she could manage. She braced herself. She never knew what her mother would come up with. Her toxicity had nearly destroyed Rachel, until Gram had taken her into her home.

"I want you out of *that* place today."

"What?" Rachel had remained in Gram's high-rise condo, which had become her home, too, even when her grandmother had entered the nursing facility.

"Dan and I are moving in."

Dan must be the latest boyfriend. Rachel struggled to catch her breath as her mind went blank. She'd have to clear out her belongings. Where would she go?

"We don't have a moving van for our things until next week. But we want you *out* by the weekend."

Maybe Gram's attorney could stop this. Rachel had realized when Gram died this would be the likely scenario. *But Gram was still alive.* But not speaking much. It was too taxing for her.

Rachel had spent her later teen years and early twenties taking care of her grandmother. She'd never had a real job. She had nothing but the dream of becoming a nurse, and a bunch of pre-nursing online college classes to her credit.

"You've been tied to my mother's apron strings for too long and now I'm *cutting you loose*."

Rachel clicked the end call button. Her friend Tasia's roommate had moved out. Maybe she could go there.

She'd need a job.

Gram's friend, the designer Sandi Browne, had called earlier in the week, asking if Rachel might be able to help at her downtown store. And she'd said if Rachel needed a place to stay, there was an upstairs apartment. She said Gram had called from the facility to see if Sandi had something for her.

Had Gram and Sandi known what her mom was about to do?

Perspiration broke out on Rachel's brow. She texted Sandi a message.

Is the job still open? And the apartment?

Her world was being shaken—like when the dollhouse Gramps had built had fallen off the table and everything spilled all over the floor. Gramps and Gram had helped her pick up all the pieces and carestakingly put them back in place. When Mom had arrived to take Rachel home and heard the story, she'd sneered. "You should have let the little brat pick them up by herself, so she'd learn not to be so clumsy."

Gramps had stared at his only child open-mouthed. He knew better than to say anything. The last time he'd corrected Mom, she'd kept Rachel from her grandparents for almost a year. She'd only given in and contacted them when one of her boyfriends wanted to take Mom to the Bahamas for Christmas holiday. Then, they'd brought Rachel over. And what a reunion it had been with Gram and Gramps.

She and Gramps and Gram had made a pact after that. If Rachel ever needed to see them, she had code words she shared. And they had to offer her mother something so enticing that she'd willingly give up control or would think it was her own idea about Rachel visiting with them.

What would Gramps do if he were alive? He'd probably say Rachel should offer to cook for Mom and Dan. Clean for them.

Placate them. But she couldn't. She could not grovel before the person who'd made her life miserable.

One year ago, Rachel had left her grandparents' high rise that week and went to the couture designer's business with a suitcase, a backpack, and a broken heart.

A gust of wind stirred a pile of leaves.

Rachel headed back to the cottage. Mom hadn't even owned Gram's condo, but she'd forced Rachel out. What would she do if she discovered Rachel was a squatter now, in what used to be her grandparents' summer home? She'd fly into a narcissistic rage and likely call whatever law enforcement personnel she could find and have Rachel escorted off the property.

She trudged on toward the sunroom. It wasn't like she had much choice. But she'd get a job and maybe that would come with an apartment, like Sandi Browne's job had. That position had given Rachel a new skillset, confidence, and the ability to take care of herself on her own. Her own earnings. Rachel had learned a lot that she took with her to her other jobs after Sandi retired and closed her shop.

What Mom had planned for evil, the Lord had used for good.

Rachel entered the sunroom. She'd go into the house's interior as little as possible. For all she knew, Mom had already sold this place—just like she said she'd do once she got ownership of it.

Tomorrow Rachel would get a job, hopefully one that offered a room, and she'd begin the next phase of her life.

And hopefully not get arrested before then.

Chapter Four

*S*eriously? Her first interview was for her fave coffee shop, but it was across from the *police* department. She'd never noticed the police department there before. *Why would I notice that anyway?* The white wood-sided station blended in with the other historic buildings in the vicinity.

Rachel stopped walking and blew out a breath that transformed into a puff of mist in the chilly air. The enticing aromas of Arabica, Columbian, and Kona coffees urged her to keep going on to Lucky Bean.

The shop on Market Street was Rachel's first job interview on the island. She needed a job. *Badly.*

But how humiliating it would be when the someone from the police department came over and arrested her for trespassing.

You gotta do this. Maybe the owner has a room for you. Move right into that and out of Gram's old cottage and you'll be all right. Leave no trace. Yeah, that's it.

Stiffening her spine, she pulled Gram's old Lucite compact mirror from her purse and checked her appearance. Same plain features, but her hair was in place, and her lipstick wasn't smeared.

She opened the door and stepped inside to the scent of freshly brewed coffee and the sounds of 1950's soft jazz—like Gramps used to enjoy. An older woman with upswept blonde hair pinned with a green rhinestone butterfly clip, eyeglasses hanging from a beaded chain, talked animatedly with the late twenty-something cashier.

The beautiful brunette at the register might be the manager. Rachel had seen her at the coffee shop the last several seasons during her limited visits to the island.

Several tables were occupied. At one, a guy stared intent at his laptop. At another, a silver-haired couple wearing dark turtlenecks and matching navy and cream wool herringbone blazers held hands as they sipped their coffee. *Adorable. Newlyweds?* Possibly long-time married like Gramps and Gram had been yet still very much in love.

Against the wall, a woman wearing a Stormy Kromer hat over straight black hair sat reading a paper. How she managed to read despite wearing tinted oversized glasses that obscured much of her pretty face was a mystery. Was that Carolyn May, the gorgeous and mysterious owner of this place? Gram and Gramps knew her dad, who had, unfortunately, passed away a few summers earlier before Rachel had arrived.

To the left, one of the baristas—a young woman perhaps twenty or in her late teens with platinum blonde chunky streaks in her brown hair—scowled at the two at the register. She stomped around from behind her counter. "Ya know, you guys might be disturbing the customers."

The manager, or maybe she was just the cashier, gave the younger woman a perplexed look.

"You're kinda loud, you know." She smirked. *Mean Girl* was stamped all over her face. Rachel had met enough of those to recognize yet another one. Too bad she'd not realized that Leesa was such a creature.

A mix of disbelief and annoyance passed over the cashier's face. "Oh, I think I'm *fine*," she said with forced cheerfulness. "We're good."

The older blonde woman's shoulders stiffened.

When the barista cast a glance in the senior citizen's way, Rachel got the distinct impression that she was really complaining about the older woman carrying on a conversation at the cash register.

Wow. Just wow. How rude. Rachel realized she was gaping when the younger woman narrowed her eyes at her.

The older blonde woman called out to the nasty barista, "When you're over fifty, you get to be as loud as you want."

The phone rang in the back room and the cashier turned around and left the register.

"You need to move over there and wait." The rude barista pointed at the very end of the glass case, near the door.

There was *no one* waiting to be served in the place. Rachel fumed as the barista sneered and went behind to her work area.

As the customer passed her, Rachel shook her head. "I'm with you. You two weren't loud. I don't know what her problem is."

If Rachel had to work with someone like that unpleasant barista every day, then her newly found Christian faith could really be challenged.

"God will sort this out. Just you watch." The older woman winked at Rachel. Her dark brown eyes didn't quite match up with her blonde hair, but they were full of good humor despite the barista's nasty behavior.

What did the woman mean by God fixing this? In the Bible, which was still new to her, Rachel had read that God did indeed deal with difficult people and with sin. She shivered—there were consequences for such behavior.

The uncaring barista prepared what looked like a cappuccino. She grabbed the milk from a stainless-steel fridge and poured it slowly into a container before pushing it under a frothing and heating machine. Smirky gal poured that into another container then expertly measured and poured syrup but added it on top of the steamed milk. Then, instead of adding espresso, and swirling the ingredients together, she went to a coffee dispenser and poured a good amount over the milk and syrup. Deep in concentration, the barista expertly frothed the milk and carefully added it to the top.

The barista turned and passed it across the counter to the waiting customer. No cover was placed on top.

"Beautiful," the customer said.

The barista pointedly ignored the woman and glanced at Rachel. "Can I help you?"

"I'm waiting on the manager."

The barista bobbed her chin in understanding, then spun on her heel.

The customer stepped to the nearby counter where cream and sugar were laid out along with napkins and stirring sticks. She took a sip of her cappuccino and frowned.

Rachel hesitated, not sure if she should speak up. But then she took a deep breath and moved closer to the customer. "Excuse me. I don't know if you're like me, but if the barista doesn't swirl my syrup into the coffee. . ." instead of *pouring* it beneath the milk, "I usually need to really get down there and give it a good stir or the flavor won't come through."

"Oh. Maybe that's what I need to do. I've never seen anyone make it like that before."

Because it was the wrong way. Rachel offered her a gentle smile. When she turned around, the manager had returned to the register and was wagging her index finger at the young barista. "You can take your apron off."

"Why?"

The brunette opened the cash register and began pulling out bills. "I can pay you cash through today or I can write you a check."

"What? You're firing me?" The sneering voice rose. "I thought you needed help desperately."

"Not at the cost of alienating my customers and friends." She directed her gaze to the corner where the woman in the sunglasses dropped her newspaper and nodded as if in agreement.

So, was the lady in the corner Carolyn May? Was that the owner? Must be.

Good gravy. Yes, the barista was rude but if they let people go *this quickly* then would Rachel get fired, too? But she needed a job too badly to turn on her heel and leave now. On the other hand, if anyone needed to be fired it was that gal.

The barista scowled as the manager counted out cash into her open palm. She didn't thank her for the pay but bent, grabbed a khaki-colored backpack and stormed off, almost shouldering into Rachel as she passed.

The blonde woman sipped her coffee. "Tastes fine now that I've stirred down at the bottom, but I think she put coffee in there, not espresso."

Rachel exhaled. "She *did.* I'm sorry. I probably should have said something."

"Oh, no, dear that's not your job. I'll ask Andrette for a freebie tomorrow. She'll accommodate me, I'm sure."

"Andrette?"

"She's the manager." The woman waved at the cashier, who rolled her eyes upwards but smiled.

The stranger playfully tapped Rachel's arm. "Go get 'em. Tiger. You're here for the interview, right?"

"Yup."

"Andrette told me she had one this morning. That's why the owner is here, too." The woman leaned in, her dark eyes showing flecks of amber. "She's in the corner scoping out that nasty employee and the interviewee—which is you."

"Ah." Niggles of uncertainty worked their way into Rachel's trembling hands.

"Best wishes. And thanks again." She leaned around Rachel and gave a thumbs up to the owner.

"Have a blessed day." And Rachel meant it.

Soon, she'd greeted the manager, Andrette Herron, and was escorted to a nearby table. The owner didn't join them but remained at the window. She should be a model with that face.

"So, you're here for our cashier job, is that right? Or barista?"

"Cashier. I have a lot of experience with that." Granted it had all come within the past year.

"But you are willing to learn barista work, too?"

"Absolutely."

"Perfect."

Rachel nodded. "Um, by any chance do you offer housing?"

Andrette cringed. "Sorry, I don't. But maybe your second job will offer it."

Second job? She tried to keep from widening her eyes in response.

"Tell me—what and where is your second job?" Andrette, arched a heavily made-up "boyfriend" eyebrow at Rachel. "And who with?"

Another job, too? Couldn't Lucky Bean Coffee House give her enough hours? "This position would be my priority." She hoped her direct gaze conveyed sincerity.

Nearby, the metallic sound of a coffee grinder whirred. If Rachel's sniffer was correct, that was Blue Mountain from Jamaica—one of her mother's favorite coffees. Anything that cost top dollar would quickly become a fave of Mom's and change the millisecond something else was labeled as better.

Her mouth watered at the thought of tasting a bit of that brew. "The position is full-time, though, right?"

"It is." A tiny tug started between the woman's eyebrows. Botox. Not twenty-something but thirty-something. *Definitely Botox* had stopped the woman's crease from forming. "Most of my employees work at least two jobs, though."

So, was a second job expected? Rachel recalled how Gram's friends had said most summer workers held multiple positions. Rachel grasped for something to say and inhaled the heady scents of the freshly ground Columbian coffee beans and vanilla muffins that taunted her empty stomach from behind the glass case.

The friendly looking Hispanic guy behind the case grinned at her and a curious warmth flowed through her. He was a nice-looking young guy of average height. He looked really sweet in contrast with his co-worker who'd just been fired.

Focus.

She'd responded that morning to that ad—sort of—in the *Town Crier* for administrative help with a remodeling job. "I, um, I've applied to do administrative assistance for a construction project."

"Ah, okay." The woman's features softened. "Even though I do offer full-time work, all my employees have two or three jobs—that's simply the way of a Mackinac Island summer employee."

Rachel's tiny fib about applying for the other job wasn't exactly one hundred percent true. *God forgive me.* Since she and the Big Guy were just getting reacquainted maybe He'd give her extra grace. At least Andrette was offering full-time work. Rachel nodded.

"I always ask about the other employment. It's not really my business, ya know, eh?" Definitely a Yooper accent going there. "But I like to know what kind of schedules my workers are dealing with." Andrette smiled ruefully.

The doorbell behind her jangled and Rachel jumped. Being slightly homeless and almost broke kind of put her on edge.

Andrette laughed. "You better get used to that sound if you're gonna be our new cashier, eh?"

Was she offering the position? Rachel exhaled a quick breath. "I'm sure I could."

"Fantastic! You're hired." Andrette extended her hand and shook Rachel's.

Warmth spread through her. A job. *Woo hoo.* She resisted the urge to do a victory dance. *Money. Food.* Payment for her cell phone. No need to steal toilet paper from public bathrooms. *Yes, yes, yes.*

Andrette pointed a long hot pink and rhinestone encrusted fingernail toward whoever had entered the shop. "Jack! We might as well get a twofer today."

Rachel cringed. What did that mean? Surely it wasn't *that* Jack. *No. No way.* There were lots of Jacks on the island, including old Mr. Jack Welling, who was either a junior or a third, who had been Gram's friend. Had been her friend, that was, when Gram and he were both alive.

Footsteps sounded behind her. She turned. A tall, dark-haired man sported designer sunglasses that would have put him back at least a couple hundred bucks. He held one of the shop's disposable coffee cups emblazoned with LB.

How did he get that drink so fast? Someone had to have shoved it into his hand as soon as he'd entered the place.

If he wasn't a body builder, with all those muscles bulging beneath his snug jeans-jacket, then she wasn't a former pescatarian. That food-choice orientation had been before she'd begun paying for all of her own groceries and eating what she could afford.

Maybe this wasn't her Jack. Why was she thinking of him as *her* Jack? No. More like goofy Jack, mean Jack, irritating Jack Welling. This guy had the chiseled features of a movie star. When he shoved his expensive sunglasses on top of his head, warm hazel eyes gazed down at her.

In horror, she realized she was gaping. Was it? Could it be? The eyes looked the same but really from the rest of him, she wasn't sure. Jack Welling had been a skinny seventeen-year-old the last time he'd taunted her. He'd worn super short hair, almost a crew cut, like his former Marine father had preferred. This guy's dark hair was longish and kind of shaggy.

Andrette gazed admiringly at what might be Rachel's former tormenter. "Jack, this is my newest employee, Rachel."

"Good for you, Andi." His deep voice held a hint of humor—like he was the type of man used to laughing a lot. Definitely not like Jack Welling. Jack was a sad sack—what Gramps had called him. And his voice was higher than this guy's. Of course, his voice might finally have changed.

"Getting no action on my ad for the remodeling job—although your twofer comment has me intrigued."

Rachel pressed her back into the chair and waited for her lie to be exposed. She'd not responded to the ad—not technically. Why, oh why, had this Jack person come in right now? He had to be the foreman on the job. He'd know that she'd *never* sent him an inquiry. Fact was, though, she did have it all typed out in a text message—but she'd never pressed the send indicator on the phone. Her fingers itched, wishing to push that icon now.

"Haven't gotten anything from ya, Rachel. When did ya send your info?" No humor in his voice now. Nope.

She schooled her face into an innocent expression and turned to look up into the man's way-too-handsome face. If he knew who she was, he gave no indication. So, this could be a different Jack. *Hopefully so.*

"I wrote my text a couple of nights ago." She turned and pulled her cell phone from her small cross-body purse—one Gram bought for her twenty-first birthday. She scrolled through her messages until she found it.

The man reached for her phone and took it. She resisted the urge to press her eyes shut and block out this whole bad situation. Jack Welling would be just as bold—grabbing her property. *How rude.*

The handsome man laughed as he read to himself. "My mom does the same thing. Writes me a text then forgets to send it. But you're kinda young for that. What are ya—eighteen? Nineteen?"

Twenty-five, thank you very much! But good—you don't know who I am. Jack Welling would probably make a crack that I was an Old Maid. Her jaw clenched.

Rachel turned as Andrette wagged a finger at Jack. "Now Jack, she's legal age to work so that's all you need to know. A woman has her secrets, eh?"

"Yeah, yeah."

Andrette pushed her chair back from the small table. "I've got work to do. Sit down and interview my new hire if you've got a minute." The warmth in her smile and voice suggested she'd known Jack a long time.

That meant he was likely an islander. Please, please, please, God, don't let this be Jack Welling. Couldn't be. Besides, there were Jacks everywhere on this island. Jack Barnwell the famous and amazing island and worldwide landscaper. Jack the owner of the stables. Jack the dock guy.

But when the gorgeous man settled into the chair across from her, and those dancing hazel eyes locked on hers, she couldn't help herself. "You're Jack Welling, aren't you?"

His features tugged in surprise—or was that mock surprise—as he set his coffee cup on the round tabletop. "How'd ya know?"

"It, um," she searched for an explanation. "You name was in the ad."

His full lips tugged together and pulled to the side. "Don't think so."

Distraction. That usually worked. Rachel gave him a huge smile and fluttered her hands. At least he hadn't said, 'Hey you're Rachel, the brat from next door.'

She swallowed hard. "Newspapers—they don't always get stuff right do they? Sometimes they print whatever the heck they want. I used to work for a small newspaper, and you wouldn't believe what the ad people would do sometimes." She was rambling. She'd worked only a week at the newspaper before they'd let her go. Then she'd gotten the waitressing job. She clamped her mouth shut. Was it too late to change her name? People did that all the time didn't they?

What were all the suggestions young Jack Welling had urged Gram to do for her over the years that he'd mocked her over? Braces-check. Contact Lenses-check. Modern clothing-sorta check. Decent haircut-check. Acne treatment-check, a year of that horrible Accutane treatment and blood tests all the time. The Rachel who sat before him now was, in a way, a culmination of his many insults—except for all the weight she'd lost from an empty-pocketbook-induced diet.

"Oh yeah?" He took a sip of his coffee and then looked hard at her. "You look kinda familiar to me." A smug look, one she knew well, tugged at his perfect lips.

He knew. He knew she was lying. He *knew* but Jack was probably going to give her enough rope to hang herself.

She snapped her fingers. "No. I'm sorry." She laughed. "How silly of me. I associated the name Jack with Welling because of that big picture at the downtown museum of the local hero, Jack Welling, Sr. The Olympian and WWI aviator. You really do look like the man. Are you related?" Of course, she already knew the answer. But she

Carrie Fancett Pagels

offered him a fake smile. Then, as if being smacked, she felt the conviction of the lie. She averted her gaze.

He dipped his chin slightly. "Yeah, that's my great-great-uncle. I'm named after him and his son, the WWII veteran. Jack Welling, Jr., had no male heirs, so my folks named me after the them."

If she remembered right, Dawn Charbonneau was Jack's distant cousin, and the Jack Welling, Jr.'s daughter. "That's a cool family tradition." Too bad Rachel's own mother hadn't passed on some kind of good tradition. Mom had been a spoiled only child who'd gone wild, and Rachel had to deal with the consequences.

"Yeah, and now I'm working on my family's cottage."

Next door! They didn't call it the Cadotte house in the ad. It was called something else. *No. No. No.* Not if she was going to keep her camping out a secret. Wouldn't matter if she got arrested for trespassing. She kept her lips tightly closed.

"I see you say you've got good admin skills."

She only shrugged in response.

"No criminal record?" He raised an eyebrow as he handed the phone back.

Not yet. "Nope. I've never been arrested."

Could be soon though.

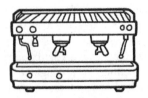

Chapter Five

When Andrette stared in her direction, Rachel made an *X* over her chest. "Cross my heart." Unless the Mackinac Island police started coming around, then Rachel might become a criminal. And since the station was kitty-corner across the street from Lucky Bean, at least Rachel would see them coming. What was the fine for squatting on someone's property, anyways?

"Andi, what are her hours here?"

The owner turned and grabbed a clipboard from the wall then joined them at the table. "I need someone at my register from two to nine each day during the week—weekends off."

"Perfect." Jack slapped the table with both hands. "I need someone seven to one."

When her jaw dropped open, Rachel quickly pressed her lips together. She'd never agreed! These two islanders, in under fifteen minutes, had put her to work for a total of thirteen hours a day. How was she going to get out of this? She'd just asked God, as a newbie praying person, to answer her needs. *God, that's overkill, thank You very much—and with the wrong guy and wrong place for work. Sorry for the sarcasm in my prayer, God, but I mean—really?*

"You're only open till sixish right now, Andi."

"Right. Sorry, Rachel. Once mid-June hits I'll need you till nine. For now, you should be done by six at the latest." Andrette inclined her head toward Rachel. "But you won't need a third job, eh?"

She didn't even *want* the second one. *Definitely not with Jack Welling.* On the other hand, if she only worked twenty hours at present then she'd not be able to pay her bills. "Right." She should say something more. "Thank you both for the opportunity to work for you." She directed her words toward Andrette and avoided Jack's direct gaze.

"No dress code at my work site. Nothing, ya know, ah, suggestive. Got young men coming on board." He chuckled, just like he had as an aggravating teenager.

She could not work for Jack. Should not. *Not ever. Never.* "I'm not sure I can work for you, then. All I own are very low-cut blouses and super short skirts." Rachel lowered her eyelids to half-mast, hoping he'd tell her right then and there that she was out. "Very sexy looking." Right now, though, she was wearing something that *no one* in their right mind would call alluring.

Andrette gave her the side-eye then pointed at Jack. "She's got you there, you sexist pig."

Jack's cheeks flushed. "You're kidding?"

Rachel shook her head slowly, enjoying tormenting the guy who had made her summers on Mackinac misery. 'Hey, Rach, why doesn't your mom put braces on your crooked teeth? Hey Rach, ya know they make contact lenses for people who wear inch-thick glasses. Hey Rach, ask your mom about Accutane for your acne.'

Her face heated as she recalled some of the humiliating moments she'd endured. And always, stupidly, she'd run to Gram crying. And Gram would make sure that whatever *Horrible Jack* had mentioned got fixed. Of course, Gram didn't call him Horrible Jack—Rachel did.

She fisted her hands.

"No problem for us here at Lucky Bean. I've got uniforms. White blouse with our LB logo and black slacks to match for my cashiers."

The baristas wore Lucky Bean emblazoned aprons over their clothing. "Great."

"Just leave me your sizes." Andrette shifted her weight. "How about you Jack? Since you require the girl to wear a nun's habit or something. Do they give you some old ones from St. Anne's to use?" Andrette chuckled softly.

"Very funny." Jack scratched his cheek. "But not a bad idea."

"It's no problem if you want to retract the offer. Especially since I have a propensity toward outrageous clothing." Rachel kept her voice low and even. Truth was, all she owned right now were a handful of basic outfits. Nothing that she'd owned before fit her anymore.

"No nun's habit." A muscle jumped in his cheek. "But since you'll be on site part of the time, best if you wear enclosed-toe shoes, long shorts or some pants, and a high-necked shirt."

Rachel raised her eyebrows. "That might give me eczema or something. I could have a really terrible rash." Oh, no, she shouldn't have said that. She and Olivia had teased Jack about his eczema when he was a teen.

Jack's square jaw dropped open. Then he closed his mouth. He slowly raised his hands as if in surrender. "I understand. I'll absolutely accommodate you on that. I'm desperate."

"That's what I told Rachel." Ms. Herron gestured around the café. "We're pretty desperate here."

His eyes widened, as if in recognition. "Rachel." He drew out her name slowly. "Rachel? Or should I call you Rach for short?" He scrunched up his nose in the way she hated and smirked at her. Oh yes, there was bratty Jack Welling and handsome mature Jack had fled.

Stupid, stupid, stupid. *I never should have said that about the eczema.*

"So, you'll front her for some cash for new clothes that don't give her rashes, eh?" Andrette's mocking tone and expression suggested she was really enjoying this.

"Absolutely." He pulled out his wallet. "Need an assistant there when I'm out. Never know when contractors will show up."

He was supposed to say *no.* Jack Welling, terrible boy that he was, would *never* have hired her. So that meant adult Jack wouldn't either. Right?

Oh, God, help me.

Pride. Pride cometh before a fall. If Jack advanced her the cash for clothes, then she could wear what she already had and buy food instead. She had almost no cash left, even after the bank in Mackinaw City had cashed her last work check using her driver's license and because the cashier knew Dawn and Jim Charbonneau who had accounts there. At some point she could go to the island bank to see about her old account that Gram had established. But who knew what was in there? Might only be fifty bucks or so.

Andrette joined them at the table. "If you can start today, Rachel, I'll also give ya an advance on your wages for a week." She cocked her hip.

Rachel almost leapt up and hugged the woman. Moisture pooled in her eyes and her stomach chose just that moment to growl loudly. Maybe Andrette wanted to see how Rachel worked, since it was Friday and she'd not be back in until Monday. She pressed her hands to her flat abdomen. "Sorry. And yes, I can start today." Right after she put something in her gut.

Across from her, Jack tapped the table. "Bring this girl and me your special egg, cheese and bacon bagels and I'll spot ya for her first weeks' wages myself."

Maybe he *didn't* know who she was. Maybe she could be super careful and he'd never find out. Maybe the extra money would be just what she needed. *God what do you have in mind here?* She should confess. But her lips wouldn't move.

"Juan Pablo," Andrette called over her shoulder, "two special breakfast bagels please."

The barista glanced over at Rachel again, his dark eyes shining. There was something about Juan Pablo that made her feel good. He looked like a compassionate soul.

"Would ya like a coffee, too?" The concern in Jack's voice almost undid her. He was being too kind now. He, too, was acting like a nice guy. But she knew better.

She did not want to eat with this man. But her roiling stomach begged her to put something in it. "Columbian with cream and sugar would be super."

"Hey, Andi, add a white sweet Columbian to that order." The way he teasingly said the words sounded suggestive.

Were these two in a relationship? *Great.* Even if she didn't work for him, she'd encounter Jack at the coffee shop.

"Sure thing, but first let's see the money, honey, eh?" Andi responded.

Jack pushed back from the table, then rose. He took the few steps to the counter and then pulled his wallet out, moistened his fingertip and slowly counted out a bunch of twenties. Heat singed her cheeks in embarrassment. She desperately needed this cash.

She slowly exhaled a long puff of air, considering.

She couldn't refuse it.

And at some point, she'd have to let Jack know who she was.

Andrette raised one bill high. "I'll keep this one and you give the rest to my new girl, eh?"

Rachel cringed. She was in her mid-twenties and no longer a *girl*.

And Jack was a grown man now and not a boy.

How had Jack Welling turned into Mr. Hunky Dude? She shouldn't think of him as a hottie. This was the same rotten person who as a teen had launched footballs over the hedgerow at her when she'd taunted him. The same creep who had toilet papered Grandma's lawn and Rachel had to clean it up. The same guy who had promised to watch her and Olivia and then spent the entire time watching a dumb Sci Fi movie while they had ridden their bike around the island—*by themselves*. When they'd returned, he'd looked up from the TV and asked, "Can ya get me some more popcorn?" Then he'd shoved an empty bag of microwave popcorn at Olivia. He hadn't even noticed they'd left.

Ugh. What a jerk. And now she was supposed to work for him? Ok, he looked amazing, but she knew the real guy inside. She knew how to manage jerks. She could handle Jerky Jack. That had been one of her favorite nicknames for Jack Welling the teen.

He slid into the chair. "You alright?"

She realized she was scowling and forced a smile. "Yeah, great. I mean I've got two jobs now for the summer. Who could ask for more?" She could add "actress" to her resume. Thirteen hours a day of work, but if she managed that for the season, maybe she'd have some to tide her over once the fudgies—the tourists—had left. And just maybe she could start nursing school in the fall if she got loans and scholarships, too.

He stared at her hard, again. "You know, you really do look kinda familiar."

She made a comical face. "I have one of those faces." One he'd taunted her about.

"You're a local?"

The barista brought her coffee to the table and slid it in front of her, sparing Rachel a moment to think. "Thanks."

"*De nada.*" Juan Pablo flashed her a gleaming smile. "We welcome you to Lucky Bean and pray you'll be happy here."

Peace cloaked her, again. "Thanks." She sipped her coffee and avoided Jack's gaze.

Jack slid a stack of what looked like nearly thirty twenty-dollar bills toward her. "I put an extra two hundred in there for some kind of work clothes. No nuns' habits, please."

Her entire wardrobe in the past year—since Mom had kicked her out of the high-rise—cost less than two hundred. A tremor began in her fingers as she reached to accept the cash. She couldn't look too desperate, despite being so.

"Hey and don't forget to ask for your share of the tips at the end of your shifts, okay?" He sounded like a big brother, lecturing her.

Too bad the Jack Welling she remembered was anything but a good big brother. He'd harassed his younger sister and when Rachel had played with Olivia, at the neighboring cottage, as they got older. When they were in middle school, he'd intrude and ask a million questions instead of leaving them alone. She gritted her back teeth at the recollection. "I'll remember. Thanks."

He leaned in. "You'll be paid as indicated in the ad, once you prove you can keep everything, and possibly everybody, straight."

She could put some aside for a room in the small college town nearby for once she was enrolled in nursing school. "I'll do my best."

Juan Pablo returned with the bagels. "Happy eating."

They smelled amazing.

Once again, she experienced the sense of peace that accompanied the server.

"Mind if I say a quick prayer?" Jack asked.

She almost asked, 'Huh?' but caught herself. "Absolutely." Was he really going to pray, right here in public? Who did that, anyway? Certainly not this pest from her past.

Jack bent his head, dark hair falling forward.

She closed her eyes.

"Father God, we thank You for this food and drink and ask You to bless Rachel's work and mine this summer. In Jesus's name, Amen."

When she raised her head, Juan Pablo was standing beside her, and he opened his eyes. "Amen." He winked at her. "I enjoy when Mr. Welling prays over his food. It's like he's asking a blessing on this whole place." He opened his arms. "The whole island."

Her former tormenter looked up. "Glad you feel that way, Juan Pablo. But when are ya going to start calling me Jack?"

"You're not like everyone else, Mr. Welling. You are special—like I keep telling you."

"You've only known me a few weeks, so ya might want to hold off judgement on that."

This new Jack, this Mr. Welling, he wasn't like everybody else. He wasn't quite like the *old* Jack.

Maybe there was hope for Rachel, too. *The new Rachel.*

And special? The old Jack was *especially* annoying but that wasn't the same thing.

"Dig in, Squirt." A muscle in Jack's cheek twitched.

She gaped at him. He *did* know. She caught his mocking gaze just as he bit into his bagel sandwich.

He chewed slowly.

"I'm quitting if you call me that again." She hissed the words at him so quietly no one else in the room could have heard.

He laughed. "Quitting *my* job or here?"

She glared at him.

Jack straightened. "Have to come up with a new nickname for ya. You've gotten too tall for that one."

Rachel had shot up five inches since she'd last seen Jack at age thirteen. And now Jack was teasing her. She was sure her nostrils were flaring. "And don't *ever* call me Rach, again."

He grinned at her. "Noted."

"Don't think that I won't throw rocks at you, like Olivia and I did, when you called us nicknames. Because I just might." Now why had she said that? *Talk about juvenile.* She took a bite of her sandwich. *Seriously yum.*

He stiffened and blinked.

Rachel wasn't done yet. "And where have you guys been these past few years, anyway? Did you make Olivia stop writing to me?"

He'd once threatened to tear up any letters that Rachel sent to their home in Grand Rapids.

Jack stared hard at her for a moment, as if he was trying to read something in her face. It unnerved her. Then he wiped his face with his napkin and pushed back his chair. "Gotta go. Come to the house seven sharp Monday morning."

Was it her imagination or was moisture glistening in his eyes? What had happened?

"See ya later, Andi," he called out as the door slammed behind him. He strode off determinedly.

Andrette glided over to the table. "What's got his goat, eh?"

"I'm not sure." She felt a little guilty about upsetting him, but gosh, that was an overreaction.

Andrette crossed her arms over her chest. "I sure love Jack. He has his moments—just like everyone does. But he's such a sweetie."

Jack a sweetie? Rachel almost felt her eyes crossing as she looked up in disbelief at her new boss. Were Jack and Andrette a couple? It sure seemed so.

So, she might end up with a double dose of Jack Welling every single day that she worked both jobs. *Ugh.*

Rachel sipped her coffee as Andrette returned to the cash register to ring up a customer. Juan Pablo carried a tubful of ice to a brown cooler at the end of the barista bar. He dumped the ice in, and she cringed at the noise.

Why did she suddenly feel so irritated? Angry even? Like she'd been when Gram had died, and she'd been furious with God. Now that familiar annoyance returned with a rush. Andrette and Jack might make her life miserable.

That just isn't true.

She could manage her emotions and what she told herself about this situation. Rachel was a grown woman, despite not acting like one, moments ago. Her cheeks heated as she finished her coffee and rose.

She should be grateful. She should be thrilled. Two jobs and cash to pay for her needs.

But all she felt was fear of being found trespassing.

And annoyance about her niggling growing concern about Jack—and what had set him off.

Why did she feel guilty? What had she done? Was this yet another Holy Spirit nudge, like Rev. Michaels told her would get stronger with time?

Andrette motioned for Rachel to join her at the register.

The customer took her coffee and muffin to a nearby table.

"Rachel, I don't know if you'd be cool with this, but if you want to go change into the shirt, in the back, you could start right now."

She shrugged. "Why not?"

A grin lit the pretty woman's face. "Come on, I'll show you where to put your things, and where the bathroom is."

"Thanks."

Soon Rachel was up front, getting the lay of the land, or in this case, the store rules and products. She was pretty familiar with what they had, since she frequented the place often over the years.

The afternoon flew by and soon, Andrette flipped over the CLOSED sign.

"Good job, Rachel." She high-fived her. "I don't think you'll have any trouble come Monday."

Except that Monday was when she began to work for Mr. Trouble himself.

Andrette went to the register and closed it out and moved cash contents to a locked bank bag.

Juan Pablo gestured to her and Rachel joined him at the end of the counter.

"This is Good Friday." His warm dark eyes locked on hers.

She'd almost forgotten.

He passed a slip of paper to her. "There is a Good Friday service tonight and Easter Sunday *la solida del sol. . .* sunrise service."

"I've never been to a sunrise service."

It sounded like he said, "I know," but she must have misunderstood Juan Pablo.

She looked at the location for the service. The Good Friday service was at a small nondenominational church but the sunrise service was in the park. It would be freezing cold out. She raised her eyebrows.

He laughed. "I know what you're thinking. But that service will be *poco tiempo.*" He held his forefinger and thumb a fraction apart. "Brief time. Then we'll go back to the building for coffee and something called. . . *bollos cruzados calientes.*"

"Hot cross buns?"

"*Si!*" He laughed. "And we will celebrate."

"I would love that." From an all-out multi-day celebration in Chicago, to fellowship with the community in Mackinaw City, to a new experience with strangers on Mackinac Island—Rachel's first Easter as a newbie Christian had morphed into the unexpected.

Suddenly her weekend alone really wasn't. And she was never truly alone. Juan Pablo's invitation reminded her of that.

"I'll be there tonight." This Friday really was turning out to be good.

Carrie Fancett Pagels

Chapter Six

Mackinac Island

Why on earth did I ever agree to work for the one person I'd hoped to never ever see again? Rachel shrugged into her sweatshirt and zipped it up. *This position could go very badly.* Rachel closed her eyes. This was Easter Monday, and she'd been so blessed by the gorgeous, though chillingly cold, sunrise service the previous morning. It felt as though her entire soul had been set on fire by the gorgeous rising sun over Lake Huron. Afterward, the church members, mainly island residents and some seasonal workers, laughed and talked and drank strong coffee and ate those amazing hot cross buns and Easter cakes. Too bad that euphoric feeling was wearing off as she faced the prospect of working for Jack. *Lord, please don't let him aggravate me. Please help me. I need this job.*

She exited Lilac Cottage and closed the door behind her. She walked through the side lawn, pausing to looked up to the third floor, squinting against the early morning light, almost expecting to spy Olivia there from her room. Jack looked down intense sorrow on his unguarded face. What was he doing in Olivia's room? Why hadn't she been there in years? And was he sad because he'd stupidly offered Rachel a job and now regretted it? Besides renovating his family's home, what was Jack doing on the island again after so many years?

Although she'd love answers to her questions, the first day of her new job probably wasn't the time to ask. But she had to find out what had happened to her friend.

She hurried to the front of Canary Cottage, up the steps, and entered as Jack had instructed her to do. Heavy footfalls on the stairs announced his descent. Just as loud as he ever was—like an elephant wearing concrete boots.

A bundle of golden fur met her first, rushing toward her from the front parlor.

"Sit!" Jack commanded and the canine complied, tail thumping the floor.

She bent and petted the dog. Could it possibly be? She looked up at Jack. "Oh my gosh, is that Goldie?"

"Yup."

A rush of joy surged through her. "Such a good girl." She patted the dog's head. "I haven't heard her barking at all since I've arrived. Is she staying here?"

A flicker of some unreadable emotion passed over Jack's face. "We're here some of the time. And she's pretty well-trained."

Rachel laughed. "I remember that she only barked on the rare occasion and when she did, *Olivia* had me go home to Gram's."

"Yeah, that's pretty strange, isn't it?" He rubbed his cleft chin. "I'd never really noticed."

Jack didn't take her bait in commenting on Olivia. "I always thought Goldie was *Olivia's* dog."

"She's *mine* now." With the way a muscle jumped near his eye, Rachel wasn't going to press further.

"Well, Goldie is still beautiful and sweet. Aren't you girl?" She petted the pup again.

"Time to get to work." Jack clapped his hands, apparently signaling an end to their discussion.

"All right."

"I've got you set up at the Captain Swaine desk." He pointed to a large, mahogany antique writing desk.

"You know he was my great-great-grandfather, right?" Her namesake, Sadie, had married Captain Robert Swaine. Rachel's full name was Sadie Rachel Dunmara, but she'd always been called Rachel other than by Gram who sometimes called her Sadie Rachel. Gram had loved her Grandmother Sadie to pieces and often spoke about her.

Jack shoved his hands into his sweatshirt pockets. "Yeah, but do you know why Captain Swaine and his wife moved into Lilac Cottage and left much of their stuff here? My folks and I wondered."

Rachel shrugged. "I always thought it was because the other house was newer, and they'd winterized it."

"Nope. This place was winterized, too."

"So why leave?"

"There were a few reasons. Legal things."

"Such as?" Maybe he was making this up.

"You don't know about the weird codicils put on this property?"

"Nope. I know your grandparents or great-grandparents or whatever aren't technically related to the rest of us."

"Right. Just by marriage, not by blood. And my great-great-grandparents had to work out an arrangement to have rights to the usage of this cottage. Peter and Ada were their names."

"Ah, yes, Ada. The once wealthiest woman in the world had married Peter Welling, who had once been Robert Swaine's brother-in-law."

"Yeah. She sure helped bail the other descendants out when they couldn't afford to keep this cottage up."

"I don't know about that part."

"My dad said it took several lawyers and decades to finally sort who inherited what property because of codicils that Jacqueline Cadotte Swaine put in her will for her heirs."

"And that was why they built their own home next door?"

"No, they'd already done that. My dad said there was something else. I guess Sadie and her husband lost a son, Robert Junior."

"Nope." This part she knew. "No, she didn't. All of her children survived."

Jack scowled. "And you know this how?"

"Because my grandmother had me do massive amounts of genealogy stuff for her. She was really into that. And Sadie and Robert's first child, Robert Junior, graduated college."

"That's what my dad said. Maybe just family lore. My folks claim there is a stipulation about our family's ownership that ends this year. Thought it had to do with Robert, Junior."

"Oh, wait." A memory came to her. "There were no documents that we could find associated with him after that college graduation. Kind of a missing trail."

"So maybe he died in adulthood?"

"I didn't think about that. I guess I should have looked harder." Maybe she still would—in honor of Gram's memory.

Jack shrugged. "Anyway, that desk is yours to use. And my dad's rolling chair."

The padded contemporary chair looked out of place with the beautiful antique desk. "That looks comfortable."

He laughed. "Yeah, we normally avoid sitting on any of the ancient wood chairs in this house."

"Why aren't *you* set up at the Swaine desk?"

"Got somethin' better." He pointed to a modern sit-stand adjustable desk. "Besides, I'm not any relation to the Swaines, like

Lilac Cottage   55

you are. My great-grandparents Peter and Ada Welling were no blood kin."

"I think Gram told me something about that. Ada bought the property when the attorneys determined that the best course was to sell the cottage and divide the proceeds amongst the heirs. I guess Jacqueline Cadotte Swaine wasn't too nice to Peter, who'd been her son-in-law, but he got the last laugh by purchasing her properties."

"Probably best that Sadie and Robert built their new house."

"All their own, so no one could take it from them." Like Mom had done to her.

"My Grandma Welling said there was something about the Swaines' son that made them move. And they'd left other things—like their bedroom furniture."

"Yeah, but if it's heavy stuff like that desk, who would want to move it?"

He gave her a cocky grin. "A few strong guys could have hauled it over there."

He was fishing for a compliment on his physique, but he wasn't going to get it. "Now you have me curious."

He pointed to the papers strewn on the Swaine desk. "Let's focus on work."

"Sure thing."

He pulled a cell phone from his pocket. "First thing. You'll use this work phone to make and receive calls and set up appointments. You need to leave it here each day after work. You won't have to use your personal phone, and I or one of the Parkers' grandsons can take calls."

"The Parkers' grandsons?"

"Maria Parker has three teenaged grandsons from her first marriage, staying with them this summer. They'll paint and do some repairs under my direction."

She was under his direction, too.

She nodded.

"They're good kids with lots of volunteer experience through their church. Their youth leader is into helping rehab homes for the elderly in their parish."

"Great."

"I thought so." Jack opened a large planner and set it atop her desk. "Here's the upcoming work schedule for the week and for the coming month."

He carefully reviewed the tasks and deadlines.

"Any questions?"

"You'll be here if I need to ask, right?" As much as she wished him gone, it would be nice to be able to get information from him in person.

"I'll be coming and going. My cell number is in that phone so you can always call if you need something. I'll have to be on the mainland to meet with people and make purchases. Other things will be shipped in."

"All right. So, you want me to reach out and verify all of these orders have been placed and the ETA on arrival?"

"Right. And introduce yourself as project assistant or whatever."

She laughed. "How about Project Princess or Her Highness of the Calendar?"

He gaped for a moment then blinked. "Good one. Whatever you want to call yourself. But I've found Project Manager is a title vendors understand pretty well."

"And will give me more authority than Royal Deadline Enforcer?"

"Well, it translates out to something similar." He shook his head. "Oh, and my mom might be coming by this afternoon possibly before you leave. Please stick to work conversations while you're on my dime, okay?" He sounded just like the same bossy older brother he'd been to Olivia.

She raised her eyebrows but bit her tongue. So much for asking Mrs. Welling about her daughter.

Olivia where are you?

Jack finished responding to the email from the electrician and sent his reply. He had to admit it was pleasant how the adult Rachel interacted with him that morning and early afternoon. She was polite, professional, deferential, and a hard worker. Her mother, Selma, had been the most glamorous young woman on the island, his father had said. Also, the most provocative and self-absorbed. The only irritating thing Rachel had done was to ask him about Olivia.

Being here after a decade's absence, in the bright yellow Queen Anne style home that belonged to another era, felt too much like reopening a wound. His visits to America had been wonderful but far too brief. Maybe he should have come back here, to what had been his father's family summer home for over a hundred years. Emotionally, this place remained a part of their pasts.

Then the visits stopped altogether when Covid had squashed his career. Two very long years. And if he was honest with himself. Two lonely years despite being aboard a ship full of merchant sailors.

Lilac Cottage   57

Rachel looked up from where she was entering figures in the old-fashioned ledger he'd chosen to use instead of a computer program. Her brow puckered. "You said you'd worked as an engineer on boats, right?"

"Ships."

She blushed. He shouldn't have corrected her. What did it matter if it was called a ship or a boat?

"Silly me, right I should have known that. My one stepfather—"

"The admiral?" An unforgettable and famous man.

She smiled. "Yes, the admiral always pointed out that a boat and a ship are very different."

"Mainly size."

Her eyes widened. Did she think he was making a suggestive comment? He wasn't.

Rachel blushed. "Anyway, when you were out on those ships, during Covid, did you get stuck? I mean, were you unable to get off or did you get trapped in port like those workers on the cargo vessels in Los Angeles?"

"That's why I'm here. All the hassles of no travel home during Covid. And my ship ended up sitting off the California coast for like *forever*." Sweat broke out on his brow just thinking about it.

She set her pencil down. "Did you. . ."

"Quit?"

Her eyes widened.

"Yup."

Rachel cocked her head, a strand of her thick, dark, wavy hair falling forward. He shouldn't be noticing how nice it looked.

"Not going back if that's what you're gonna ask. I'm one of the *pandemicly rearranged* people. I don't know if that's a word or not, but that's what I call it." He smiled. Mei never understood his little word jokes, but Rachel would.

She chuckled, a nice sound that zinged around inside him in a way he shouldn't be enjoying so much. "I like that."

And he liked this newer, kinder version of Rachel. Would Olivia have also morphed into a new version of herself? Coming here was stirring up so many memories. Was he so *Olivialy rearranged* and never to recover? Was it fair to not tell Rachel that Olivia had died of leukemia eleven years earlier?

"So that's why you've come back here to fix up the place this summer?"

When Jack shared his plan to leave the merchant ships, his father begged him to come renovate the house—so they could create new memories there. But had Dad really just wanted him to rid the place

58   *Carrie Fancett Pagels*

of Olivia and her presence? Or was there some other motive for having Jack here? Dad was acting more evasive than usual when Jack questioned him on almost anything. His defensiveness worried Jack. Mom and Dad rarely came to the cottage since Olivia's death—usually just to ready it before the season and to do winter prep at the end. Other extended family members had made use of the place during the high season. But it was time to move on, and face summers without Olivia.

He drew in a slow breath. He needed to tell Rachel about his sister. "Hey, Rachel, there's something I should explain."

"Hello!" The front door swung open, and his mother stepped in carrying a box marked Mackinaw Bakery. She set it on an antique mahogany console, covered with an old sheet.

Jack gave her a big hug. "Hi Mom! Any problems on the ferry?"

He released her.

"None at all." She stepped back. "I just can't believe you're back in Michigan to stay."

First, he'd need to find a job, but he didn't want to discuss that in front of Rachel.

Mom glanced at Rachel and gasped. "Selma?"

Rachel's eyes widened.

"Oh, no, of course not." Mom's breath seemed to have caught in her throat. "Rachel?"

Jack cleared his throat. He should have told Mom. "Rachel is working for me this summer."

"My son didn't tell me." Her voice emerged as a loud whisper.

"It's so lovely to see you, again, Mrs. Welling."

"And you, too." Mom continued to stare.

Was she wondering what Olivia would look like now, at the same age, if she were alive? Every time Jack looked at Rachel, he'd tried to imagine his sister at her age. But all he'd come up with was a memory of Olivia as a sick young teen.

Rachel's dark eyebrows tugged together. "I keep expecting to see Olivia come through that door."

Tears welled in Mom's eyes. Jack reached for the box of Kleenex and handed it to her. She grabbed two tissues and blew her nose.

"Oh no, I'm sorry." Rachel's face grew pale. "Is something wrong with Olivia?"

Mom shot him an accusatory stare. If Jack had told Rachel, then Mom wouldn't be suffering this right now.

He shoved a hand through his hair. "I'm sorry. I should have explained."

Why could he never say the words? Because it made it real. He wasn't ready for that. "My sister died. That's all I want to say about it."

Mom sniffed. "Leukemia. It's been over a decade now."

Rachel raised her palms, her eyes glistening. "Oh no. I'm so sorry. She was an amazing person. My best friend, really."

Jack gave her a hard look. Was she kidding? Those two only saw each other in the summertime. Sure, they'd been constant companions, but he'd always believed the Chicago girl had a bunch of chums back home. Best friends? Olivia had possessed a swarm of friends in their Grand Rapids neighborhood, most of whom abandoned her when she got sick.

"I think. . . I'm sorry, but I need a little time to myself." Rachel swiped at her eyes. "Before my next job starts." She returned to her makeshift desk and grabbed her beat-up little purse.

"Yeah. No prob." That was what normal people did when they grieved a loss. They didn't run off to sail around the world as an engineer on a merchant vessel. They hit the pause button on their lives and grieved. But he hadn't. Nor had his folks.

In both of his condos, he had a family picture of himself, Dad, Mom, and Olivia. It was as though they were caught there for all time. He'd dumped one of his girlfriends after she asked about Olivia and why he never spoke about her. That's how emotionally immature he was. After that, he'd put the photo frame away if he had someone over and he'd take it out as soon as they left.

Being here in this cottage brought all the ghosts back to life.

When the door closed behind Rachel, Mom sank onto the faded velvet divan that needed reupholstering. "I thought I'd seen a ghost when she looked at me. It was as if young Selma Dunmara was here." She shook her head. "I'm not sure if I've seen her since the Parkers' belated twenty-fifth wedding anniversary party—other than in a few magazines after that."

"When was that?"

"Oh gosh, before Rachel was born. Maybe that year before." Mom shrugged. "But she sure looks like Selma—so beautiful with that dark hair and ivory skin."

Jack shifted uncomfortably. The sleeping beauty he'd spied next door was indeed Rachel, his old nemesis. "Well, I can't be paying attention to that stuff—she's my employee, Mom."

Mom splayed her fingers. "You know I'm a stickler for boundaries so of course I don't expect you'd cross any lines. I was just observing how she's changed so much."

"I bet Olivia would be just as pretty as you, if she were still here." This was a first step. He had to say something that could start the conversation that needed to be held. The sharing of their loss.

She swiped at her eyes. "Thank you for saying that." She sniffed back tears. "Seeing Rachel helps me imagine what Olivia could have been like as an adult."

"Instead of remaining a teenager forever?"

"Right."

Jack joined her on the divan, which creaked ominously. They both laughed.

"I hope it doesn't break."

"It might." Mom patted his hand. "But it's far worse to have a breaking heart and no one to share that with."

He wrapped his arm around his mom and pulled her close. "I'm here, and I'm ready to talk about losing Olivia."

Rachel had to pull herself together. She couldn't go to the coffee shop with her eyes swollen from crying and her nose red. She'd remembered that their maid Yolanda had used theatrical makeup for her stage productions on the island. The maid loved acting in local plays. Rachel went into Yolanda's room and located the set in her dresser drawer. The stuff looked in great shape. *Just this once.* She didn't like using someone else's make-up, but her normal foundation wasn't going to cut it. She carried the kit into the bathroom and dabbed the lightest nude color onto her nose. Soon the redness had completely disappeared. No wonder actors loved the stuff.

Olivia gone. Olivia dead. Leukemia.

She had to stop. It was reminding her that Gram was gone too, and the grief still so raw.

Rachel bent over the sink and let the tears fall in there. Would she fill the porcelain vessel if she let herself cry it all out? She gently blotted her eyes with a dry washcloth. Her eyes needed some actors' makeup, too. She couldn't quell the swelling, but she could cover the redness.

Why didn't Jack tell me? Poor Mrs. Welling—having to explain to me. But why hadn't they ever told her or her family about Olivia's death?

Or had they?

Mrs. Welling said she'd died ten years ago.

The same year Gramps had died. *What a crazy time.*

Had the Wellings told Gram, and she'd been too distressed over Gramps' sudden death to tell Rachel?

Mom had flipped out after Gramps had died. She'd acted like she might be next. Gram, too, had morphed into someone Rachel hadn't recognized. For the first time she could remember, both Gram and Mom sought to control her every movement. They'd taken her out of her private school in Chicago and the two of them had packed her up and sent her off to Virginia. She hadn't even been allowed to attend the funeral.

Maybe they'd been too distressed with their own grief to mention Olivia.

A strange noise, like metal grinding, sounded from behind the door that led to the basement. She cringed.

The grating sound stopped. What had that been?

She listened. Nothing.

Rachel exhaled a sigh.

That's all she needed—for something in the basement to go haywire. She'd never been down there, and she didn't want to start now.

It wasn't her house. She was just camping out until the new owners arrived. They could deal with the strange noise in the basement.

Not my problem.

Is it, Lord?

She was a newbie to this faith thing. Not every weird thing that happened was some kind of sign from the Lord. Her nerves were already on edge. That's probably why she felt this odd tug in her spirit. She wasn't supposed to be here in this cottage. Maybe she should beg Jack to let her rent a room from him.

No way. Especially since she didn't want to get in his and Andrette's path on their date nights or whatever.

Her phone sounded for a text message. She didn't recognize the phone number.

This is Jack's dad. I'm looking for Toni. She's not responding to my texts. Neither is he.

Rachel frowned. Why wasn't Jack's mom answering?

What was Mr. Welling doing with her cell phone number? Had Jack shared it with him? And if so, why?

She lowered her head. She'd have to talk with Jack about boundaries—especially with her cell number. But this was her neighbor. Love thy neighbor and all that.

Just saw them. They r fine. Maybe no signal. Spotty up here. She texted her message back. Then she added, *u need them to call u?*

Had he even tried to call them? Sometimes texts worked when the phone didn't though.

You doing ok? Sorry about your grandmother.

How did he know about Gram? She'd really need to talk with Jack about not sharing her information. *Ugh.*

Or had Mom told him?

Her stomach sank. Was Jack's dad her father? If she was completely honest with herself, she'd considered Mr. Welling a candidate for a long time now.

That would make Jack her half-brother.

She didn't want to deal with any of this.

TY. Gotta run to work.

Rachel jogged up the alley and most of the way to town, slowing only when she got to the library.

She ignored the ping of her cell phone until she got to Lucky Bean.

Andrette is a great boss. Mr. Welling's message was true—Andrette seemed really nice. Obviously, he knew Jack's sweetheart well or at least thought highly of her.

This was such a small-town kind of place. Why did she think she could keep her secrets to herself?

And she hadn't shared any info with anyone but Jack. She couldn't trust him with anything.

Same old Jack.

Just like a big brother reading a diary.

But Jack had kept Olivia's death a secret all these years.

Something didn't jive.

Chapter Seven

Mackinaw City, May 2022

*A*s if they were about to depart onto the Titanic rather than on a Mackinac Island ferry, Kareen Parker clutched Zuzu's carrier tightly lest they sink.

"Good morning, ma'am." The young dock worker scanned Kareen's ticket.

"Beautiful day." The nip in the air stirred her blood.

He offered a crooked grin. Old Kareen would have been annoyed by his cocky young male attitude, but *New Kareen* found it charming. "Yup. No ice to get stuck in out there today."

She arched a brow. Fortunately, she'd never experienced such an ordeal.

"Don't eat too much fudge over there," he advised. *Definitely cheeky.*

The ferry line employee must be about the same age as her youngest grandson, Carter. Carter had worked for another company, Sheplers, for a couple of years before he left for college.

Kareen stepped into the queue. Zuzu made snuffling noises. Most passengers wore labor workers' attire. With her fancy couture outfit from Cassie Browne, with its matching long ivory coat, she must look as out of place as a dolphin arcing up in this harbor.

She climbed the stairs and took a seat, setting Zuzu's carrier underneath as best she could. "There, there, we'll be to the island in no time." Her chihuahua wasn't a fan of the water but if Kareen held her little snuggler in her arms then Zuzu would yip the entire trip over. No point in upsetting the other passengers.

As the ferry departed the dock, Kareen's heartbeat skipped with the waves—not in anticipation but in a mix of hope and dread. The scent of fresh lake water churning was so different from the briny scent enveloping her new husband's yacht when they rode up the Intracoastal Waterway. Gianni in Florida was her new life. Her deceased husband Hampy and many of their friends on the island were now gone. Some from age, some from the dreaded pandemic, and some like Hampy from self-destructive behavior.

Fifteen minutes earlier, before she'd arrived at the dock, an irrational thrill of hope had sped through Kareen when she'd spotted Margaret Dunmara's sedan parked in front of Butterfly Cottage. But her former dear old friend was terribly ill and in a nursing home. So, Margaret wouldn't likely be there at the Straits. Kareen touched the navy, yellow, and white silk scarf at her neck, a long-ago gift from Margaret Dunmara—pinned with a gold clasp from their mutual friend, Dawn.

The owners of Butterfly Cottage, her longtime friends Dawn and Jim Charbonneau, wouldn't be up North until June. At least they were doing well. When Kareen's sweety got there, she hoped they'd accept him. She chewed her lower lip. Dawn and Jim didn't know yet about Gianni. Nor did hardly anyone. How silly that as senior citizens in their seventies, both widowed, she and Gianni felt they had to protect their families from the truth of their love. Still, since Hampy had passed away only in the past year, Kareen and Gianni felt an obligation to wait until they saw their families in person again.

The ferry underway, Kareen caught a clear view of Butterfly Cottage with the luxury late-model sedan parked out front.

If Margaret hadn't parked her car at Dawn and Jim's place, then who had?

Rachel? Rachel Dunmara—Margaret's granddaughter and someone the Parkers were forbidden to see. Supposedly Selma Dunmara believed the Parkers might be a bad influence on Rachel. Judge Dunmara knew the story of the Parker family's criminal background in Chicago, but that had been so long ago it seemed ridiculous. When Selma's daughter began coming to the island with her grandparents, Kareen and her family were given the cut supreme. Margaret froze her out. Periodically, though, the Dunmaras sent a Christmas card. Kareen had suspected Selma's mandate of no contact by the Parkers with her child had something to do with her son, Hamp.

The ferry horn sounded, and Kareen jumped. She ought to be used to the noise after all these years. She grabbed a treat from her purse, bent, and offered it to her pup, who grabbed it. "Now Zuzu, where are your manners?"

Kareen straightened. The chill Lake Huron breeze cut through her flimsy coat, and she shivered. Why had she sat atop the ferry instead of sitting underneath as she and Hampy had done for decades? Because there was *no* Hampy anymore, other than his ashes which had been shipped to their son. Their son? Sweat broke out on her brow as she contemplated her next steps with her son. *Too many secrets for far too long.*

The announcer came on the speakers, offering island guides for sale.

Dread worked its way up again yet mixed with some anticipation. Truth be told, she'd yearned for the hotel, or their "resort" as Hampy like to call it, to come into view. This might be the first of the *lasts*. This would be first time she saw the pillars of their majestic white hotel on the East Bluff for this season and when she left it would be the last time that she'd be greeting it for the season.

If Gianni got his way, then by September, she'd have completely turned over the running of Parkers to Hamp and Maria. And have figured a way she could transfer ownership. They'd earned it. And as Gianni repeatedly pointed out, she didn't need to continue her co-dependency with Hampy's legacy.

She inhaled deeply, wishing Gianni was there to hold her hand and tell her it would be all right. This should be an interesting summer—preparing her family to accept her new husband, whom they'd never heard about and trying to straighten out the estate.

Husband. Thinking of Gianni as her husband made her smile. For the first time in her life, she felt like someone had her back. And she trusted him with the secret she'd kept for over fifty years.

A shadow cast over her shoulder as someone neared.

"Kareen Parker?"

Not her name any longer, but she'd answer to it this summer. Kareen swiveled to look up at Joy Ellis, their bank's assistant manager. "Hi there." Wow, her words sounded bright and cheerful, not like the old Kareen.

Joy's eyes widened as Kareen beamed up at her. Oops, she should be looking sad—like a grieving widow. But the last six months of Hampy's drawn out self-inflicted death from alcohol addiction had cured Kareen of most grief. And the Co-da meetings, counseling, rediscovering her faith, and finding Gianni—and new love—had brought an intense healing.

"I. . . uh, how are you doing, Mrs. Parker?"

"Great." Kareen scooted over into the empty seat next to her on this early ferry crossing, the vibration of the ferry coursing through her thin leather flats.

"I thought I saw you get on board, but I wasn't sure." Joy's light eyes held concern. "You look so different."

With Kareen sporting a new hair color, carefully applied makeup, designer sunglasses and a wardrobe of colorful new stylish clothes she'd almost not recognized her own self in the mirror that morning. "I'm doing really well, thanks."

"I'm glad." Joy chewed her lower lip.

"How's work at the bank? Is that where you're going this morning?"

The younger woman gaped at her for a moment. "Uh, yes, I'm the manager now."

"Wonderful. Well deserved." Joy was a hard worker and always had a smile for every patron.

"I don't know about that, but it has allowed us to buy my parents' house on the lake near Cheboygan." Joy brushed her long blonde hair over her shoulder.

"That's super."

"They've moved to Florida."

"That's where I am now. Where are they?" Gianni would love meeting the vibrant couple.

"At the Lakes."

The Lakes was a massive and popular development intended only for senior citizens. "Oh, my goodness, that's where Gianni and I are." Kareen stiffened as she realized her slip. Should have stopped and bought coffee that morning at the Mackinaw Bakery. Yes, from now on she must be fully caffeinated before she talked to anyone.

Joy's tawny eyebrows tugged together. "Gianni?"

Kareen waved her hand. "Oh, Hampy and I met Gianni and his wife on a riverboat cruise down the Danube a few years back. Friends ever since." Much *more than friends* and she'd omitted the fact that Gianni's spouse was now deceased.

"Oh. Yes, it's good to have friends at a time like this." Joy exhaled a sigh.

Nodding, Kareen understood how deeply the pandemic had affected everyone—sometimes too much to verbalize it. "I'll have to look up your mom and dad when I return to Florida. Did they come up here this summer?"

The pretty blonde laughed. "Yes, they're our guests now, which is kind of fun. They're in my old bedroom and complaining about using the hall bathroom."

"Gotta love that."

"Yup." Joy's expression grew serious. "I do need to see you some time—about a banking issue."

Kareen frowned. "Sure. I imagine you mean about taking Hampy off the joint accounts. I was planning on coming in this week."

"Good. We can talk then."

"Is it okay if I bring Zuzu?" Once she got on dry land, she planned to bring her pet, a gift from her new husband, everywhere she went.

Joy cringed. She must not be a dog person. "Is that her *nickname*?"

"Yes, that's what we call her." Kareen cast a surreptitious glance down at Zuzu's carrier.

"I'd wondered who she was since she'd never come in." She splayed her hands. "And we had no address."

What was Joy talking about? Kareen sat, struck silent.

"She'll need to come in, too, to change over those other accounts." The bank manager was all efficiency now, sounding very serious.

Kareen's hands shook as she bent to pat her chihuahua through the opening in her tiny pink carrier. "This is Zuzu and she's been a champ on this whole trip up north." She straightened.

Joy's face reddened. "Oh, I'm sorry. I misunderstood. I, um. . ."

Were there bank accounts with someone else's name on them with Hampy's? From the woman's horrified expression, Kareen guessed there were.

Joy stood. "I better get back downstairs."

With her fair Irish complexion, Joy didn't benefit from all that sun streaming down but it was probably that mention of the mystery account that had her departing.

"Joy, I'll see you probably tomorrow afternoon." Some of her old cranky Kareen nature kicked in as she realized her husband may have had another woman on some accounts. "I'll bring Zuzu if that's okay, and we'll let her *sign* for that other gal if you want."

A mix of emotions danced over Joy's lovely face. "Sorry. No pets in the bank. I'll track down the . . .the um, the not-Zuzu." With a tight smile, Joy fled.

Kareen closed her eyes. *Lord, You and I are just getting to be buddies again. You've got me through so far. You brought me healing. Carry me through yet another of Hampy's pain-inducing behaviors. Amen.*

Why wasn't she furious that there may have been another woman? For one thing, the notion seemed impossible. For another— who was she to point a finger at him?

As people pulled out their phones to take pictures of the West Bluff cottages and the Grand Hotel, Kareen considered what her husband had told her before she'd left Florida. "You've got to tell them the truth, Kareen."

The truth could destroy her family.

But it had to be shared.

Rachel strode purposefully past the Grand Hotel, intent on getting to the lane behind Gram's house—until something bit the bottom of her foot.

"Ow!" She stopped, her muscles tensing.

What was that? She lifted her right foot, where a jagged rock pierced a hole in her two-year-old espadrilles from Target.

"Dang." She caught herself from saying her previous favorite swear word. Those shoes had given her a ton of mileage. She pulled the offending stone from the shoe and tossed it aside. A couple of tourists, dressed in the required evening attire for after six at the hotel, cast her a wary look. The man, in a well-fitting Armani blue jacket and pants with matching tie, wrapped his arm around the woman in a marine blue floral dress with a matching long sweater jacket. He opened the door for her near Sadie's ice cream place, as if he was keeping his lady from viewing the local riffraff.

She stood with most of her weight on the foot that wasn't throbbing.

As Rachel's online nursing instructor would say, "This was a conundrum." Only in this case instead of a complex medical question, her problem was a rip in the bottom of her shoe. Should she divert from her path and walk "home" past the other houses on the West Bluff as she owned the place? Or should she cower in fear like the squatter she was?

Would the "blue couple" look out the window of the Grand and point at her? *"Hey look there's that girl who has worn her shoes out. What's she doing here?"*

No way could she walk up the graveled roadway leading to the back entrance of the cottage. Maybe she could put some duct tape on her shoe when she got back. She'd take her chances and walk past the hotel and then through the West Bluff arches and onto the sidewalk.

Since her return, she'd not spotted any West Bluff cottage occupants other than Jack. She limped on, now really calling attention to herself if anyone saw her on the sidewalk.

With determination, she moved past the Jeffries' pretty cottage, with two stuffed horses seated on the white wicker settees on their front porch. Only two more houses to go.

"Hey!" A lanky blond guy in his early twenties waved at her as he jogged from the Jeffries' cottage toward the street.

Oh no. She was pretty sure he was Carter Parker—the younger of the two brothers she was to have nothing to do with. She'd seen a Christmas photo card Mrs. Parker had sent to Gram.

He continued toward her. *What does he want?* Carter had been just a little younger than Olivia and Rachel and she'd not seen him in years. Mom had deemed the Parkers, "Unsuitable people." More surprising was that Grampa Dunmara had *gone along* with Mom's wishes, since Kareen and Hampy Parker were Grams' friends. Although Rachel wasn't especially oppositional, she'd kept her eyes open for the Parker brothers, who were about five years apart in age—the elder being two years older than Rachel and Carter three years younger. Still, she'd never, ever, interacted with them.

Rachel stopped and waited, forcing a smile. "Hello."

"Saw you were limping and was concerned." Light eyes surveyed her and then focused on the sidewalk behind her. "Hey, you're bleeding."

Rachel turned. Sure enough, a trail of red dots showed where she'd walked. "Ugh."

"Yeah. Ya need a Band-Aid or somethin'? Anything I can do to help?"

"Simple abrasion or laceration which will require cleansing, as soon as I am able, and application of antibiotic ointment." Which she did not have. "And a bandage."

His eyes widened. "Wow. You a doctor or something?"

"Something." She bit her lip. Heading into her seventh year of trying to complete her nursing studies.

"Well sounds like you know your stuff. Anything I can do besides all that medical stuff?"

"I'm almost. . ." She'd been about to say *home* but since she was technically homeless, that might not be a good idea. And she should have kept her mouth shut about treating the cut.

"Almost home?"

She dipped her chin. "Almost to where I'm going."

"Oh." His thick blond eyebrows drew together.

She stared down at her sore foot. If Gram hadn't left any first aid stuff in the maid's bathroom downstairs, which Rachel had been using, then she may have to venture upstairs. Her stomach clenched at the thought of what could happen if she was caught there, trespassing.

"I'm Carter Parker. I work with a landscaping business."

Interesting that he left out the other stuff about his family owning one of the nicest resorts on the island.

"I'm Rachel and I. . . work at Lucky Bean." The words sounded odd to her ears. For so many years her identity had been as Gram's caregiver. But she was gone.

"Love that place. Best frappes on the island." Carter grinned. He had a boyish charm that would have had the girls at her boarding school in Virginia swooning.

Rachel dipped her chin. "Nice to meet you."

"Whatcha doin' up here?"

"I love the Pontiac Trail walk." That was true, but she wasn't going on it. She stared down at her throbbing foot.

"Maybe you better head back to your rental and do like you said—clean it and put on bacitracin or something."

"Um, I think I'll be okay." She needed to change the topic. "What about you? What are you doing?"

"Just finished checking on the Jeffries' back garden. Mr. Jeffries runs the Mackinac State Parks and they stay at their house up there most of the time, but the family owns a place here, too."

She knew all that. Her foot spasmed and she sucked in a breath.

"Aw, I'm sorry. That really hurts, doesn't it?"

She compressed her lips.

"Sure I can't help you? I can call a taxi."

"No!" That came out way too loud. "Sorry."

His cheeks reddened. "Aw, I'm sorry. That's me overstepping."

Or had he thought she was broke and couldn't afford a ride? Also true. "I'm working two jobs."

"Yeah, yeah, who wants to shell that out to our carriage drivers?"

"Right." She needed to pay for other necessary things like groceries.

"But the taxi drivers gotta make a living, too."

"Yes."

She bit back a gasp as her foot pain ramped up.

Carter seemed like an okay guy. Mom had warned Gram that if she allowed Rachel anywhere near the Parkers then she'd never let Rachel go to Mackinac Island again. But Gram was gone to heaven now and Rachel was an adult.

Mom's threats were null and void.

"I got an idea." Carter pulled a blue handkerchief from his pocket. "This is clean. If you put that under your foot, it might stop the bleeding and make it easier to walk. But you really might want to rethink the whole Pontiac Trail thing."

She should refuse to take the cloth. But then he might persist in trying to help her. Still, it was nice to have someone care. "That's super. Thanks. The pressure of my foot in the shoe won't staunch the blood flow when I lift that foot to walk."

"I like how you talk. I mean—who says staunch and blood flow?" Carter grinned as he handed her the clean bandana.

She tucked the cloth into her shoe and slipped her foot back inside as he held her arm.

"How does it feel?"

He seemed so sweet.

The sensation of a connection between the two of them budded somewhere deep in her soul. Since she'd become a Christian, these strange responses were occurring more frequently. Rachel wasn't sure she liked them.

"I think much better." She really needed to get going before anyone else saw her who might recognize her. "I bet I could still do my walk if I go super slow." Like so slow that she almost wasn't hiking Pontiac Trail, which she wasn't.

"All right then." He grinned and a dimple showed in his cheek.

"Thanks." He was a cutie. And there was something about him that seemed so vulnerable. Gram had said losing his mother had really affected him.

He gave her a little wave. "Nice to meet ya, Rachel."

"You, too." *After all these years.*

She limped down the sidewalk, finally stepping off and onto the adjacent soft, albeit cold, green grass. Soon she passed the yellow mansion where she'd begun working for Jack. So far so good with that, but this was early days.

She headed around the side of the house to the rear sunporch and servants' quarters on the back and unlocked the outer door. When pushed open, the door's hinges protested. WD40 was just what it needed. She'd start a list. She stepped inside the sunporch and then unlocked the inner oak door.

Rachel headed into the maid's bathroom to clean her cut.

Her foot throbbed. This had been Yolanda's bathroom when she used to work for them in the summers. The past several years' brief trips, Rachel hadn't required a maid or cook. She rummaged through the medicine cabinet and found some recently expired antibiotic cream. *Good enough.* She found a box of Band-Aids, too.

She stepped inside the clawfoot tub and ran some water on her sore foot and then washed it well. She got out, dried, and tended her wound.

With only three pairs of shoes, she needed to replace the ruined pair. And she really should purchase some antiseptic that wasn't past its due date.

Tomorrow, she'd stop at the bank after working for Jack and before she started at Lucky Bean. Doud's Market was near the coffee shop and she'd find ointment there, and the bank was one block further down. She'd only been in the bank one time—when Gram had opened a small account for her. All of her communication with them had been for Gram's accounts and much of that had been done online like Rachel did most other accounts.

When Rachel had taken over Gram's bill-paying she'd not had her send anything to that account nor had Rachel ever seen paperwork for it. Maybe Mom received the statements and had never shown them to her. Likely spent what was in there. Technically that would have been illegal since the account was in Rachel's and Gram's names, not Mom's. Still, Mom had been known to pull all kinds of tricks to access something she needed—or wanted. Or to tick someone off.

Dear Lord, I need some emergency money in there in case I have anything more serious happen to me. Amen.

This foot injury was a wake-up call.

Hopefully, there'd be no surprises at the bank.

Chapter Eight

*W*as this what Kareen's therapist, Dr. Mary Svendsen, had called *dissociation*—this strangeness in her experience of what should be familiar? How could walking into the office she'd worked in for fifty years feel so foreign? The place was quiet. *Neat. Clean.* But it had always been those things.

No—Hampy had made it a *noisy* place.

She gave Zuzu a quick squeeze before setting her down. Always, before, guilt would grip her over her annoyance at Hampy's disruptions. *It wasn't his fault.* A huge part of the disruption he'd supposedly caused was only in Kareen's own mind. A mind that could never rest because it was too busy being co-dependent with her husband, her daughter-in-law, and her son. A mind that was only now becoming fully her own responsibility.

Zuzu must have sensed Kareen's mood because she whined and sat, gazing at her with doleful eyes.

"It's all right, baby. We'll be back home before you know it." *Florida.* Simply thinking the word brought comfort.

She strode across the sunny room to her desk and turned her computer on. She'd become another person now. A person with a *quiet* mind. Someone freed from the responsibility of other people's addictions.

Kareen chewed her lower lip. People had no idea what her life had been like. Was it terrible to be so relieved? Comforted in knowing Hampy was finally at peace?

Kareen sat in her ivory leather rolling desk chair, toes barely touching the floor, and lowered the seat. Clearly her son, Hamp, had been using it. She tipped her head back and gazed at the swirls in the plastered ceiling. For the first time since she could remember, she didn't feel irritated by being in this room. She was here of her own volition and could leave anytime she wished. A slow grin bloomed.

"*Hola suegra*!" Maria carried in a small tray with a steaming mug and a large cinnamon roll slathered in butter.

"Good morning, sweetie." Kareen grinned at Maria. "I love being your mother-in-law. My son sure was fortunate to have found you."

"I tell him that every day." Maria laughed a bell-like sound as she slid the tray onto the desk.

"Thank you." Kareen inhaled the scrumptious scents of hazelnut coffee and cinnamon. "I missed you guys when I was gone."

"Or did you miss my cooking?" Maria laughed and clucked her tongue.

Kareen laid her hand atop a green binder full of printouts. "I bet these books are in great shape." The information was also in the computer.

"I'm glad you agreed to step back into this spot for now." Maria shook her head slowly. "I'd forgotten what I have to do to get ready for all those grandchildren."

Although Kareen had just two grandsons, Maria had four, bringing Kareen's grandson total to six. A big blessing. "They are wonderful kids. I look forward to spending more time with them."

"Gracias. It will be great having them here." Maria pushed back a lock of dark hair from her pretty face. "But I think Jack Welling will keep them busy, too."

"Oh?"

"Yes. The boys will help Jack with the remodeling and redecorating of his parents' cottage."

"Gosh, I'm not sure that place has ever had an update." She cringed. "*Ever.* Something to do with a legal situation."

Maria shrugged. "All I know is the boys will work almost full time, but they will only have that job, and they will have family time, too."

"Good." If only she and Gianni could spend time with her grandsons—together. He'd love them. Kareen sipped her coffee. "This is perfect."

Maria gave her two thumbs up. "I want to keep you working on those books so I can hang with my grandsons."

"All right, all right. I'll get to work." She winked at Maria as she forked a piece of gooey roll into her mouth. *Perfection.* Then set the silverplated utensil down.

"Something has changed with you." Maria shook her finger at her. "You've got a secret."

She needed to change the topic. "Well, it's no secret that I've survived the pandemic. I'm sure grateful for that."

Maria slacked her hip, her expression growing somber. "A surprising number of early arrivals at the hotels on the island again this year."

"Which is good for business. Reservations for the upcoming high season are more typical—more like 2019."

"Typical. That's a word we haven't been using for a while." And nothing in her life had been typical for ages.

"Right. Gracias for pushing Hamp to take over the family quarters."

Kareen waved her free hand as she sipped her coffee.

"Don't be giving me the *de nada* wave. It's a big deal to surrender the family suite to us."

She set her coffee on the tray. "Simple logic. The cottage is too small for you, Hamp, and the grandkids—who by the way truly are just so. . ," she searched for the words.

"Lovely? Handsome? Funny?" Maria giggled like she was in her teens instead of her fifties.

"All that. I am so grateful to be their bonus great-grandmother."

"They love you, too."

"And I'm happy to help you and Hamp out while I'm here. But I am not going to be the drudge I was for Hampy." She raised her eyebrows. She'd make clear to Hamp that he'd better readjust any expectations he had of her managing the place. Because she wouldn't. Time for the baton to be passed.

"I understand. And again, we are glad to be here with *mis nietos* coming. The cottage was fine when it was just us, or when Carter was home from college."

"I'm sorry he decided to do that, but it made sense." Especially financially. "Kind of silly to go to college and then sit in your dorm and do online classes."

"His heart had to heal, too." Maria flipped her palms over.

"True." How that girl could dump her wonderful grandson was beyond Kareen's understanding. She raised her coffee mug to Maria. "Thanks for the breakfast. I'll nibble on that excellent bun while I'm reviewing the Excel files."

Maria dipped her chin and then left.

Kareen powered on her wireless keyboard and then adjusted the height on the monitor screen. Gianni would get a kick out of this. At almost six foot six, he was always having to change the height on things for her. Any time he saw that she needed something, he'd spring into action. *What a guy!* What a miracle God had brought about by bringing that man into her life.

Forget starting work just yet—call your man. Was that God giving her a nudge or her own instincts? At this rate, she'd never get anything done. Regardless, Kareen grabbed her cell phone and scooted her rolling chair away from her desk. She called her husband.

"Hello, my favorite girl." He made a smooching sound.

"Hiya, my favorite guy." She kissed back. "I guess we're pretty blessed."

"Yes, ma'am, we surely are." His smooth drawl was thick today.

She loved his Southern accent.

The first time she'd laid eyes on Gianni, he was seated at a small table in a corner of Mayflower European cruise ship's massive dining room. Dinners were intended for mingling with other guests but he and his companion, a woman with thinning silver-streaked red hair, remained off by themselves.

While each successive course was served for the Captain's Dinner event, Hampy grew progressively louder, his speech more slurred. Kareen had caught the strangers' glances in her direction. The man, who she later learned was Gianni, had been attentive to his wife, Sylvia. At one point he'd flagged down a waiter for something. The couple possessed what she'd always wanted in a marriage—devotion, love, and respect emanating from their every movement, punctuated by occasional laughs.

As guests left the dining room, she'd remained at the table with Hampy. He'd insisted on drinking the last of the wine bottle, despite having consumed multiple glasses. Only they and the couple in the corner had remained. The gentleman shot her a look of compassion, stood, and retrieved a wheelchair.

She hadn't known it then, but Gianni's spouse of fifty years had been dying of cancer while Kareen's own husband killed himself slowly with alcohol.

"You there still, honey pie?" Gianni's concerned voice brought her back to the present.

"Oh, yes, sweetie, I was just thinking about when we met. It seems a decade ago."

"Covid," they said together.

She huffed a laugh. "Yeah, it really made those years stretch out during the worst of it."

"Yes, my darlin', but we're just going to focus on what's ahead."

"Right." She giggled, feeling like a schoolgirl. "I miss you so much."

"Miss you and your snuggles."

Her cheeks heated. "I miss that, too."

"You sure you don't want me up there for the scattering of Hampy's ashes?"

"It's all set up. And yes, I'm sure. Let's wait for after that."

"Have you told them yet?"

"No. But I'm going to tell them about us soon."

"Don't put it off too long, babe."

"I won't. Call me tonight, would you? Before bedtime?" That was the worst time of day for her. She and Hampy hadn't been very affectionate for years. She'd not realized until the very end how much his stealthy alcohol habit had impacted them.

"Will do. Love you, Honey Pie."

"Love you, Gianni Joy!" They exchanged phone kisses and then ended the call.

She sat there, warmth cloaking her from the love shared with her new love.

"So, you want to tell me who Gianni is, Mom?"

She turned to see Hamp standing there, frowning.

"Didn't I teach you to not eavesdrop?" She cast him her best stern mom look. This really wasn't how she wanted this discussion to take place.

"Have you already found a replacement for Dad?"

She blinked at him. *Not now. Not yet.*

"Mom, are you already seeing someone?"

"Yes." A little more than that, actually. If she blew this conversation, then how would she tackle the more important one they needed to have?

Her son stomped out of the room. If the notion that she was dating upset him, then how would Hamp react to news of her marriage

"Hamp?"

But he left, giving a raised flick of his wrist in goodbye, without a backward look. How many times she'd seen his father do that same gesture over the years? How would her son react when she unloaded all her news on him?

Would that parting gesture be the last one she'd see of him, when he learned of his parentage?

Rachel crinkled her nose. *If Jack hadn't kept me late, to deal with the plumber, I wouldn't be in this situation.* She'd have gotten to the bank and bought nonexpired antibiotic for her foot. Granted, it felt much better today. She could stop by Doud's after work at the coffee shop, but the bank would have to wait until tomorrow.

Rachel cast a wary eye at the police station as she approached Lucky Bean. What if law enforcement got notified that an unauthorized person was camping out in the back sunroom at Lilac Cottage? Chills ran up her arms. How humiliating. She could almost hear Gramps tut-tutting over the illegality of her behavior.

A gust of wind rippled a nearby flag and she shivered. She really did need to find a room to rent once she discovered what money she had, if anything, at the bank.

She stepped into the coffee shop, the scent of fresh coffee, Kona if she was correct, making her mouth long for a sip. *Not until break time.* She'd have to suffer for a few hours more.

"Hola, Rachel," Juan Pablo called from behind the case.

Juan pointed to a petite woman with spikey blond hair peeking out at impossible angles from beneath her pink knit hat. How did she manage that? Her youthful face reminded Rachel of a pixie or elf. "This is our new barista, Starr."

"Nice to meet you, Starr."

"Thanks!" Her high-pitched, girlish voice matched her face and hair. The new employee sported a dusty blue, pink, and cream plaid long-sleeved shirt over a pair of baggy khakis covered by her Lucky Bean black and white apron.

Rachel waved at Andrette, who was on the phone. Probably with Jack, who had only spared Rachel enough time to grab her peanut butter sandwich and eat it as she hurried down to the coffee shop.

What did Andrette see in him, anyway? *How many women go for tall, dark, handsome and intelligent guys?* She fought back a chuckle. If they knew Jack, they'd put his appearance aside and focus on just how truly annoying he could be.

She walked to the back and set her purse into its assigned slot. She hung her hoody on a metal hook above it.

Her phone chimed but she let it go. No phones allowed at the register, and she was in danger of being late to take her station from Andrette.

She stepped out to the register and caught Andrette's attention. Her boss motioned for her to go ahead and take over. The front door opened and a trio of red-haired men, ranging from twenty or so to late thirties, ambled in. Their walks were so similar, and their builds so close, these guys had to be brothers. All wore work uniforms of quilted dark green jackets emblazoned with Patrick Brothers' Shipping in white lettering. Except she knew they didn't really ship stuff. It was just a fancy way of saying they barged stuff over from the mainland and back.

"We'll have three giant cups of joe to go," the center man announced around the toothpick in his mouth.

The other two men nodded, their own toothpicks moving up and down as if they were chewing on them.

Smile, Rachel, smile. She forced a grin.

"Hola, Patrick brothers!" Juan Pablo turned and grabbed the coffee carafe of the Americano brew.

"I've heard about you three." Starr's voice came out in such a shy way, that it caught Rachel's attention.

The youngest man may have thought she was flirting with him, because he turned his full attention on the new barista. This Patrick brother offered a megawatt smile that improved his average looks immensely. "What have you heard?"

Rachel handed change back to the paying brother.

The man leaned in. "I can't wait to hear this," he whispered.

The youngest brother moved closer to the case.

Starr cocked her head. "Juan Pablo told me that I would like you."

Juan Pablo secured lids on the coffee cups. He turned and cast Starr a cautioning look. "I tell her you are very nice men. *Sympatico*."

"Nice? What about handsome?" The third brother asked.

Juan Pablo set the cups atop the case. "She's very new here, so don't make me change what I told her."

All three laughed and the tension in the room was broken.

Juan Pablo leaned in and said something to Starr.

The young woman shook her head.

The Patrick brothers left, the youngest waving at Starr as the door closed behind them.

Rachel sprayed hand sanitizer on her fingers, something she did if she'd handled paper money. Probably overkill, but with no health insurance, she needed to be careful. Yesterday's injury proved that.

What she wouldn't do for a cup of coffee right now. Coffee, coffee, and not a drop to drink—for her just yet.

Starr gasped. "Oh heavens! That's Linda Sorensen coming in!"

The door opened and a woman in police uniform, without the jacket, walked in. She sported a light blonde pixie cut.

Breathe. Just breathe.

"Your hair is so pretty," Starr gushed, touching the stray wisps around her own face.

Juan Pablo cast the girl a warning look.

Linda's eyes widened. "Well, thank you. I sure like it. Great to keep it cut now that I can get into the hairdresser again."

"Oh, yes, that must be hard when you have hair." Starr nodded solemnly.

Rachel stiffened. *What a weird thing to say.*

Linda stared at the barista.

Oh, wow, what if Starr had been a cancer patient like the pediatric patients her pediatric oncologist stepfather had treated? Rachel nodded solemnly. "It's a blessing to have hair. For people who've lost their hair due to chemo, it's a real trial." Mom had always asked that short-term stepdad to not speak about 'such dreadful drudgery' at home.

When Linda's straight shoulders relaxed, so did Rachel's. If Starr had been a chemo patient, she didn't share that. Maybe she'd had a brain tumor and that explained some of her odd behavior.

The cop leaned in toward Starr, who stood behind the barista case. "My name is Linda Sorensen, and you'll probably be seeing a lot of me. What's your name?"

"Don't you recognize me, Mrs. Sorensen?" Starr cocked her head at Linda. "I'm one of your ATMI—Addicted to Mackinac Island—original members. I'm Starr Bourne."

Linda's eyes widened slightly. "I'm so sorry, I must be having one of those days."

"No wonder. You do so much." Starr splayed her fingers and then moved them like a jazz dancer. "Police administrator extraordinaire. Addicted to Mackinac Island Facebook group leader with over 20,000 members."

Not a cop. The tension left Rachel's shoulders and threatened to take her knees out with it.

"That's so wonderful," Rachel chimed in. She hadn't been allowed on social media for so long that it had become a habit to avoid it. Maybe she should join Facebook and some other things out there. Gram was gone so no censor. What was the harm? Still, she sure didn't want certain people knowing where she was. Definitely not. Besides, her low budget cell phone plan had very little internet usage time. *Nix the social media for now.*

"What can I say?" Linda Sorensen's light eyes sparkled. "I love what I do."

"Welcome back." Starr smiled.

"I just got here this morning." Linda's soft voice held just the tiniest edge.

"I know." Starr scooped some coffee beans into the grinder.

Juan Pablo shot Starr the side eye as Linda headed to the register, looking a little perplexed. If Rachel herself met someone who knew her, but Rachel didn't know them and that person knew that Rachel had just gotten to the island—she'd feel a little strange, too. In fact, simply having a law enforcement employee in the place had shifted Rachel's world.

The sound of the coffee beans being crushed cut into her thoughts as Linda pulled her wallet from her compact purse.

When the noise stopped, Rachel smiled tentatively at Linda. *Please, Lord, if she's somehow involved in my arrest later, make her like me.* "I'm Rachel and I don't know you. Or at least I didn't until Starr told me who you are just now. I'm new here."

Starr and Juan Pablo had their heads together. This wasn't looking good for the new hire. At least Starr did seem very sweet.

"I'm having the mocha frappe, and I'd like a German chocolate muffin, too, please." Their customer's voice was too sweet for a police department worker. But, then again, maybe you needed to have a nice gentle voice for dealing with people about legal matters.

"Sure thing." Rachel rang up the purchase, and Linda slid her card into the machine.

In a few moments, Rachel handed a Lucky Bean emblazoned frappe and the bagged muffin to Linda.

"Have a blessed day!" Linda called out as she left.

"You, too!" Rachel replied as Juan Pablo nodded at the woman and Starr made an odd waving motion.

Andrette emerged from the back room, clutching a chihuahua with a pink collar and matching halter and lead set. She raised her index finger to her mouth and looked around at them. "Don't anyone tell Linda I've got a dog back here, eh? I don't need the police to know I'm violating an ordinance. She's a real stickler—makes that place run like clockwork."

Rachel looked out the front window as Linda crossed the street.

"You'll be seeing her a lot." Andrette added.

Not what I want to hear—even if she is super nice.

Chapter Nine

Kareen returned to her office, determined to search through Hampy's desk for anything that would explain his mysterious bank account. Fortuitous that Joy slipped and asked her about it.

In two hours, she'd cleared most of Hampy's drawers in his so-called work desk. Her old, banished friend, *Resentment*—with a capital R—had shown up in full force that morning and dressed in a tailcoat ready to do full-on business. *My husband didn't work. Hampy just schmoozed. He drank and hid the bottles.* Kareen waved her hand through the air to banish the thoughts. She visualized Resentment with a big red *R* on his tuxedoed chest, vaporizing. Dr Svendsen had taught her a trick or two in the last year, as had attending church with Gianni. Kareen's Co-Dependents Anonymous meetings had been critical in her recovery and she'd made some good friends in the CoDA group.

Focus. She needed to focus on this endeavor.

This search was over. *Not quite yet.*

She'd pulled on the heavy last drawer. She bent and tugged but met stubborn resistance. "Come on old gal." She was talking to the drawer and not herself. Still, if anyone walked in, they'd probably wonder. She chuckled.

The drawer jerked free, releasing the bottom section. Several envelopes jammed the side. She pulled them free. Old letters from Margaret addressed to both of them—she set those atop the desk. Next was a yellowed letter addressed to their son with no return address. And then bingo! A bank statement addressed only to Hampy. All of their other bank documents included her name. Maybe this was it. Her heartbeat clicked as fast as a stenographer taking court notes.

Kareen opened the envelope. A checking account. In Hampy's name. No one else's name mentioned. Dated ten years earlier. Over two hundred fifty thousand dollars in there at that time. Only three checks written from the account in that month.

"My Lord, Hampy. What did you do?" She shook her head.

"He's not here, Mom. And what did Dad do?"

She slapped a hand to her chest. "You've gotta stop sneaking up on me like that, Hamp." At least he'd finally stopped grumbling about her 'dating' Gianni.

He kissed her cheek and deftly pulled the checking statement from her hands. "What's the problem?"

"It's only in *his* name."

Hamp's eyes narrowed. "So? That's yours now, right?"

Acid filled her gut. She wished she'd remembered to take her Prilosec earlier. "It's a little complicated."

"Why?" He flexed his shoulders.

"Joy said there was a woman's name on the account, too."

"No way." His eyebrows pulled together.

"Yes." She took the papers from him. "This is the only statement I've found that I don't recognize."

"But it only has Dad's name on it." Hamp ran a hand back through his thick hair, so much like his father's—his biological father's.

The reminder that she had made her own blunders made her want to downplay this issue. "Yup."

"But it's an account with another woman's name on it according to Joy?"

"Yes."

"Oh, Mom. Whoa." Hamp slumped into the adjacent burgundy leather chair.

Kareen kept her voice low, "Joy wouldn't tell me who—only that it was someone who wasn't on the island as far as she knew."

"We need to get to the bottom of this." Even the shape of his hands reminded her of the man she'd mainly known only through his movies.

"I'd like to know who it is, but I don't know how I can get that info."

"I wonder if there are more."

"No, Joy only mentioned the one account. And your Grandpa Parker was the son of a criminal, so it's no wonder he kept things secret." *Ha-ha, who am I to point the finger?*

"Huh?"

"Don't act like we haven't told you." She and Hampy had explained it to their son and grandsons in case they ever came across any unsavory stories about the Parker family's criminal past. Not that they were biological relatives to any of them, in fact.

He shrugged. "Let's not dwell on that."

"All right."

Her son shook his head. "I never saw Dad with another woman. I can't imagine he'd have cheated on you."

She stared at her only child. There was a reason he was the *only one*. A dark reason. A reason he knew nothing of. She reached for the roll of Tums on top of her desk. But even if Hampy had been unfaithful, how could she throw the first stone?

"I'll go with you to the bank tomorrow, Mom, and we'll get this straightened out."

"No, no, I'll go on my own. I'm a big girl—and I'm your mother in case you forgot." She'd have to watch her tongue—she was beginning to sound like her old self rather than the new less-cranky version. "Sorry, dear." She patted his hand. "I know you want to help."

"I do. We'll get a lawyer if we have to."

"That's a bit extreme."

"Mom, what if this person tries to," he gestured around the room, "take the resort from us?"

"Now you're getting carried away. As I've told you and Maria, it was our intent to turn the property over to you." With the hope that Hamp could at least partially buy them out. Her son and grandson had lost money on all of their international properties during the pandemic but were beginning to turn substantial profits now. If only things would turn around. Worst case scenario, though, she'd retain partial ownership.

He nodded slowly. "Is your. . . friend Gianni coming for the memorial?"

That was a quick change of topic. "Are you okay with that?" She'd have to tell him soon that Gianni was his new stepfather.

"Yeah. I think so. Maria and I want to meet him."

She cocked her head. "I'm thankful that you'd even consider it."

Hamp shrugged. "You said he was Dad's friend, too."

"Yes."

They'd set up a Sip n Sail cruise into the Straits, to scatter Hampy's ashes. It would be the kind of memorial service her husband would have wanted.

Hamp rose. "On a different note, your friend Margaret Dunmara's granddaughter seems kinda lost. I've seen her around town. The kid looks around a hundred pounds lighter."

"Really?"

"And she kinda dresses like a homeless person sometimes."

"I didn't know you kept track of her." Kareen cast him a hard look.

His cheeks turned pink. "She's a good kid."

And he would know this how? Kareen's mommy antenna began to vibrate. "How old is she?"

He shrugged. "In between Parker's and Carter's ages."

Born during the time he'd separated from his wife. *Oh no.*

"Her narcissist of a mother will likely swoop in and sell off their family's legacy." Hamp snapped his fingers. "Just like that. Selma will live the high life she's always wanted."

"Her grandparents enjoyed that lifestyle on occasion." She recalled her twenty-eighth anniversary event at Lilac Cottage, thrown by the Dunmaras. They were supposed to have had a silver anniversary party several years earlier, but Hamp had gotten married, then his wife was struggling with addiction, and Parker was born. Her eldest grandson was just a baby when Margaret and the judge threw the belated party and Hamp was in his early twenties. Selma had flirted outrageously with Hamp the entire night. Hamp had briefly separated from his wife later that year. "They sure knew how to show their friends a good time. Pulled out all the stops."

"Until the death threats started." Hamp exhaled a sharp sigh.

"Right." She moistened her lips. That had been a terrifying time for Margaret. And then look what happened. *Tragic.* "You never dated Selma, did you?"

He scrunched up his face in what might be mock disgust. "No." He turned away from her—a habit of his when he wasn't being fully honest.

She looked hard at her son's broad shoulders. Had he failed to carry his own burdens? Margaret had said her granddaughter was the result of Selma having a one-night hookup. Had it been with Hamp?

He swiveled around. "What's the matter? You look like you've seen a ghost."

Had Hampy tried to cover for Hamp? Was the real reason Selma forbade Rachel to have contact with any of the Parkers more to do with a connection between them? All this time she'd thought it had been because of her daughter-in-law's drug and alcohol struggles.

Before Kareen accused her son of anything, she'd get to the bank. She'd lean in on Joy a little bit and see if she could find out who was on that account and if this checking account slip was for the same account.

And she was ordering DNA kits online as soon as Hamp left the room.

Those results could serve multiple purposes.

The burden she'd carried for over fifty years would finally lift.

"No, I'm so sorry, Mrs. Parker, but I can't disclose anything about your husband's accounts that don't have your name on them." Joy scratched at her arm as though she had a vicious mosquito bite or a sudden outbreak of eczema.

"But that's my husband." *Was* her husband, and her correct name was now Mrs. Franchetti. "Per state law, I now own those accounts."

"There are other state laws that preclude me from disclosing certain accounts to you, ma'am." Joy's lips compressed into a firm line.

The dreaded *ma'am*. In the South ma'am meant nothing particular, but here in the North it was the kiss-off. Kareen worked up a head of steam.

"Mrs. Parker?" an unfamiliar voice asked from nearby.

She turned to spot Selma Dunmara and gasped. Only it couldn't be that little trollop. She'd be close to fifty now. No amount of work at the most renowned plastic surgeon could have made such a transformation. Must be her daughter. Zuzu yipped and jumped down from the young woman's arms, but she held tight to the leash. "Andrette asked me to bring her over to you. Sorry."

"Ma'am, we can't have a dog in here."

Kareen wasn't sorry, although that still small voice was trying to tell her that she should be. Instead, she turned and offered an acid smile to the manager. "I'll be back—with something from my attorney."

She swiveled around. The young woman wore a Lucky Bean uniform. With that long dark hair and porcelain skin she was almost a dead ringer for Selma Dunmara. Kareen stepped closer. Gorgeous light blue-gray eyes lit the girl's face. That sweet expression differentiated her from Selma's usual smirk of superiority over other mortal beasts. But that facial structure sure matched.

"Thanks for bringing my baby to me, sweetie." She liked how that last word rolled off her tongue. Old Kareen rarely used endearments. Gianni, and God's work in her life, were having a good effect. Could this be her own granddaughter?

"No problem."

Kareen cringed. She detested that expression. Why couldn't young folks simply say, 'You're welcome' instead of acting like something might have actually been a problem?

As she strode off, she heard the stranger's words to the bank teller, "I have an account here, but I have never accessed it."

Kareen froze, then swiveled around, heartbeat ticking upward.

Despite Joy casting her an evil look as though urging her to go out the door with Zuzu, Kareen hesitated.

"And I had a question," the young woman said. "If someone has a joint account with someone and that person. . . um, passes away, does that account go to the other person whose name is on there?"

Kareen held her breath. Was Selma's daughter here to claim Hamp's mystery account? Could it be? And what was the connection?

"My grandmother died, and we held a checking account jointly."

The floor stopped shifting under her feet. Kareen exhaled sharply as she exited the bank building. The young woman was asking about her grandmother's accounts not about Hampy's. But she had to mean Margaret had died. Kareen's mind could not process that information. Margaret Dunmara gone, too. Like Hampy and so many of their friends.

What if something happened to Kareen? She in her mid-seventies now. Who knew how long she had left.

Didn't her son and grandson have the right to know the truth?

Chapter Ten

A loud noise ripped into Rachel's consciousness. She startled. Was her landlord pounding on the door again, demanding payment? She shook herself as an engine roared nearby. She wasn't in Chicago awaiting eviction, like she'd dreamed about. She tried to wake up from her nightmare. She was here at Gram's place—without permission. If someone showed up, she'd have to deal with it.

What day was this anyway? She rubbed her eyes. *Saturday.* Her sleep-in day. Instead, someone was mowing the lawn nearby.

She peered out the window. The guy she'd met when she'd torn her espadrilles, Carter, roared past on a riding lawn mower. *What the heck?*

She sat up. She was still wearing the frilly, dotted Swiss, maxi dress that she'd worn to work at the café the previous night. She'd been too tired to change clothes for bedtime.

When Carter turned and mowed toward the back enclosure, his eyes locked on hers. He startled and suddenly turned off the mower. He jumped off and jogged toward the back porch.

I don't need this right now. What she needed was sleep—three or more hours of blessed deep sleep. Crud. And no nightmares, thank you very much. But lawn maintenance happening must mean someone intended to stay here at the house. *Dear God, guide me.*

Carter stood outside the locked enclosure of the back sunporch. "Sorry," he mouthed, waving his hands over his head.

Poor kid. Okay, not that much younger than her, but he seemed more like a kid. Not like Jack, who'd become a man. *And why think about Jack?* She saw him every weekday. She slipped her feet into Grandma's slightly small pink slippers and went to the porch door and unlocked it. She stepped outside as Carter backed away.

Rachel frowned. "I thought you said you did this for people during the week." *Great—aggravate someone who can tell someone else that you've camped out in their new home.*

"Yeah, I was supposed to, but we're short-staffed right now—as are a lot of places—and the crew has to pick up the slack."

"So, you're going to be doing yardwork back here on Saturdays?" *Great, just great. But if anyone shows up here to take control of the place I won't be living here anymore anyways.* She had to find another place.

"Not sure. At least the next two weeks."

Perfect. Did that mean someone would be moving in for the summer at that point? She sure wasn't going to ask. She wanted to ask him to wait until the afternoon to mow. She gave him a sheepish grin as she brushed her bangs out of her eyes. "I'm working two jobs during the week, and I only have the weekends free."

"You have the entire weekend off?" Carter stared incredulously at her. "I haven't had free weekends in the summer since I was thirteen."

This probably wasn't the time to share that she'd been Gram's caretaker until she'd had to move to the rehab facility. "Yeah, on my old job I often worked weekends, too."

"At least we have off during the school year, right?" He grinned, his perfectly straight teeth an excellent advertisement for his orthodontist. "Or aren't you in college?"

"I'm in college." *Sort of. Very, very, part-time and online.*

"I'm at UVA, the University of Virginia, studying Computer Science."

"Nursing for me." Although she'd be over forty by the time she completed, if she kept on at this snail's pace. Still, if Lake Superior State University accepted her, and offered her scholarships and financial aid, then maybe it could happen sooner.

"Yeah?" He scratched at his scruffy chin. "I took one year off during the pandemic. My dad and stepmom didn't want to shell out money for me to sit in a dorm and take online classes."

"Yeah, I get that." But she'd never been onsite during any of her six years of classes. She was itching to get started in the nursing program.

"I guess I better get back to work."

"Yeah. Hey, Carter, I need a favor."

"What's that?"

"Please don't tell anyone that I'm staying back here." She rolled her eyes upward. "It's kind of a secret."

"Sure thing. You're paying the bill, after all."

She was about to protest but clamped her lips shut and nodded.

Was she, though? She'd set up automatic payments to so many accounts. She could go online and see if Mom had frozen out that account.

It couldn't hurt to look. Could it?

Jack stared out Olivia's window down at Carter Parker. This whole thing with Rachel staying in the servants' quarters in the rear of the house was getting weirder by the moment. Clearly, the yard crew was taking care of the property, but who was paying for that if Rachel was so hard up?

Not my problem. Not my business.

Jack hurried downstairs, making more noise than usual, and not caring a bit. He went to the kitchen and poured himself his third cup from his Mr. Coffee. That old thing was still chugging along more than a decade after he'd left. And he was still concerned about Rachel Dunmara.

Why?

Maybe because she got to *live*. Maybe because her mom was such a loser while his own was amazing. Maybe because she'd *noticed* him. He'd been the healthy kid. The *ignored* one.

At home, and at school, conversation had become all about Olivia. Her treatments. When the next doctor appointment was. The prayers for his sister. But on the island, all had been kept secret.

And maybe because of that, Rachel had treated him like he was *there*. He'd enjoyed tweaking her because she always gave him a very real reaction. Like he was a real person. Like he really was present and mattered to her even if in a bad way.

He should make it up to her. *Gosh, I was a brat.* He shook his head slowly. Rachel Dunmara had set his sails aright. He'd loved to sail when he was younger. He and Dad would go out regularly until Olivia had gotten so sick. Thank God Livvie had insisted Rachel be kept in the dark about her condition. If she hadn't, would Rachel have been just like the others? Would she have treated him like the nonentity he'd become? The *healthy* sibling?

Nah. Rachel was too spunky for that. Even if she'd known about Olivia, she'd have noticed *him*. She noticed everything. Everybody. She had a heart for people, something he'd been accused of lacking. She was "good people" as Grandad liked to say.

Jack needed to man up and be there for Rachel. Although she did great work and kept the schedule on track, something was definitely off. Maybe it wasn't his business, but maybe this was God pushing him. Maybe this was the Holy Spirit like Mom liked to talk about, kicking his butt to make him act.

He'd help her. He'd ask her forgiveness for being a *tool* when they were younger. He'd watch over her.

And he'd make darned sure Carter Parker didn't run his mouth about Rachel being on the property. That was something Jack could take care of right now.

Carrie Fancett Pagels

Chapter Eleven

Late May

*D*ear God, don't let any police come out and run across the street and arrest me. Rachel exhaled her prayer as she peered out Lucky Bean's front window after her shift ended. Her heart clenched as administrator Linda headed toward the shop.

Juan Pablo moved alongside her, bringing with him that faint scent of cedarwood and incense. "You know, we have a rear exit door, mi amiga."

How did he sense her fear? Maybe because she was clutching her small backpack to her chest as if her life depended upon it.

"Better get your bike registered soon." Starr nodded solemnly. "That lady is like the Santa of naughty lists when it comes to having a license."

Juan jerked his thumb toward the back. "You can avoid Miss Linda if you exit onto the side street."

She shrugged the tension from her shoulders. How did Starr know her tag had lapsed? Rachel had pulled her old bike out from the carriage house and had pumped up the tires. But she'd not replaced the old license. A bike license was the least of her worries. No way was she going in to get a permit for it. Maybe she could ask someone else to do it for her. If she went into the office and the office administrator started quizzing her on anything, Rachel would run. And that would not be good.

"Go on." Juan waved her toward the back.

Andrette cast her a strange look as she passed by. Rachel nodded and went to the back and exited onto the side street. No Linda in sight and thankfully, no police. Three weeks she'd trespassed on the property, and no one had tossed her out. Good thing high blood pressure didn't run in the family, because her level of anxiety ramped up daily.

She rode home, passing carriages of tourists. She was reminded of her races with Olivia through downtown. They'd been daredevils.

When she got to the hill at the Grand Hotel, she jumped off the bike and pushed it up the hill.

Soon, she'd reached the cottage and the savory scent of meat grilling carried over the hedges. Jack was welcoming the work crew. These were the Parkers' grandkids by marriage. Jack had invited her to eat with them, but she'd turned him down. He'd probably just harass them the entire time by going over every little thing they'd do on the job. *Ugh. No thanks.* But her stomach growled its protest over her decision. She'd had only a peanut butter and jelly sandwich today and a frappe at work.

She went inside and changed into the few casual things she owned. She returned outdoors to check on the seeds she'd planted in the garden. The yard smelled earthy where she'd turned the soil in what would be a little vegetable garden—if she didn't get kicked out before the plants matured. She bent and her khakis sagged down her hips. She grabbed them. She was still losing weight. These cargo pants had fit okay three months ago. Down from a size twenty to a six in the year since she'd been kicked out of Gram's high-rise and now more. At least the work clothes from Lucky Bean fit.

She bent to touch the baby green tendrils pushing up from a row of spring peas and grinned. A breeze carried the scent of grilled meat, teasing her senses. Her stomach growled loudly. There were supplies in the cupboards—Doud's had delivered lots of canned and boxed food. She'd kill for something fresh, though. Payday was tomorrow. She'd buy produce then. Thank God she'd found the French press in the kitchen cabinets. That thing was a life saver.

Jack jogged around the side yard straight toward her. How could someone look so gorgeous even in a ratty paint-streaked hoodie and sweatpants? "Hot dogs and hamburgers almost ready. Sure ya don't wanta join us? The guys wanta meet ya."

Male laughter carried over the hedge.

She brushed her hair back from her eyes. "I can't believe the school year ended. Seems early."

He shrugged. "A lot of schools in the south let out in May."

She locked eyes on him. "It's really sweet that you're doing this for them." Jack had mentioned earlier that Maria and Hamp had a huge influx of guests tonight at the resort. Another cruise ship had arrived.

He tugged at his shirt. "Me? Sweet? Did you just say that?"

She crinkled her nose but then another waft of beefy air hit her nostrils. "That smells so good."

He waved her forward. "Come on then." He jogged off.

She was not going to admire how athletic his physique was—even in sweats. *Nope. Not doing that. Argh!* Surely a sneak peek didn't count. And his sweetie, Andrette, wasn't here. That didn't seem fair, since she cooked for him so much. The manager told the staff about all the yummy dinners she made for Jack at her place.

In Jack's backyard, three young men in their teens clustered around the grill. All sported dark hair but in differing styles. Two of them waved at her while the third eyed her warily. The youngest one had greenish eyes while the other two had brown. They were all really cute—each in his own way.

"Hey guys, this is Rachel Dunmara, I told ya about her. She's the admin assistant who'll keep us all in line." He turned toward her. "Including me."

"As if that's possible." Rachel rolled her eyes.

The newcomers laughed.

"I'm Sean and these are my brothers." The youngest of the three guys, or at least the shortest, gestured toward the other two. "RJ and Austin."

"Nice to meet you."

"RJ is the oldest of us here," Austin stepped toward the grill. "And we have an older brother at college."

"Any sisters?" By Jack's cringe, maybe Rachel shouldn't have asked.

"Nope. No sisters." RJ grinned. "Just a band of brothers."

Sean pointed at the meat on the grill. "Yo, Mr. Jack, I think these are done."

Mister Jack, that was funny. It made Jack sound so old. She exchanged a glance with him, and his sheepish expression suggested he thought so, too.

"Just call me Jack." He stepped toward the grill where hotdogs crisped and hamburgers were looking a tad overdone with dark flat edges.

Just call him Handsome Jack. Handsome, athletic, intelligent Jack Welling who was also a pain. *Pain in the heinie Jack.* But he was also being generous and kind. Ugh, that all didn't really fit together. *Stop thinking about Andrette's guy!*

Jack transferred the meat to a ceramic platter.

Buns, coleslaw, and beans were laid out on a newspaper-covered picnic table. A lemonade jug weighed down paper plates. It was a little chilly, but the sun shining down warmed the open area.

Something prompted her to ask Jack, "Would you like to say the prayer?"

He cast her a quick glance as he set the hot dogs and burgers on the table. "Absolutely."

Sean removed his baseball cap, emblazoned with *Houston Astros*, and clutched it to his chest. All three brothers bowed their heads and closed their eyes, and she did the same.

"Lord, we thank You for the travel safety You gave these guys and for filling their grandparents' place with guests. You're a good God. Thanks for bringing Rachel to help us, too. Bless our efforts as a team. And bless this food to Your glory. Amen."

Tears pricked her eyes at his blessing of her, too. "Amen."

The three teens made the sign of the cross.

"All right, we start with our lone lady." Jack swirled his hand forward as he bent at the waist.

He looked pretty adorable. She grinned. "I'd love a hotdog."

He placed a hotdog on a bun and then waved toward the other food. "Help yourself, milady."

"We don't have to call her milady, do we?" Sean's expression almost looked serious.

Rachel spooned some coleslaw on her plate. "Actually, I prefer Princess Preciousness or Her Royal Assistantshipness to Milady for my title."

"Is that a word?" RJ stepped in next and accepted a hamburger from Jack. "Assistantshipness?"

"Nope. But I like it." She laughed.

Austin took his plate with two hotdogs and a burger. "I do, too."

"Stick with just Rachel." Jack's grumpy voice brooked no argument.

"Call him Your Royal Grumpiness." Rachel pointed her plastic utensils at Jack.

"He seems so chill to me." Sean secured his own plate.

"Because I am." Jack blew on his bent fingers and then brushed them against his broad chest. "Chill is my middle name."

"Since when?" Rachel poured herself a short glass of lemonade.

"Since I said so."

"Definitely not sounding chill." Austin elbowed Sean.

Rachel snickered as she took her plate and cup to the Wellings' second picnic table. This one was a large, rectangular, glass one with high-backed aluminum seats with blue chair pads. Ketchup, mustard, relish, and pickles clustered in the middle of the table. "You know that expression about *not as I say but as I do*?"

"Yeah." RJ slid in beside her.

"That applies here." She quirked her eyebrows.

Austin set his plate down on the other side of her. "Do you two always, bicker like this?"

Sean sat beside RJ. "I can tell they are like sister and brother. How long have you known each other, Miss Rachel?"

She cringed. *Miss Rachel?* Yikes, that definitely sounded old. Maybe it was just because these guys were southern. "Oh my gosh, almost all my life I've known this big baboon." She gave Jack a syrupy smile.

"Not exactly." Jack sat opposite her. "That would be what nineteen or *twenty* years if I'd known you all your life, right? By your behavior maybe you're younger."

RJ sat straighter. "My brother David is twenty."

"I'm not twenty. Or nineteen." She glared at Jack who had just chomped a huge bite of hamburger. And how could he appear so good-looking despite a mouthful of food swelling his cheeks like a chipmunk? "But our boss is right about something. I have not seen *him* since he was about eighteen. He went AWOL from Mackinac. And since Mr. Welling here is what, maybe *forty* now. . ."

"You look so young, dude." Austin gulped down his lemonade.

Rachel chortled as Jack continued to chew and shot her the evil eye.

"He's thirty soon, not forty." Sean pointed at Jack. "Grandma said Miss Andrette is throwing him a huge party, and we'll be invited."

Just what Rachel needed—a reminder. Remembering Andrette and Jack's relationship sent her errant attraction to her employer racing off. *Yup, chill all right—a chilling effect in this case.* Suddenly, contrition coursed through her.

She squirted generous amounts of catsup, relish, and mustard onto her hotdog. Probably not a good plan but she loved all the fixings and this wasn't going to be a Chicago dog. When she bit in, wow, it was worth the layer of goo. Sure beat peanut butter and jelly sandwiches.

"Watch it!" Jack leaned forward as if he might come across the table at her.

Rachel stiffened and stared down in horror as mustard, relish, and catsup squirted out and smeared on her shirt. One of the few shirts she owned. She grabbed a napkin and swiped it, which resulted in a worse mess. "Drats!" Only two casual shirts that fit her. She needed to change out of this top, but she didn't have anything clean to put on.

She pulled the wet gooey part away from her chest. "I've got to go and soak this before the mustard sets." The pale-yellow top would still show a mustard stain if she didn't do something, plus the ketchup would stain, too.

"I've got Persil in there but no stain remover." Jack jerked his thumb toward his cottage. "Sorry."

That strong odor-killing detergent might work on stinky clothes, but probably not on stains. She pushed her chair back and stood. Her pants started slithering down her hips. She gasped as she grabbed them.

Jack's features tugged in concern. At least he had the good sense to keep quiet for once.

"Thanks for dinner. Nice to meet you." She grabbed her plate with one hand and held her pants up with the other. She walked away with as much dignity as she could muster. This had to be what the British called having a stiff upper lip, because she sure did.

Oh Lord, what am I to do? I don't even have a bare minimum of clothing These conversations with God were getting a lot easier. It really could be like talking to a friend. Pastor had said to ask and pray, and God would show her the answers.

Rachel shoved the back door open and then stripped out of her shirt. She headed to the bathroom and pumped liquid soap onto the stain. Then she put the stopper in the old-fashioned sink and filled it with water. She plunged the shirt into the cold water then exhaled a puff of breath.

In the mirror, she realized she'd continued to lose weight in her bust, too, because her bra wrinkled where there had once been more bosom.

She had to do something about her clothes.

Seek and ye shall find.

Gram had left summer items upstairs in the past—things she either didn't plan to wear in Chicago or couldn't. Had Gram done so the last time she'd been here? Rachel inhaled a deep breath as she stepped out into the hallway.

Dare she go further into the house? Only four steps ahead of her, the burgundy, green, and gold hall-runner beckoned. It needed a good vacuuming. What if Rachel did something in compensation for her being there? Clearly Mom had not sent anyone to empty out their belongings, especially their personal effects.

What if Rachel went up and removed Gram's clothing? That made sense. *I'd be helping.*

She strode down the hall, the thick rug offering cushiony comfort beneath her feet. *I'll vacuum, too.* That would only better things. She mounted the stairs, the walnut baluster rail smooth beneath her touch.

How many times had she run up and down these stairs? Usually, she'd be calling out for her grandmother. *Oh, Gram, I miss you so much.*

Carrie Fancett Pagels

She reached the top, then stepped down the hallway and entered her grandmother's room. She paused, tears filling her eyes. The bedroom smelled faintly of old damask roses and eucalyptus or something minty. She pulled back the sheet covering the bed. The bed was made, pillows still there, as if Gram would be back any moment. *Never again.*

Rachel couldn't help herself. She lay down on the soft bed and pressed her face into the pillows. These smelled of her favorite perfume—Cinnabar. Tears burst free.

Oh Gram, why did you have to go? God, why did You take her? I need you, Gram. I miss you so much. I keep expecting you to step out of one of these rooms.

When she'd poured her grief out to God, she grabbed a Kleenex from the inlaid wood tissue box on the bedside table and blew her nose.

Focus. You're in a pickle, as Gram would say.

She needed to look for something she could wear and then go back to her section of the house before anyone saw lights on up here. There were no bedroom closets because of the house's age, but Gram and Gramps had a large armoire. She opened it. Inside hung an array of outdated garments. Surely something could pass as merely vintage, whimsical clothing. Most items hung from old-fashioned heavy wooden hangers. Some bore the initials of Gram's grandparents, Sadie and Robert Swaine. They were Rachel's great-great-grandparents, and she'd heard stories about them from Gram all her life. Sadie supposedly was a very stylish woman in her later years. Gram always had been, too.

Rachel started in the middle of the closet. Hot pink jumpsuit— definite no. But the whole Barbie look was making a comeback. Make that a *maybe* if she only used it for casual wear. She couldn't imagine Gram in that outfit, but then again, she used to love trendy things. Slinky backless cocktail gown, nope. A garish brown, lime-green, and orange sixties mini-dress—super no. Whoa, then there was a white tunic with a Nehru collar. And behind it hung a pair of black bell bottoms.

She could take the bell bottom legs in later but right now they might do. A polyester black, white, and fuchsia button-up top with an attached necktie could go with this look and was the right size. She'd look through the rest of the closet and trunks later—if she didn't get kicked out before then.

Rachel donned the outfit and then went to the mirror and pulled the white sheet from it. Photographs fluttered down onto the wood floor, and she retrieved them. The glossy first photo showed young

Mom with Gram at the Grand Hotel about thirty years earlier. In another, Gram sported a toga for one of her parties and Mom dressed like her twinsy. They appeared loving and close in the pictures. Perhaps that was why Gram had kept them on the mirror. How sad that they'd grown apart.

Rachel adjusted the tie at her neck and examined her reflection in the mirror. *This is as good as it was gonna get in this outfit.* She headed back downstairs to her little hideaway. She'd go back up during daylight and also check Gram's drawers to make sure there was nothing special, or very personal, left in them.

The next morning, Rachel prepared her French press coffee, ate her instant oatmeal, and headed off to Jack's. She looked ridiculous in this outfit, but luckily, the seventies styles were making a comeback. The baggy pants that young stylistas wore didn't look quite like these super flares though.

She arrived at the Wellings' cottage to find Andrette standing in the doorway, chatting with Jack. She turned and surveyed Rachel head-to-toe. "Oh my gosh, I love that look! I thought Jack made ya wear work boots and a nun's habit—he can be so weird about women working around men. But wow, you should wear vintage to work—I love it."

"You'll make an exception for me?" If she kept losing weight, then she'd have had to ask her boss for a smaller uniform, anyway, which she didn't want to do. And she wasn't ready to wear a size two. She'd been that size when she was ten, maybe.

Andrette grabbed her shoulders and twirled her around. "Oh, yeah, if you've got anything more like this you have my complete permission to wear them to the shop. Customers will love that, eh."

Rachel nodded but didn't reply. *Vintage* was what Andrette called it. So, it definitely wasn't passing for the return-to-the-seventies new clothes vibe.

Jack cast her a quizzical look. "The shirt is fine, but those pants are a tripping hazard here at work."

Yup, there was the reminder that she was his minion. She saluted him. "I'll fix the wide bottoms."

Grinning, Andrette patted Jack's shoulder. "She can sew. Did you know?"

"Nope." He scratched his chin.

"I'm pretty sure Rachel has time-traveled to us right from the seventies—the era of clothing she's wearing." Andrette arched a brow slightly or maybe as much as her Botox would allow. "My mom and grandmother tried to teach me to sew—they'd sewn their own clothing when they were young—but I refused."

"Necessity caused me to learn." Rachel bit her lip as Jack's tugged in a doubtful pout. "You know—a spare button here, take in an inch or two there, mend a tiny rip."

"That's right. You were off at school in Virginia. I had a repair kit myself, at the Merchant Marine Academy."

"And we're very proud of you, Jackie." Andrette patted his cheek like he was a little kid. That was so weird. But he just beamed back at her as if he loved her. He reminded Rachel of a dog about to start wagging his tail.

Andrette turned toward Rachel again. "You said you worked in a couture shop and had some sewing skills."

"I did sales but yes, I can stitch things up." Preferably, one day as a nurse practitioner or physician's assistant she could do the kind of stitching she'd rather do. Rachel had needed to learn how to fix secondhand clothing so she could wear it. Some items, like her khakis, simply weren't cooperative with a needle and thread. "No time traveler here—just a watcher of Sandi Browne in the shop. And many YouTube videos."

"Some moms and even grandmothers aren't into that kind of thing—sewing or stitching." Andrette shrugged.

Jack closed one eye. It was the look he often did when he was fighting back the urge to say something smart-alecky.

"And certainly, I don't sew." Andrette shrugged. "I don't know any women my mom's age, even, who do."

Rachel's mom was into 'new boyfriends preferably potential rich husbands.' On the rare occasion, she'd hand Rachel a wad of cash and tell her to take a taxi downtown and pick out a new outfit. Mostly though, she ignored Rachel's needs. Gram had often bought Rachel's wardrobe.

As far as her dad—who knew where he was? Mom claimed Rachel was the result of a one-night stand. Gram had described Mom as a party girl prone to clubbing. Her father could be one of any of the millions of men in the Chicago area, or some young guy from out of town who'd visited a club one night and slept with her mom. If Rachel could afford it, she'd do a DNA test and see what came out in the wash. Not that she'd do anything about it necessarily. But as a budding medical professional, she'd wondered if she ever needed a transplant or something—yes, she was ridiculous for thinking about such things—but wouldn't it be good if she knew who her biological family members were other than Mom and Gram?

"Hey, Rach, it's okay if you wear them today. But get them fixed before next time, okay?"

She gritted her teeth, but she wasn't going to react to his unwanted nickname for her. "Sure. Thanks." She headed toward her chair.

RJ stopped scrubbing the nearby wall, which would be painted. He ran toward her office chair and pulled it back for her.

"*Gracias.*" She smiled up at the young guy.

"*De nada.*"

Jack scowled at them.

What was his problem?

Chapter Twelve

*T*hose guys are young and full of testosterone. I don't need them hanging all over Rachel at work." Jack scowled as he hissed his complaint to his aunt.

Andrette's low laugh reminded him of his father's, her half-brother. "Oh, Jackie, they're almost boys. Don't get so freaky, eh?"

He tapped his chest. "I once was a kid and I know what teen boys can get up to."

She rolled her eyes and frowned. "Why do you care if they flirt with her? They're Latino guys—they're gonna show a little more flare than you ever did."

"I cannot believe my own auntie would actually say that about me. I'm crushed."

"Nah. You aren't." She tried to pat his cheek again, like she had earlier, and he'd ducked away.

Jack wagged his finger at her. "You run your shop the way you want and leave me to handle this reno the way I want." He crinkled his nose at her and then instantly regretted it.

"You just reverted to snotty little Jackie when you did that nose thing." Andrette shook her head. "Wait till your uncle gets here and discovers how you've been treating me."

He raised his eyebrows. "What? I've been squiring you around the island to your events. I've used my personal carriage, which I have to pay for by the way, for said events. And I've stayed at your place when you've gotten scared or lonely at night."

She raised her hand. "I don't get lonely."

Sore point. Uncle Marques didn't want her up here by herself. Marques sure as heck didn't want Andrette running a coffee shop by herself when he was downstate working at his law practice. "Sorry. Shouldn't have said that."

"I've got to go."

"See ya later?"

"Maybe." She cocked her hip. "If I need to be *squired around* somewhere." She whirled and stomped out of the room.

"Aw, come on!" Jack followed her out, feeling every eye in the place on his back.

His phone rang. The electrician. He had to take this call. "Hello?"

"This is Dean from Les Cheneaux Electricians. Is this Mr. Welling?"

"This is Jack Welling."

"We got a guy on the ferry coming out right now. You at home?"

He took a deep breath and lowered his chin to his chest. It was continuing with the electricians. The specialists were coming *whenever* they felt like it. Thank God he had Rachel because she'd already had to stand in for him when the plumber showed up unannounced. "Yup. I'm here."

"Good. You got a carriage to pick him up?"

A carriage? Seriously, this dude not only was gonna send someone unannounced, but he wanted a ride up to the bluff? Jack wasn't letting this jerk off that easily. "He knows the address and how to call a taxi, right?"

There was a long pause. Scored a hit. "Most folks up on West Bluff send their personal drivers down to get our electricians. We're busy, you know—"

"Yeah, yeah," Jack cut him off. "And I have absolutely *nothing* to do myself."

Another pause. "Well, he'll be there on the St. Ignace boat, Star Line, next arrival. Has our orange shirt on with the white lightning bolt logo front and back."

At least he'd have no trouble spotting the dude.

Rachel moved alongside him, concern in her eyes.

She'd always been the sensitive type. That was one of the reasons Mom had loved having her hang out with Olivia.

"What's going on," Rachel mouthed.

Jack covered the phone's microphone. "The electricians have finally decided to get someone over here."

She nodded.

"Okay, Mr. Welling, you'll send your driver or not?"

"Yeah, I'll send my driver." Which was himself.

"Fine." The guy hung up.

Jack scratched his forehead.

"You're having a rough morning, aren't you?" Rachel held out a refilled coffee cup to him.

"Thanks." He sipped it. "Tastes better than mine."

"Anything would." She gave a little shrug. "Ditchwater probably wouldn't."

And here he'd just been thinking how great she was. Just like he had with his other girlfriends. *Other girlfriends?* This wasn't a girlfriend. Not a friend. This was an employee. "I'm off to pick the dude up. Can you hold down the fort?"

"They're supposed to scrub those walls and baseboards, right?"
"Yup."
She saluted him. "Aye, aye, skipper." She dropped her hand.
One thing he had to give Rachel—she wasn't boring.

So, what had Jack and his lady love, Andrette, argued about that morning? Rachel couldn't believe they'd stood there fussing at each other while the work crew was present. *None of my business.* She must have told herself that twenty times while she'd scarfed down her tuna salad for lunch and got ready for her second job. And he'd been ticked off at the electrician, too. Not that she blamed him. Jack said the man had quoted a price triple what Jack remembered.

Luckily, Rachel had found the contract which proved the correct quote.

Jack had actually thanked her. Told her that she'd really helped him out and was doing a great job.

And the boys had gotten the entire wall and baseboards cleaned up and had moved onto the next cleanup area. They were so cute and sweet. With brothers like that, she might have had a chance at a happy childhood.

Not with Mom for a mother, though. And she wouldn't wish her mom on anyone.

She rode her bike down Market Street to Lucky Bean and arrived to find a line fifteen deep out the front door. LaDonna, the morning cashier, shot Rachel a look of disbelief. "What kind of outfit is that?"

"Andrette approved it, so here I am." Rachel didn't appreciate the older woman second-guessing her clothing. She grabbed her own register tray. "Go ahead and let's swap out."

LaDonna raised her stubby index finger at the next customer. "One moment please, I'm changing out the till."

As soon as the other cashier completed her tasks, Rachel got set up. "What can I get you?" she asked the pink-haired teen girl.

"Love the whole vibe." The teen motioned to Rachel, her hot pink fingernails matching the accent color in Rachel's polyester shirt.

"Thanks." Rachel pressed a hand to Gram's shirt, almost tangibly feeling her grandmother's love.

Footsteps sounded behind her.

"Let's add this." Andrette swirled a chiffon pink scarf around Rachel's upswept hair, then tied a bow at an angle on the side of her head. Her tone was bright despite the fight with Jack. "Brings out your pretty eyes, too."

The Admiral had always said she had the prettiest eyes. Where was he now? Probably in DC. He was a good guy. No wonder he'd figured Mom out and beat a hasty retreat.

"Thanks, Andrette."

"I'm gonna help." The manager smiled brightly at her as though this simple act had made her immensely happy. Maybe Andrette and Jack had kissed and made up. "I'll go take orders from outside, eh, and you ring them up as they come through."

"Thanks."

Only two baristas were behind the counter, so Rachel tried to assist them when she could, especially since their manager was helping her.

Finally, after a solid hour, the influx of customers slowed.

Andrette joined Rachel at the register. "I'm heading out in a minute. I've got a big order coming in."

"Really? We just took one yesterday." A massive dray load of goods had been brought to the store.

Andrette tilted her head and shoulders to the side, playfully. "Well, it's one of those secret things."

"Okay." Not that it was up to Rachel to okay the manager's work. Maybe this secret was the reason her bosses had quarreled that morning.

"See ya." Andrette headed out.

Rachel and her co-workers waved goodbye.

Starr was working again today. She had the habit of chewing her lower lip and frowning as she intently worked on crafting a frappe for a customer. Right now was no exception as she finished prepping a mocha frappe for a nice-looking dark-haired customer about Rachel's age.

When the man left, and they were momentarily empty, Juan Pablo came around from behind the baristas' counter. "This look suits you, *mi amiga.*"

"Thank you." Rachel yawned. "I think I'm ready for pajamas now."

He laughed. "Later."

Starr wiped the counters off. "Do you think Andrette would let me come in wearing something shiny? Something sparkly?"

Juan Pablo's eyes widened as he turned toward the young woman. "Don't ask."

It sounded like he'd softly added, "The big boss wouldn't allow that."

Funny how those two acted like they'd known each other a long time. Rachel sprayed sanitizer onto a cloth and wiped the register. "Where did you and Starr first meet?"

Starr did her jazz hand wave. "It was far, far away from here." She giggled.

"A long time ago," Juan Pablo grumbled.

Was Starr maybe once a juvenile delinquent who Juan had helped? He sure seemed like a grumpy older brother—like Jack acted toward Rachel sometimes.

Starr giggled. "John Paul recommended me for this place. I've not been here in—"

John Paul? Ah, the English version of Juan Pablo.

"Okay, we better get back to work." Juan Pablo scowled. "There are people coming."

As Juan hurried around the counter, Starr looked contrite.

Rachel squinted out the front windows. "I don't see anyone."

Starr crossed her arms over her chest. "He always knows."

What the heck did that mean? Why had Juan interrupted the new worker? "When were you here on the island before, Starr?"

"Oh, I just meant in general I hadn't been here," she gestured around broadly. "You know. Like in an existential way."

Juan Pablo closed his eyes and shook his head slightly, muttering something under his breath.

Maybe Starr truly had some cognitive issues. It was all right—she was super sweet.

The door opened. Juan was right. Then again, they regularly got customers all day long.

These aren't regular visitors. Rachel stared at the couple smiling broadly at her. She squealed like a teenager as she came around the side of the counter to hug Dawn Charbonneau. "What are you two doing here?" Warmth surged through her as she approached the older woman.

But Dawn only stared at Rachel, as if she had no idea who she was. Jim Charbonneau, too, gaped at her.

"Oh my." Dawn gaped. "You look just like Selma. Or like she did. Is that really you, Rachel?"

"We wanted to surprise you." Jim blinked as he opened his arms to her and gave her a bear hug then released her. "We're early birds. But you've surprised us, too."

Dawn tilted her head. "You're not anorexic, are you, dear girl?"

"No, no." Rachel raised her palms. "Just a lot going on this past year."

"Well, we're here for you." Jim squeezed her shoulder gently. "Any time you need something, you let us know."

Oh no—can't put this off any longer. Guilt assailed her. She needed to tell them about Gram. She took two steps back, closer to the register in case anyone needed her. "You two are the best! Thanks again for letting me stay at Butterfly Cottage. It was lovely." Until Dawn's sister and niece had unexpectedly shown up, but that wasn't the Charbonneau's fault.

Dawn adjusted her purse strap. "Are you at Lilac Cottage by yourself again?"

Rachel surreptitiously looked around in case anyone had heard that question. She stepped forward again. "Yes." Truly alone this time. *And not supposed to be there. A trespasser.* "And I have something I need to share with you two."

Jim cocked his head. "What's that?"

"It's about Gram."

The older woman touched the pointed collar on Rachel's blouse. "Oh my. That's like something Margaret and I would have worn back in the day."

"As it happens—this is Gram's." *Or was.*

"Thought so." Dawn flashed her a quick smile then turned to Jim. "Do you remember the parties thrown at the Reynolds' house? I think Mags wore that outfit to their very last party before. . ."

Rachel frowned. Before someone died? She needed to tell them. *Get this over with.*

Jim cocked his head. "How's Margaret doing?"

She pulled in a fortifying breath. "I am so sorry that I'm just telling you this." She hung her head.

"What is it?" Jim asked.

"My grandmother. . . she passed away." Rachel raised her head.

Dawn's light eyes widened. "Ohhhh, oh my gosh. I'm so sorry, Rachel." Her eyes pooled with tears.

Rachel wished she'd notified all of Grandma's friends, especially these precious folks. More than that, she wished Mom would have done so and spared Rachel the pain.

Dawn's tears overflowed. "She was an amazing friend. I've missed seeing her."

Jim shook his head. "That's hard to believe both Margaret and the judge are gone."

Dawn swiped at her tears. "They're together now. They loved each other so very much."

The two held hands, and Jim pressed a kiss to Dawn's brow.

"I am so sorry I didn't tell you earlier." Rachel sure hadn't meant to disclose this here at the shop. She shook her head. "I think I was having a hard time believing it myself."

Grams' dear friends moved in to encircle her with their arms. Warmth, comfort, and forgiveness spread through that group hug. Rachel sniffed back tears.

When she looked up, Juan nodded at her. "Why don't you take a little break?" Juan Pablo gestured to Starr and himself. "Let us wait on you?"

"I got some training in how to minister to people." Starr turned and pulled three mugs from the back shelf. "I've been wanting to practice."

Jim leaned in. "I guess you could say that a cup of joe right now would be a good form of ministry, right?"

Dawn and Rachel both laughed softly.

"Sit down over there and I'll bring you some walnut brownies." Juan Pablo smiled at them. "Definitely good for the soul."

"Are they?" Dawn arched an eyebrow.

Rachel made the Girl Scout sign with her fingers. "Scouts' honor." The Admiral had made sure she'd gotten to scout meetings. *A shame it'd been only one season.* He'd even been the cookie parent when Mom failed to complete the job after signing up for it.

They sat at the table. Starr never had asked how they wanted their coffee, and when she set the mugs in front of them, they all looked up.

Starr pointed around and indicated which had cream, which had sugar, and how much of each.

"That's exactly right." Dawn sipped her coffee. "Perfect."

Starr nodded slowly.

Jim winked at the girl. "Guess you do know your coffee ministry, young lady."

Rachel could only stare at her co-worker. No one was that good. Good guesser? Or something else?

Juan Pablo slid a small ceramic box of sugar and sugar substitutes in front of them and fresh cream in a stainless-steel container. "In case she didn't get it quite right." He nodded slowly.

"Thanks, Juan."

The three of them sat there drinking their coffee. Dawn wiped at a tear that rolled down her cheek. "I was afraid things had gotten worse when I didn't hear from her, or you, for a long time last winter."

"To be honest, I'd kind of hoped my mom would let people know." Rachel cringed.

Jim crinkled his nose like he did when he was skeptical about something. "Selma wouldn't notify anyone of anything unless there was something in it for her."

"Jim!" Dawn swatted at his hand. "I can't believe you said that! Selma's her mother, after all."

He shrugged. "It's true."

Rachel drew in a deep breath. "She kicked me out of Gram's high-rise the minute we had Gram moved into the long-term care facility."

"She did not!" Dawn slapped the tabletop.

"She did. And moved her newest boyfriend in with her."

Dawn gaped. She set her mug down. "Oh, Rachel, I'm so sorry."

"It's not your fault." That sounded so silly.

"Where did you stay, then? That was your home since you were, what, sixteen?"

Rachel glanced around the room, her life situation suddenly front and center again. "Oh, I managed. I worked for one of Gram's friends and lived above her shop for a while."

"If we had known, we'd have had you go to our place in Rolling Meadows." Jim angled his body towards her.

"I got another job, and I had my very first roommate." Rachel forced a smile. A roomie who ripped her off and booted her out. "So, I've had some life experiences that have helped me to grow up a little more."

Dawn coughed. "As if being Margaret's caretaker since you were sixteen hadn't made you grow up too early."

Jim mumbled something under his breath.

"That Selma. If I see her anytime soon, she'll be sorry for putting you out of your own home."

"Well, it was Gram's home."

"Yes, but not Selma's. And I'm pretty sure Margaret planned to leave it to you." Dawn exchanged a long glance with her husband. "Right, Jimbo?"

He shrugged. "People say a lot of things, but what matters is what they put into writing."

"Speaking of writing, my granddaughter Jaycie told me that Mimi Vendue is doing a book signing this summer here and wants me to get her an autographed copy. I hope to make it back over for that." Dawn tapped her fingers on the table. "And at least you've got Lilac Cottage."

"Glad you can stay there." Jim sipped his coffee. "But you're always welcome at Butterfly Cottage, too."

Rachel stiffened. She couldn't tell them she was illegally staying at Gram's cottage. If she did, couldn't they get in trouble? Aiding and abetting or something like that? There was no need for them to know. *Is there, God?*

Dawn's phone rang and she looked down at it. "That's Kareen now—we'd better get a move on."

"Yup." Jim scooted his chair back.

"We're meeting with an old friend who lost her husband. He was also our dear friend, like your grandmother." Dawn sniffed.

Jim's eyes grew moist. "A lot of losses since the pandemic plus these two close friends. It's hard getting old."

"You're not old, Mr. Charbonneau." Rachel gave him a quick hug. "You're well-seasoned."

"Give this well-seasoned lady a hug, too." Dawn grinned.

"Should we stop by your cottage before we go back?" Jim donned his ballcap.

Before Rachel could protest, Dawn shook her finger at him. "You promised me a late dinner at the Pink Pony, mister, and you're not getting out of it."

Jim shrugged. "Another time then, Rachel?"

"Sure." Like *never*. Not while she was camping out there. She'd not implicate them in her criminal activity.

She'd tell them one day. She really would.

Just not today.

Chapter Thirteen

K areen, have you heard about Margaret? We just found out."
Dawn held Kareen by her shoulders as Zuzu looked up at
them.

"I overheard her granddaughter say that at the bank, recently."
Jim compressed his lips.

Kareen frowned. "I knew Margaret had been in that rehab facility
since before I went to Florida, but I hadn't heard anything about her
death."

Jim pulled off his baseball cap.

Kareen gestured for her two friends to sit on the couch in her
private living room.

Once she sat, Dawn's blue eyes flashed. "It would have been nice
if Selma had notified her mother's friends."

Jim barked a laugh.

Zuzu jumped onto Kareen's lap.

"I know you and Hampy didn't see Margaret much." Dawn
removed the pillow from behind her and set it aside.

Since the Judge had died, they'd only seen Margaret Dunmara a
few times.

Jim tapped his palms on his knees. "But she used to be your and
Hampy's dear friend."

"Yes, the Judge and Margaret were our close friends—even threw
a silver wedding anniversary for us at their cottage." Kareen reached
for a carafe of water on the table and poured three glasses. "Albeit a
three-year delay from our twenty-fifth anniversary due to Hamp's
wedding, Parker's birth, and other things." Like her daughter-in-law's
addictions and their brief separation. What a memorable night that
party had ended up being—in all the wrong ways.

She set Zuzu down. She rose and offered a glass to Dawn and Jim,
who set them on the glass-topped coffee table.

"Hard to believe that was so long ago." One side of Jim's mouth
crooked upward.

"Twenty-six years." Kareen sat. "That was one crazy night." One
of the worst nights of her life, when a ghost from her past had shown

up in person. Perspiration broke out on her brow. This Holy Spirit thing that Gianni had been pushing on her wouldn't let go.

"We ran into Margaret's daughter at Lucky Bean." Dawn pressed her hands to her face. "That girl looks just like Selma did at her age."

"When I saw her at the bank, I thought she was a clone of Selma Dunmara."

"She works at Lucky Bean." Jim scooted back further in his seat.

So that was the young woman who'd come to the bank—Selma's daughter, Rachel.

Dawn gave a harsh laugh. "Can you imagine what the judge would say if he were alive?"

"If he found her working there?" Jim shook his head. "He'd have grabbed Rachel, shoved her into his carriage, and brought her right back to the cottage."

"He was definitely one for privacy, even when I first met him with Hampy." Kareen recalled Hampy's words. "He called the judge paranoid, but honestly—if I were a federal judge, I'd want security and discretion, too."

"I don't think Mags minded." Dawn huffed a sigh. "But I wonder if Selma and Rachel had to pay a price for that."

Kareen frowned. "How old is Dunmara's granddaughter now?"

"I think she was twenty-five on her birthday. I sent a card." Dawn grinned. "You know me and my penchant for fancy cards."

Dawn was so thoughtful. But would she be so understanding about Kareen's marriage to Gianni? "I am so sorry to hear about Margaret. She was very kind to me."

"She's in a better place." Jim gestured upward.

"Yes." Dawn covered Jim's hand with hers. "But we're here to help you, Kareen, with Hampy's memorial. And Hamp told us on the way in that you have to work again tonight at the resort."

"Yes, we've got a huge group coming in. But I did want to talk about Hampy's service. You two have been such dear friends all these years."

Compassion etched Dawn's features in concern. "You know we'd do anything for you."

"How can we help?" Jim cocked his head.

"Thanks so much. I really appreciate this." Kareen rose and went to the sideboard and grabbed her notes. "Let me tell you what I've got planned so far."

"Kareen, is there something else you want to tell us about?" Dawn's plaintive voice made Kareen cringe.

She turned to face her dear friends. They deserved to know.

"Yes, there are some things I need to share. And you might be shocked."

"Oh?" Dawn and Jim exchanged a puzzled look.

"For one thing, my name is now Kareen Franchetti." She arched an eyebrow.

Jim tucked in his chin. "How's that?"

Dawn blinked rapidly. "Isn't that your friends' last name?"

Sipping her drink, Kareen watched as realization dawned on her pals' faces.

"Oh!" Dawn clapped her hands together.

Jim gaped, then clamped his lips shut.

"And if you're willing to listen, I'd like to share some of what Hampy put me through before he passed."

Both nodded slowly.

Now, several hours after her chums had left, Kareen still felt drained. She sipped on her iced tea and gave her eyes a little break from working on her computer.

Now that she'd told Dawn and Jim about all the horrors Hampy had subjected her to in his last days dying from alcoholism, Kareen had a weight lifted from her shoulders. They'd taken the news of her remarriage very well. Better than she'd thought. Now she would need to tell her family about Gianni—and about so many things. Some she wasn't quite ready to verbalize just yet.

She set her drink down and completed her Excel spreadsheet on her MacBook laptop and saved it.

Someone tapped on the door and Zuzu barked. Kareen had stopped leaving the door open after Hamp had eavesdropped on her phone call with Gianni. She desired to be completely open with her son about their situation, if only she could. Hamp had been so upset simply thinking that she was going out with Gianni that Kareen allowed him to believe that she and her husband were only dating.

She went to the door, Zuzu hot on her heels. She opened the door to find her daughter-in-law standing there. "Come in."

Maria entered, carrying a tray with two plates. "Burritos California with refried beans and cilantro rice."

"Oooh, my favorites. What did I do to merit such favor?" If it had been left to Hamp, they'd probably have banished her from the family table for "seeing" Gianni.

Zuzu sniffed the fragrant air. Maybe these were her new favorites, too.

"You've been working so hard, Mama Kareen. Let's go out onto the patio." Maria inclined her head toward the exit. "Can you open the door for us?"

"Sure thing." Kareen opened the glass doors to the private patio. "Thanks so much. I'll go grab a couple of Cokes from the mini-fridge."

"Gracias." Maria set the tray down on the outdoor table.

Kareen grabbed a dog treat for Zuzu and two cans of Coke and brought them outside. She handed one Coca-Cola to her daughter-in-law. The old Kareen would have asked about how Hamp was doing with his drinking. That wasn't her job, though. It never had been. It was Hamp's own responsibility to work his AA program and stay sober.

Maria took her seat. "I want to tell you I'm proud of you for starting over and not being afraid after what your husband put you through."

Kareen raised her eyebrows. "You knew? Or rather, what exactly did you know?" She sat down.

Maria pointed to her own dark eyes. "I can see."

Kareen took a deep breath. "I'm finding out a lot more people were seeing more clearly than I was."

Her daughter-in-law set her napkin on her lap and clasped her hands. "Why don't I say the prayer."

She dipped her chin in agreement.

"Father God, we ask Your blessing on this food and on our conversation. We love You, Lord, and we trust You. We ask You to bless this food and our fellowship. In Jesus' name, Amen."

"Amen." Kareen sipped her Coke. "But what exactly did you see going on around here with Hampy?"

"Ah." Maria waved her fork in the air. "I knew right away he was a mad crazy drunk—sorry I'm just calling it like I see it."

"Really? How was everyone catching on but not me?" *Codependency, that's why.*

"You see, I would take our trash out to the garbage cans. I did it at night. I don't mind it. And I'd see all the alcohol bottles in *our* bin."

Kareen tugged at neckline. "I didn't realize Hampy had done that, but I'd figured he must have disposed of them somewhere. It would have been easier for him to have tossed them in our hotel cans."

"I think the staff would have seen him." She raised a dark eyebrow. "This way, he would take a walk over to our cottage and when he was there, away from prying eyes, he'd dispose of his bottles into our trash."

"Oh boy. I bet you thought my son, Hamp, was the one guzzling all that booze. Or Parker."

"I wondered at first, but I never saw either of them drinking. So, I started watching your husband." Maria sipped her Coke.

"That was smart." She took a bite of the burrito and rich flavor exploded over her taste buds. Maria was an amazing cook.

"I can only imagine what he put you through all those years. Aye yi yi. And I am glad you found someone else. I'm going to get Hamp to come around, too, about your new sweetie. He's just having a hard time realizing what had been going on."

"Did he read my journal?"

"He started. But it was hard on him. He was upset for his dad but also for you and really, he was embarrassed that he hadn't stepped in to help you."

Kareen waved that suggestion away. "I wasn't in a place where I'd have accepted help. I was so completely humiliated, and I didn't want anyone else to have to suffer like I did. So, it's not his fault."

"You seem much more content now. Tell me some more about Gianni." Maria took a bite of her burrito.

There was one big thing they all needed to know—at the very least, Hamp. But not today. "Maria, I need your advice."

"Anything."

"How do I tell my son that I'm *remarried*?"

Maria's dark eyebrows shot upward. "Remarried? Mama Kareen! *Estoy sorprendida!* Maybe that's the wrong word. Maybe not shocked but surprised. I mean this is a good thing, si?"

"If I get that kind of reaction from you, then what is my son going to say?"

"'Curiouser and curiouser' as your youngest great-grandson, my grandson, would have said." Maria waved her hand, as though she held a magic wand. "You know Hamp—you have to slowly lead up to that announcement. Keep giving him hints."

"My son always did despise surprises—as you discovered the hard way when you threw that surprise birthday party for him."

"Si! And he stomped out." She snapped her fingers. "Just like that."

"You got past that, thankfully."

"We did. But no more surprises, and I love a happy surprise."

"Well, he won't find my remarriage a good surprise." Kareen gave a curt laugh.

A seagull swept onto the patio floor, squawking for food. Kareen normally would have shooed the pests away, but today, she tore off a bit of her food and tossed it to the bird. Zuzu chose that moment to bark, chasing the seagull away.

"Mama Kareen, I am very happy for you that you've found love again. Gianni sounds like a really decent man. It's just that. . ." Maria gestured around them to the resort. "With a business that you owned, and invested your life into, I guess I'm a little surprised that you'd remarry so quickly."

"I, or rather Hampy and I, had already known Gianni and his wife for a few years." She waved dismissively. "And Gianni and I got a pre-nuptial agreement."

"You did?"

"Yes. Gianni wants his estate to go to his children, and I want mine to go to my son."

"Well, you know my situation, and how I too remarried. It's complicated to start life over. And for me, and my grandchildren, and now you—we've all been blessed to have each other and to have love. That's the thing that matters much more than money. And a pre-nup was never considered with Hamp."

"Gianni came from. . ." her husband came from great wealth, but it sounded so crass to say that. His family's fortune made her portfolio look like pocket change. "He has some assets he wants to keep in the family just like I do."

Maria's expression suggested she was biting her tongue. Kareen pointed to Maria's plate. "Eat up. Before you know it, there will be some emergency you'll have to attend to."

"Hamp will handle things." She forked into her food.

"This is delicious." Kareen savored the spices and meat.

Her daughter-in-law grinned. "Is it pride to enjoy your own cooking so much?"

Kareen shot Maria a look of disbelief. "Honey, if I cooked like you, I'd shout it from the heavens!"

"Gracias."

Zuzu begged at her feet. Kareen set her fork down. "Maria, do you guys need anything from Petoskey?"

"Hamp usually has a list going. Why?"

"I have to run down to pick up a piece of art I commissioned with Wendy Shoults."

"You *didn't*?" Maria's red lips formed an 'O'. "You commissioned a painting of Zuzu?"

Zuzu looked up expectantly, and Kareen bent over her beloved little dog. "That's right. We're talking about you, you little scamp." She handed the pup a bite of her meal.

"Wendy will do a great job. And yes, I'll get you that list tonight."

Going off island to get stuff was a regular occurrence. "I do love these eight miles of precious island, but I sure do miss the convenience of all the big box stores on the mainland."

"I know I want some more cases of Coca-Cola. The boys are already putting a huge dent in my stash."

Maria sipped her cola then patted the can. "Oh, how I love that sugary sweetness and the caffeine kick this gives me, but I really should cut back."

Kareen shrugged. "Good gravy, you could have much worse things to drink." *Like the alcoholic beverages that killed my husband.*

"Yes. So, more Coke it is."

"No problem."

Maria laughed. "But back to what you asked—how do we let Hamp know that you are married? That's a tough one."

"I thought if he read my journal, it might help him to understand what I've been living with for over twenty-five years."

Maria took another drink of her Coke. Kareen's daughter-in-law was definitely not giving Coca-Cola up anytime soon. Maria set the can down almost reverentially. "But you were married over *fifty* years."

"The last half were the problem. Our first twenty-eight years were glorious."

"What happened? What on earth would drive someone to drink and to alter their personality?" Maria shook her head, her dark tresses bobbing. "Mid-life crisis?"

"No. I don't want to say right now, but I'm investigating something I think might have caused Hampy to morph into"—she raised her hands—"someone else."

"Is that why you asked us last night about doing the DNA tests? I mean, do you think it's a genetic issue?"

"I don't know." Kareen puffed out a breath, feeling a little cagey. "I want to get to the bottom of some things that may be going on. But please don't tell Hamp. Just keep the pretense that it's for genealogy purposes."

Maria averted her gaze. "I really have been wanting to do my genealogy, especially now for the boys' sakes. It's good to feel connected to our families. Among the Hispanic people, it's a thing of pride and a matter of course to have huge close-knit families. Growing up, I had a much smaller family than my other friends in Texas."

Kareen had forgotten that. "You had just the one sister, right?"

"Si." Pain flitted over Maria's pretty face.

"Hamp's friend, Tamara's ex-husband, was married to her, isn't that right?"

"Si."

Tammy was Hamp's dear friend. She'd been married to Brad. Brad had been Maria's brother-in-law, and she'd shared that she'd despised him for years because she held him responsible for the death of her sister and the unborn twins.

"I only had one sister, and my mother was an only child. Her father died in Mexico—I don't know anything much about him other than his first name was Roberto—before her mother moved her to Texas. My mother met my father in our Hispanic community there. My father had what I now think of as an average size family with four siblings. But most of my friends had like maybe fifteen or more aunts and uncles and dozens of cousins."

"That's amazing. I had a small family, too." Kareen ate the last bite of her burrito. "But maybe you'll find a bunch more cousins or other family members if you do that DNA testing." Wouldn't hurt to have Maria do it, too.

"Wouldn't that be something?"

Kareen stared at Maria. What would this woman think if she knew whose daughter-in-law she biologically was? If she knew the secret Kareen had kept far longer than that of her marriage to Gianni—that Hamp's father was one of the biggest silver screen stars in history?

Zuzu made little whining noises.

"Come here you little beggar." Maria gave the dog a tiny piece of her food.

"You, too?" Kareen laughed. "I swear she has everyone wrapped around her little paw."

Maria bent and patted the pup's head. "How about Gianni, does he like your adorable pup?"

Laughing, Kareen pushed away from the table. "You should hear him talking to her on the phone. He calls himself PopPop, and she knows who that is. Watch."

Kareen patted Zuzu's back. "Where's your PopPop? Where is PopPop?"

The tiny dog sat, her entire body shaking as if in anticipation. Her little eyes wide as she looked around but remained seated and shivering. Kareen scooped her up. "Awww, I sorry, I sorry. I shouldn't have teased you." Her sing song-voice wasn't one she usually used around Maria.

"You are so changed, it's almost unbelievable. Gianni must be good for you."

"Yes, for me and for this little sweetie." She stroked Zuzu's head. "I'll call PopPop later and you can talk to him then, okay?"

Zuzu barked, almost as if she understood.

Hamp stepped through the door. "Who's PopPop?" His eyebrows bunched in confusion.

"That's what we call Gianni."

"I think it's cute," Maria interjected.

Thank you, God, for that—before Hamp can start quizzing me.

Carrie Fancett Pagels

Chapter Fourteen

*R*achel laid down on what had been their maid's twin bed, in the servants' quarters, and closed her eyes. Working two jobs and taking her last online nursing course was catching up with her because oblivion claimed her immediately.

Mom's boyfriend lunged toward her. He transformed into a giant octopus—a massive purple creature. She broke free and ran down a long golden hall and opened a huge pink door covered in frilly eyelet. Inside, Mom stood smirking, wearing Rachel's prom dress, and behind her was Zack, Rachel's date.

A grating metallic sound wakened Rachel from her nightmares. She panted several shallow breaths. Those horrid dreams had once been her reality.

What had that weird sound been? She rose and listened.

Her phone alarm sounded. The chimes repeatedly tolled like loud brass bells.

"Why did I change to that annoying sound?" She sighed. "Because I needed something noisy enough to wake me."

She checked the digital clock. This alarm was for her bedtime, so she'd get up on time in the morning for work at Lucky Bean, but she'd fallen asleep even earlier.

She went to the servants' quarter's bathroom and washed up for the night. She removed Gram's sapphire heirloom ring and placed it on an antique china ring holder on the counter. Gram said the ring had been passed from her Grandmother Sadie Duvall Swaine to her mother and then to her. Mom would just have hocked it or thrown it in a drawer—that's probably why Gram had given it to Rachel and why Rachel's name was on the checking account and not Mom's.

My name is on Gram's checking account in Illinois. Rachel had checked online and the Chicago bank account was still active. And it *had* paid for the lawn service Carter had done.

But it was Gram's money, not hers. Rachel had taken care of the expenses, though, for a long time—all those that weren't on automatic payment set up by Gram.

The car was Rachel's since she was also on the title. And according to the bank, if there were two names on a checking account then the survivor owned what remained. She splashed water on her face. She knew exactly what was in that account when she'd checked it last week. She'd expected Mom to try to close it out. But she couldn't if Rachel was also listed as owner, could she?

If Rachel did use Gram's checking account, then would Mom accuse her of stealing from the estate? Could Mom try to take legal action and dispute that Rachel was on that account properly? Tomorrow she'd ask the bank manager about what the specific rules were for joint accounts and what if someone contested the secondary person's ownership.

Maybe it wasn't such a great idea to have blown most of her pay on this last pre-requisite course for the RN program. But that was her future she was investing in.

She wasn't going to be a trespasser forever. But if she got a conviction for doing so, would she still be able to get her license as a nurse?

God help me. If I need to leave Lilac Cottage, help me to do so.

After showering and preparing her morning French press coffee, Rachel went outside and sat in the backyard. This might be her last lazy morning at the cottage and she wanted to enjoy it. The antique Zephirine Drouhin roses were finally climbing the trellis again and buds had appeared. A text pinged her cellphone.

The exam has to be pushed back a few days. Rachel's nursing class instructor sure knew how to ruin a day.

"What the heck?!" Rachel was tempted to throw the phone against the wall if she had another one for back-up. But the three-year-old iPhone 10 had to hold her.

She gaped at the message from her professor. That text meant she could not do her test on the weekend. Working on her studies at the library each weekend had been fine, but it wasn't going to cut it for WIFI for the exam. At least it was after her second job. Should she ask to use the WIFI from Jack's house? No. She was not going to bother him. He'd no doubt have some lame crack about nursing as a career. But desperate times called for desperate measures.

"Wassup?"

Rachel startled at the male voice and pressed her cell phone to her heart. "Way to scare a person."

Carter chuckled as he strolled around the side of the cottage. "You said mow in the afternoon, didn't you?"

"Yeah, yeah."

"And it's afternoon."

"Just barely," she harrumphed.

"What were you yelling about back here?"

"Ugh. My professor changed an exam again and it's now at a time when I don't know if I can get to WIFI."

"No WIFI here?" His lips curled in.

"Nope. And I've got only a minimal cell plan."

"Which is pretty spotty on the island."

"Yup." And her internet time was severely limited on her phone.

He pulled off his navy baseball cap with UVA emblazoned on it. "I know most of the passwords for the businesses around here—and a bunch of the residents', too."

"Really?"

"Happy to share."

Wasn't that like stealing? She pressed her eyes closed. When was she going to be able to get all her ducks in a row for this God thing?

"Hey, can't you use the café's WIFI?"

"It's not for customers. Only for business use."

Carter snorted. "I have the password if you want. Just don't let Andi see you doing it or Carolyn if she's in there."

If she was going to finish this class and be considered for Lake Superior State's Nursing program, then she had to do something. "What about someplace between here and the café? Besides the dock—it's too distracting there."

"Joann's Fudge has some WIFI and there's that hallway outside where you could sit."

"Still too noisy."

"You work right by Doud's. Go sit behind that old Frenchman's shack—no one ever goes out there—and login to the Doud's store WIFI."

She exhaled slowly. That could work. "Alright. I'll try it."

"Open your contacts and add this under Doud's." He gave her a moment and then rattled off the password, which she'd never have guessed in a million years.

"Thanks, Carter."

"De nada as my nephews say."

"You have nephews?"

"Yeah, *hello*, you're working with them—Sean, RJ, and Austin."

"What?"

"Those dudes are my step-nephews. They're my stepmother Maria's grandkids."

"Maria is great. She brings us empanadas in the morning and sometimes burritos at lunchtime."

He rubbed his flat stomach. "She's like the best cook ever."

"Definitely." And Rachel had eaten in some high-end restaurants with her family in Chicago, but Maria's cooking was amazing.

He looked around the backyard. "No one's gonna see you back here."

"Huh?"

"Jack said I'd better not talk about you being here or he'd hurt me bad."

"He said that?" She stiffened.

"Well, he didn't say how he'd do it, but. . ." Carter raised his hands.

She rolled her eyes upward. "I'm sure he thinks he's looking out for me."

"Oh yeah, totally. He told me that his dad has him watching over you."

"What? That sounds a little creepy." She frowned.

"Nah, that's just Mr. Welling. I think it's the old Marine thing, ya know?"

"My grandfather was in the Marines, too."

"Grandpa Parker said that's why Mr. Welling worked for the judge—because they were both marines."

"When did Jack's dad ever work for my grandpa?"

"That's how he met Jack's mom. So, I guess, what, thirty years ago or so?"

"So, before I was born." No one had ever mentioned it around her.

"My grandmother used to see him up here doing yardwork and said he was the biggest slacker she'd ever seen." He laughed.

"Yeah? Hard to imagine Mr. Welling being lazy."

"She said he'd be down at the street leaning on his lawn mower, looking around, like he had no cares in the world."

Rachel laughed. "Sounds like a lot of young guys."

Carter pressed a toe of his white Converse retro sneakers into the grass. "I better get this yard taken care of before my grandmother starts calling me a slacker, too."

"Huddle time!" Jack made a circle with his index finger and RJ, Sean, and Austin joined him.

He rubbed his hands together. "We're gonna tape off the kitchen tomorrow. Today we're gonna wash it down with some good old elbow grease."

Sean raised his hand.

"You don't have to raise your hand, Sean." RJ elbowed his brother. "You're not in school."

Jack shot RJ a hard look before mussing Sean's hair. "What's your question?"

"What's elbow grease?"

"Yeah. What is it?" Austin crinkled his upper lip. "That seems weird to put on a wall."

RJ made a face of disgust. "You goofs! It means you use your guns." He flexed his upper arms, muscles bulging. "And bend your elbows a bunch working."

"Oh." Sean's cheeks turned pink.

Jack waved his flattened hand to stop the chatter. "Okay, enough about that. We're, or rather you three, are gonna wash the kitchen walls from top to bottom with this Borax solution."

"Don't tell grandma we did this, or she'll make us clean the kitchen in her house." Sean wagged a finger at his brother.

"Carter can do that himself." Austin frowned. "He's got the place to himself now that we're staying inside the resort."

Rachel looked up from the desk, where she was comparing three contractor's line-item quotes. "Carter has a house to himself?"

Was she thinking of asking him if she could get a room there? Jack's face heated. Maybe she should stay here. Not that he didn't trust Carter, but. . .

RJ leaned in. "Rachel has a big exam today, Jack. You sure you want her working on those numbers?"

Jack cast a look back at Rachel, who was bent over the desk again, comparing the printouts. She rubbed the side of her head. She looked beautiful despite her scrunched up forehead and pursed lips. She was the heart of their group, with her little pats on the backs for the boys and her words of encouragement to them.

She'd actually thrown a few morsels his way.

Austin waved his hand in front of Jack's face. "Hey, no ogling—just like you told us."

"I wasn't ogling," Jack growled.

"Yeah," RJ agreed. "He's worried about Rachel taking her nursing exam."

"*Nursing* exam?" She'd never mentioned it to him.

"Didn't you know she's studying to be a nurse?" Sean bent and peered into an old plastic bucket.

Jack didn't respond.

"She used to take care of her grandmother." RJ grabbed a metal pail and a sponge.

Austin took the last pail and two rags. "Rachel lived with her and took her to appointments."

He knew she'd helped her grandmother, but not how much. He'd thought they'd hired full time nursing assistants. And she wanted to become a nurse now? "You guys get to work and be careful on the ladders."

Sean saluted.

Jack saluted back as the trio marched off. He'd completed his requirements for the military college, for service. But if they ever needed him, the government could call him back up to serve.

Dad never talked about his years in the Marines. Definitely a harder gig than what Jack had done. In fact, Dad was secretive about a lot of things, including his work discrepancy and now his plans to retire. And Rachel didn't talk about much, either, besides work. Why did that bother him that the boys knew something he didn't know, and she was with him every day?

He went to Rachel's desk. "You doing okay?"

Tension was etched on her beautiful face. He could still see some of the vulnerable girl in her eyes. "Fine." She turned her attention back to the sheets.

"The guys said you've got a test today."

"I do." Her hands shook as she highlighted a line on two of the sheets and searched the third.

"Do you want to take a break from this? To study?"

"Nope."

"Well, okay then." If she was going to be like that then so be it. "I'm heading to the mainland to meet with the plumber."

She gave a curt nod.

"If you need to knock off early, that's fine."

She shook her head.

"All right then. I'm off."

But as he headed out the door, conviction hit him. *Lord, what can I do for her? Show me.*

Rachel shifted the computer bag as she approached what Carter had called a shack, but was a quaint white structure. The old building was small, but back in the seventeen hundreds there were probably a bunch of houses like this on the island. She'd seen the little house a number of times, but Gram always steered her away from entering the building.

Her chest throbbed from where she'd gotten accidentally burned, earlier at work. Rachel squared her shoulders. What would she do if that Girl Scout guarding the entryway, who looked to be no more than fifteen, came around back and kicked her out?

"Do you have your admission?" the scout asked.

Rachel displayed her pass. Thankfully, Carter had told her earlier to go up to the booth and get a day pass. "Here you go."

The kid shoved her glasses up. Her hair was braided in tight cornrows tied off with tiny pink ribbons. Maybe she was thirteen not fifteen. "Welcome to the Fisherman's Cottage, circa 1780. This house was inhabited until the late eighteen hundreds."

"The late eighteen hundreds? Seriously?"

"Yes. The last family, the Duvalls, were islanders." The girl's dark eyes fixed on Rachel's chest, where the coffee burn was still tender. "Are you okay? I mean, no one did that to you did they?" She pointed, compassion painting her young features.

"Oh, no! Just me. I work at the coffee shop down the street, and I grabbed my boss's coffee to bring to her and didn't realize the top wasn't fastened."

The Girl Scout nodded solemnly as her gaze searched Rachel's face. Did she really think someone had done this to her?

"I'll be more careful next time, Scout's honor." Rachel made the sign with her fingers and the girl grinned.

"Go ahead and look around. It's a nice piece of history that a lot of people overlook."

"Will do." Something made her add some truth. "And it's all right if I sit out back, too, right?"

"Sure."

"It's so pretty out there."

"Bring me a caramel mocha latte tomorrow and you can stay as long as you want."

Fifteen, not thirteen, or maybe sixteen or more. Rachel laughed. "Will do."

She ducked inside the dark building, which was actually a log cabin inside, despite the white covering on the wall's exterior. It was maybe twenty feet by twenty feet, max. Pictures lined the fireplace mantel. One drew her attention. She moved toward it. That was the same woman as in a photo at Lilac Cottage, of her great-grandmother. Sadie was scrawled across the bottom of the picture. She gaped. Sadie Duvall Swaine was the wife of Robert Swaine, a prosperous ship captain and businessman. Was this tiny home part of Rachel's own history? Chills coursed up her arms.

She needed to get her exam started instead of researching who'd lived here. She moved to the tiny kitchen area and exited out the back. Had her great-grandmother Sadie, who'd traveled the world, grown up here? It sure looked that way. And if so, why hadn't Gram told her?

No time for that now.

Thank God it was another gorgeous sunny Mackinac day. She sat on the wooden bench by a rustic picnic table and pulled her old laptop out of its case. She attempted to log-on to Doud's WIFI.

It didn't work.

She tried again, carefully entering each letter and number and symbol.

Noooooo!

Jack watched from the sidewalk as Rachel's face turned pink, then red. She gaped at her computer.

Rachel stood and clutched the computer to her chest. "Oh my gosh, oh my gosh."

Jack strode forward and then hopped over the fence that surrounded the Mackinac State Parks cabin. "What's got you so upset?"

She blinked at him through tears. *No, please. No tears.* Tears were fatal. Tears made men do weird things.

Her nose crinkled adorably. He reached into his pocket and then shoved his clean handkerchief at her. "Blow your nose and tell me what's wrong."

"No WIFI."

He glanced at the parks' oldest building. "They didn't have it back in the day."

She stared at him.

He laughed. "Definitely not in the Duvalls' time." Was that why she chose to do her test here? Dad said Mrs. Dunmara's grandparents, the Duvalls, had owned this humble home.

She scowled. "No. I'm trying to use Doud's."

"Doud's? They don't have public WIFI."

She sniffed. "Carter gave me the password, but it won't work."

"They probably changed it." Because of people doing what Rachel was trying to do.

She stared at him as if he was an idiot.

He raised his hands in surrender. "I guess you figured that out. But why didn't you just ask to use my WIFI?"

"I knew I couldn't get back there in time, for one thing."

"And the other?"

"Because I don't like asking you favors." More tears dripped down her pretty face.

"Oh, don't. . ." He wouldn't say cry. Cry was a cuss word as far as he was concerned.

"I should never have signed up for this class."

"Why did you then?"

"I'm trying to study to be a nurse."

Who worked two jobs on the island taking an online course in the summer? *Someone desperate.*

She sniffed. "I've been taking online classes for *years* including in summer. This is my final class before I can continue on for my BSN."

The way she said *years*, she meant it.

Today's distress was revealing. Rachel might act tough, but she was like a chocolate chip cookie dipped into one of Andi's mochas—the cookie would collapse in the heat if left there for more than a second.

He pulled out his cell phone. "Sit down, Squirt." He pointed to the picnic table.

She huffed. "I need to find WIFI somewhere."

"I'm setting my phone up for a hotspot. Let's see if it works. It should. I use it at the cottage sometimes when the WIFI is down."

"Really?" She sounded hopeful. "I don't have enough on my plan to do that."

"I do, and I've got great reception in town."

Rachel sat at the table and opened the laptop.

"Go into settings and search for Olivia's name." He'd set his phone to his sister's name, planning never to forget her.

"Olivia's name?"

"Yup. Do ya see it?" That wasn't wetness in his eyes, it was allergic irritation from summer flowers. There were baskets hanging everywhere downtown and blooming in every yard.

"Yes. Got it."

"Password is all lower case." He read off the string of random letters and numbers he was using that month. "Are you in?"

"I'm in!" She beamed up at him. "But my test will take at least an hour."

"I'll leave my phone with you." Only his mom, Dad, and Andi had this number. He used his other phone for business and the remodeling jobs at the cottage.

"Are you sure?"

"Make sure you can log onto your exam. Do that before I go." He sounded, even to his own ears, like the big brother he once was. Wasn't he still? Wouldn't he always be Olivia's older bro?

She focused on her screen, bent in, and typed something.

A seagull landed on the sidewalk nearby and squawked at them. Jack made a shooing motion at the pest. Didn't need the bird distracting Rachel during her test.

"I'm in!" She jumped up and ran to him.

Before he knew it, Rachel had launched herself into his arms. And he pulled her close, inhaling the scent of apples in her hair and a hint of roses. He released her and she looked up at him with wide eyes. Warmth surged through him.

"Sorry, that was out of line. But thank you." Her blush almost matched the burn on her chest from earlier. Andi had told him about the accident.

Good thing I came to check on her—between the lack of internet and that burn, she's had a rough day.

"No prob." Definitely no problem. *Maybe a problem.* Felt like aboard ship when they'd hit a massive wave. Yes, a problem—she was his worker. "We'll just pretend that never happened."

Her jaw slacked, but then she ran back to the table. She didn't look up as she sat and began her test.

"You can leave the phone with Andi, and I'll get it from her later."

Rachel glanced up, nodded, and then stared back at the computer.

Why had he lied? He wasn't going to pretend that hug had never happened. Not with the way she made his heart zing or whatever it was doing right now.

Rachel Dunmara definitely wasn't a kid anymore.

Jack was in no situation to be thinking the thoughts rumbling in his head. He had no job as a merchant mariner anymore. He had no desire to go out on the high seas again. And he couldn't imagine himself working as an engineer in a shipbuilding company like the position he'd been offered in Virginia.

He needed to set up that interview with the Great Lakes Shipbuilders School soon.

Why did Rachel make him want to have something to offer a woman?

He wasn't ready to answer that question.

Chapter Fifteen

I can't bring her back, Goldie." Jack retrieved the dog from Olivia's former room yet again. "You're gettin' too old to be sleeping on the wood floor."

He'd have to put a chair in front of the empty room. The guys had done a great job clearing it, scrubbing the walls, and repainting both the walls and the ceiling. Rachel had cleaned its small chandelier-type light fixture. Almost every trace of Olivia had been removed. At least he no longer had anxiety when he approached that bedroom. His sister would always be with him in his heart and in his best memories.

This was his third consecutive night in his own bedroom. Seemed weird sleeping again at the cottage. That was one reason he often accepted Andi's invites to stay in town. Sometimes, here at Canary Cottage, he'd lie awake and feel like he'd been transported back in time. Due to the cost of transporting the family's heavy antique furniture off the island, the pieces remained in the cottage. Both his apartment and his condo had been minimalist and ultramodern. Maybe that was in reaction to the ornate Victorian furnishings of this place, or perhaps so he'd never conceive that he was putting down roots in those ports.

One girlfriend had ditched him because she believed his behavior announced he had no intention of remaining for long. *She was right.*

The hinges on the front door groaned as someone opened it downstairs. He stiffened. The door had been locked.

"Jack?"

"Mom?" What was she doing here?'

"It's me and Dad. We brought Trenary Toast."

He stifled a groan. He hated that stuff. Mom and Dad loved the hard sugary and cinnamon dried-up toast that they dipped into their coffee to keep it from breaking their teeth.

"Also brought you some of Miss Lorinda's bear claws—fresh this morning." Dad's voice boomed.

"That's more like it." He patted Goldie on the head and scrambled downstairs.

Mom opened her arms to him. "I just missed you so much after seeing you again, and I begged Daddy to bring me up."

"It's a surprise." Dad rolled his eyes. "I know how much you love those."

"Actually, it's you who can't stand surprises, Dad, not me."

Mom elbowed him. "Yup. He called you on it, *Mr. No Surprises Ever.* Not *ever* never."

When Jack arrived in Michigan, he'd stopped by his father's workplace for the school district. The receptionist there, a new hire, said she'd never heard of his dad. "Talk about a surprise, I got one when I stopped by your office."

Dad scratched the back of his neck. "We'll talk about that some other time." He snuck a glance at Mom.

Mom brushed something from Jack's shirt. "How's it going with Rachel?"

"She's a good worker."

"That's what my sister says, too."

Andi was Dad's half-sister, but he didn't refer to her that way.

"Pretty sure, though, that the teen boys working for me all have a secret crush on her."

Dad's lips twitched. "And does their boss?"

Jack scowled. *Beautiful, funny, intelligent, compassionate, and hard-working.* Why would he have a crush on her?

Dad clapped his hands. "Well, are you gonna give us the tour?"

"Yes, sweetie, show us what all you've done so far." Mom squeezed his arm. "I can see all the painting and it looks great."

"Come on." Jack waved them toward the stairs. "Let me show ya the bedrooms and our progress."

When they'd finished examining the completed projects, they returned downstairs.

"It's coming along great." Dad clapped him on the back.

"Thank Rachel for that when ya see her. She's got that Chicago pushback and doesn't put up with much from the contractors."

"Good." Dad flexed his shoulders. "You have to be firm or nothing will get done on time.

"Let's go outside." Mom gestured to the back. "It's so pretty today."

They went outside to the back lawn at the more formal wrought iron picnic table.

Dad pointed at the trellis. "Needs painting and the vines needed trimming. You want some help with that, Son?"

"Nope. Colton Byrnes and his crew are coming over here later. Owed me a favor." For getting him away from Dubai and back to the states, stashed in Jack's room on a freighter.

"He's back?" Dad frowned.

"Sort of." Jack reached for a napkin. "He's got a new show starting soon."

Mom laughed. "That's right. Didn't his co-host Sue Pentland run off with some fabulously rich guy from Dubai and leave him in the lurch?"

Dad cast Jack a knowing look. "Didn't realize he was working on the island again. But I saw him not too long ago with a gorgeous gal at the Lumberjack Show in Mackinaw City."

"Yeah, that's his new love interest, Cassandra. She's not only an engineer, but she's also hosted podcasts on 'Landscaping Meets Engineering'. Cassandra Crafts Nature is the name of her show." Jack slathered his bearclaw with butter. "And she and Colton's new HGTV show will be called 'Cassandra and Colton Craft Nature'."

"A lot of C's in that!" Mom laughed.

Dad scanned the yard and house. "Do you mean they're fixing *this* backyard and HGTV might be coming in, too? Or is that a separate thing—because I'd like to know." His gaze settled on the cameras he'd installed. Maybe he'd not run them through the island board. Did he need approval for that?

Jack raised his hands. "I didn't tell them yes for sure, Dad."

"It's fine. Go ahead. But can I be here for it?" Mom's eyes grew wide.

"Colton has already requested your brownies."

"Really?" Mom squealed like a teenage girl.

Everyone loved his mom's brownies—and his mom. He'd been so blessed to have such a warm and caring mother and father. Poor Rachel, she'd been raised by someone, in Jack's opinion, who was even worse than his friend Parker's mother. At least when Mrs. Parker was sober or straight, she really did try. And she loved her sons.

"We wanted to ask if you've decided what you want to do next." Dad dunked his Trenary Toast into his black coffee.

"Not that we're trying to push. But it's been so lovely being able to see you again. Especially since. . ." Tears filled Mom's eyes.

Especially since his sister was gone. *What a selfish jerk I've been.* Jack reached across and covered his mother's small hand with his own. "It's been great seeing you two more, too. Those once-a-year visits weren't enough."

"We'd love to have you closer to home, Son, but we want what's best for you."

"And we're prepared to both retire and fly to where you are—when you're in port for extended times."

Maybe that's why Dad wasn't at his jobsite. Maybe he'd already transitioned to another location before his retirement.

"I'm not going back. The pandemic made ship life a nightmare." Sometimes they'd been stuck sitting in the water for months waiting to unload. "I am done with that." But he didn't have a next act planned. He had saved enough that he could go without work for a long time.

"My buddy at Michigan State has asked if you might consider doing remote teaching."

"I don't have an advanced degree, Dad." Nor did he intend to put himself through that excruciating pain of engineering classes ever again.

"You have life experience."

"I'll be honest, I have a lot more interest in teaching boat building in Hessel.

"Really?" Mom shrugged. "I never saw that one coming"

Neither had Jack. *Now why did I say that?* Maybe because he'd run into Garrett Christy, the master builder, on a mainland hardware store run and the older man had suggested it.

He ran his thumb over his lips. Mom would say that was God giving him a nudge. "I think it could be an answer to. . ."

Mom frowned. "To your prayers?"

"Yes, this could be."

"I'll toast to that." Dad raised his nasty bread. "Get it? Trenary toast?"

Jack shook his head in feigned disgust. "Nah. I don't get it. I *never* buy that stuff. Don't know why the bakery carries it."

"More for me, then." Dad grabbed another piece of the rock-hard stuff and dunked it in his coffee.

"We can't convert you, then?" Mom arched an eyebrow.

"Not to Trenary toast."

He'd started the day mourning the absence of his sister, and now here were his parents wrapping Jack in love. He turned his head and swiped at his eyes. Mom moved in and wrapped an arm around him. Dad, too. They stood like that for a moment.

Olivia may be gone. But they still had each other.

From her vantage point on the third floor of Lilac Cottage, Rachel could see Jack and his parents seated in their spacious backyard. When she and Olivia were young, they'd strung white fairy lights across the back and the place had seemed magical. Family lore held that several marriage proposals had occurred there.

Not her great-grandmother Sadie's and great-grandfather Robert's, though.

When she was young, Rachel had never thought she'd ever want to be married. Not from what she'd seen and experienced in her mother's relationships. Granted it had been her mother who had manipulated and destroyed her marriages—all but one. And that still galled Mom, no doubt. As had the other man who had gotten the better of her, Dr. Gentrey.

The handsome young pediatric oncologist had met Mom at a soiree for the hospital. Ironic that their breakup should occur there, too, one year later. Gram had contributed to the Barrington Hospital Christmas toy drive for the kids on the unit and had been invited to a posh party at the Drayton Hotel. Gram had been sick. She was supposed to bring Rachel with her. Instead, Mom ended up going and brought a recalcitrant Rachel. About age ten, she'd realized her mother was different from all the other moms.

Dr. Gentrey, a rising star, had made a beeline for them as soon as they'd entered the room. Mom, attired in a glittering ruby red gown, and Rachel in a white and silver dress with itchy chiffon poufing it out underneath, stood out. But that was part of her mother's modus operandi. To get as much attention as possible. While the waitresses and waiters had made sure Mom and Rachel got whatever they needed, Dr. Gentrey never left their sides.

Looking back, he really didn't only have eyes for Mom. He'd been overly nice to Rachel, as well. He'd been gracious and kind until one of the other doctors joined them. Then the physician had become downright surly. Afterward, Mom insisted it was because he'd been jealous of the other man.

One year later, at the same event, Rachel had searched for her stepfather down one of the hotel hallways. Her mother was dancing with the hospital CEO and had a steady line of companions while her stepfather had disappeared, leaving Rachel on her own. When she found her stepdad, who'd spent the entire past year making sure everyone on the hospital staff had met his little girl, she'd learned the truth. The doctor who'd interrupted them the previous year had been the jealous one.

She discovered the two doctors embracing. It was clear that this wasn't a simple friendly hug. Dr. Gentry and his friend were gay and in a relationship. Rachel had been shocked. It looked like they might kiss but then Dr. Gentrey saw her and she ran back to her main gathering room.

When she told Mom later what she'd seen, Mom had gone off like a keg of ignited dynamite. That was the first time Rachel had heard the word narcissist. Mom had hurled the word at Dr. Gentrey, and he'd volleyed it back at her.

Took one to know one. That was when Dr. Gentrey had unknowingly excised consuming shame from Rachel's brain. Shame that she wasn't good enough for her mother to love. Shame that her father hadn't married her mother. Shame that there must be something wrong with Rachel, something terrible that caused Mom to hate her. Or to at least not care about her like other moms cared for their kids. Rachel had looked up the word *narcissist* and began reading all about narcissism. And Dr. Gentry's surgery of words had freed her.

Almost.

Strange waking up with his folks asleep upstairs. Almost like the old days. Jack slid his cup of coffee by his spot at the kitchen table and took his seat. He'd finished over half his mugful when he spotted a familiar home in an ad. Jack almost lost hold of his Detroit Free Press. Lilac Cottage. For sale by a reality company that wasn't local. He gripped the paper, crumpling the edges, and re-read the ad. What had his dad said? Hadn't he said last night, over s'mores making, he thought Mrs. Dunmara would have left it to Rachel? Something stank here.

"I don't believe it." He looked around the kitchen which would soon transform from pale yellow to Mackinac blue.

Mom tied her robe as she entered the kitchen. "What don't you believe?"

"There's an ad in the Free Press for sale of the Dunmara's cottage."

She frowned. "Let me see."

He pointed to the ad featuring a large black and white image of the house and grounds.

"Wow. Have you seen the realtors up here?"

"Nope. There are always tourists taking pictures of the houses on West Bluff, so I don't think I'd have noticed."

"Rachel didn't say the family was selling the property?"

"No."

Mom took the paper and sat down across from him at the table. "Your dad said to watch for anything unusual going on with Lilac Cottage, and I'd say this qualifies."

"Might be why Rachel has been looking for a place to live." Turned out Mom and Dad already knew about Rachel staying at the cottage because of the cameras.

"Really?"

"Yup. Aunt Andi doesn't have any rooms for her and told Rachel. Same at the Island Bookstore at Doud's. Nothing. And if the cottage sells. . ." Maybe she could stay there. *No. That would not work.*

"Wow. I never thought they'd let Lilac Cottage go out of the family." Mom tilted her head. "Margaret said neither her property nor this one can be sold outside of the family. The inheritance is structured so that it's nearly impossible."

"Yeah?"

"I wonder if Selma is trying to pull a fast one, hoping that no one contests it. I'm going to ask your dad." Creases furrowed mom's forehead.

Dad ambled in wearing rumpled pajamas. "What are you going to ask me?"

"About someone trying to sell Lilac Cottage."

Dad scowled. "They can't just sell it. There are legal contingencies in place."

"What do I need to do to help Rachel?" How many times had he asked himself this very question?

"Well, for one thing, let's get Andrette's husband in on this."

"All right." Jack grabbed his phone and texted his uncle a quick message.

"The Robert Swaine, Junior, clause expires this summer on this house. That's why we wanted to go ahead with the renovations." Dad glanced around the kitchen.

"I thought you just wanted it done, and I was available."

"That's part of it." Mom covered his hand with her small one.

"But the will specifies that if no heirs of Robert Swaine, Junior, are located by the end of this summer, then the property leased by Peter and Ada Welling may have full ownership. Otherwise, it remains owned by the surviving heirs, if any, of Robert Swaine, Junior."

Jack's family had been here for decades. Seemed unlikely someone would show up now to stake a claim. "I'd like to take a look at that will sometime."

"Sure thing. It's in the lock box, and we've got a copy with our attorney."

"When's the last time you looked at it?" Jack tossed back the last of his coffee, which tasted nothing like the stuff Rachel made when she was there.

Dad shrugged. "Probably before we had Livvie."

Mom and Dad exchanged a mournful look.

Before Livvie. Before she got sick, so sick for so long, and died.

"I miss her. Especially how feisty she was, despite being ill."
Despite knowing she may die.

"That's what kept her with us so long." Mom swiped a tear from her eyes.

"She's still here with us." Dad tapped his fist to his chest. "Always."

Goldie pranced in and got a head pat from Mom and Dad before dropping down at Jack's feet. "We've still got you, girl." He bent and rubbed the fur on her back.

"And, not to compare with Goldie," Mom raised her eyebrows, "but having Rachel here working for you has to be a comfort. She was almost like family. Olivia's best friend."

A comfort?

Maybe she was.

Chapter Sixteen

*B*ouncy joy, at finally being able to get to the bank to find no huge line, tumbled with gurgling anxiety in Rachel's gut. Nearby, the manager's door was open and a feminine voice in a familiar language—possibly Polish—rose in anger. Rachel cringed.

The elderly lady ahead of her at the counter tucked her packet of cash into her 2010 Louis Vuitton purse. Mom had that one and had discarded the pocketbook in the trash the next season when the newest version released. Not so this lady, who clutched it to her side like a beloved child—something Rachel had never been. *Beloved grandchild, though, yes, I was that.*

"May I help you?" The teller compressed her lips as once again an outburst emanated from the office.

Rachel tugged at the bottom of her Lucky Bean shirt. "Yes, I would like to cash these checks and I have a couple of questions."

"Do you have an account here?"

The squirrels in Rachel's stomach chased each other's tails. "Um, well that's the thing. I did have an account here, but I don't have the numbers."

"Do you have ID?"

"Sure." Rachel pulled her Illinois driver's license from her wallet and handed it to the woman.

The clerk entered the info into her computer and stared at the screen as though it possessed the answers to the universe. What would it be like to hold all the wisdom of creation? The pastor at the island church Rachel was attending had preached that it was a good thing that God didn't let us understand all, for it would drive us mad. Rachel's puny human brain would explode no doubt.

The teller grabbed the driver's license. "Checking the birthdate, too."

Hope blossomed. "So, you've found it?"

The woman grabbed a piece of paper and jotted down some numbers. "This one you're primary on."

"There's more than one?" She tucked her chin in.

"Yes. We do have the death certificate for one of the others." She cast her a hard look. "I didn't know Mr. Parker had a granddaughter."

Parker? Rachel stiffened. "Dunmara was my grandfather's name."

The teller's face reddened. "Our manager, Joy Ellis, isn't here today but our regional director is here if you want to speak with him."

Rachel pulled in a breath. Could she possibly be the Parkers' granddaughter? *Oh my gosh, is that why Mom really didn't want me around them? No. No way.*

"Or you could come back when Mrs. Ellis is here."

"No." It had taken weeks to actually find time to get in to the bank and not have a huge line of people waiting. She'd finally exhausted the amount Jack had advanced her, though.

"Uh oh." The clerk's dark brown eyes widened.

Rachel swiveled. A frowzy redhead stomped out from the manager's office and departed the small lobby. *Guessing that didn't go well.*

The gray-suited man standing in the office door shoved his glasses higher on his thin nose.

When Rachel turned back around, the teller raised her hand and called out, "Mr. Heissner?"

The teller tapped Rachel's work checks. "Would you like me to cash these or deposit into your savings account?"

"Cash please."

"Excuse me," a deep man's voice sounded behind her. The fiftyish man moved alongside Rachel but gave her plenty of room. Might be habit from Covid or maybe he just understood about personal space. To his credit, the manager didn't look the least bit flustered by the problem client who'd just departed in a huff.

"Mr. Heissner, Miss Dunmara has accounts here, and we've received the death certificate on one."

"Sorry for your loss, Miss Dunmara." Heissner's eyebrows drew together, emphasizing a growth on his forehead.

That looked an awful lot like squamous cancer. *Should I say something?* Nope, she'd not go around imparting her limited medical training. "Thank you." Her heartbeat stuttered. She'd lost Gram, not Mr. Parker. She wasn't a granddaughter of the Parkers.

"I'd be glad to assist you." His words sounded like they came through a glass bottle as Rachel wracked her brain. Hamp Parker, Carter's Dad, and Mom had never dated. Had they? Or had they hooked up for a night?

"Here's your cash." The teller handed Rachel the money in an envelope, and she slipped it inside Gram's old Michael Kors' purse.

Mom never thought much of purchasing clothes for Rachel much less a purse. Rachel had always thought it was because her mother was so self-centered. But had part of Mom's stinginess been because she'd been punishing Rachel because Hamp Parker hadn't married her but someone else? *Wait, he had to have already been married because his son, Parker, is older than me. So, he was already married.*

"Here's the account info, Mr. Heissner." The teller handed the man a Post-it note covered in numbers.

He nodded, then turned to Rachel. "Come with me."

She followed in a daze. The patterned carpet beneath her feet swirled. She should leave. *Breathe.* Hadn't she always wondered who her father was? And if Hamp Parker was her dad, then she'd have a brother. Two brothers. More grandparents. But Mr. Parker had died. She'd have another grandmother, too. Her breath hitched. Shivers coursed down her arms as tears pricked her eyes. She blinked them back.

Mr. Heissner gestured to the squarish chair on her side of the desk. The pink desk accessories didn't quite fit this man. He sat down and began typing on the keyboard.

The small office smelled like lilacs and something minty. Pictures dotted a nearby corkboard A tall man and two boys were photographed standing in front of the Paul Bunyan statue in St. Ignace. She'd not been to Castle Rock in years. *When I go up for my nursing interview, I'll stop.*

"Okay, I see we did receive the documentation from the Executor."

She needed to clarify. "So, this is for Mr. Parker? Right?"

He blinked at her. "Is that how you refer to him, excuse me, *referred* to him?" He shook his head. "Sorry, not my business."

"I. . . um," did she tell him that she had no idea what Mr. Parker was to her? "I think there's a mistake, maybe, because my name is Rachel Dunmara. Not Parker." Maybe they messed up.

He glanced at the screen. "Rachel Dunmara of Chicago?"

She nodded.

He rattled off one of her childhood addresses and Rachel's birthdate.

She closed her eyes and lowered her head. This was too much. What was going on?

Heissner cleared his throat. "That's you, correct?"

She compressed her lips and nodded. She couldn't help but stare at what was likely a cancerous growth on his face. It had all the hallmarks. Maybe she wasn't a doctor, not a nurse yet either, but she'd been reading a lot in the past seven years while pursuing her hopes of becoming a medical professional. She surreptitiously reached into her purse.

"I've had this happen a few times, where a joint account has been a surprise." He shrugged. "It can be for many reasons. Sometimes the person simply wants to reward someone."

She found her pen and small notepad and jotted down 'squamous cell cancer – Google it', on a sheet of paper. She'd hand it to him when she left. She shouldn't, she really shouldn't, but all her years of studies were kicking her to do it.

His eyes narrowed, as if he was appraising her. "Perhaps this Mr. Hampton Parker enjoyed talking with you at your job." He pointed to her Lucky Bean shirt.

What was he implying? She stared at him. Hampy Parker, she was told, was more a martini guy than a coffee aficionado. And she'd never run into him there after the place had opened.

He laced his fingers together. "Maybe he figured, if you're a *local* island girl, that you could benefit from some funds to go to college or buy a house on the mainland." His tone had changed to one of condescension.

Still, what he'd said triggered a recollection. *College funds.* Gram had bonds in her name and Rachel's for college. She'd forgotten all about them, but they were in the high-rise. In the lockbox.

"Possibly Mr. Parker had no other family, Miss Dunmara." His patronizing manner grated on her last nerve.

This guy was completely clueless. Obviously, he had no idea who the Parkers were.

Rachel swallowed. "How much was in Mr. Parker's account?"

He named the amount.

Even if she never laid her hands on the bonds, she could use these funds to pay out-of-state tuition at Lake Superior State even without any scholarships. "And that's now *my* account?"

"Yes, indeed it is."

She could earn her RN degree. She'd be able to support herself if Mom had inherited everything else from Gram, like she'd claimed she would.

"Would you like to keep this account open, Miss Dunmara?"

Rachel's phone alarm sounded. She had to get back to work. "Yes. Thank you."

Mr. Heissner was saying something else as she shoved her cautionary note at him, turned and hurried out. She had to get back.

As she exited the bank, Mrs. Parker and step-grandsons were heading up the walkway. Rachel froze and gaped at the woman. *Is she my grandmother, too?*

Tears pricked her eyes, and she swiped at them.

"Oh, Grandma Kareen, there's Rachel. We work with her." RJ waved at the young woman, who hurried off in the other direction as though fleeing a fire.

Looks like Rachel is crying. Compassion touched Kareen's heart. Was Margaret's granddaughter struggling? No doubt losing her grandmother was more like losing a mother, since by all accounts Selma wasn't much of a mom. But who was Kareen to point fingers? *I've been so stifled emotionally by my codependency that I've failed as a parent, too.* But she wouldn't fail these boys. She loved her bonus great-grandsons to pieces.

"I bet she's late from her lunch break." Sean elbowed RJ. "She's wearing her uniform."

"Yeah, let's stop by Lucky Bean afterwards and buy Grandma Kareen a frappe."

"A frappe?" She snorted in a very unladylike way. "Only if it looks exactly like an Earl Grey tea, is hot, and tastes just like it."

"Aw, Grandma Kareen." Sean wrapped an arm around her. "We want to buy you a treat for opening accounts for us."

She'd told them the previous night that she'd opened savings accounts for them in joint accounts for each boy. Should have done it earlier, when Maria and Hamp had married.

"Thanks, Grandma. And it's a good idea to deposit some of our work checks into the savings account."

"You can come in here any time that you like, after we set up these accounts, and you can do what you want." She shrugged. That was between them and their parents, who were two hard-working ER nurses.

"Dad would probably say to deposit it all." RJ crinkled his nose.

"We can only buy a few things with what we've earned so far from Jack." Sean rolled his eyes. "And I plan to spend mine."

Kareen chuckled. "Part of it on my Earl Grey flavored hot frappe?"

"Yes ma'am."

These cuties, her bonus great-grandchildren, had brought her so much joy. She loved her two Parker grandsons, too, and with nudging from her newly renewed relationship with the Lord, she wanted to bless them, too. *But will they let me, once they know the truth?*

"You all right, Grandma?" RJ opened the door to the bank for her.

"Yes, thank you."

They entered the building. Instead of Joy in her office, a man about Hamp's age stood in the doorway chatting with one of the tellers, Camille.

"Hi, Mrs. Parker." Camille blinked furiously.

"Have you got something in your eye, dear?" Kareen frowned.

Camille shook her head in a small sharp movement,

"Parker, you say?" The gentleman adjusted his cheap eyeglasses.

She extended her hand. "That's correct," or it *had* been, "and I'm here with my three great-grandsons," her heart swelled with pride, "to open joint accounts for them."

Now the man was blinking at her, too.

"Mr. Heissner, a department head, is here from the main office today while Joy is out for some training." Camille glanced between Kareen and the bank officer. "Would you like to come back when Joy is here?"

But Mr. Heissner lurched forward and shook Kareen's hand, an almost mischievous look in his hazel eyes. "I'd be delighted to help Mrs. Parker and her grandsons." He waved them into the office while Camille swiveled around and left them.

Soon they were bunched up in the small room. Joy's handsome sons' and husband's picture hung on the wall, beaming down on them. Probably better that Kareen meet up with Joy privately soon. She'd try one more time to worm out of Joy who was on Hamp's other account.

After dispensing with niceties, Heissner gathered their basic information. "And you understand that you cannot remove someone from a joint account?" He looked at her long and hard.

"Of course." She frowned.

He returned to inputting information. RJ patted her hand. "Thanks, Grandma."

Heissner cast her a sympathetic look. "Please accept my condolences on the loss of your husband."

How would he know? He was a mainlander.

When she didn't respond he sniffed. "Hampton Parker was their grandfather?"

"He was our step-great-grandpa," RJ shared.

"So, he had quite a few grandchildren?" The man sounded just like a police officer. "Any granddaughters?"

What a weird question. "All grand*sons*. No granddaughters. Maybe a great-granddaughter one day." She beamed at the boys.

"Why do you ask?" RJ scooted up. *Nothing got by that one.*

"No reason." But the banker's smug expression irritated Kareen.

RJ leaned in further. "We saw our friend, Rachel, on our way here. Did she finally get her banking stuff done?"

The man's hand covered a piece of memo paper so quickly that Kareen couldn't see what was on it. "I can't comment on confidential bank business."

RJ pushed back into his chair, again. "Right. I understand." RJ was an avid crime stories reader. He and Kareen watched Acorn and BritBox murder mysteries nightly. They snacked on kettle corn and drank ginger ale and cackled like they were detectives themselves when they'd solved the mysteries.

Her TV-watching sleuth buddy knew something. *RJ saw something.* She couldn't wait to ask him what it was.

When they'd finished and left the building, she and RJ turned to face one another at the same time. "What did you see, RJ?"

"That paper, it said Hampton Parker and it had numbers. It said Rachel Dunmara and joint account. That's what you set up for us, right? Why would Grandpa Hampy make one for Rachel?"

Kareen tried to catch her breath. *Deflect.* She needed to deflect until she could work this out.

"Well, we can't be *sure* that's what it meant." She tried to give him a stern face but failed. She'd had too many years of making Cranky Kareen faces at people.

"What else could it mean, Grandma Kareen?"

"Let's ask Rachel." Sean waved his hands high, and people seated on a nearby bench gawked at them.

"No! We can't ask her." Horrified, Kareen gripped Sean's shoulders. "Please don't do that."

"All right, Grandma Kareen." His look of contrition reassured her.

She made a circle gesture with her hands to include them all. "Nobody says a word to her. I'll sort this out first. Okay?"

"Honor!" RJ stretched out his arm and his brothers laid their hands atop his.

Kareen placed her hand on top. "Family honor!"

"Agreed!" they all chorused and released their hands and grinned.

Maria was the one who had taught them the honor pact, and Kareen appreciated its use right now. *Oh, Hampy, what is that all about? Did you cover up something our dear boy did and keep it secret from me?* Like mother like son. Shame washed over her, but God had cleansed her of her sins. She had to keep reminding herself of that truth.

When they reached the coffee shop, the youngest opened the door for her.

"What a gentleman you are."

"De nada."

"Hey! There's Carter. Who's he talking to?"

Carter, slouched at the side of the register while a customer pointed between a wide-eyed Rachel and him. He was angled in toward Rachel and didn't see them.

"I'm telling y'all, ya look like kin." The forty-something blonde woman, attired in red from her headwrap down to her patent leather kitten-heeled sandals, pointed a long crimson fingernail at the two.

Rachel shook her head. "No. Just friends."

The flashy gal shook her head. "I'm an artist, and I'm telling you, both of you have distinctive features I'd normally see in siblings."

Carter mumbled something that Kareen couldn't hear. Rachel shot Carter a decidedly dirty look.

"Do you know who I am?" The woman placed her left foot in front of her right. Her skin-tight crimson ankle pants pulled up higher, revealing a rose tattoo on one ankle.

"Verdina Rosen." Rachel's face looked wan. She barely resembled the girl who Kareen got glimpses of with Margaret on her island visits, before the pandemic hit.

The woman snapped her head to the side. "Say what? You know my name? My work?"

"We, or rather, my grandmother, bought your Bright Days."

"Oh? A print?" Her shoulders slumped a little.

"The original." Rachel gave the woman a strange look. "I was there when you delivered it to us in Chicago."

The artist gaped. "Ohmygoodnessgraciousmeohmy, child." She ran all the words together except for the last. "Here I was bragging about my artist's eye, and I couldn't see you were a Dunmara. A chip off the Judge's block, God rest his soul. Please forgive my impertinence."

Rachel smiled and did a drop wave as if dismissing the issue. "It's all right, I've lost about half of *me* since then."

"I didn't want to say, honey, and I still shoulda recognized those glowy blue-gray eyes of yours." She pressed her small bag to her bosom. "And thank y'all for filling my order so fast. I better get my sorry self outta here before I stick my big old size eleven tootsies in my mouth again!"

The flamboyant woman pushed past them. The Dunmaras must have had deeper pockets than Kareen realized to have bought a Verdina Rosen original. But that wasn't shocking. Not compared to the realization that yes, this young woman and her grandson might possess some similar facial features.

This young woman could well belong to her son, Hamp. *But Hamp was too smart for the likes of Selma Dunmara.* Kareen cringed. But Selma was a gorgeous woman, just like her daughter was now. That liaison had to have happened when he'd been separated from his wife, God rest her soul.

If Rachel was Carter's half-sister, then Kareen needed to put the kibosh on any budding relationship between those two. She exhaled a sharp breath.

"What's wrong, Grandma?"

"No Earl Grey on the menu." She gave a curt laugh.

Hamp had a daughter. She'd always wanted a granddaughter. Was this really all that different from her bonus step-great-grands? Moisture overflowed her eyes. Standing right in front of her could be a new family member. Between Gianni's grandchildren coming into her life and Maria's, Kareen was getting blessed beyond all her wildest imaginings when it came to grandchildren and family. Would Hamp, Parker, and Carter feel the same way when they heard her news about Gianni?

Probably not.

Carter turned toward her. "Grandma! Nephews! What are you guys doin' here?"

He raised his hand and the boys took turns high-fiving him. Carter's blissful grin contrasted sharply with the anxiety that painted Rachel Dunmara's pretty face. Rachel *Parker.* She could have had Hamp's name. She could have had a father.

Kareen sucked in a breath that wouldn't leave.

She'd never told her son about his real father. He'd never had a chance to know him. But he was still alive.

Today.

She'd tell him *today.*

Rachel Dunmara's looks didn't come just from her model mother. They also came from one of Hollywood's leading men.

First, she had to tell Hamp about her new husband.

Next week, she'd tell him about his birth father after he'd digested her news.

That was the best thing.

Shame whispered in her ear. *Shut up, shut up, shut up. I'm a child of God.*

So was her son. He was also the biological son of the man he so strongly resembled, that complete strangers had mistaken him for the film star.

No one in their right mind, though, would ever have suspected— not even her own husband—that a senior from Bryn Mawr College in the 1960s, a conservative Christian girl, a stick-in-the-mud could ever have met, much less produced a child with Wayne Stephens.

And that meant that poor Hampy had no heirs. No true biological heirs. Which would make it all the easier to turn the property over to Hamp and Maria. But she would get the truth out of Hamp, and if this girl was his daughter, he'd need to step up to the plate.

He needed to acknowledge Rachel.

Before that happened, Kareen needed to make some acknowledgements of her own.

Chapter Seventeen

A book signing? How long had it been? Years since Rachel and Gram had gone. But since Dawn had asked Rachel for a favor, she headed off to the Island Bookstore. Mimi Vendue, tagline the Parisienne Dabbler, was signing her newest novel there. Dawn Charbonneau's daughter, Jaycie, loved the author's books which were set in Paris and featured a late teen girl having adventures of a lifetime. Jaycie was in Switzerland, and Dawn couldn't come over to the signing, so she'd asked Rachel to snap up an autographed copy.

When she got to the entrance to the wide corridor leading to the bookstore, she stopped as the caricaturist who was usually there did his magic. Except this was more like dark magic as the picture emerged looking vaguely like Jack Welling dressed in a Hawaiian shirt. Seated there, sporting a garish red, orange, and teal tropical button-up shirt, Jack scowled at her.

"What're you doing here?" Jack growled.

She poked her index finger in her cheek. "I've never seen that before on you."

Passersby glanced, some staring openly, at the handsome man attired in a truly hideous shirt.

Jack crinkled his nose. "You won't see it again."

She half-circled around him. "Why not? It suits you."

The artist chuckled. "Sounds like she's got your number, Jack."

"Be quiet, Byron," Jack snapped.

"Hey," Rachel pointed over the artist's shoulder. "Shouldn't that be a more ginormous head, maybe kind of swelled up?"

"Maybe so," the caricaturist agreed. He added more hair, fluffing out in all directions.

Rachel laughed. "That big hair on a big head looks great for him."

"Very funny." Jack's brows bunched together.

"I like this girl." The artist enlarged Jack's nose in the picture.

Voices from in front of the bookstore caught her attention. She'd better get in line before Mimi was done with her signing. "Ta ta for now, boys. I've got better things to do than to chit chat with you."

"Is that what they call verbal harassment these days?" Byron raised his eyebrows.

Rachel walked around the short group in line. The author's pert turquoise beret was cocked sideways over glossy dark curls. Her linen and lace blouse looked straight from a Paris boutique. Rachel stepped inside and up to the register. This wasn't her first rodeo, or in this case first book signing. Rachel needed to purchase the novel before the author signed it outside.

Tamara, the sweet manager of the store, wasn't there. The young woman at the register looked to be about Rachel's age. Her nametag read, Emma, and she looked familiar.

Rachel lifted a copy of the novel from on top of a short stack near the register. She slid it toward the pretty cashier, who rang it up. Rachel passed her a stack of ones and fives for the total.

Emma locked a light-eyed gaze on her.

Oh no. She didn't know she was granddaughter of Dunmara's did she? Had they met at something?

"You work at Lucky Bean, don't you?"

Rachel exhaled a slow breath.

Emma grinned. "I thought I'd seen you there and the dollar bills confirm you're working someplace they do tips?"

She forced a smile. "Right. I thought I'd seen you somewhere."

"Coffee addict." Emma shrugged.

Rachel accepted her change. "Thanks."

"Hey, I heard the author is doing something over at Pink Pony afterward. But I'm not sure if it's an open thing or what."

"Oh. Okay." Rachel slid the book out of the protective bag that Emma had put it in.

She went outside as the last visitor walked off, beaming.

Was it her imagination or did Mimi's brow wrinkle in irritation as she glanced at her watch?

Her *watch?*

Maybe it was a memento from Paris. Mimi Vendue, who wrote teen girl fiction, sported a petite filigree gold watch. Pulling out a smartphone during a book signing to check the time might not be so cool.

Rachel approached the table, which was festooned with the woman's signature colors of cream, rose, teal, citrus orange, and purple. On her Instagram account, her background was swathed in these colors as a surreal Paris sunset. "Hi, I was hoping to get a book signed." Well, duh. How dumb was that? Obviously, since she was standing there shoving a book at the author. *Ugh.*

Mimi smiled. Her pancake makeup was thicker than Mom's usually was. Kind of like stage makeup. Hadn't Rachel read that Mimi's brother was one of those old-Hollywood cowboy movie stars?

Mimi tapped long elegant burgundy nails, French-tipped in white, on the tabletop then turned the cover to the signing page. With a flourish, she signed her illegible signature. "How should I make out the inscription?"

"Make that to Ray Ray, or Rache, or slug-bug!" Jack Welling wrapped an arm around Rachel, and she slapped it off.

"If this book was going to be personalized for you, Jack, I'd have Miss Vendue put, 'To the big head, no brain, hare-brained, pig-faced nincompoop'!" Her face heated. Now, who was using juvenile language? Oh my gosh, and this guy was her boss. *Maybe not for much longer.*

Wide-eyed, Mimi frowned up at them.

"Mom! Mom! Can I have a quarter for the gumball machine?" A red-headed boy of about eight elbowed past them and shoved his open palm toward Mimi. His Indiana State t-shirt was covered with what looked like chocolate ice cream drippings.

Mimi yanked the book away and glared at the child. "Go ask your father."

"Aw, he said no."

Jack dug in his pocket. He passed the child several quarters as two other boys joined them.

"Thanks, dude." The eldest of the boys, a young teen of the exact age—wrong sex—of Mimi's targeted audience, did the head bob that cool kids now affected.

"You're welcome, dude." Jack stretched out his fist for an air fist-bump.

"Merci." Mimi beamed up at Jack. "Now, how should we really personalize this book?"

Jack jerked a thumb toward Rachel, and she cringed.

"Please make it to Jaycie."

"Spelling please? I want to make sure it's exact." Mimi's classic Revlon Cherries in the Snow lipstick had faded to a pale sheen. *So busy she'd not had time to touch up her lipstick.*

"Hey, Meems! Sorry, but the boys got ahead of me." A middle-aged man with a bleached blond mohawk ambled toward them, pulling up on his sagging jeans shorts.

When he reached them, he cocked his head at Jack who stood almost a foot taller. "Hey, you're not that pro football guy, what's-his-name?" He snapped his fingers. "The one who keeps sending my wife those letters?" He balled his meaty fists.

Jack raised his hands. "Nope. Just a lowly ex-ship engineer."

Mimi rose. "Rufus Zenkowicz, knock that off right now or you'll be paying for your tow-truck business all by yourself."

The teen boy tapped his dad's arm. "Yeah, Dad, we've dealt with that football dude. I sent him a cease-and-desist order using a template off the internet, and he finally stopped bugging Mom."

"A budding attorney." Rachel reached for her signed book, wanting to get out of the place before she learned any more of Mimi Vendue's secrets. *TMI.*

"Hey, dude, who was it?" Jack placed both hands on his broad shoulders. "Who's the player I look like?"

"Zack Fluor, can you believe it?" The teen did the head bob again, and Rachel averted her gaze. Weirdly, Mimi's son reminded her of Carter Parker at this age.

Jack elbowed her. "Hear that? I look like Zach Fluor. Voted best-looking athlete of the year." He chortled and turned toward Rufus. "Thanks, man. I needed that today after she shot me down over there." He pointed at Rachel and then jerked his thumb toward where the caricaturist was working on another picture.

Rachel shook her head.

Mimi leaned in toward Rachel. "This is why I spend a *lot of time* in Paris. Because otherwise, I'm right at home with these guys in Podunk, Indiana. Unless my brother flies me out to California to visit with him and his star friends." She made a face as she fluttered her hands.

"Mom, can I get a copy of—"

Mimi scowled. "Stop! You've spent your allowance, and your dad is taking you on a carriage tour while I have *my thing* at the Pink Pony with Uncle Wayne."

Wayne Stephens—that was the famous actor's name—Mimi's brother. Gram had loved his movies.

Rachel tucked her book back in its protective Island Bookstore bag and turned to leave, away from Mimi and her family but mostly from Jack. If she hurried, she could make it out without. . .

"Rachel! Let me give you a ride to West Bluff." His voice was loud enough to carry through the entire corridor, which was packed.

She whirled on him. "Why don't you just announce to everyone where I am staying, Mr. Zack Fluor?" she ground out through clenched teeth.

"Ya know, Zack rhymes with Jack." He stroked his chin. "And I've got his strong jawline."

"You are so ignorant," she mumbled as she headed to the sidewalk. But Jack, an engineer, was a smart guy—just not careful enough. Who knew what her mother would do if she heard from someone that Rachel was camped out in Gram's cottage?

Mimi, the Parisienne rambler, was a middle-aged mom from Indiana who lived in a Paris fantasy world. Maybe Mom was a little bit like the writer. Mom kept pursuing her idea of a perfect husband. Perfect marriage. Perfect home. But in her heart of hearts, was Mom trying to find someone like Grandpa had been? The educated judge who overcame humble beginnings as the son of Irish immigrants. The man who'd acquired position after position of authority and cases that received national attention. Was that why Mom had moved her latest beau into the high-rise just as soon as Gram had entered the nursing home? Mom had modeled for a short time, but she'd quit that after becoming disappointed because she hadn't received top rankings as an elite cover girl in New York. She'd always tell people she should have been, and Mom's hangers-on wine-mom friends would agree.

Mimi didn't hide her less than perfect family away today—not like Mom used to do with Rachel. And maybe the bestselling author didn't totally live in a fantasy world. Maybe she just liked writing stories set in Paris, perhaps during a time in her life that was less stressful. Mom liked to focus on her pre-Rachel years. Maybe that was the least stressful time in her life. Before she'd had a child to raise.

Maybe she should give Mom a little bit of slack. But every time she did, Mom would come back with behavior even worse than her previous stuff. Hadn't Rachel's therapist advised her to stop making excuses for Mom's awful actions and words?

"Wow, you are like a million miles away." Jack clutched her arm.

"You're still stalking me?"

"I'm not stalking you. I've got my carriage right out front."

Jack had to stop their bickering. He and Rachel were acting like teenagers. And he was thirty not thirteen.

"Hey, I'm sorry for back there." He helped her into the carriage.

Rachel's irritated expression morphed into one of regret. "Me, too. I'm sorry. I don't know what got into me."

He slid in beside her. "I was easy prey."

"What were you doing with the caricature?"

"Andrette asked me to do it."

"Oh, Andrette." She raised her eyebrows high.

"A late joke gift for my birthday.

"Ah." Rachel compressed her lips.

Turning thirty was a touchy subject, and his aunt wanted to make him relax about it. "So do you think I look like Fluor?"

She turned toward him and closed one eye. "Nope."

"Come on. Not even a little?"

She faced forward. "You're *much* better looking than him."

Whoa. Had she just said that? Rachel thought he looked better than the Athlete of the Year? He waited for her to add a punchline. But she didn't spring one on him. "Ya mean that?"

"Yeah. I met him at a party in Chicago with my Gram. In person, he doesn't have those nice cheekbones you have and all that thick hair. He's got kind of a flattish face which might work great for photos but not so much in person."

"Really?"

"Whereas your photographs usually look like a great big loon." She turned and smirked at him. "Like those goofy pics on your Facebook page."

"You looked at my Facebook page?" He flexed his shoulders. "Thought you didn't do social media."

"I just started."

Jack shrugged.

"You ought to take the one down of you drooling down on the ex-girlfriend who ripped you off."

He should never have told her about Mei. But recently, when they'd been alone and she'd confided about her mother's antics, he'd shared about his ex. "I should remove it. But I don't go on there much, anyway."

"Someone—a friend—ought to fix that for you." She shook her head. "I wonder if Mei's modeling agency has any clue what she did to you."

He crinkled his nose. Rachel had shared that she'd once actually seen Mei in Chicago.

"Mei is the busiest plus size model in the world—even Sandi Browne had her model her 2018 collection—and she has to rip off her engineer boyfriend? Sheesh!"

Jack waited for her to make a crack about him dating a full-figured woman. Curvy or thin, a dishonest girlfriend wasn't what he wanted. It would take a long time for him to trust again. "So, remove the pics?" He'd known it, but he'd never worked up the energy to bother.

"Just sayin'. That's what I'd do."

"If you were my friend?"

"Yeah. If I was."

Weren't they? Hadn't they spent hours and hours together talking? Hadn't he helped her out? But he was her boss.

Pure and simple, he *employed* Rachel.

And things needed to stay professional—pure and simple.

Nothing with Rachel had ever been simple and some of the thoughts he'd been having about her weren't as pure as they should be.

Jack needed to rein those thoughts in.

Chapter Eighteen

Lake Superior State University
Sault Ste. Marie, Michigan

I'm here about the nursing applicant interview." Rachel clutched her hands together at her waist. She wore a retro outfit that was actually back in fashion—a simple short-sleeved navy dress with a flared skirt and white trim around the collar. Zipping the back had been a struggle, but she'd run next door, and Jack had helped her with the last bit.

Jack. He was turning out to be so very different from the aggravating teen he'd been.

"The Dean has a bit of a back-up. Have a seat." The secretary, whose purple hair was shaved on the sides indicated a nearby vinyl padded seat next to a girl in her mid-teens. Was someone that young there for an interview, too?

When Rachel took her seat, she smiled at the teen. "Hi. My name's Rachel. I'm applying to transfer in."

"I'm MoonBeam today."

"Today?" What did that mean?

"I don't like my name, so I change it up."

"Oh." Rachel scratched her neck. "MoonBeam has a nice ring to it." Maybe this chick was related to Starr—at least in her outlook.

The girl laughed. "Yeah. It's so boring here that I have to do something different."

"Why are you applying then?" The girl sure wasn't sounding like a typical nursing student.

"I'm just here to aggravate my mother."

"How?"

"She's the dean. Dean Dean in fact." The girl laughed. "Dean Latisha Dean if you can believe that."

"Oh." She'd known the Dean of Nursing's last name was Dean but to hear the daughter call her Dean Dean almost made Rachel laugh, too.

"And I graduated in June—I'm sixteen—but she won't let me go away on my own."

Memories flooded Rachel. "I uh, I had to leave home when I was your age."

"Really?"

"It wasn't a choice. And it was hard out there." She'd been shuffled off to Virginia immediately after her grandfather's sudden death.

The girl tucked her legs beneath her on the chair. "But it's way more exciting than here, I'll bet."

"Depends on what you call exciting." Boarding school certainly wasn't. Neither was working low wage jobs and dealing with rotten roommates—that was not exciting, it was frightening.

"My mom's problem is that she cares too much and wants to keep me a baby."

Rachel almost snorted. "You have no idea how great that is that your mom cares about you and wants to take care of you."

"Didn't yours?"

"Nope." She'd let that chunk of negativity shoot past her lips. Unlike some of her friends' stories of helicopter parents, Rachel really couldn't remember a time when Mom had shown interest in anyone but herself. The therapist had said even when Mom seemed like she cared, she was only displaying behaviors that were to her advantage. The pediatric oncologist stepfather had been the same way.

"Yeah, but look at you now." The girl pointed a stubby finger at her. "You're on your own and applying to nursing school and you're what—nineteen?"

"Twenty-five."

"Really?" She angled her chin down.

"Right. And I don't really have the money to pay for this even if your mom picks me as one of the new transfer students."

"Whoa. Really?"

"Right. I'd have to keep working while finishing nursing school. And I'd have to find someplace to live if they don't give me any financial aid."

The girl slumped back into her chair. "Was there anything good that happened to you once you left home?"

Besides this summer and the time with Gram, *not really.* "I got away from a guy who chased me down an alley with a knife. I count that as good." She shuddered at the memory.

The girl's eyebrows scrunched together. "You're making that up."

"Nope. And it was good that I always had a paycheck given to me, unlike some of my other friends whose employers stiffed them."

"They didn't get paid?"

"One friend worked a month and then when he should have had his first check, he was fired and given no pay."

"How can someone do that?" Outrage tinged the girl's words and the secretary glanced at them.

Rachel raised her hands. "Stuff happens out there in the real world."

"What happened to him?"

"He went home to his folks. They were happy to have him back." Unlike her mom would have been if Rachel had to do that.

The door to the office opened and a red-haired twenty-something woman exited, attired in a slim navy pantsuit.

Oh no, I'm not dressed right. Rachel brushed at her skirt.

A woman with a chic bob and gold wireless eyeglasses shook the younger woman's hand. "Thanks for coming in."

As soon as the redhead left, the dean scowled at her daughter. "Mopey, or Dingbat, or Moonie or whoever you are today—what are you doing here?"

The secretary chortled. "She's your newest applicant."

The dean pointed to the exit. "Go home and pack your bags, I've had enough of this."

Rachel pressed her back into the chair, shocked that the woman would behave so unprofessionally.

The girl shot to her feet. "No way. Not after what she just told me." She pointed at Rachel.

Shrinking into her chair, Rachel averted her gaze. The dean took two steps closer.

"Oh, what did Miss—"

"Dunmara," the secretary supplied.

"Tell you?"

"Said that for three free hots a day, a bed, a roof over my head, I should kiss your feet."

Rachel gaped at the girl, horrified. She glanced at the dean, but the woman was smiling and shaking her head.

"Glad someone is speaking the truth to you and happier yet that you're not going to Aunt Ruthie's farm to work."

"What?" The girl almost shrieked the word.

"Because we need you to do your online classes, here, where you actually have WIFI and are not in Amish country."

"Yes, Mom." With that, the girl temporarily named MoonBeam left.

158   *Carrie Fancett Pagels*

The dean tilted her head back. "She will be the death of me yet."

The secretary rolled her eyes and motioned Rachel toward the office. "Ya want some gin, Dean Latisha, or just water, like usual?"

"Bring the whole bottle."

"Gin or water?"

"Gin in a water bottle is fine, thanks."

From their playful banter, it was clear there'd be no gin brought in—but for a moment, Rachel wondered.

The dean closed the door behind her and took her seat behind her desk. "So, what did you really tell my daughter?"

Rachel sat and summarized what had been said.

"That's impressive. But my kid is gonna think I put you up to it."

"I'd hate to see anyone go through what I did."

There was a rap on the door and the secretary brought in a carafe with a glass turned over on top of it.

"Thanks."

"You're welcome." She closed the door again.

"I've looked at your file." The dean poured herself some water and sipped it. "What type of nursing do you ultimately want to go into?"

"I thought I wanted to do pediatrics, but I'm feeling more drawn to either psychiatric nursing or possibly drug and alcohol outreach. I'm hearing there's a strong need for both in the area."

"And you hope to stay here after you graduate?" There was a skeptical look on the woman's face.

"Yes." Mackinac Island was officially located in the Eastern Upper Peninsula, despite seeming like a special little world of its own.

"And you understand that you will be charged out-of-state fees, which can be substantial?"

"I would need loans and hopefully scholarships, if I'm eligible."

"With that excellent GPA and your recommendations, I'd imagine you could qualify for the Sadie Duvall Swaine scholarship."

Rachel stared at the dean. Was she joking?

"And since you're, shall we say, a little more mature student, you'd also be eligible for housing at that same benefactor's namesake building. The Sadie Duvall Swaine house is located at the perimeter of the main campus."

Rachel managed to dip her chin in acknowledgement.

"Mrs. Swaine was one of the foremost nurses in the Eastern Upper Peninsula, and she left a legacy here for us. She believed in helping those who truly wished to help others."

Moisture threatened in Rachel's eyes.

The dean pointed to a framed portrait on the side wall. "That's a picture of her pinning our first scholarship graduating RN."

"I, um, she was my great-great-grandmother."

"Sadie Duvall Swaine?" The dean pushed her chair back from her desk.

"Yes."

A slow smile blossomed on the woman's face. "The girl in that photo—that's my own grandmother. That scholarship made it possible for her to have a better life."

"That's wonderful. My grandmother told me that Sadie was a nurse, but I had no idea. . ." Rachel opened her palms.

"Well, I think it would be lovely for her legacy to bless you, too."

If Rachel had a large scholarship and a place to live, then maybe she wouldn't have to work and could focus on her studies.

And finish her degree.

And start her life.

Wayne Stephens Hosts Event for Author Sister, read the headline. Kareen slumped onto her sofa in her private apartment. Her heart hammered as she scanned the story. The movie star's sister, an author Kareen had never heard of, had signed books at the Island Bookstore and afterwards her brother splurged for a huge party at the Pink Pony. Kareen set the paper down on the coffee table. This changed things— like accelerant on a fire. Was Wayne there to disclose his own truth to Hamp? She swallowed hard, then texted her son to come see her.

She'd work her Co-Dependents Anonymous's Twelve Steps. *I can't. God can. I think I'll let God.*

Her fingers itched to text one of her CoDA friends. She sent out a quick message to her sponsor and asked if she could call her later.

No more delaying, I have to let my son know about my new husband.

When Hamp joined her, she gestured to the upholstered chair adjacent to her.

"We need to talk." Not about everything, though. She chewed her lower lip as she sat.

"I imagine this is about that guy."

Not about Wayne—he had no clue about him. "Gianni is his name."

Hamp huffed a dramatic sigh and sat. "Okay, Mom, what's up?"

"First of all, thank you for how well you've run this resort while still giving major input to Parker on your other properties."

He crossed one leg over the other and leaned back. "Thanks. You know I love our resort."

"I do, and your dad and I wanted to turn over the resort to you and Maria. You know that." She clutched her hands in her lap.

He nodded.

"But your dad died before we could work out the specifics."

Hamp swiped at his eyes. "I can't believe he's gone."

"I know. And I also know he'd want me to get moving on making that transition happen."

He uncrossed his legs and bent forward. "Do you mean soon?"

"Yes. I have been working with my financial planner on sorting everything out. I'm still wrapping up the last of things here and then I should be good to tell you what I can do for you and Maria."

"We don't expect you to just give us this place."

"I would if I could, and absolutely this will go to you when I pass." Which was why she had to tell him about Wayne. Before the man showed up and did it for her.

"Not any time soon, Mom." Hamp drew in a deep breath.

"Hopefully not. I want to explain some things I've put into place to protect that inheritance."

"Such as?"

"I signed a pre-nuptial agreement with Gianni."

Hamp blinked. "You mean—as in getting *married*?"

"Your inheritance is protected in my pre-nuptial agreement with my *husband*." She let that sit there.

"Your husband?" He flushed to his hairline.

At least he hadn't exploded. "You may recall that you and Maria married somewhat quickly."

His cheeks puffed out, and he expelled a sharp breath. "Yeah, but Mom. . ."

She raised her hand. "Your dad and I knew Gianni and his wife for years before your dad died. He's a really good guy, and I hope you'll like him."

He stared blankly, as if in shock. How then, would he take her other news when they received it?

"Your father and I discussed what we'd do if either of us passed away before the other. We wanted each other to be happy. We always encouraged the other one to remarry if we found someone who made us happy. And I have." There. She'd finally spit it out.

Her phone dinged, indicating an incoming text message. Her sponsor could talk later. *Fantastic, because I'm going to need that conversation.*

Hamp ran his hand back through his hair and looked exactly like his birth father in one of his mid-career movies. Her breath caught in her throat. This secret had gone on far too long.

"On a different topic, but still family related, I got those DNA kits in the mail today." And he'd better do his. If he didn't, then at least Carter would. She needed to use those results as a starting point for their conversation. "Maria says she's going to do one, too, so I ordered an extra one for her."

"Great." His grunting tone said otherwise.

She rose and went to the counter and brought him back three of the tests and mailing envelopes. "One for you, one for Maria, and one for Carter."

"All right." Hamp rose and took the kits from her. "You know I don't really care about these, right?"

"I do. But it will be. . ." Maria would have called it fun, but this wasn't about something fun. It was about, "revelatory."

He arched an eyebrow. "If you say so, Mom."

She opened her arms, and he gave her a hug. "I love you so much. I hope you know that, Son."

"I love you, too, Mom."

Enough to bear up under the truth?

She prayed so.

Chapter Nineteen

*C*arter grinned at Rachel. "What is this, our fifth Saturday hangout session?" They'd also attended church together a few times. Jack usually sat with them in the pew and joined them for sandwich picnics in the park afterwards.

"I haven't kept count." But she'd enjoyed their budding friendship.

The weekends had become fuller now that Carter visited with her after he'd finished the yardwork. He'd keep working on it as long as the automatic payments continued. So far, no one had kicked her out of the cottage. But that could happen any time.

"I love spending time with you." Carter dangled his long legs over the back porch steps and inclined toward Rachel.

"I love spending time with you, too." He was a really sweet guy.

"You're such a great listener." Carter grinned in a way that reminded her of someone else. Someone famous, but she couldn't put her finger on who.

"You're a great listener, too." She winked at him.

"Aw, you're just imitating me."

"No. I'm not." She raised her hands. She was careful how much she shared with Carter, but he had recently begun to tell her about his life. And she'd unloaded about her trials and tribulations with her mother and lack of a father.

"Hey, I think I may have a present for you." He pulled something out of his backpack.

"What is it?" A robin flitted past to its nest in the house she'd placed there on a whim the previous year.

"It's a DNA kit." He waved the rectangular box.

"Looks more like a Covid kit."

"Kinda does. But it's not." He passed it to her.

"Thanks. But how'd you get this."

He shrugged. "My dad refuses to use it. I don't know when she got into genealogy, but my grandma and Maria are both pushing it, and I don't mind."

She held it out. "So, this is for your dad?"

He shook his head. "He's refusing. He's mad at Grandma. Besides—you said you wanted to do one."

Rachel drew in a slow breath. What if she finally found out who her father was? What would she do about that. *It's time.* "Thanks. I'll do it."

"Great. We'll see if we find out anything interesting like if we're descendants of King Tut or something."

She just stared at him. She could mess up some family's lives if they discovered she was a missing daughter.

"Oh, gee, sorry. That was insensitive."

"It's all right."

"You're so chill. I appreciate that." He patted her back. "And thanks for not judging me about Abbi-Renae."

"Judgement free zone." She stiffened her hands and jabbed sideways. Abbi-Renae was the so-called ex-fiancé who still texted him.

"I really thought this summer I'd be married." He swiped at his eyes. "And beginning my life helping manage my family's resort."

"Instead, you're still schlepping around doing the landscaping."

"I don't really mind. But. . ." he lifted the back of his shirt, revealing a large red splotch.

"That's not good. With Lupus, and with your doctor telling you to knock yardwork off your list of activities, I can't believe your dad would still push that on you."

Carter shook his head. "He doesn't know."

She stiffened. "About your Lupus?"

"He knows but not about what the rheumatologist told me."

Rachel gently shook her head. "Why not?"

"I'm sensing some judgement." Carter elbowed her.

"I'm sensing some *lack* of good judgement." She elbowed him back.

"Touché."

"First of all." She raised one finger. "When your ex-fiancé keeps texting you every day maybe she doesn't think she's your ex. Right?"

He nodded.

"Secondly, you're the guy your family counted on to run a landscaping business that other people have abandoned, which isn't fair. Especially with medical advice against it—sorry, buddy, that's all on you." She pointed at him and closed one eye.

"Got it. Texting ex-fiancé is still attached. Failing to disclose to Dad is bad." He took a swig of his Pepsi as his iPhone pinged.

She laughed. "A message from her?"

Carter pulled out his phone and looked at the screen.

Rachel extended her hand, palm up. "Let me see that."

He obliged.

"CC I miss u n cant wait to c u again." Rachel read aloud and frowned. "What's that about and who is CC?"

Carter's cheeks redden. "She calls me her Cutie Carter or CC."

"Oh my gosh, gag me already. Don't ever let Jack hear that one." She jerked a thumb toward the Wellings' property. *Why am I concerning myself with what Jack thinks? Sheesh.*

"Whatever. But I don't know why she keeps talking about seeing me, because I won't be back to UVA until the end of August, and I have no intention of getting crushed by her again."

Rachel scowled at him. "Then why do you keep answering her texts?"

He shrugged. "I miss her. She was like my best friend." His ears turned red.

"You still love her. Don't you?"

He drained the rest of his can of pop. "Maybe."

"No maybe about it. Either you do or you don't."

"But it's over."

"Are you sure?" She pressed her hand over his and bent toward him.

Jack strode around the corner, dressed in tailored khakis and a close-fitting white oxford shirt that showed off his physique. His loafers looked new. And expensive. If only he wasn't her boss. Then what?

Forget it. He's Andrette's.

"What's over? Your little tête-à-tête with Carter?" He crinkled his nose.

Carter tossed his empty can at Jack. "Who speaks like that? Tete-a-tete?"

"Apparently, I do—since I just said it—*oh ye who are illiterate.*"

"I have a three point seven GPA at the University of Virginia so don't give me that, Mr. United States Merchant Marine Academy. I heard they use crayons for writing implements at that place."

"That's for deckies. I'm an engineer, in case you forgot."

"You're an engineer? A marine?"

"He's not a marine." Rachel interrupted. "That's a boat academy."

"Merchant Marine is a branch of our military for ship engineers."
Jack strode toward them, hands in his pockets. "And a ship is different from a boat."

"Whatever." Carter hopped down. "I'm gonna think about what you said, Rachel."

She pointed at him. "You do that."

Carter jogged off, playfully brushing Jack as he passed him.

"Man, I *wish I had a brother*." Jack sighed loudly.

"Huh?"

"Not!" He gave a quick hard shake of his head. "I don't know how Parker puts up with him."

Rachel had always wanted a sister. Like Olivia. Or a brother. "I'd take him in a heartbeat."

He raised his eyebrows. "You would, huh?"

"Yeah."

His features tugged as though he was considering something. "How so?"

"As my brother—as we were just discussing, you numbskull." She elbowed him as he sat down beside her.

"I'm a numbskull now?" His attempt at looking offended didn't cut it, and she laughed.

"You've always been a numbskull."

"Wow." He turned and looked hard at her. "You're harshing my mellow."

"What?" Since when had he started with the weird sayings?

"My dad says that expression. I'm rarely mellow, though, so I haven't borrowed it till now."

"You can *look* sort of mellow sometimes."

"I am when I'm with you."

Rachel cast him a sideways look. "Like this morning when you were screeching you couldn't find the inventory for the upstairs blue bath?"

"Screeching?" He placed his hand over his heart. "Do I screech? No, I don't screech."

"You do." She took a swig of her Pepsi. "Big time. I heard you all the way over here."

"Hey. That's not nice to say I'm a screecher."

"Who said I was nice? Certainly you never did." No matter what kindness she and Olivia had done for him, like baking him brownies when his mom couldn't. "Maybe you're secretly nice."

"Me? Not sure anyone says that."

"Andrette thinks you're nice." More than nice, apparently. *Focus, Rachel, Jack is with Andrette—stop this flirting.*

"Andrette thinks *everyone* is nice."

"Truth." She laughed.

He made a face of mock horror.

She raised her hand, and they did a high five.

"I wish Andrette wouldn't be so nice to that. . ." Jack rubbed his fingers over his mouth. "That idiot of a husband she has."

"Husband?" her voice came out in a croak. *What husband?* Jack was in a relationship with a married woman? Rachel wasn't about to touch that topic. She needed her job. She swallowed hard, feeling bile rising in her throat. "Can I get you a can of Pepsi?"

"Yeah, sure."

She rose and went to the back door. *Calm down. This is for them to work out. God help them.*

"Hey Rach, I need a favor."

She turned around to face him. He'd sure floated her some favors this summer. But working for two cheaters wasn't such a great thing, was it? "Sure."

His hazel eyes widened. "Sure? That's not the response I expected but I'll take it."

"Ask away." Heck, things were going from bad to worse. "Anything."

"Seriously, anything? Wow."

She rolled her eyes. "What is it?"

"I need a date."

She stiffened. "Huh?" He was asking her out?

He waved his hands like an umpire calling a foul ball. "Not like a real date."

She arched one eyebrow. So, the cheater was going to cheat on the woman he was cheating with? *Ugh.* "For what?"

His Adam's apple bobbed. "I need someone to accompany me to the annual medical center auction and ball."

"Why not Andrette?" There, she'd asked.

"Wants her absentee husband to take her." He crinkled his nose.

"Oh." She crossed her arms. This should be good. "And why do you need to go?"

"I need to be there because it's a family tradition, and I don't want to go alone."

She stared at him for a long time.

"What?" Jack made a silly face. "Why are you looking at me like that?"

She uncrossed her arms. "*Jack.* You're tall, dark, intelligent, and gorgeous—all you have to do is hang out at the Pink Pony at night instead of with Andrette, and you'll find a date in"—she snapped her fingers—"two minutes, five tops." Which was another reason why he shouldn't be hanging with a married woman. Maybe his church attendance was out of guilt rather than faith.

"You really think that?"

"Yeah, but after a half hour she'd figure out you're a big geek engineer." She shrugged. "Ask her in the first fifteen minutes and you're golden."

He started to chuckle. It began deep in his chest and then burst into a head back full-on hooting laughter. Tears streamed from his eyes, and he swiped at them.

She crossed her arms over her chest and tapped one bare foot. "What's so funny?"

"You." He took a deep breath, still chuckling.

"I'm dead serious."

"That's what's so funny. I think you *are* serious."

"I'm not trying to be humorous. I'm telling the truth." He needed to end that relationship. Get right with the Lord. Jack had a lot of nerve praying to God all the while he was messing around with someone else's wife.

"Your version of the truth."

"Which happens to be the real truth."

"So, I'm gorgeous?"

She waggled her hand. "Maybe just really, really, handsome."

"I already knew I was tall, and my hair is dark, but at the Merchant Marine Academy in my class of engineers, I was not the smartest guy on the block."

She widened her eyes. "Hello! You have an engineering degree and that alone makes you a smartie pants."

He raised his hands. "I'm a smartie pants geek?"

She nodded, trying to make her face look very thoughtful. "Yeah, that's it." Apparently not smart enough to stay away from married women.

"Well," he sighed, "my offer still stands if you want to accompany me to the event, because I'm just *all that*."

Rachel hesitated. Why had he repeated his offer after she'd given him a clear way out?

"Tell ya what, Rach, I'll pay you to go with me. It will be just like going to work but you'll be. . ." He gestured head to toe. "You'll be all dressed up."

The only fancy dress she had was one Sandi and Cassie Browne had gifted her with—a chiffon lilac formal gown that they claimed showed off her dark hair to perfection. Who knew what condition it was in after sitting in her car trunk for so long. "So, it won't really be a date then, will it?"

"I guess not." He looked a little disappointed.

Maybe she really should think of him more as a friend and not as her boss or her friend's irritating older brother. "You don't have to pay me. I'll be your date. As your friend." If the purple formal couldn't be worn, she'd have to dig through Gram's closet some more.

"My friend?"

"I think you're my pal, aren't you? You saved my butt on that nursing exam—thank you very much."

"I guess I did."

"All right. It's a date."

"My first event without Aunt Andi at my side."

Rachel almost choked as her back spasmed in disbelief. "*Aunt* Andi?"

"Yeah, she'll be with annoying Uncle Marques at the medical center auction and ball."

Shock mixed with relief with a big paddle cement stirrer pulling up something else. Maybe hope? No, that couldn't be it. She grabbed a breath. "Let me get you a Pepsi, and you tell me about this event my buddy is taking me to, okay?" Her buddy. Her friend. She swiveled and headed inside.

Rachel let the door slam behind her, its thud echoing the impact on her heart. These feelings she'd been having for Jack had free rein now. *Noooo!!!* She closed her eyes and leaned against the wall, her heart stuttering.

Andrette was his aunt.

She'd accepted Jack's invitation.

What had she just gotten herself into?

Chapter Twenty

July 18th

"We'd better get our golfing days in before it gets hot out." Kareen's friend Jill pointed to the electronic screen in the hotel lobby where temps in the high seventies, some rainy, showed for the next five days.

"This would be a balmy spring day in Florida." Kareen arched an eyebrow at her longtime pal, a librarian from the mainland.

"I made the reservation for eleven, is that good for you?"

"It is, and don't be surprised when you see my vast improvement from years' past."

"Oh?" Jill's little laugh sounded doubtful, but Kareen would show her how lots of practice had gotten her into her best-ever form. "I'm mostly hoping we'll run into Wayne Stephens. He's here on the island, you know."

Kareen tried to breathe. She still hadn't found out where Wayne was staying or how long he might be there. But thank the Lord, he'd not contacted her, Hamp, nor Carter.

"Mom?" Hamp strode toward them, his tan linen pants expertly pressed and white cotton shirt immaculate. Good thing he had Maria since there was no dry cleaner on the island. Her daughter-in-law was a saint.

Too bad Kareen wasn't.

"Hi Hamp." Jill offered a tentative smile to Kareen's grumpy-looking son.

"Are you all right, Hamp?" Kareen cast her son a warning glance that had worked before to tamp down his irritation. *Not today.* His reaction to her news had been stone cold silence. They'd not spoken of it since.

"Mom, we keep getting deliveries from Gianni."

She shrugged.

"Who's Gianni?" Jill frowned.

Kareen gently squeezed her friend's arm. "I'll tell you about him later."

Hamp rolled his eyes. When he'd been young, if she'd refused him something, he'd always gone to his dad. Hampy would cave in like with the red Corvette convertible that had gotten crashed within a month of purchase.

"Gianni," he elongated his name as though in distaste, which it probably was, "sent special food deliveries, new pillows for your room, and now we've had a dozen vases of mixed roses and tiger lilies show up this morning."

Warmth surged through her. That was so romantic. If only her husband could be there with her sooner.

When she didn't reply, Hamp added, "The note said the flowers were *not* for the memorial. That's all it said."

"What's going on?" Jill turned toward Kareen. "Who is this Gianni guy?"

"My dad's replacement." Hamp rubbed the side of his nose.

Kareen glared at Hamp. "He's not Hampy's replacement. But Gianni Franchetti is my *husband,* and you'd better show him proper respect when he arrives."

"Your husband?" Jill's eyebrows soared.

"Yes. I was going to tell you all about it later." But her son had spoiled it. She looked pointedly at him.

"What do you want *done* with those flowers?" He sighed.

"There really isn't room in my office and bedroom combined." Kareen crossed her arms. "Save me several but put the rest in the guests' rooms. I've still got the potted plants, the ferns he sent last week." She was not about to apologize to her adult son about her decisions. But if he didn't get his act together soon, she might have to reconsider how long she could stay.

Hamp gave a curt nod and turned around.

He was so worked up, albeit silently, and Hampy wasn't even his father. If these special deliveries set him off, then what would happen once he knew the truth about his parentage?

Would he go ballistic? Would her son then freeze her out completely?

Would Wayne show up here at the resort and make a scene?

A haze crouched above the water all across the Straits of Mackinac, as Rachel brazenly sat on Lilac Cottage's broad front porch and sipped her newest coffee creation. *Perfection.*

Strange to have a Monday off from the coffee shop. Andrette was training a new cashier so they could stay open longer and to have more relief workers. Covid had reared its ugly head again and lots of places had workers out sick. The manager wanted to get ahead of the game.

Tourists passing by in carriages gawked at her. Rachel waved and some waved back. She'd had it with hiding. Jack had showed her the ad to sell the cottage. If someone was going to kick her out, she might as well enjoy the property for the last time.

"Got any left in the pot for me?" Jack, attired in ripped-off-at-the-knee jeans and a paint-spattered USMMA t-shirt, clunked up the front steps in his work boots.

She almost spit out her mouthful of coffee. "What're you doing over here?"

"Can't a neighbor visit?"

"Yeah, but. . ."

"Just figgered if you're gonna be open about squatting at your grandmother's house—even if you're not really—" he scratched the back of his neck, "then I'm gonna flaunt it, too!" He grinned, his white teeth with the one just a little crooked caused her heart to give a little leap.

"Sure. Sit down. Maybe wave at that next group of tourists in the carriages passing by. Maybe even raise a cup of joe to them and point to me and shout, 'Hey, guess what, she's here illegally!'"

He shook his head.

She rose. "Let me get you a mug of my latest brew."

"Kinda sounds like a witch's thing."

"Very funny, ha-ha." She opened the door and strode inside. She poured him a mug filled with half cacao beans French-pressed, the other half regular brewed Columbian, and then poured a dollop of cream, two heaping teaspoons of demerara sugar, and then stirred it.

She carried the beverage to the porch. "It's a little sweet."

"Like me?" He pointed to the middle of his chest where a paint splatter of reddish-orange looked curiously heart-shaped.

"No comment." She adjusted the cushion on her chair and then sat.

He took a big gulp. "Where's the whipped cream for this thing?"

"Oh my gosh, you are such a baby." She started to push back her chair, but he grabbed her arm.

"Nah. Just teasing. Tastes like something Olivia would have loved, though." He stared out at the water view. "And she'd have demanded a huge topping of Reddi-wip."

"I don't remember her ever *demanding* anything." Rachel used her free hand to sip her coffee. Jack left his hand loosely holding her arm. She didn't want him to lift it. She savored the warmth in his touch. For some reason, his hand on her forearm felt reassuring.

He leaned closer. "Livvie knew she could get me to do anything because I was her caretaker."

"Her *caretaker*?" Rachel drew her eyebrows together.

"I'm the one who watched her. The one who did anything she asked."

"Not when I was there." She sipped her coffee. Some whipped cream would improve it.

"Because when you were with her, I knew she was in good hands, and I could get a break."

"But why would your parents put that duty on you?"

He shrugged. "Dad was gone a lot of the time, and Mom was at work, too. Even when we were up here, Dad was mostly unavailable until later at night. Mom was distracted by her grief and denial. Those two didn't accept her illness, and Olivia went right along with it. She knew the leukemia upset them."

"Oh my gosh, that's awful. So, you had to be the voice of reason?"

"I'm sure they didn't see it that way. I wanted a normal teenage dude job on the island. I did get that one summer but then after she got sick. . ." He released her arm, sat back, and took another drink from the Chicago Bears emblazoned mug.

"I think your parents asked a lot of you." She sipped her drink, which was cooling despite the warm day. "They asked too much."

"Maybe so."

"And that's why you left for sea?"

"Part of it." His voice grew husky.

They sat there, sipping their cacao-coffee drink. Birds sang in the nearby maple trees as the leaves on the birches rustled as though someone was whispering comfort to them. The breeze picked up and blew a paper napkin from the table.

They both bent to retrieve it and bumped heads.

"Ow! You broke my noggin." Jack patted his dark hair.

"I don't think so. I'm almost a nurse-in-training, and I think I'd know."

"Almost?" He cocked an eyebrow. "Did you pass your exam then?"

"I did." Her cheeks heated. "Thank you, again, for helping me with the WIFI."

"You can give me credit when you're a famous nurse somewhere."

"Sure thing." Would she be like her ancestor, Sadie? Well known. A nurse for decades.

"But you're not a nurse now. I've gotta get back over to the house and get working. You, *too*, soon."

She glared at him. "Um like, no? You interrupt my peaceful enjoyment of—"

"Flaunting it?" He laughed. "That you're right here on West Bluff in a fancy cottage?"

"Whatever. I'm off the clock—off your clock. So, I'm sitting here on the front porch for what could soon be the last time."

"You can come sit on my porch if you make more coffee like this." He waggled his eyebrows. "But first I think you'd like to come help me and the guys a little longer."

"That's a *super* no."

"Since Andrette gave you time off, you should come back and help us."

"What?" Her voice came out in a little shriek of disbelief.

"Just sayin'." He winked at her then slugged down the rest of the contents of his mug.

"You know, Jack, that coffee is meant to be savored—not gulped."

"One man's savor is another man's swig."

She made an exaggerated cringey face. "Where do you come up with these goofy sayings?"

"I made that one up all by myself."

"I can tell." She huffed a laugh.

"See ya later."

"Maybe." She scowled at him.

"Maria is bringing us burritos, taquitos, rice and beans, and empanadas tonight." He stood. "Just for the workers though."

She loved Maria's cooking. She loved Maria. There was something so special and warm about her.

"Too bad you're gonna miss out, Squirt."

She swatted at him, but he jumped back.

No one else got under her skin like Jack Welling did. He knew just how to trigger her.

"I'll come over and work for the fifteen minutes before Maria gets there."

"Two extra hours or no deal."

"One hour."

He extended his hand. "Deal."

A buzz shot through her at the warmth in his strong hand as he grasped hers. "Deal."

Hey, my dad says he's coming back up on Thursday. Supposed to be a bad storm on Wednesday. I'll pick you up from Andrette's in the carriage tomorrow and Wednesday, too, if it rains.

"I have an umbrella," she drawled.

"And I have a carriage and horse that I'm paying for."

She nodded her acquiescence.

"Can't have my right-hand gal getting wet and getting sick, either." Concern, genuine unease reflected in his face.

The storm wasn't supposed to be anything unusual. She was about to tease that getting wet wouldn't kill her, but she bit her tongue. He'd lost his sister. He couldn't do anything about it. And Rachel hadn't been able to do anything to stop Gram's disease from progressing, either.

"I appreciate your thoughtfulness, Jack."

His eyes darkened as he stepped closer and grasped her hands. He bent his head as his gaze locked on her parted lips. Was he going to kiss her?

"You've got a little bit of coffee foam on your lip." He ran his thumb over her top lip.

Heart hammering, she stared up at him. *Thank you, Jesus, that he can't read my mind right now or I'd be in trouble.*

Chapter Twenty-One

Without Starr and Juan Pablo, the coffee shop seemed oddly quiet—despite all of its usual noises. There was an absence Rachel could sense in her spirit. She was getting to be super fond of those two fellow employees.

Recently, their boss spent evenings schmoozing with local business owners but tonight Andrette had been with the crew. That she was Jack's aunt, not his sweetie, made Rachel grin.

The last customer carried his iced coffee out the door, and Andrette turned the lock. By her twitchy shoulders, she'd seemed rattled about something.

"Thanks for locking the door." That was usually Rachel's job. She pitched in with the clean-up, and tonight was no exception.

Andrette cast her a wary look. What was the matter with her? Had she heard Rachel was going with Jack to the ball and didn't approve?

The baristas emptied the coffee pots and would do their clean-up routine. Meanwhile, Rachel grabbed the can of Clorox wipes and went over the keyboard of the register until it shone. Then she wiped the front of the counter and sprayed glass cleaner onto the dessert case and wiped it.

Andrette transferred the few remaining desserts into an aluminum tin with a cover. "I'm taking these to the Parkers' house tonight." She gave Rachel a pointed look.

What in the world was her problem? "Cool."

Usually, they split the leftovers amongst themselves. Sometimes they brought them to someone on the island who needed a lift. "Colton Byrnes really liked those cream-cheese turnovers yesterday." The landscaper usually came by right before closing and chose a few treats to take home after his work was done. They'd all felt so sorry for him yesterday, because of the big story on Entertainment Tonight about his ex, Sue Pentland, that the crew bagged up the rest of the turnovers and sent them home with him.

"I'm glad he's back. He's a good guy. I can't believe that designer dumped him, eh?"

"Apparently you and most of America, given the comments I've heard."

"We take care of our own." Again, an irritated look flashed in Andrette's eyes like a warning.

"Okay, I've gotta wind down." Lulu, their new barrista made a little swirl in the air. She could prepare a killer vanilla-orange frappe, and Andrette had added it to the lineup. She had a night shift job, too, and always had to leave a little early.

Rachel moved to the front of the glass case, which always required extra care. Lulu quickly dried the remaining dishes.

Andrette joined Rachel in cleaning the glass front.

"Ya know, he's a little young for you, eh?" her boss asked softly.

Rachel frowned. "Who?"

"The Parkers' grandson."

"Carter?" He was only a few years younger than her. And why was Andrette making that comparison anyway?

"He's graduating college next year."

Rachel stopped wiping and straightened.

"He told his grandparents that he's hoping to date one of our workers. And Jack told me Carter has been hanging out with you. So, I thought I'd come by and see what's going on at night."

First, Rachel needed to be sure Carter hadn't squealed on her—and it didn't seem he had. Second, she needed to throw Andrette off the whole notion that she was cozying up with the Parkers' son. "I haven't seen Carter in here but maybe once or twice. He has talked about Starr a little."

"Starr? Oh my gosh, she probably is right up his alley after that crazy girlfriend he had at UVA. The Parkers have been really good to me. They helped me get this job managing the store when I wanted to come up here to work. Mr. Parker was such an exuberant and helpful man. I can't believe he's gone." Andrette shook her head.

"That's what Carter said. He's really grieving, too." Rachel would leave out the fact that she was more of a sympathetic ear than girlfriend-type material. "And I believe Starr has really helped him with that."

"How?" Andrette blinked at her.

"Carter attends a mid-week church service that Starr and Juan Pablo do for islanders. I only recently learned about it myself." When she'd attended the Holy Week services with Juan Pablo, he'd participated but not led them.

"Really? That's why they needed off on Wednesday?"

Rachel hadn't been able to attend because of her work hours. "A Wednesday evening meet and greet, small dinner, and a short message on faith. Starr often talks with Carter afterward. He thinks she's super cool."

"Has Starr ever mentioned Carter here?" Andrette pointed her index finger down.

Rachel shook her head. "Never."

"Good. He needs to get that degree finished and stay away from women."

What should Rachel say to that? "He has become a good friend to me. He's so nice."

Again, that cautionary look. "Oh?"

Rachel splayed her fingers. "If anything, I'd say I'm much more interested in. . ." Who? Her mouth hung open like a trout.

Andrette's eyes widened. "Jack?" The word came out on a breath.

"Colton, actually." Rachel spit out the lie so easily she shocked herself. Old habits died hard. "But please, please don't tell him, okay?" *God forgive me.*

Her boss did a long exhale. "Be careful. Colton Byrnes is one of those guys who is friends with everyone. He's always chatting up the ladies especially since he bought that cottage in Hubbards' Annex and hosts his television buddies. The summer workers all think Colton has the hots for them but he's just being nice."

Rachel nodded attentively as if absorbing the importance of Andrette's words. "So, he's really not into me? He's just coming by to get a snack?" *More lies. Ack!*

The owner cast her a sympathetic look. "Yeah, hon, I hate to break it to you. I saw him tonight and that's just Colton schmoozing. He's dating his co-star from his new HGTV series that starts in the fall."

"Oh." Rachel exhaled and lowered her shoulders. *Oh Lord, don't let me go back to lying about everything. Help me.*

"I think Jack introduced Colton and Cassandra. He knew her from some engineering thing."

"Oh." Her vocabulary was getting seriously diminished.

"And Jack hasn't, I mean. . ." Andrette chewed her hot-pink lip. "He's not come on to you, has he?"

"No!" That was God's honest truth.

"You look horrified!" Andrette laughed. "I guess no swooning over young Carter—or Jack, eh?"

Rachel made a face. "Nope."

The woman looked positively relieved. And why did that bother Rachel more than it should?

Lulu joined them. "I'm done. See you later." She made a little waving motion.

"Goodnight." Andrette followed Lulu to the door, let her out, and then locked it again.

"Who's that man out there?" Rachel pointed to the guy in the dark suit who was pacing the sidewalk and talking on a cellphone. "He keeps looking over here." It was a little creepy.

"Oh my gosh!" Andrette unlocked the door, leaving it wide open, flew across the street, and threw herself at the stranger.

He shoved the phone in his pocket, picked Andrette up, and twirled her around. Then he kissed her like there was no tomorrow. Rachel turned away, cheeks hot.

She finished cleaning and soon heard Andrette talking as the twosome walked back toward the café.

"What are you doing here early, honey?"

"Needed to see my gal." But the man's tone of voice sounded false to Rachel.

"I'm so glad you could get free to come up."

"Me, too."

Surely, he missed his wife. Then why had he left Andrette up here by herself for the past two months? Although the café manager really wasn't alone. She had friends and family on the island.

The two stepped into the café.

"Rachel, this is my husband, Marques." Andrette beamed as she clutched her man's arm.

"Rachel Dunmara?"

"Yes." The handsome man looked vaguely familiar.

"I knew your grandfather well. I was his clerk before. . . everything."

Andrette tugged hard on Marques's arm.

Rachel searched her memory. "I think I remember you." But the image that flashed through her mind was of a young Marine saluting her grandfather's coffin in the private ceremony they'd had. This was the same man. She was sure of it.

He nodded, his rich brown eyes assessing. "I'd hope you would. I accompanied you on your trip to Virginia for school."

Straightening, she tried to recall that long drive. The chauffeur. The silent young man who sat beside her. She'd sat looking straight ahead, listening to her CD player on headphones, since she wasn't allowed any electronics with social media access on them. All she'd remembered of that guy was how sad he seemed. And ashamed. Like he'd made some terrible mistake. *Worst travel companion ever.* But that wasn't his job. He was like a babysitter, and she was already a teenager. "That was you?"

"Yup."

"I never wanted to go there, ya know." And she'd hated almost every minute, especially being away from Gram.

"I wished I'd never had to take you there. I wish it had never happened." Were those tears glistening in his eyes?

"Marques," Andrette hissed.

"Sorry. I just loved your grandfather. He was a great man."

"Yes, he was." This was one of the few people who ever spoke about him, though. After he'd died it was as though he'd never existed. "I miss him." Her own eyes watered.

"See what you started?" Andrette poked her husband's chest.

"Sorry." He shrugged.

"Come on, let me lock up, and let's get out of here."

Rachel headed to the back and grabbed her purse. When she returned to the front, Marques and Andrette were kissing. "Excuse me." She walked around the two and exited.

Raindrops started as soon as she'd taken three steps toward her locked bike.

"Milady?" Someone called out in a fake British accent.

Jack pulled his carriage to a stop as more rain pelted her face.

"Come on, you'll get drenched!" That hollering loud voice was all Jack—no fake accent involved.

She hopped in beside him as Marques and Andrette hurried into the back seat, the carriage rocking.

"I'll get my aunt and uncle to the Parkers, then I'll bring you back to Lilac Cottage." Jack flicked the reins and the horses moved forward.

"Thanks, Jackie!" Andrette called out.

"Hate it when she calls me that," Jack mumbled.

He was seated so close to her that his thigh rubbed against hers. But there was nowhere to move to on the narrow bench.

On the street, people ducked into restaurants and out of the pouring rain.

Luckily, the scalloped overhang on the carriage prevented most of the deluge from reaching them. Jack tugged at the blanket covering his lap and pushed half of it over on her.

"Is your dad really retiring?" Marques called out over the noise of the horses' hooves, the wheels, and the rain.

Jack shrugged. "I suspect my dad already retired and didn't tell my mom yet," he said, loud enough for only Rachel to hear.

"Yeah? Why would he do that?" She snuggled a little closer to him, which she'd not thought possible, and away from the rain pelting the side of the carriage.

"Don't know. But I'm going to find out. You want to help me?"

"Sure. Nothing illegal though, right?"

"Nah. Just make a few calls for me tomorrow at work."

"Sure. And thanks for the ride."

"I'll bring you down here again tomorrow since you've got your bike at the shop."

"Thanks." She cast a sneak look at him.

Jack was focused on the road. His handsome profile was so near. If she were an artist, she'd capture that image in a painting, not a caricature. She could get used to looking at that face every day. She gave herself a mental shake. What was she thinking? She had two more long years of school ahead of her and needed to make a life for herself.

"Rach?"

"Yeah?"

"Don't want to upset you, but I saw a man in a business suit hanging around outside your cottage today."

Chill from the rain made her shiver. Or maybe it was this news. "Yeah?"

"Older guy, silver hair, fancy shoes, tailored suit."

"Did you talk with him?" She longed to press her head onto his shoulder and rest it there.

"Yup."

Jack directed the horses to make a sharp turn around a corner. In the back, Marques and Andrette chuckled about something.

"Who was he?"

"Attorney named Arthur Lyonis."

"That's my grandmother's executor. He's handled their trusts for ages."

"Didn't say. But he's looking for you."

The downpour and the cloudy sky turned the evening's end into murky gloom—matching her mood perfectly.

The man standing in the Parker resort lobby looked like a drenched rat—Kareen's own drenched rat! She strode forward as he removed his soaked raincoat and handed it to one of the valets, along with his umbrella. Tears overflowed her eyes.

"Gianni! What are you doing here?" She opened her arms to the husband she'd been missing so much that it felt like a perpetual hurt inside her heart.

He pulled her close into an embrace and kissed her cheek. "I couldn't let you go through this alone."

She tilted her head back. "You mean you'll come to the service?"

"You and Hampy were there for me when Sylvia died, weren't you?"

She kissed him. "Yes." This good man was hers. Her husband. Her cheeks warmed with happiness.

"It was quite a trip to get here." He chuckled, that adorable deep laugh he had.

"I have missed you so much." They embraced again.

"Okay you two, that's enough PDA for our lobby." Maria chuckled as she moved alongside them.

Kareen stepped back but held onto Gianni's hand. "This is my husband, Gianni, and Gianni this is my wonderful daughter-in-law, Maria."

"Nice to meet you, Maria." Gianni inclined his head toward her.

Her sweetheart was truly here. Oh, how she'd longed to beg him to come, but hadn't.

Hamp joined Maria and extended his hand to Gianni. "I'm Hamp Parker, Kareen's son."

"My new son-in-law."

"Yeah, I guess I am." A sheepish grin flitted over Hamp's face.

"I'm delighted." Gianni waved around the lobby, which was well lit especially against the rainy backdrop, evident through the glass.

"You're spoiling my mother." Hamp wrapped an arm around Maria. "And I think she deserves it."

Had her boy really just said that? "Thank you, Son."

Would he still believe that after she told him who he really was?

Chapter Twenty-Two

*H*ampy's memorial service was finally happening. Kareen could scarcely believe it. Parker arrived only that morning, in late from Switzerland. Hamp and Maria and the boys—Sean, RJ, and Austin—were in the inner cabin speaking with the pastor about some last-minute additions to the speeches. Dawn and Jim Charbonneau, attired in shades of navy, had waited on the dock for Kareen and Gianni and had given her their heartfelt hugs. Dozens more of her and Hampy's friends were now boarding the vessel. Andrette and Marques stood in the back of the boat with Jack and his parents. Kareen's grandson, Carter, had a Lupus outbreak, probably from the stress, and had his oxford shirt buttoned to the top and his tie tight. He looked very uncomfortable but stood by Parker at the rail.

Veronica, the owner of the boat, weaved through the passengers toward Kareen and Gianni, trailed by Hamp. When she reached them, she pointed to the captain. "He'd like to head out on the time we scheduled."

"That's fine," Kareen reassured her younger friend. Veronica was a sweetheart and had made the planning very easy.

As she watched Veronica depart, a woman with an over-sized, wide-brimmed white sunhat attired in a flowing white jumpsuit stood out garishly in the sea of dark colored clothing worn by mourners. This was not a celebration of life, like some services were. This was a simple return to the Straits of a man who'd deeply loved this area and its people.

"Who is that?" Kareen hissed to Hamp.

He exhaled sharply. "Oh my gosh, Mom. I think that's Selma Dunmara."

"What's she doing here?" And dressed like that.

"You okay, pumpkin?" Gianni leaned in and squeezed her hand.

"Do you want me to ask her to leave? Hamp frowned at the out-of-place woman, who was accompanied by a strange man who looked Eastern European by his attire and distinctive features.

Kareen didn't want to make a scene. This was hard enough already. Thank God Gianni was with her. "No."

"Who is that woman?" Gianni whispered in her ear.

She leaned back and looked up at him. "She's the daughter of the people who had once been our closest friends. Both of them have passed now."

Gianni shrugged. "Do you think she's here to represent her family? I know my daughter, Takisha, has had to do that for me. She attends in my absence."

Kareen compressed her lips.

Hamp touched her back. "Mom, I can ask her and that guy with her to leave if you want."

"It's time to get underway."

"Mom? Veronica is still on board. Last chance." Hamp inclined his head toward Selma, who was talking with the man she'd brought.

Kareen raised her palms. "Let's just go." The sooner she got this over with, the better, which was an awful way to summarize an over fifty-year marriage. At least half of those years had been good. The second half—not so much.

"Okay, then."

"I'm glad we did this for your dad." Hopefully, Selma wouldn't make her regret the decision.

"We should probably circulate a little, once we're underway." Hamp leaned his head against hers for the briefest of moments, reminding her of the adorable boy he'd been. They'd been so close before he'd married and before his wife's and his addictions disrupted everything. But they had a fresh start now. *One day at a time.*

A cool breeze chilled Kareen's face as the ferry headed out away from the island. Passersby on the Starline ferry waved at them from the open top. What would they think when none of those aboard waved back? From the corner of her eye, she spied Selma waving, using her other hand to clutch her fashionable hat. Same old Selma, always wanting attention. The last time she'd seen Margaret's daughter was at the anniversary party, twenty-six years earlier.

They passed the channel marker and then Round Island lighthouse, the beacon to the harbor. Then they were out in the Straits of Mackinac, with a slight chop playing across the water's surface. The sun shone down on them. "Your dad is at rest now." Kareen looked up at her son. Hampy was the man he'd known as his father. For all intents and purposes, he was his father. If the Holy Spirit hadn't convicted her that she needed to tell her son the truth, then she wouldn't have. What would he think when his DNA results came back?

Today was about Hampy. She'd honor his memory. "Come on, Son. Let's do this."

Gianni released her arm and Kareen and Hamp moved toward the front of the ferry, where Jim and Dawn Charbonneau were standing. What a comfort to have such dear friends there.

Someone tapped her shoulder. She turned. Carter wrapped his arms around her. Parker stood behind him, his eyes red.

"Grandma, what is Rachel's mom doing here?" Carter frowned.

Kareen shook her head gently. "No idea."

"I'm gonna find out." Carter crinkled his nose like he did when he was about to be defiant. Off he went.

Hamp patted her hand.

Parker moved forward. "It seems strange for that Dunmara woman to be here when she always kept her daughter away from us. Acted like we were lepers."

Selma had always been fond of Hampy. Her own father had often been absent because of his court cases and public duties. Judge Dunmara took his work seriously. A little too seriously. And Selma had been emotionally neglected. Of course, she'd made up for it with her outrageous attention-seeking behavior once she became a teenager.

Kareen swiveled to see Jack Welling, eyes narrowed, staring at Selma and her friend who were chatting with Carter.

Was Selma there to take possession of Lilac Cottage? Was this memorial simply coincidental?

Carter would find out.

Or Jack would.

If Kareen knew anything about that young man, it was that he had a tenacious spirit. He'd sure needed it after his poor sister had died.

"Are you ready, Kareen?" The officiant moved alongside Kareen, clutching her Bible.

"Yes. I believe I am."

Time to lay Hampton Parker, Sr., to rest.

Voices carried through Gram's cottage and all the way upstairs, where Rachel was sleeping in her old bedroom, having finally given into the impulse to do so. Rachel sat straight up. Someone was here. *Oh my gosh, I've got to get up and out of here.* She'd slept in because

Jack canceled work since he and the guys would be at the memorial service for Mr. Hampy Parker.

The bedside alarm clock read eleven. She cringed as she hopped from her bed and shoved her feet into slides. Was it the police? Had Linda finally sent someone up here to check? Who'd Rachel be fooling if she ran now? And why wasn't Gram's attorney, Mr. Lyonis, returning Rachel's calls?

She pulled on Gram's robe and tied it at her waist. Clearly her bed, in her old bedroom, had been slept in. She had no time to straighten anything.

Someone laughed. Police wouldn't be laughing, but people were definitely inside the house.

"From what I'm seeing, this place has been kept up," a woman's voice proclaimed. "That will help with the resale."

Resale? She'd known this might happen, but her stomach sank to the oak floor. Someone had put an ad in the paper, but this was their family cottage. This was the one place she had happy memories of being part of a family. The one place that felt like home. That was why she'd come here. Why she wouldn't give up without a fight.

She squared her shoulders. She had every right to be here—well, maybe not, but it felt like she did in her heart. She quickly straightened her bed and exited the room. "Hello! Who's there?" she called over the banister rail.

"Oh!" the woman's voice carried.

"Hello? This is Rachel, the owner's granddaughter, and who is here?" She headed toward the stairs.

A gray-haired man with a paunch peered up at her, frowning. "I'm the realtor tasked by the estate."

Rachel stared down at him in what she was hoping was an imperious manner. "Why didn't anyone notify me?" Time to bluff. She had to reach Gram's lawyer.

A blond woman wearing a pink boucle suit that could have been grabbed from Grama's closet stood beside him. "We didn't know, dear. Is this an okay time for us to come through?"

The relief that flooded through Rachel almost made her stumble as her muscles relaxed. Her ploy had worked. If she sent them away, then they'd surely report that she was staying there. They might anyway. She needed to buy some extra time and get them out of there. "It would be best if you could come back later." *Or maybe never.*

The two exchanged a glance and then looked up at her. The man reached into his pocket and pulled out a shiny silver case. He pulled a card from it. "I'll leave my business card here on the console and you call—"

"Or text," the blond woman interrupted. She grinned up at Rachel. "My daughter always texts."

The man scowled. "Fine. Either way we've got to get this done before next Friday. The executor wants this moving forward."

"I'll be in touch." Rachel squared her shoulders again. "Since you obviously have a key. . ." and where had they gotten that from? "You can let yourselves in if I'm not here."

The man dipped his chin, but the woman narrowed her eyes slightly. Did she suspect? Rachel summoned up her courage. "Did Mr. Lyonis call you? He's the attorney."

"No, it was Selma, the executor and owner of this house."

Rachel's gut clenched as she backed away from the rail. She tried to catch her breath. So, it was true—Gram had left Mom the cottage just like she'd always said she would.

"Have a good day, dear," the realtor called out as she and her co-worker left.

The front door closed. When Rachel didn't hear the lock engaging, she went downstairs and locked it herself. She walked through the front parlor and stood at the side of the window. The two agents were still in the yard, pointing up at the roof. She stepped back. Shouldn't they have gone on their merry way, as Gram would have said? Instead, they lingered as if she hadn't just told them to basically get lost.

She pressed her hand to her head and slumped down into the nearby divan, still covered with a white sheet. What was she going to do? Once they realized she wasn't supposed to be there, they'd no doubt take action. She had to get another place to stay.

Poor Rachel. That was all Jack could think of during Hampy Parker's memorial after speaking with Selma. *What a piece of work.* And the guy with her looked like Russian mafia. Jack had come into contact with some of those types at various shipyards around the world. A rich criminal type. Probably trying to hide out here.

And Selma was lying about everything. That woman, who'd had the nerve to show up in a flashy white outfit more fit for a nightclub, had all the marks of a con artist. Jack's ex had those, too, but he'd overlooked them—for too long.

He headed away from the wharf, intent on getting to the county offices to check on the deed for Lilac Cottage. Did Selma own it? If not her, then who? Then he'd track down that attorney, Lyonis, if it took the rest of the day. If that nasty woman was actually telling the truth, then he'd have to get Rachel out of there. That boyfriend of Selma's was getting nowhere near Rachel—not on his watch.

He moved through the ferry dock building and then crossed the street. Jack weaved through tourists on the connecting street and headed to Market Street and a quiet area near the café. He called his dad.

"Hello, Son. We're sorry we missed the memorial. Had a little medical issue here to deal with, but all is well now."

Medical thing? Mom just texted that they couldn't come. "You're alright?"

"Yeah. Your mom is fine just a stomach bug. But what's up? How did it go?"

"You knew Selma Dunmara?"

"Sure." It sounded like Dad's wooden chair was scraping the floor. "Why?"

"Didn't you say our cottage and theirs have a similar legal situation? As far as selling them? Different from the stipulations shown in our documents, but didn't the Swaines put something on Lilac Cottage, too?"

"Absolutely."

"Doesn't Lilac Cottage have to remain in the family?"

"Oh boy. At this point, it's a little complicated." It sounded like Dad was scribbling something on paper. "All of the heirs have to agree."

"For both our cottage and Lilac, right?"

"Yes, that was a stipulation when my grandparents, who were not direct descendants, bought the place. The other family had to have veto rights on the sale."

His back started itching. Was his eczema about to explode? "Has Selma asked you?"

"No. But I just got a message from some guy, Lyonis, who is the executor of the estate."

Jack scratched his lower back. "He stopped by here and left his card, but I haven't been able to reach him."

"He's staying at the Grand. Maybe stop by there if you can't get him on his phone."

"Will do. I think Selma is trying to pull a fast one, Dad."

"We may have to get our own attorney involved, but I can't buy her out, if she inherited it and decides she wants to sell."

"Let me get ahold of that guy." At least now Jack had a legitimate reason of his own, and not simply for Rachel's sake, to speak with the attorney.

Carrie Fancett Pagels

"Do that and get back to me."

"Sure thing."

Now to find the guy.

"My mom is here on the island?" Rachel gaped at Jack then handed him the café Americano he'd ordered. Lucky Bean's walls seemed to shrink in around her.

"Go on. We'll cover the register. No one's coming right now." Juan Pablo gestured to the door.

What was it with that guy? He was usually correct in his predictions. "Okay. Thanks."

Rachel came around the counter and she and Jack stepped out into the early evening sun.

"Your mom was at Hampy Parker's memorial for some reason." Crinkles formed around Jack's eyes as he squinted at the sun. He pulled his sunglasses from his pocket and put them on.

"She's not been here for ages. And she's not a fan of the Parkers."

"Yup. Ya told me. But Hampy Parker also had ya on a joint account."

She exhaled hard. "I haven't touched it, and I still don't know why."

"You should do like I said and go ask to look at the old bank statements and see what he used that account for."

"My *morning boss* would have to let me off work."

"I'll let you off. I'll even come with you, if you want." He looked so sincere.

Someone had her back. Jack wanted to help her. "Someone showed up at Lilac Cottage this morning. Real estate agents."

He closed his eyes. When he opened them again, fire flashed in their hazel depths. "I bet that's why your mom is here."

She frowned at him. "And you talked with her?"

"Yup. Claimed to be here to look at the family property before it was sold. Said she was the executor. But it's a lie."

"What? That's what the real estate agents told me, too."

"Mr. Lyonis is your grandmother's executor."

"That sounds right. That's what she said she'd do."

An older woman on a bicycle nearly collided with the dray horses as they turned the nearby corner and both she and Jack stiffened. She shook her head. "Gosh, I thought I was going to have to use some of my nurse's training skills."

"She was lucky he didn't clip her." Jack touched her shoulder lightly. "But back to what we were discussing—your mom didn't inherit Lilac Cottage."

"No?"

"She can't sell it for a lot of reasons but there's one huge one."

Laughter carried from a nearby shop.

"Which is?"

Jack gestured to a bench. "Sit down."

She slid onto the wooden seat, and he sat beside her, his body angled toward hers.

Jack took her hand in his, his fingers warm. "Rachel, you own Lilac Cottage. I found that out by going to the county offices today."

"What? I do?" She pressed her free hand to her chest. "How? Really?"

"Yeah, the attorney, Lyonis, wouldn't tell me anything. He was looking for you. Wants to talk only with you, which actually makes sense."

She stared at Jack. He had gone out of his way to look after her interests. What would it be like to have someone do that every day? She blinked back tears.

"He's at the Grand and can meet us tonight."

"Tonight?" She looked down at her Lucky Bean uniform, which she'd worn that day instead of something vintage.

"Need to clean you up and get you into evening clothes—me, too—but yeah."

Maybe there was hope for her. Gram hadn't forgotten her. But with her mom and how crazy she could get, obviously this wasn't going to happen without a fight. "But my mom has realtors coming in here."

"Yeah, and she no doubt had that ad placed, but she can't sell what isn't hers."

"No. Not unless she tries taking this to court." Rachel chewed her lower lip.

"Don't borrow trouble. Let's talk with Lyonis and see."

"You'll really come with me? What if I'm wearing a 1970s lime green cocktail dress?"

"Of course." A look of affection painted his features.

"Thank you. And I can accessorize that with a hot pink feather boa."

"I don't mind." He leaned in closer. "I'm not letting you go through this alone." He stood and pulled her to her feet. Then he embraced her.

Jack smelled like fresh air, pine trees, and sandalwood but as great as those scents were, his hug was ever better.

He leaned back. "And Rach, the guy your mom is with looks like a thug." This close, Rachel could see the amber flecks and green that rimmed his eyes.

"That would be a first for Mom. A thug. Wow. She must have dumped Dan. He was super clean looking. Kind of nerdy."

"Maybe things have changed now that your grandmother has died."

"I don't know. We haven't talked since she kicked me out of the high-rise."

Jack clasped her arms. "Listen, I'm going over and asking Linda Sorensen about the legality of someone trying to sell what isn't theirs. Ideas about what to do next. Like do we need some kind of court order, or what? And we'll also see what Lyonis says tonight."

There was no *we*. But hearing Jack say it, made something inside of her hope for more.

"And I think you should stay at my place till you can get your locks changed. Didn't you say the realtor walked right in? Unlocked the door?"

"Yeah. My mom must have given them keys."

Her phone pinged.

"Go ahead. Check that."

Rachel pulled her phone from her pocket. "It's Carter. He says my mom and her boyfriend are staying at their resort."

"Some nerve." Jack ran his hand through his hair. "This is getting weirder by the moment. Why would she stay someplace where she doesn't like the people who own it?"

"Maybe it was just Hampy Parker?"

"I don't know."

A couple walked past pushing a baby stroller with an adorable little boy in it. He waved at her, and she waved back. What would Jack's little boy look like? *Stop those thoughts!*

"My mom is the type of person to cut you off if you say anything at all critical to her. If anyone in that family dared badmouth her, she'd have made sure she never saw them again." She made a slashing gesture. "Completely cut off."

"When Hampy Parker had a few too many in him, he was known to spout some rude stuff at people. Kareen would always get him home, though. Once she had to come down to the Pink Pony and get him and I thought she'd take him by the ear and pull him outta there."

"Carter really loved his grandfather. He's told me numerous stories about him."

"Carter's brother, Parker, did, too. But Hampy and and his grandson, Parker, had the same problem."

"What's that?" Carter hadn't said.

He shoved his hands in his pockets. "Alcoholics, but the fun kind. Most people gave them a pass."

"Hmm, maybe my mom didn't. Or wouldn't." After the Admiral had left her, the only man to do so, Mom had shredded all the print pictures that she had of him.

"About the locks—I'll call John Hubel to come replace them, but it'll probably take him a day or two." He dipped his chin. "Hey, I really would feel better if you came over and slept at my house until those are changed."

She raised an eyebrow at him.

"Stay in my sister's room. Would you do that? For your safety? My dad insisted that he wants to run a check on your mom's boyfriend, too."

She ran a hand across her face as a carriage full of tourists rode past. How she loved this place. And now it was hers. "I don't want my mom to run me off, but I'm going to trust your judgement."

"Really?" Jack rocked back on his heels and smirked at her. "Since when did that happen."

"Today." She poked his chest. "But don't push it."

He saluted her. "I'll pick you up after work."

"Thanks."

"See you later then."

She nodded, then headed to the coffee shop in a daze.

She wasn't trespassing. She was Lilac Cottage's owner.

Oh, Gram.

Hours later, attired in a long meadow green summer dress borrowed from Jack's mother, the two of them mounted the red-carpeted steps to the Grand Hotel. Jack opened the door for her, and they entered the grand parlor to the sound of harp music.

"Mr. Lyonis said he'd meet us at that large vestibule outside the music hall." Rachel paused as a woman so tanned that her skin appeared like leather pushed past her and Jack. *Why do people do that to themselves?* In her reading on skin disorders, they always cautioned against excessive sun exposure.

"I bet that's him."

Attired in a perfectly tailored black suit, Gram's attorney stood, arms crossed, within the elevated vestibule.

Jack tugged at his tie. Dressed in that white dress shirt and navy slacks, he looked especially handsome tonight.

Rachel moved forward and mounted the steps, with Jack trailing her.

"Good to see you, my dear." The old-world-style gentleman gave her a kiss on each cheek. He smelled like lemon candies and peppermints.

"So good to see you, too, Mr. Lyonis."

Jack extended his hand. "I'm Jack Welling, we spoke on the phone."

"I'm glad you are taking care of Rachel—like your father always took good care of the judge."

Jack exchanged a quizzical look with her. Before she could ask Mr. Lyonis what he meant, he pointed toward the parlor.

"I've reserved one of the side chambers for our discussion. Follow that young man in the white jacket."

A dark-haired, slim man, about Jack's age, and wearing an ear wire quirked his finger at them. He had a European air to him, which made sense since the hotel had been bought out by a European conglomerate.

Mr. Lyonis offered his arm to Rachel. "Come with me, my dear."

Jack ambled ahead of them, closely behind the white-jacketed worker.

They were admitted to a smaller room off the Grand's main huge parlor. Inside, coffee and tea service had been set up on the large, polished oak table.

Mr. Lyonis pulled a heavy antique chair out for her and then sat at one adjacent. Jack sat across from her. He winked at her, and she smiled back. This thing of having someone there with her was feeling really good.

The attorney unlocked a slim attaché case and pulled out legal-sized documents. He reviewed each one with her methodically, including her mother's claim against the estate. Jack had refilled her coffee cup several times before Mr. Lyonis finished. She'd be up all night at this rate.

"So, you see," Gram's attorney shoved his dark metal glasses onto the bridge of his nose, "you inherit, or rather, inherited everything."

"Except the ten thousand dollars she gave to her mom. Right?" Jack leaned in, elbows on the table.

"And the use of the house in the suburbs during her lifetime." Rachel added.

"Correct." Mr. Lyonis slid the documents back into his leather briefcase. "That was done to ensure the court knows this person, in this case Selma, was indeed considered."

"I remember hearing about in the old days them putting just a dollar in there." Jack tapped his fingers on the table.

Rachel raised her eyebrows. Mom must be furious. "Inflation."

The attorney chuckled. "That's pretty much it."

"Selma is living in what is Rachel's high rise, still?" Jack frowned.

"Correct." Mr. Lyonis spun the locks numbers on his case.

"What can she do about that, sir?"

"Well, there are several options. And really, Selma should be back in her own house since she has no right to usage of the high-rise."

"What about her suit against me?" Rachel shrugged, her shoulders stiff.

"She doesn't have a leg to stand on." That looked like a secret smirk on the man's face. "I made this thing watertight. Your grandfather demanded that I do it how I did."

Gramps must have really regretted how he'd spoiled Mom when she was younger. Or was there something else. Did it have to do with Mr. Parker? *Maybe so.*

"I'd suggest I outline your options for handling your mother and that after her court case is heard, we meet up again and go over what you'd like to do. We could do that tomorrow if you wish."

This was surreal.

"Of course, because of how Margaret set up all her bank accounts and investments, those are already yours. There will be paperwork that needs to be filed but you can discuss that part with my paralegal, Jeannie."

Mr. Lyonis pushed away from the table.

Jack started to rise so Rachel did, too. Mr. Lyonis hurriedly pulled her chair free. "Thank you."

"Mr. Welling, if you ask this lovely young woman to marry you, I assure you I'd have her draw up an extensive pre-nuptial agreement."

Rachel gaped, glad that the attorney couldn't see her shocked expression. Jack did, though, and he grinned.

"What if I wouldn't sign it?" Jack crinkled his nose.

"My mother never would sign any of those offered her." Rachel gazed upward at the coffered ceiling, remembering how her mom had taken her husbands for anything and all she could get.

"I'd advise Rachel to not marry you if you won't sign." That was a genuine smirk as the lawyer linked his arm through hers again, and escorted Rachel from the room, Jack trailing them this time.

Rachel tilted her head toward Mr. Lyonis. "We're just friends."

"I'm her boss, actually." Jack's voice held a tease.

Mr. Lyonis looked over his shoulder. "Is that what they call it these days?" He stepped back, released Rachel's arm and gestured for Jack to move forward. "I sense your relationship with Rachel is nothing like your father's was with the judge. But I do think you'll take good care of her, won't you?"

Jack wrapped an arm around Rachel. "Yes sir, I will."

"Good. I've got another meeting tonight with some of my colleagues up in the Cupola. I'll leave you young people on your own." He raised his hand in a short wave and headed off through the parlor.

Jack leaned in. "I couldn't help Olivia, but I want to be there for you."

So, his attentiveness was simply out of guilt for losing his sister? Still, she needed an ally. Her own mother tried to sell Rachel's inheritance and was suing her. The whole thing was mind boggling.

"Listen, let's get you back to the house. We'll run you a big clawfoot tub full of bubble bath. And you can sleep on this overnight. Your grandparents wanted you to have what they worked for. Just be grateful."

"I am." She'd been waiting to share her happy news about the email she'd received that day. "And, Jack, I've got some extra special stuff coming up, too."

"What's that?"

"I've been accepted in the nursing program at Lake Superior State." Saying it out loud suddenly made it real. Her dream was coming true.

Jack lifted her off the floor and spun her around. "That's wonderful. I'm so proud of you, Rach!"

Pure, unadulterated, joy morphed into something more when he set her down and locked his warm hazel eyes on her.

Dare she wish for that something more?

Did she have the right to ask God for anything more at all, after how He'd blessed her?

Jack still held her arms, his grip warm and firm. God wasn't limited in His blessings. She'd trust in the Lord to give her just what she needed.

When Jack released her and stepped back, she was pretty sure he was having similar feelings.

"Hey, we're still on for the fund-raiser event, right?"

"Oh, yikes, I haven't picked my dress up from the dry cleaners in St. Ignace. I dropped it there when I went for my interview." It had smelled of old car trunk when she'd brought it, but otherwise it had been in good condition.

"I can get it when I go to the Soo for those lamps I ordered."

She cocked her head at him. "Would you?"

"No problem. I'll even pay for it, since you're doing me a favor."

The warm fuzzy vibe she'd had faded. This was about favors being returned. That was all. "Thanks."

Chapter Twenty-Three

*M*aria carried a tray of mint tea and peanut butter graham crackers to the outdoor table where Kareen and Gianni were seated. "Mama Kareen, are we really doing a Wayne Stephens movie fest this week?"

"Mom, he's not even staying here." Hamp shook his head. "He's at the Grand Hotel and his sister and her family are staying with Colton Byrnes in Hubbards' Annex."

Kareen shrugged and Gianni smiled his approval.

"Not only that, Mom, but I thought you hated his movies." Hamp accepted a tea mug from his wife.

"I'm a huge fan." Gianni grabbed a plate of peanut butter slathered grahams, and their tea. "In more ways than one."

Kareen's husband, when he'd learned of Hamp's true parentage, had voiced how glad he was that she'd had a son given to her—regardless of how she got him. Plus, she had her two grandsons because of that awful night. "I think you might enjoy watching some of those forbidden movies with our guests."

"Forbidden?" Hamp snorted. "Dad and I watched them when you went to bed."

"Really?"

"Every red-blooded American guy in Dad's age group watched all those Westerns he did before he switched to thrillers."

Gianni nodded.

She splayed her fingers. "Okay, okay."

Maria plopped down next to Kareen. "I am positively emotionally wiped out from that ceremony yesterday."

"Me, too." Kareen cupped her tea mug in her hands, wishing it held liquid strength. She had to lean into the Lord for grit and determination.

"The beautiful service brought back memories of my first husband's funeral service." Maria sighed. "I'm glad we had a long and good marriage."

Hamp covered Maria's hand.

Kareen set her tea down. "We've been blessed to have found new love, too. I think God worked that out for both of us, Maria."

"For all of us." Gianni raised his mug.

"I'm glad, too, Mom." Hamp looked genuinely sincere.

"We are all blessed." Maria beamed at them.

And would Hamp consider being the son of one of the most famous movie stars in the world a blessing, too?

Maybe it was good that Rachel had a second job. Less time to obsess over the pending drama with her mom. No time to be freaking out about what Mr. Lyonis had told her. Still, a headache was working its way into MRI machine-like rattling in her brain. But she tried to be pleasant to their customers at Lucky Bean.

"Can I get a French press—black?" The clean-cut yachty-type guy offered Rachel a totally flirty smile despite his girlfriend clinging to his arm.

Rachel exhaled sharply. Lucky Bean didn't do French press. Too time consuming. She cast a glance at Juan Pablo.

"*Señor, nada* on the French press on our side." Juan Pablo pointed to himself and Starr. "But the pretty cashier—she can do *muy bueno*."

Rachel raised her eyebrows so high at him that her bangs tickled them. "Juannn?" She drew out his name in warning.

He pointed to the couple. "For once is no line." He motioned for Rachel to come around.

The customer's girlfriend made a cringey face. "We don't want to make a problem."

The guy shrugged. "Hey, if they're willing." He did the sexy grin again, and Rachel wondered if that was just his normal smile. Nobody gave her that kind of look.

Juan Pablo grabbed an apron and handed it to Rachel as she came around the back.

"You are going to get me into so much trouble," she whispered to him.

"De nada."

"It's something to me. I can't get fired." Until they figured out what Mom might legally try to do to contest the will. She wanted to be on the far side of any court cases before she stopped working.

"Do your magic," Starr encouraged.

Rachel opened the cabinet and pulled out her own personal French press she kept at work. This was her one splurge this summer, so she'd have one at the shop. She also pulled down a canister of her favorite coffee.

"Filtered water, right?" Yachty guy called out.

Rachel gave him a thumbs' up as she poured from the Brita pitcher into the kettle.

"I'd just like a cappuccino." The woman pointed to the board.

"Absolutely!" Starr hummed to herself as she worked on the other drink.

Before long, the water in the electric tea kettle reached the correct temperature. She'd just completed the pour-over for the French press, when Andrette entered from the back.

Uh oh.

The manager sported freshly manicured nails with turquoise and navy stripes and tiny yellow crystals. She placed her hands on her hips. "What's going on here?"

Juan Pablo finished wiping off the case. "It's Rachel's break, and she was just about to start her French press when this delightful young couple walked in."

"If you're the owner, then give this girl a raise," Sexy grin guy said, "because when I asked if she minded making me one, too, though it's not on the menu—she did." He had the same smooth style even with the manager.

"Thank you," the girlfriend called out. "You have no idea what he's like if he doesn't get his French press coffee. You're the only place that was civil to us about it."

"Well, I bet you know the reason." The steam seemed to go out of Andrette.

"Yes, we do." The sexy grin came on strong. "Even the yacht club won't make it for me."

The girlfriend pretended to draw a tear trailing down her cheek.

"Oh gee, I know who you remind me of." Andrette clapped her hands together. "You're Bunty Braeburn and this is your fiancé, eh? You're Michigan's biggest social media whiz."

Rachel looked harder at the young woman. With the oversized sunhat, sunshades, touristy khaki shorts, a floral shirt, and a pair of white sneakers, she blended in well.

"Yup. And you're Andrette Brown Herron, who I've been stalking." When Bunty smiled, she transformed from plain to lovely.

Andrette blushed. "That's me."

Bunty pulled a phone from her purse and handed it to her boyfriend. "Get a pic of me and Andrette together. I've been following this shop for the past three months trying to get an interview with the market's hottest manager."

"I am so sorry." Andrette pushed a lock of hair from her face. "I bet you've heard that I'm a recluse in the off-season, eh?"

"Yes, but I also know you're getting accolades all over the place. I want an article for my new magazine."

Andrette and Bunty wrapped arms around each other's waists as yacht guy snapped some pics.

Bunty pointed her index finger upward. "Raise the phone and angle it down a little." She stood taller and smiled seductively.

Bunty could match her boyfriend on the grins when it was for social media.

Rachel brought the French press coffee and Bunty's cappuccino around as Andrette and Bunty viewed at the pictures and chose several for Instagram.

"Ought to get one with you, too." Bunty angled toward Rachel.

"No!" Rachel barked and all eyes focused on her. "I um, I'm sorry, but I look awful." Ack, she was lying, she looked no different than usual.

"She doesn't allow pictures." Juan Pablo winked.

"Right," Starr agreed.

"Ooh, I sense a story there." Bunty lowered her sunglasses and examined Rachel.

Her boss looked sad. "She's the granddaughter of a really important Federal judge."

Rachel straightened to her full height.

"And quite terribly," Andrette cocked her head, "he was murdered and covered in a high-profile case for years before these latest difficulties our countries' judges have been having."

No! Not true. Heart attack. Rachel stared at her boss.

Bunty nodded solemnly and yacht guy looked hard at her.

Why would Andrette make up a lie like that? Rachel wanted to yell at her. But her heartbeat ticked up so fast, she wondered if her body knew something she didn't. And Rachel couldn't say anything to her boss right now.

"Go ahead and take your break, Rachel. Jack's back there grabbing some stuff for the cottage."

Rachel slipped around the counter, grabbed her own cup of French press coffee, and exited out the back.

Andrette's voice carried, "Her family owns one of the cottages up on the West Bluff. Lilac Cottage. It's beautiful, eh."

She felt yacht guy's gaze on her, even before she turned to catch him watching her. When she swiveled around and continued walking, head down, she almost bumped into Jack.

"Whoa there, Rachy Woo."

Another of his horrible nicknames for her. But it had saved her coffee. She expelled a breath. "Sorry."

"What's up?" He turned and pulled a box of pre-ground coffee from the shelf.

"Ew, I can't believe Andrette buys that for you."

He beamed. "Ha. Even better—the owner gets it free and although she'll never use it here at the shop. Carolyn gives it to me." He sounded so cocky.

At Lucky Bean, everything was ground fresh. "The beans are the thing." The shop's owner, Carolyn May, had made sure they all understood.

"For me, free is an amazing thing." Jack winked and patted the tin of coffee. "I'm happy to share."

She raised her hand. "No, thanks. Andrette lets me have the real deal when I'm on the clock. I just have to use my grandmother's French press."

"Andi described your enjoyment of that ridiculously time-intensive coffee as *euphoric*."

"Maybe not euphoric." She took a sip and closed her eyes, enjoying the taste. She opened her eyes and the look on Jack's face made her cheeks heat. He looked like. . . like he was *attracted* to her. "More like enjoying the wait for something truly memorable."

He cast her a dreamy look that was so unlike him.

"I want to ask you something." Jack's parents and grandparents knew Rachel's grandparents.

"What?" He tucked the coffee into a cardboard box and pulled a sleeve of filters from the shelf.

"Andrette said something that is. . ." she was going to say *a bald-faced lie*, "crazy."

He frowned. "That's not like her."

"I know." She chewed her lower lip.

Rachel sipped her coffee as Jack continued to pull stuff from the shelves and pack them into the box.

"Well, snookums, are you gonna tell me?"

"Snookums?"

"Your grandmother used to call me that." He laughed. "Your grandfather would always yell at her for calling me that."

Gramps had died from heart failure while he was at work. Why would Andrette say otherwise?

Her boss entered the workroom, her heels clicking on the linoleum floor. "I'm sorry I said anything to Bunty about your grandfather."

"Who's Bunty?" Jack asked.

"A social media megastar who has been emailing me for a few months. She showed up here today."

"What's that got to do with Rachel's grandfather?"

Andrette waved her beautifully manicured hands around. "Nothing, I just gotta little flustered. When they asked why Rachel won't be photographed I just. . ."

"Made up something?" Rachel drew her eyebrows together.

Her boss blinked at her. "Well, no. . . What do you mean?"

But the manager had lied.

Andrette shook her head slightly. "I thought that was why you were so careful about no photos. I thought you didn't want the hoopla like after your grandfather's death."

"Having a judge murdered in his own courtroom. . ." Jack touched her shoulder.

She flinched. "No." Rachel raised her hands. "That's not true!"

Andrette and Jack exchanged a glance.

She had to get out of there. She looked for her purse and grabbed it. "I gotta go."

Her boss wagged her finger at Jack. "See what you've done?"

"Me? You're the one who brought it up in front of complete strangers! And I've told you to leave her alone about the pic thing."

Rachel headed out the back, trying to catch her breath.

As she rounded the building, she spied Bunty and yacht dude. She turned to walk the other way, but she heard someone running toward her.

"Hey, Rachel, stop."

She kept going to the corner, to the French-Canadian cabin where her great-great-grandmother Sadie had grown up.

Yacht guy caught up with her. She turned away from him and looked at the small cabin. This was how her family had started.

"I'm really sorry about how this has gone down." Gone was the megawatt smile.

She looked at him. "What are you talking about?"

He glanced toward Bunty, who was walking slowly toward them, almost teetering in her heels. "Listen, before she gets here, you need to know I'm a federal agent, and I'm assigned to your case."

She almost burst out laughing but yacht guy looked serious.

She noticed the lines on his forehead and around his eyes. "What case?"

"One assigned to me and a few others."

A few others? Who? This was absurd. "Is this some kind of joke? If so, I really don't appreciate it. My grandfather died of a heart attack while he was at work." But maybe not. Jack and Andrette wouldn't lie about that, would they? Both seemed genuinely convinced.

Keeping his eyes focused on Bunty, the guy leaned in. "Your grandfather's murderer is due for release. He's very sick and an old dude, but we think the guy's still as crazy as ever."

Rachel's head throbbed. This was too much.

He angled his back to Bunty, reached into his shorts' pocket and pulled out a white business card. He handed it to her. "That's my private, encrypted phone number and several ways you can contact me."

"What are you two gossiping about?" Bunty called out.

He turned and waved at her. "Trying to get you another interview while we're here on the island, babe."

When Bunty reached them, she lowered her sunglasses onto the bridge of her nose. Rachel was surprised to see crow's feet around the social media darling's baby blues. Bunty touched Rachel's arm. "You didn't know, did you?"

Rachel stiffened and drew back. Bunty dropped her hand.

"I could see it in your expression. You didn't know your grandfather had been killed, did you?"

"I, uh, I've gotta go." Rachel turned and jogged around the corner and into a crowd of tourists.

She continued on to the corridor to the Island Bookstore and then ducked inside the store.

Tamara Tomac, the manager, stood at the register ringing up a customer, a silver-haired guy with a Yacht Club baseball cap and matching navy and white clothing down to his navy boat shoes. Tamara stiffened her neck. "What's up, Rachel? You look like you've seen a ghost."

The older guy accepted his receipt and book and left as Rachel approached the counter.

"I just had a huge shock."

Tamara raised her eyebrows. "What happened, hon?"

Rachel ran her tongue over her upper lip, tasting salt and coffee. "I, um, you knew my grandfather, right?" *Ack, of course she did.*

Since Rachel had been a tiny girl, she'd been coming to this bookstore and had known Tamara. The store manager's look right now was one of total avoidance.

"Yeah, yeah, I sure did." Tamara moved stuff around on the countertop and averted her gaze.

Rachel leaned forward. "Someone told me he was murdered, but that's not what my grandmother and mother told me."

"Oh, hon, I'm sorry."

Rachel swallowed hard. "Sorry someone told me that he was killed or what Gram said to me?"

By the way Tam gazed at her, with sympathy etched on her pretty face, Rachel had learned the truth today. Which meant that Yacht guy might really be Federal agent guy. She pulled his card from her pocket. Shane Wade White was the agent's three-monosyllabic name. She'd been about to tell Tam about him, but hesitated.

A group of giggling Girl Scouts swarmed into the store.

"Listen come back tomorrow and I'll take my lunch with you, okay?" Tam reached across the counter and patted her shoulder.

"I can't, but will you be here Saturday?"

"Yeah, yeah, this Saturday I will be."

"See you then."

Rachel exited the store. One of the girls pointed to the latest Mimi Vendue book.

She walked through the crush of tourists and headed to the hallway that adjoined the Joann's fudge shop. She got good cell reception there, so she sat on a bench and googled her grandfather's name. All kinds of stories popped up.

Dunmara Murdered at the Bench.

Judge Dunmara Killed at Work.

No Motive Known for Judge's Murder.

Chicago Tribune, Detroit Free Press, and Washington Post all had stories in their online archives related to her grandfather's death.

This was surreal. How could she not have known? How could no one have ever said anything to her about it?

Rachel rubbed her forehead.

She and Mom lived in a suburb. Mom used whatever husband's name she was married to at the time. Rachel had used her first stepfather's name for a long time, despite it not being her legal name.

Recollections flooded her mind. The strange people who came to the high-rise after her grandfather had died. The extra security they had. Being sent off to school in Virginia almost as soon as Gramps was buried. The limits on her social media.

It all made sense. It was like one of those card shuffling things where all the cards slid right into place although it looked like they shouldn't.

She replayed what the agent had said. She googled her grandfather's killer. Due for release after over a decade in prison.

Was that fair?

She couldn't go back to work. She texted Andrette her apology.

She should go back, though. She'd be letting her co-workers down.

A voice nearby caught her off-guard.

Mom.

Carrie Fancett Pagels

Arguing with a man with a heavy Eastern European accent.

Rachel ducked her head, spun on her heel and hurried back into the fudge shop. She weaved among the customers and exited out the front door, then hurried toward home.

But she couldn't go there, even if it was hers. Jack wanted her to be careful.

This was nuts, truly nuts, but all she wanted to do was to get away, so she hurried to Cindy's Stables. A long queue of riders left as she arrived. She went inside. Definitely crazy. She hadn't been on a horse in years. But she was a good rider.

Before long, Rachel was astride a beautiful bay mare. They meandered into the center of the wood-shaded island. She rode for hours, until the horse was due back at the stables. By the time she got back, she and God had spent a long time talking or rather she'd given Him all her troubles in a big basket and He'd taken them.

Now to let Him carry them.

Chapter Twenty-Four

*K*areen slipped the DNA records into her capri pants' pocket as she followed Gianni out of their suite. She'd give Carter his results after the outdoor service tonight. He wasn't a half-sibling to his new friend, Rachel. Instead, his results showed Selma's daughter to likely be Carter's aunt. And that meant that her husband, Hampy, had fathered Rachel, not Hamp—as Kareen had suspected.

She took Gianni's strong hand as they headed out through the lobby. "Do you think it's crazy to be relieved that Hampy had his own secrets, too?"

Her husband quirked an eyebrow at her. "No. I think it might help your son accept what you need to tell him."

Would it?

Gianni assisted her into the private carriage that waited for them on their drive. Soon, they'd arrived at Marquette Park, where the Wednesday evening service would take place, in the back corner. Carter was to meet them there.

As they walked across the verdant lawn and around the lilac trees now devoid of flowers, music carried.

Gianni squeezed her hand. "You said Hampy did his DNA for the same ancestry site last year, right, sweetie?"

She nodded. "I'm glad now that he did. But at the time, he was acting so strange and drinking so much that I refused to do my own."

"Well, you did it now."

And she had shown as a match on Carter's report. Nothing there for Hampy, of course. Mimi Zenkowicz, or Mimi Vendue as she went by, showed as his great aunt. And Horace Przbysleweski matched as grandfather. "Did you know Wayne Stevens' real name was so awful?"

"Nope. No wonder the guy changed it for Hollywood."

"What do you think Carter will say? And why don't I have Hamp's results back?"

"Let's hope for the best with Carter. He's got his head on right. As far as Hamp—my bet is, he tossed the kit."

A breeze stirred her wrap, and Kareen pulled it closer around her.

"Grandma!" Carter jogged away from a group of twenty-somethings who were clustered near a makeshift stage. "You really came."

Kareen hugged him, and Gianni patted his shoulder.

Carter waved for them to follow him.

They joined the group and a few of the younger people greeted them. She recognized a bunch of islander kids whom she'd known for years. Not really kids anymore. They were growing up, like Carter was.

Carter pointed to a dark-haired Hispanic man who stood on the stage. "That's Juan Pablo. He's like an itinerant minister. Starr is his assistant." He waved toward a girl with spiky multi-colored hair who was passing out leaflets.

"Didn't we see them at Lucky Bean?" Gianni rubbed his face.

"Yeah. They both work there, and they do this ministry on Wednesday nights."

The young woman moved closer and handed Kareen a sheet with words to some songs she didn't recognize.

"Carter! So good to see you here." Starr practically bounced as she greeted Kareen's grandson.

"I love what you and Juan Pablo are doing. It's a lot of fun."

Starr turned back to Kareen. "I've got a special song for you tonight, Mrs. Franchetti."

Kareen stiffened. How did this young woman know her correct married name? What had Carter said to her? And why a special song? "Oh? Well, thank you."

Soon, Starr joined Juan Pablo on the platform, and she began playing guitar while the itinerant minister sang. People in the audience sang along. Kareen followed the words but didn't try to sing them. She didn't know the melody. But her eyes filled with tears as she read the song's words about God's heart being full of love and not shame. For too many years she'd carried the shame of her son's birth. Her shame at misleading her husband into thinking that he had fathered her son.

Juan Pablo went on to preach about how God forgives sins. He read scripture confirming when you confess your sins to the Lord they are as far as the East is from the West.

Gianni wrapped his arm more tightly around Kareen and leaned in. "I think this message tonight was especially for you, my Sugar Bear."

She swiped at her tears. Carter was watching, and listening, in rapt attention. Would her grandson be so forgiving as God was? Would her son?

She'd soon find out.

Was the cottage really hers? Rachel kept sneaking looks out the window as she worked at Jack's place. She'd slept dreadfully, despite the lovely bath she'd taken. Way too much recent excitement. The guys were out back painting the window frames and trim today. Jack was in the middle of a call with the guy about the heat pump that should have been delivered yesterday. She needed to get some more of her things from the cottage.

Rachel slipped out and headed next door. Gram's colorful hollyhocks were climbing high alongside the cottage, next to heady damask roses whose scent carried on the breeze. This place was Rachel's now, but the upkeep would be her responsibility, too. Gram had kept everything on autopilot for years. Could she do the same?

When she rounded the building to the back, someone stepped out from beneath the shadows of the tall evergreen hedge.

A man wearing dark close-fitting casual clothing stared at the second story.

Rachel took a step backward. She trusted her instincts, turned and ran all the way to Jack's. She rushed up the front stairs, pushed the door open, and ran smack into Jack.

He grabbed her shoulders. "You okay?"

"There's a strange guy skulking in my backyard."

He strode to his desk and jerked opened the bottom drawer. He grabbed a gun.

"Didn't know you had one of those."

"Yup. Stay here." Jack exited the front door and jogged toward her cottage.

Should she call the police? How bizarre that just yesterday she was still concerned someone would call law enforcement about her camping out at the cottage. *But it's mine.* She called the island police department and breathlessly gave them the info.

"We'll send some officers right away, Miss Dunmara."

"Thank you." She ended the call.

Jack's dad had cameras. She called him and got his voicemail. "Mr. Welling, can you please check the cameras that show my cottage? Someone is in the backyard." She'd said it. *My. My cottage. My backyard.* "And I don't know who it is. Jack's over there now." *And I hope he doesn't shoot someone.* She touched the End Call icon on the screen. She hated to interrupt Mr. Welling when his wife was sick, but this was scary. She and Jack had also agreed to ask his dad what his relationship had been with her grandfather, but now wasn't the time for that.

After what seemed like an eternity, Jack finally returned. "Nobody there. But my dad called me. He's sending me some close-up images from the cameras. What did the dude look like?"

"Slim, dark clothes and shoes, dark hair, medium complexion. He was too far away for me to get a good look at his face."

Jack's cellphone pinged. "My dad sent some images."

He moved closer and showed her a picture. "I was wondering if it was the creep with your mom but it's not him. Do you know this guy?" He expanded the picture, so she got a close-up of his face.

"Nobody I know."

"You're definitely gonna keep staying here with me at our cottage. No arguments. And Dad is coming up as soon as he can."

She began to tremble from head to toe

Jack wrapped her in his arms. "Might be nothing. Could be someone thinkin' that since the place is advertised for sale, then now's a great time to break in."

Rachel pulled away and looked up at him. "And that's supposed to reassure me?"

"Well, no, but it's better than some other options."

She slapped his arm. "Again, thanks for that. Not!"

"Someone has to look after you."

Maybe he had a point. No one had been looking after her best interests for a long time. "I called the police department and they're sending someone."

"Great."

At least the police weren't coming for her.

An hour later, after the cops left, she called Andrette to let her know that she'd be late for work. After skipping out yesterday, she really didn't want to leave her boss and the crew in the lurch. Rachel normally kept her commitments. But her life was becoming too complicated.

Luckily, her afternoon at the coffee shop went smooth as silk. The Patrick brothers had shown up during a lull and the youngest one flirted with Starr, again. She invited him to come to the Wednesday night services and all of the brothers had agreed. Rachel hoped she could get to one, too, before summer was gone. The weather was good, and she rode her bike to and from work, instead of letting Jack drive her.

When Rachel arrived at Jack's, a bag of popcorn popped in the microwave. "Wanta watch some of the old family videos I found, from way back when?"

"Sure." She stretched. "But I've got to catch some shut-eye soon."

"There's one marked the Parkers' silver wedding anniversary. Want to look at that? In honor of Hampy?"

The man had bequeathed her money that would cover her nurses' training. Why not learn more about him?

Jack grabbed two Cokes and the popcorn and set them down on the antique coffee table. Then he started the video and sat beside her. Goldie stood in the entryway to the room, watching them.

"Look at that." He pointed to two couples standing on Lilac Cottage's veranda in the video.

"Gram and Gramps." She covered her mouth with her hands. They were so much younger than she'd ever remembered them.

"This thing looks almost thirty years old."

"Not quite." She pointed to Jack's young parents. His mom held a squirming boy in his arms. "Look! Your hair is blond there."

Jack patted his head. "Got dark when I started school."

"But you were actually at this party."

He put the video on pause. "Kinda remember it a little. Mrs. Parker got all flustered when someone arrived." He pushed the play button and the video resumed.

"Turn up the volume."

Jack accommodated her.

The videographer followed the Parkers and Gram and Gramps and the Wellings inside. The place was packed. "I've never seen so many people crammed into Lilac Cottage."

Gramps stood on a wooden box and waved his arms. "We've had to delay our friends' silver anniversary a couple of times but we're celebrating now!"

"Here! Here!" People cheered.

"Since we first planned this shebang, Hampy and Kareen have welcomed both a daughter-in-law and later a grandchild into the fold!"

More applause.

Gramps talked about how happily married the Parkers were even after twenty-eight years. "Like newlyweds," He proclaimed.

"There's your mom." Jack leaned forward and pointed to the right side of the screen. "She's holding a martini glass or maybe that's champagne."

Waiters in suits circulated through the room pouring bottles of champagne. "She does love that stuff."

"Oh, now I remember. The cowboy dude arrived." Jack pointed to the four-year-old version of him was running toward a tall blond man in a flashy white suit who'd come through the front door.

"That's the actor Wayne Stevens. What would he be doing there?" Goldie plopped down on Rachel's feet.

"Don't know, but I remember running up to him, and he was really chill with me."

In the video, young Mrs. Welling scooped Jack up into her arms and chatted for a minute with the actor, looking starstruck. Mr. Welling joined them.

Rachel leaned forward and pointed. "Look at Mrs. Parker, though. Put it on pause."

Jack obliged. "Looks like she's seen a ghost."

"Yup. And look at my mom." Rachel's gut clenched. She'd seen that calculating look on her mother's face way too many times. "She was up to something."

"My ex used to get a look like that." Jack pressed the play button on the remote.

Gramps gestured to Kareen Parker, who was staring dumbstruck, while Hampy grinned and waved at their guests. "Mr. Parker looks like the happiest man in the world."

"There's their son, Hamp. Wow I think he might be younger than we are now."

"And there's his wife tossing back her entire glass of champagne." Rachel cringed. The poor woman had died from her addictions.

"That really is a crazy look on your mom's face."

"Yeah, that's her evil demented look. She has a few of those." Onscreen, Gramps finished his toast, others began to chime in. A half dozen people raised their champagne flutes and proclaimed the Parkers to be the happiest couple on the island. Meanwhile, Mom edged closer to Hampy and Kareen. Hamp Parker cast a wary look at her but then returned his attention to his giggling wife. The toasts ended and Kareen Parker made a beeline for Wayne Stevens. "Looks like Mrs. Parker is having a big fangirl moment there."

The camera scanned the partygoers and settled on Mom talking with Hampy Parker. With a seductive smile plastered on her face, she leaned forward, revealing far too much cleavage. *No. Oh no.* It was like watching a train wreck about to happen. Was this where everything started? Rachel pressed her spine hard against the couch's back. The camera moved back, pausing on Mrs. Parker, whose enraged expression surprised Rachel.

"Apparently, Kareen Parker was not a fan after all," Jack deadpanned. "But I wonder what she's got against America's hero?"

The next footage was of Hampy Parker's suited back as he followed young Mom, her hips swaying suggestively, toward the hall that led to the back of the house. As the two disappeared out of sight, Hampy turned and glanced back into the room of revelers. Everyone was talking, laughing, drinking, and eating hors d'oeuvres. And Kareen Parker walked out the front door with Wayne Stephens, her hands visibly shaking.

"What year was this, Jack?"

He looked at the box. "Twenty-six years ago."

Rachel ran her tongue over her upper lip. Her narcissist mother may have decided she couldn't stand all the attention that the Parkers were receiving. She'd likely wanted to show Kareen Parker that if she, Selma, wanted Hampy then all she had to do was snap her fingers and that belated silver wedding celebration of love could be broken. *So evil. So Mom-like.*

"You okay?"

She pushed her hair off her forehead. "I, uh, I need to get to sleep."

Jack stretched. He picked up their Coke bottles and the popcorn bag and brought them to the kitchen. "I'm glad the guys put a different bed in Livvie's room and that nightstand and lamp. Were you comfortable in there?"

"Yeah, it was fine. And Jack, thanks for helping me. And letting me stay here." And for showing her that video. Shame that had always chased her as she grew up was nipping at her heels. But God would never do that. He'd never want her to feel ashamed of being there on His earth. And she needed to follow His purpose for her life.

Goldie looked up at her with baleful eyes.

"Do you care if I bring Goldie in with me tonight, Jack?"

"She'd love that."

"Thanks. I would, too." If Olivia were still alive, then Rachel could tell her all about her suspicions.

"Rachel?" Jack turned off the kitchen lights. "I think you saw something I saw on that video."

She compressed her lips. "My mom and Mr. Parker?"

He joined her in the living room. "I don't know what went on that night, but I've got a pretty good suspicion."

Rachel dropped her head. "I think I know why Mr. Parker had an account with my name on it."

"What do you mean?"

"They told me at the bank that Hampy Parker held a joint account, a checking account, with my name on it, too."

"Why? How?"

"I don't know. But I bet when I look at the past records they are pulling up for me, I'll find checks sent to my mother."

Jack rubbed the back of his neck. "Hate to say it, but I think you may be right."

Those DNA tests couldn't come soon enough.

How would Carter feel about discovering that she was his aunt? Or his father finding out he had a sister?

"Rachel, if Mr. Parker was your father, what are you going to do?"

"What do you mean?" She exhaled a puff of air.

"Do you know if he stipulated anything in his will for you? Are you possibly an heir?"

She raised her hands, then dropped them. "I don't know."

But she sure didn't want to lose her relationship with Carter.

Chapter Twenty-Five

Rachel cross-checked the figures from the two quotes they'd gotten on the roof. She rubbed her eyes. How was she supposed to focus? Sleeping in Olivia's bed, down the hall from Jack, hadn't helped.

The front door opened, and Maria stepped in, a look of shock and determination on her face. For once, she came empty handed. She strode right to Rachel's desk.

"I need to talk with you."

In the kitchen, RJ shouted, "Grandma's here!"

When Austin and Sean came through the door, Maria waved them back. "Not now. I will speak with you later."

Expressions downcast, the two returned to their tasks.

"Could you come outside with me?"

Jack cast them a quizzical look. He was on hold with the roofer.

"Do you mind, Jack?"

He shrugged.

Rachel followed the older woman outside to the back yard.

Maria slumped into a lawn chair. She gestured to the one beside her. "Sit. I need some help from you."

"What is it?" Had Mom done something stupid at the Parkers' resort? Had Maria found out about Hampy being her father?

"I need to know about your family."

"My family?"

"Si. Your grandmother, great-grandmother. The Swaines."

"Why?" She frowned. "What's going on?"

"You took a DNA test, right?" Maria removed an envelope from her crossbody bag.

"Yes, Carter gave it to me—"

"That's all right. No worries."

"The results aren't supposed to be back for a few weeks."

"I got mine already." Maria's dark eyes flashed.

"What does that have to do with my Gram?"

"Do you have an aunt named Honoria?"

"Yes. My great-aunt."

"Si. Good. Honoria is a cousin to me."

"What?" Rachel frowned. "That should mean my grandmother was your cousin, too."

"Yes, and you also, it shows as my relation."

Rachel dipped her chin.

"That's what it shows, but I don't know how."

"Tell me about your family. There has to be a connection to mine."

Maria raised her hands. "My mother never knew her father. He died when she was a baby. My step-grandfather was the only grandfather my sister and I knew."

Rachel nodded.

"My grandmother's people were all from Mexico. She said her family there referred to my grandfather as a gringo. When he died, my grandmother came to the states. She never returned home. 'Bad blood' was all she said about her brothers who took over and ran her husband's shipbuilding company there."

"That must have been hard."

Maria wrapped her fingers around Rachel's wrist. "But this is the thing. That company was named Swaine—not a Mexican name. Lopez was my grandmother's maiden name." Maria released her wrist.

Rachel pressed her fingers to her lips. "Swaine? That's my great-great-grandparent's name."

"I think we descend from the same line, and I want to find out more. Do you have your family charts?"

"Yes, Gram had some she kept in her desk." Rachel groaned. "But that's in her high-rise, and my mom is living there." Though not for long if Rachel had her escorted out. Maybe she should get the locks changed at the high-rise while Mom was here on the island. But that would be too mean.

"Do you think she would help?"

"I doubt it. Not unless there was something in it for her."

Maria clucked her tongue. "That's too bad. I think I may be a descendant of your Sadie and Robert Swaine. It's the reason I asked my daughter to name her son Roberto, at my own mother's request, for her birth father's name."

Wasn't there a family story about a missing son? Robert, Jr.? Wasn't it tied somehow into their property rights? Jack said something about it. Rachel rubbed at the tension starting in her neck. "So likely you and your family are all related to me?"

"Looks like it."

"That's pretty cool." She had more family if that was true.

"My *abuela* was very secretive about my grandfather's past. He died young. She left all her family behind in Mexico. She always seemed very distressed about that. About them." Maria chewed on her lower lip. "She remarried in the states."

"Did she talk about her first husband?"

"Abuela always clammed up whenever anyone asked her about her family's reasons for leaving Mexico.

"And here you are back at the Straits of Mackinac where your grandfather would have started his life if he was Sadie's son."

"God works in mysterious ways." Maria made the sign of the cross.

"He does." What would he reveal to Rachel via her own DNA results?

Did she really want to know?

Jack ended his call. "Hey you, two, what's up?"

Their family had always been at the cottage on borrowed time, but it had never really felt like it to Jack—until now. He listened as the two women gave him a recap of their conversation. His gut sank.

He tugged down his t-shirt as he stood, towering over Maria, who might be one of the long-lost descendants of Robert Swaine, Junior. He pointed to Rachel's desk. "That belonged to Captain Robert Swaine."

The tiny woman's eyes glowed as she caressed the desktop she'd seen numerous times before. "I think he would have been my great-grandfather, then."

"Yes, if your DNA results are accurate."

"Why wouldn't they be?" There went Rachel with attitude.

He shrugged and scratched the side of his head. "Stuff happens."

"I plan to gather whatever records I can find, and Rachel is going to help me with some that Sadie Swaine left."

"There's some next door, too, in a lock box somewhere and my folks have some legal paperwork that may help." Yeah, help Maria and her grandkids claim this place as their own. All of his father's investment and Jack's hard work could go right down the drain.

Maria clasped her hands to her chest. "I am so excited to have more family. And so very many people were listed on my papers. Many cousins who live all over near here. I cannot believe it!" Her dark eyes filled with tears. "All my life I've prayed for a bigger family. And now I have it."

"Me, too." Rachel pulled Maria into a hug. "I'm glad to call you my cousin."

"And the boys, too!" Maria cupped her hands around her mouth, "My grandsons come here and meet your new cousin!"

RJ, Sean, and Austin trailed into the room, all looking skeptical.

"Roberto James, you were named after your great-grandfather, Robert." Maria gestured around the cottage. "He was born in this house."

"This belonged to his parents. They were my great-great-grandparents, so we're distant cousins." Rachel wore an expression of shock on her pretty face.

"Not so distant." RJ rushed forward and lifted her off the floor.

"Easy there, boys." Jack moved forward in case he had to intervene, but Rachel was laughing.

He really needed to talk with his folks. "How about you guys and Rachel take the rest of the day off? Go do something touristy together. How does that sound, Maria?" He opened his wallet and pulled out some twenties and handed them to the boys. "Bonus for your hard work."

The three waved their cash around like trophies.

"Gracias, Jack. I'll send them over again tomorrow." Maria gave him a quick hug.

Each boy slapped Jack's outstretched hand as they departed. "Tomorrow dudes."

Rachel waved goodbye.

"Yo! Tomorrow," Sean called out over his shoulder, then shrugged. "Or maybe I'll sleep in."

If Maria's family turned out to be legitimate heirs then they could all do their sleeping at this cottage. Who would have thought that after all these years that these descendants of Robert Swaine, Jr., would be found? For Sadie Swaine to put that into the legal documents, she must have harbored that hope—even stipulating it out over a hundred years.

The front door closed shut.

The scope of this project now changed. Jack had wanted to erase the memories of Olivia from the cottage. Would God simply take it away from his family? He dropped his head. *Lord, You've worked like this in my life before. You've taken away what I thought was mine. Help me release my grip and not grasp tightly to what is going on here. Let me be in Your will. In Your plan.*

He swiped at his eyes with the base of his palm. He wasn't crying. That was sweat.

But the sadness and anxiety enveloping him was real.

Rachel left Jack's house with Maria and her grandsons, but she had other plans. "I've got to work at Lucky Bean later, so I can join you for a little bit. Maybe get some ice cream at Sadie's?"

Seemed strange that the ice cream place was the same name as her great-great-grandmother's and Maria's and these boys'.

Sean raised his arms. "I love all their flavors."

"That's where all your money goes." RJ elbowed his younger brother.

"Does not."

"Does too."

"Stop arguing! Mr. Welling gave you enough money to get lots of ice cream." Maria scolded.

Austin shoved his hands in his cargo shorts' pockets. "Let's walk down there and get a taxi into town afterwards."

"I'd rather walk, boys, since you have the afternoon off."

"Yo, Grandma, can you power walk it?" Sean tugged at Maria's hand.

Maria quirked her face and pointed ahead. "You get started and Rachel and I will roar right past you. Watch and see."

The boys took off. Austin, though, lagged and turned to look at Rachel and Maria, who were merely strolling along. He gave them two thumbs up and then sped off.

After Rachel ate her chocolate fudge mint sundae at Sadie's, she texted Carter. *Did you get ur DNA results?*

Yup

Another text from him popped up. *I have urs*

Can u meet me she texted back.

Where

Pontiac's Trail

She headed past the Grand Hotel's main entrance and continued on. The Jeffries' stuffed horse still sat on a porch seat, looking like it was waving a welcome to her. She'd met Carter several months earlier right here. So much had happened since then. She grinned, glancing down at the pair of New Balance tennis shoes Jack had bought for her months earlier on a trip to the mainland when he'd discovered she only had two pairs of shoes.

By the time she reached the trail's entrance, Carter zipped in on his bike.

"Come on." She pushed through the turnstile. "And watch out for poison ivy."

"You seem pretty chill, given you're about to find out about who your dad is."

She glanced over her shoulder. "I've got a pretty good idea."

They moved forward onto the path along the cliffside.

"Not too sure these results aren't switched or something."

"Why do you say that?" She stopped at an area wide enough for them to stand side-by-side.

Carter handed her an envelope. "I wonder if your results and mine have gotten switched."

She chewed her lower lip. She needed to spit this out. "I'm pretty sure when we open mine, it will show your grandfather as my biological father."

Carter stared at her.

"Which would make you my nephew, which seems weird." She pushed her hair back from her face then opened the envelope.

Leaning over her shoulder, Carter pointed to his grandfather's name. "How'd you know that? I thought you didn't know who it was?" He stepped away.

"Jack and I watched a video with my mom putting the moves on your grandfather at a party twenty-seven years ago." She shrugged. "And we guessed."

Her friend, now known to be *her nephew*, frowned. "Well, mine is hosed up so yours might be, too." He opened his letter and showed her the names.

Rachel scanned them. "Where's Hampton Parker, Sr., on here?"

Carter snatched the sheet back. "Right. Where is he? He's on yours and not mine."

"But your grandmother's name was on there and the relationship. Kareen Parker."

"Yeah." He crouched down on one knee. "Somebody's been lying to me, to us, then."

"That doesn't make any sense that he wouldn't be on there."

He huffed a laugh. "Doesn't it? I'm not so naïve that I don't get what that means. My grandfather wasn't my dad's father. Some other dude was."

Rachel rocked back on her heels, dirt and pebbles crunching beneath her feet.

A breeze swirled up the side of the cliff. "What do I say to my dad? He didn't do his test. You did his."

She took his hand and tugged it. "Come on. Let's finish our walk and talk about this."

"I don't know."

"Why don't you tell me about your grandfather, and let's make a plan about how you can talk with your grandmother. Okay?" She was beginning to really feel like an aunt. Or a big sister. But what if he wasn't actually related to Hampy Parker?

He blinked at her, and Rachel pulled him in to a quick hug. "It's going to be all right."

"Thanks, Rachel. Yeah. Let's walk and talk."

"Did you guess the first time we met that I wasn't really going to walk Pontiac's Trail?"

"Kinda. But I liked you right from the start."

"Do you still?"

"Of course." He quirked an eyebrow. "But I'm feeling a little mixed up right now."

"But you don't hate me? I mean if I am your grandfather's daughter and you've got a different grandpa out there somewhere?"

He tipped his head back, as if searching the cerulean sky. "Why would I hate you for something my grandmother did?"

A seagull swooped low past them, squawking as it went.

"Don't hate on your grandma, either. At least you're here because of her."

"One way to look at it."

"Come on. Let's go."

They hiked along the path, careful of the poison ivy.

"I wonder if this means I'm not really a Parker, then." He shrugged.

"That's who raised you." But was she now a Parker? She rubbed her arms.

"But I feel like I don't know who I am now." He tapped her shoulder. "Have you felt like that?"

She stopped and turned. "I guess when I was younger, more so. Lately, though, I've owned my Dunmaraness. My grandfather was really my psychological father."

Carter ran a bandana across his brow. "I guess we're sorta the opposite because your father was my psychological grandfather."

After a moment, they hugged.

"I'm glad you're my friend, Carter."

He released her. "And I'm glad you're mine."

"How do you think your dad is going to take this news?"

"That's the big wild card."

Kareen's hands trembled as she followed the hostess to her table at the Fort Tea Room. This was her favorite tourist spot on the island and the safest place for a meeting.

Wayne looked up, his yellow polo shirt almost as bright as the tables' umbrellas. He pushed back from the table, but Kareen motioned for him to remain seated, and thanked the hostess. Gianni had accompanied her and was strolling the grounds, ready if she needed him. She gazed down at the three-carat rose gold cocktail ring Gianni had placed on her finger that morning. What a joy to have a husband who wanted to shower her with evidence of his love. A smile tugged at her lips, despite the tense situation—and that, no doubt, was exactly what her husband had wished for.

She sat and placed her handbag on the adjacent seat.

"I'm glad you contacted me, Kareen."

She nodded.

"The weird thing is that when I came here the last time, over twenty-five years ago, at my friend Ray Dunmara's request, I didn't even know your name. But I knew immediately who you were."

"I knew your name, of course." The newspapers, television, and magazines wouldn't let her forget.

"But you didn't *then*, did you?"

"No." She understood implicitly what he meant by *then*.

The waiter stopped at their table and took their drink orders.

When the server departed, Kareen straightened stiffly in her chair and placed her hands on the tabletop. "I hated you for a long time. Years. Decades."

"I'm sorry. I truly am."

She raised her flexed fingers, her ring flashing sparkling light. "When I read a piece about your sister, and her rise to fame, and about how the two of you had been raised on a farm in Indiana, I realized you weren't the monster I thought you might be."

He shook his head slowly. "That night was my first time at any of those parties. I was just a small-town boy lost in Los Angeles, and I'd just landed a bit part in a movie."

Kareen nodded. "I wondered that, after reading some of Mimi's interviews."

"When I saw you at your anniversary party, I didn't mean to upset you. I mean, I had no idea who you were. But when I saw your son, and when you unleashed your fury on me, I got a clue."

Kareen pressed her eyes closed, recalling that horrible night. She'd finally had to confront the truth. She locked gazes with Wayne, a now-famous man who she really didn't know other than in the biblical sense. "I was a student at Bryn Mawr, engaged to Hampy, when my roommate suggested I come home with her to California. 'We'll have a blast with my Topanga Canyon chums,' she'd said." Kareen huffed a laugh. "Nowadays, the kids call that kind of gal a frenemy."

The waiter returned and slid their glasses onto the table.

"I remember the woman who brought you—she ended up being a bigtime party girl after she came back from college. Her dad was a producer in Hollywood."

"Right." Kareen's jaw spasmed. "She brought me to that party knowing there would be all kinds of things going on—drugs and all that—figuring her conservative, naïve roommate needed educating."

"And my buddy brought me"—Wayne patted his chest—"the hayseed from Indiana, to let me experience more of the so-called glamourous lifestyle out there."

She raised her glass. "To people who have overcome the results of what others have inflicted upon them."

"Amen." Wayne touched his glass of iced tea to hers. "At least we didn't end up like some of those a few years after us."

Shivering, Kareen recalled the shock and horror she'd had at reading of the Manson murders only a couple of years after her visit to Topanga Canyon. "Can you imagine?"

"Thank God we weren't there."

"Yes, thank the Lord." She took a sip. "Are you a believer?"

"I am." Wayne's Adam's apple bobbed. "And believe me, I didn't deliberately do what I did that night. I ate a brownie or two and had a couple of cups of punch. Then I woke up in the morning… and you and I were there." His suntanned cheeks turned pink.

She stared hard at him. "That's exactly what happened with me. Except that a few weeks later I realized something was wrong."

"I'm so sorry."

"I dropped out of college, horrifying my parents, and eloped with Hampy. And just under eight months later we had Hamp, Junior. Then I spent another twenty-eight years trying to convince myself that my son was also my husband's."

Wayne took a long drink.

A ferry horn sounded in the distance, and he flinched. "Do you ever get used to that sound?"

She laughed. "Only took me a decade."

"It's beautiful here. I'm glad Hamp got to live here and not. . ."

"Not in California?"

"No. But if I'd known about him, I like to think I'd have helped. Although after our encounter at the Dunmaras', it was crystal clear you didn't want me butting in."

"I've told him. Today." Kareen wrapped her hand around the cold wet glass. Hamp had said nothing. He'd just walked away from her.

"My wife has known for a long time. Since we didn't have children, she'd wanted me to reach out to him. But I'd told her it wasn't my call. That was yours."

"I don't regret that I have him." Kareen couldn't believe she'd uttered those words, but they were true.

"No? I'm glad."

"We made a beautiful son, through no design of our own, but God has blessed me, and him. I pray you can have some kind of relationship with Hamp."

"I'd like that."

The waiter returned to the table. "Excuse me, but there is a gentleman who wishes to be seated with you. Will you allow him?"

Kareen turned to see Hamp striding toward them with steely determination. As he neared the table, he slowed, a look of indecision wobbling over his features.

Wayne rose. "It's all right. That's my son."

The server moved away, and Hamp stepped forward. He extended his hand. Then Wayne pulled her boy into a hug.

Tears filled Kareen's eyes. She slipped away from the table. Time to let father meet son.

Chapter Twenty-Six

July 22nd, 2022

*H*ow had Rachel, in such a short time, settled into this familiar routine with Jack? She didn't know, but this would all come to an end once she started nursing school in late August. Mr. and Mrs. Welling had insisted Rachel stay at their house until the realtor's ads were removed, and her mother received her cease-and-desist order. At least she'd not run into Mom, after that near call, and now she and her boyfriend were back in Chicago.

Jack tapped her shoulder as he went into the kitchen. "I really enjoyed the medical center auction last night."

"I did, too." Except for all the people who kept asking when they'd started dating—which they hadn't. "You gave some exceptionally clever responses to people about our impending triplets."

"I got some good medical advice about that, too." He chuckled as he poured himself a glass of tea. "You want a glass?"

"Sure. Thanks."

She followed Jack into the living area. She set her iced tea down on a coaster on the coffee table. Jack ambled toward the new built-in unit they'd assembled the previous day. "Our team sure did a great job installing this thing. My dad's gonna love it, although I don't know what we'll do if Maria decides to kick us out."

"She won't kick you out." Rachel scowled at him. "The Parkers have their own drama going on. They've invested their money into hotels in Europe, with their son, and into the resort here on the island."

"Even though they say they won't try to make us leave and take legal action to sell the place, we won't really know that until the dust settles."

"True. But I'm trusting in God."

"I spent most of the last church service praying about this mess instead of listening to the pastor."

"I'm sure he'll forgive you."

"The pastor or God."

She laughed. "I guess both."

He pushed a lever on the cabinet's front to reveal the new flat screen TV. "Want to watch the news before we have dinner?"

"Maybe so." Rachel flipped her hair over her shoulder. "At the coffee shop, we're hearing about inflation, the gas prices on the mainland—which doesn't affect me here on the island thank God. But also, electricity prices."

Jack grabbed the slim remote and touched some buttons. He changed the channel to one with a news anchor in a sport coat. The broadcaster looked even more serious than usual. Jack sat on the couch.

Rachel moved a pillow at the end, placed it between her and him, and sat as far from Jack as she could. It would be dangerous to sit too close.

"A recap of the week's news, fires across the United States as well as Europe, dangerous heat waves around the world breaking records, Europe joins the US in a head toward a recession, Ukraine's First Lady visits with the president and pleads with Congress for more military aid, Covid cases ramping up as President Biden tests positive."

Her pastor in Chicago might be right—these could be the End Times. She cast a glance at Jack, who was wrinkling his nose. She rose and took the remote from him and turned the TV off.

She huffed a sigh and returned the remote to its spot on the cabinet.

"So much for that." Jack laced his fingers, inverted his hands, and cracked his knuckles.

"As much as I hate you doing that—I hate the news even more."

He raised his eyebrows. "At least the local news, per my phone feed, wasn't as dire."

"Whitecaps in the Straits and vehicles slowed to twenty miles per hour on the bridge? Is that what you mean?"

"And temps hitting eighty on the mainland." He laughed. "Big news."

She made a face of mock dismay. "Thank God for those stiff breezes off the Straits."

"Yup."

Lilac Cottage 225

"I bet they won't put in the Town Crier about us being granted a Cease-and-Desist Order against Mom."

"Probably not. Not the kind of thing you'd see in there."

"But we got it, thank God." The judge issued the order immediately after seeing their paperwork.

"I'm so glad my uncle was here and could help us."

"Pretty handy to have an attorney for an uncle."

"Yup. But Marques has no idea how to prepare fresh fish from the Straits." Jack waggled an eyebrow at her.

"You grilling fish tonight like you promised?" She loved his fish.

"Packet cooking—not right on the grill."

"Same thing."

"It's not. Grilling would be directly on the grill. This is in foil."

He had to argue about everything. If he ever got married, how would his wife stand it? "No propane, though? Right?"

"I've got charcoal." He grinned that slow crooked smile that made her catch her breath.

"And lighter fluid and matches, I presume."

"Yup. Got whitefish filets from St. Ignace and some awesome smoked trout dip and crackers. And Carter left us a salad earlier, from Maria."

"That's a feast." But that meant she'd have to spend even more time with Jack as he prepared the coals, cooked the meal, and then they ate. But now that the order had been received by her mother, those ads should be pulled from the newspapers. Which meant Rachel could return to Lilac Cottage, her home now.

"Hey, you want me to check out those noises in your basement after we eat?"

"Yes, thanks. Probably squirrels." Metallic sounding squirrels. Every time she went over there, particularly at night, she heard at least one creepy sound from below stairs.

"Squirrels would be in the attic. Maybe some rats in the basement."

"Ewwww. Don't say that."

He shrugged. "Could be true."

He started the charcoal grill. She chopped the veggies in the kitchen, which was still a construction zone. Then he returned and began to assemble the fish packets.

"It's amazing to me that even with this kitchen torn up, you know where everything is." She was impressed.

"Spices are different all over the world. I got to try a bunch of different things in my travels. I definitely always know where my spices are." He tossed a cherry tomato in the air and caught it in his mouth.

She shook her head. He was going to choke on one of those and she'd have to do the Heimlich maneuver. "Do you think you'll miss the whole merchant mariner thingy?"

"No," he said without hesitation.

She passed him the veggies. "Can you see yourself working at the boatbuilders' school in Hessel?"

"Yeah. Yup." He grinned. "But first they'd have to hire me."

"They will. Why wouldn't they with your credentials?"

"I don't know." He added onion, peppers, and the tomatoes to the packets. "I've never taught, for one thing."

"You're really good with the guys. They respect you."

"Are you angling for a raise?" He dipped his chin.

"No. It's the truth."

"Thanks.

Jack shook salt and pepper over the fish filets. He sealed off the aluminum foil and placed the packets on a large stoneware plate. "Do ya mind tossing Maria's salad again? It's in the fridge."

"No problem."

Jack took the packets to the grill and returned in a few minutes. "Tonight I'll even share a couple of the peanut butter Long Johns that Lorinda sent over on the boat today."

"You get those delivered to you?"

"A buddy works on the docks and rents in Mackinaw City. He buys them for me."

She wagged a finger at him. "You've been holding out on me, Jack Welling."

"Do you think if I kept those out in plain sight that all those boys would leave them alone? They're teenagers—not a chance." He curled his lower lip in, looking adorably like a young boy himself.

"You're right." She gave the salad one more good toss.

"Wanta sit outside?

"Of course."

They sat at the picnic table and ate their salads drenched in ranch dressing.

"When I get a place on the mainland, I'll get a gas grill."

"Place on the mainland?"

He ran his hand down the side of his face. "For a lot of reasons, I have to get something. For one, if I get hired then I'll need a little place to stay in Hessel."

"Right. And with that whole thing about descendants of Robert, Jr., having a right to the property."

"Yup. There's that."

"I'll be staying on the mainland, too, once I start the fall semester at college."

His hazel eyes darkened. "I prayed hard for ya to get in."

She blinked back tears at his confession. "I appreciate that."

"I could use some prayers, too."

She pointed both index fingers at him. "You got 'em!"

"It took being dumped, being ripped off, being stuck in port during the pandemic, and giving up my job sailing to finally convince me of my need for God." He tugged at his short's waist. "But it was worth it to get right with Him."

She speared a piece of cucumber. "It took some truly outrageous behavior from my mom to wake me up and get me back on the path. And some truly wonderful people that God placed there. I've really been blessed."

"Am I one of those blessings?" He took a bite of salad.

She set her fork down. "Yes, I think you are." She touched his bare arm, her fingers tingling.

"Good. I think you're a blessing to me, too."

"Super." Something inside her warmed, and her heart beat stronger.

Jack jumped up. "Better get those off the grill." He jogged over and slid the packets onto the platter, then brought them to the table.

Soon they both sampled the fish.

"Yum. This is why I love your fish. It's soooo good." Rachel took another bite.

Was he blushing? His cheeks were pink beneath his light tan. "I aim to please, ma'am," he drawled.

She shook her head. "I think that's the voice you used when you were the cowboy in the little plays that Olivia and I performed."

He pretended to blow smoke from the end of his upturned index fingers. "Yes, ma'am."

Jack often made her smile. But he also aggravated her—although that was getting less common.

They finished their fish, with the sounds of wind and waves carrying up from the Straits.

"I'll get some iced tea to go with the pastries." Jack rose and went to the house.

"Thanks."

He returned. "It's like getting a three-course meal."

"I think you're right. This is really nice." She could get used to this—but she'd better not.

"Are you ready for your studies to start?" He sounded concerned.

"I am so thrilled. But I am a little nervous. I'll be so much older than the other students." But her ancestor, Sadie, had started later, too, and she'd had a long career.

They talked about what movies they hoped to see once they were on the mainland and the places they wanted to go. Almost seemed like Jack was feeling out whether they could do some activities together.

Rachel nibbled on the last of her flaky Long John, savoring the peanut butter cream filling and frosting.

"Ya missed some." Jack took his thumb and swiped something off her cheek, the act feeling rather intimate. Like something a boyfriend would do, if she ever had one. "Got it."

"Thanks." She placed her hand on her face, still feeling the warmth of his touch.

"Here. Let me carry our dirty plates in." Jack stood and took hers as well as his into the house.

When Jack returned, clapped his hands. "Come on. Let's go find that noisemaker in your cottage."

The two of them walked through the hedge and over onto Gram's property. No matter that she now owned it, the cottage would always be Gram's in her mind. But it could still be her home.

Jack went ahead of her inside.

The bird bath was empty, and she quickly filled the basin before entering the cottage. Jack stood there, hands on hips, frowning.

The strange noises carried from the basement. "See!" she shouted triumphantly. "I told you so."

"That sounds more metallic than anything. Like something grinding on a ship."

"Or whirring."

"Like something working too hard." Jack waved toward the door. "Ya got a dehumidifier down there? Those things have to be cleaned out periodically, ya know?"

"I don't think so. Gram didn't allow anyone to go down there. Nor did my grandfather."

"You got the key?" Jack leaned in as the groaning sound resumed.

She pulled her circlet of keys from the wall where she'd hung them. "I know I'm a sissy, but it never occurred to me there might be a dehumidifier running. That part makes sense—but then why all the warnings to stay out of the basement?"

"Maybe something unsafe down there?"

"Right. Maybe the basement stairs are like some I've seen where they would be seriously out of code if someone built them today."

"Like we're dealing with next door."

"Right." She unlocked the door and a light flickered on, apparently automatically. It was bright enough that she had to blink.

"These stairs are later twentieth century." Jack pointed to the heavy wood treads that were wide and deep. "Not like the ones I've got."

"Yeah, yours were doozies. And a pain to get replaced."

Jack moved ahead of her, and another set of lights flashed across the stairs. "What the heck?"

"Probably for safety. Those automatic lights can be helpful."

"No. I mean all this." He waved forward.

Rachel descended a few more steps. "What in the world?"

The room was like a fortress with thick cement walls, and rifles and other guns hanging from racks. Older-looking communications equipment hugged one wall. There was another room within the basement, the door closed. Rachel strode toward it and another light glowed. She tried to open the door, but it was locked.

"This is like a *safe* room." Jack frowned. "Didn't your grandparents ever have you practice coming down here?"

"No! Like I said, they wouldn't allow me near the basement."

A whirring sound came from the right and they both turned. What looked like a video camera emitted a mechanical groan as it tried to swivel on its mount.

A chipmunk raced past them.

Rachel shrieked as she launched herself into Jack's arms.

Jack held Rachel close. "Listen, your grandfather was a federal judge. He had some pretty heavy cases according to my dad."

Rachel stepped back from him, fear lingering in her expression.

Behind him came another whirring sound. Definitely not a chipmunk and not the surveillance camera.

Rachel pointed. "What's that?"

Doors creaked open on a heavy gray metal case. Jack flinched at the case's grating noise and jerky movements. Rachel grabbed his arm and squeezed hard. *What was that thing gonna do?*

Inside was an old bag phone, a green landline phone like his grandparents had owned, a walkie talkie, and a primitive flip phone.

"Ack! I wondered if that thing was going to fire something at us." Rachel released his arm.

"Me, too." He ran his knuckles across his jaw.

"I wonder what those do?" She pointed to several switches on the wall.

One toggle was white, another red, and the third was black. Rachel flipped the red one before he could stop her.

"Hey, don't touch any more of those," Jack called out as a grinding sound at the top of the stairs commenced.

Rachel raced up the stairs as a metal panel slid in front of the door. "No!"

Jack hurried to the wall and flipped the toggle down. *Nothing.*

By the time Rachel reached the top of the stairs the panel was nearly closed. Would they be locked in?

Rachel shoved her cell phone sideways in between the panel and the doorjamb.

It sounded like an ice machine spitting out cubes as Rachel's phone met its crushing death.

Jack stared at the toggle. "This must be a latch switch, meaning that once it was engaged then it could not be reversed."

"What are we going to do?" Rachel remained staring at her phone which kept the door only about a half inch open.

"I'm afraid to touch any more of those buttons but we probably have to." He shouldn't have said *afraid*, he should have reassured her. "We'll figure it out." That sounded more confidant.

"Gramps or Gram should have told me about this."

"Did they ever say anything about going down to the basement if anything happened?"

"No, like I told you, but. . ." Rachel turned around and descended the stairs. "I swear I saw the yard guy coming down here, now that I think about it. But my grandfather told me I must have imagined it. I was a little girl then."

"The yard guy? My aunt's husband worked for your grandfather after he got out of the Marines after Afghanistan."

"Andrette's husband? I thought Marques was a lawyer."

"He is a lawyer, but he and your grandfather were part of that old Marine '*Oorah!*' bunch. My dad, too."

"Your dad?"

Jack's phone rang. "Speak of the devil."

He took the call. "Hi Dad, I'm glad you called."

"Oh? What's goin' on?" Dad's voice sounded strained.

Jack didn't want to worry him too much, but they had to get out of here. "We're down here in the Dunmaras' basement, but it looks more like Fort Knox."

"Oh yeah?" Dad's voice cracked. *Something definitely going on.*

"We're kind of stuck down here. I may be an engineer, but this stuff isn't exactly ship-grade material. Ya know anything about this?"

There was a long pause.

"Dad?"

"I'm here." It sounded like he was scrambling around in the drawer for something. Metal jangled on metal.

"Who's there with you?"

"Me and Rachel. We're both here, stuck in this crazy safe room or safe basement or whatever this is. I could start messing with the toggles, but I don't know what will happen next."

"Don't touch anything!" Dad barked.

"All right." Jack ran a finger under his neckline. "Ya know about this place, then?"

Images flashed through his mind. Dad asking Sis if she'd heard from Rachel. Mom sharing about the letters from Rachel's grandmother. Dad re-reading Margaret Dunmara's letters, later, a far-off look in his eyes. Was he taking his Marine buddy thing a step too far?

"Roger that."

Whoa, Dad was slipping into military lingo.

"What are you going to do, Dad?"

"Call the team. Get you two out."

Team? "Who? How?"

"Don't worry about that. Sit tight."

"Sounds like we don't have a choice." He rolled his shoulders, releasing the tension gathering there.

"Just don't touch *anything* in there." He sounded just like he did after going to a Marine reunion. Jack half expected him to shout 'Semper Fi!' but instead, Dad just ended the call.

Jack tucked his phone away.

Rachel stared at him with wide eyes. "I could hear some of the conversation. Wow."

Jack ran his fingers over his evening scruff. "My dad is somehow involved with all of this." He pointed around the room.

"Sounded like he knew about this place." She frowned.

"He's coming to get us out."

"He couldn't just tell you how to do some kind of override?" Rachel flipped her hands over.

"Apparently not."

"At least we've got your cell phone. Mine is crushed." She closed her eyes hard, for a moment.

"You can afford a new one."

"Right, but I'm worried about my mother suing me."

"Lyonis said she doesn't have a leg to stand on."

They sat there in silence, the cool musty air enveloping them.

Jack's phone rang. "Dad?"

"On the move. Put me on speaker."

Jack put his phone on speaker. "Go ahead."

"Listen, I did retire this year, but not from the schools—although I worked for them some. Mostly as cover, though."

"Cover?" Rachel asked.

"Hi Rachel. Your grandfather helped me get a federal government job after I got out of the Marines. I was assigned on detail for him off and on over the years."

"On detail? You mean you protected him?" Jack processed his father's words.

"Part of the time. The rest you don't need to know."

Jack exchanged a look with Rachel. "So, you weren't an online teacher for the schools?"

"Some of the time. Kind of liked it, too." A car horn blasted in the background. "Darned semis, they think they own the interstate."

"Yeah, well they do, so be careful." Was he really telling Dad, a retired federal agent, to be careful?

"It worked out great for me to be on assignment at the Straits with the judge next door. And when I couldn't be there, I asked Marques to step in. He was with the agency after he got out of the Marines. I introduced him to your Aunt Andi. But he's a bona fide attorney now. I've called him and left a message to see if he could help and another for a different agent."

"Thanks." He angled his body toward Rachel.

"I. . ." There was a pause filled with muffled traffic sounds. "Rachel, I wish I had been there the day your grandfather was killed. I've blamed myself. But Olivia was so ill at that time—"

"Oh, Mr. Welling, I just found out how he died. You can't blame yourself for what that criminal did."

"It's hard not to. I loved that guy. The judge was a father-figure to me. A great man."

Rachel swiped a tear from her eye.

Jack forced himself to breathe. His 'safe in the boring suburbs' life had been an illusion. And his sister's death hadn't been the only thing that had rocked his father's life.

"Mr. Welling, do you know anything about a guy staying at the yacht club? An agent?"

"I called in a favor when I heard your grandfather's killer was released. Supposedly too frail and ill to cause anyone harm, but it doesn't take a lot of energy to pull a trigger."

Rachel shivered.

Jack took her hand.

"I better sign off. Lots of traffic."

"See ya, Dad."

"Bye."

Rachel squeezed his hand. "So, your suspicions about your dad not working at that school were right."

"Looks that way."

"Thanks for not yelling at me about pulling the red switch. I can't believe I did that." Rachel tugged her hand free. "Just an impulse decision and now look at us."

"We can play games on my phone until my dad gets here." He laughed. Rachel was not a game player, in more ways than one.

"I've been thinking about Olivia more, since I've been staying with you. I really miss her."

"I spent the first month up here just kinda soaking in the fact that my sister wasn't ever going to be there anymore."

"I'm so sorry. I wish I had known."

Jack shook his head. "That was Olivia and my mom wanting to keep up a front of all being well when she got sick. And now knowing this about my dad—I guess he and Mom have that in common about keeping up an image."

"Do you think she knows what he really did for a job?"

"I don't think so." He raised his eyebrows. "But maybe."

"You're not some kind of secret agent, are you, Jack?" Rachel swatted at his shoulder.

"Nope. Just an unemployed engineer hoping for a new career start. Still waiting on the boat building school in Hessel to call me."

"I think you could use a hug." Rachel opened her arms.

He embraced her, inhaling the strawberry scent of her hair. "Thought I told ya that fruity shampoo attracts mosquitoes."

"Will you forever be trying to micromanage me?"

He didn't release her. She smelled so good. *Shoulda kept my trap shut.* She felt perfect in his arms. *Right.* She belonged there.

Rachel shivered and he pulled her closer. If she tipped her head back, he could kiss her.

Someone pounded on the panel door. "Rachel? Jack?"

"We're here!" Rachel screamed. Was that the sexy grin yacht guy?

"Agent Shane White here. I'm gonna get you out."

"Thanks, man!" Jack called out.

"First, I need you to keep back from the panel."

"Okay."

"Keep far away from both this panel door and the switch case. Turn your backs to both in case any debris goes flying."

Jack wrapped an arm around Rachel's shoulder and turned her around.

"I'm going to try to remotely disengage the mechanism, but if I can't then I'll need to take this panel down."

"Is there any other way out of here?"

Jack texted something.

"Not that I know of. I'm following directives from Welling."

They waited. A grinding sound came from the switches.

Jack patted his pockets, then pulled out a Swiss Army knife. "Agent White, nothing happenin' down here except a bunch of noise."

Jack's phone pinged. He read the message, "My uncle is on his way and says to look for a vent."

"A vent?" Rachel frowned.

"I've got another idea, though."

"What?"

Jack jogged up the steps. "Agent White, I want ya to shut down the electricity to this place and I'm gonna take apart that switch panel. See if I can release the toggle manually."

"I think this is set up electronically."

"I'm a merchant marine engineer and I might be able to figure out a work-around." Jack turned to her. "Where's the electric box, Rachel?

She explained where it was and he relayed that to Shane.

Jack went to the wall and eyed the switch panel. "I need you to hold my phone, with the flashlight on."

"Wouldn't this be better?" She pointed to two flashlights on the table.

"Do the batteries work?"

She tried them and one lit. "That's surprising."

Footfall sounded overhead. Was that the back door opening and closing, too?

"Jack, this is Uncle Marques."

Jack cupped his hands around his mouth. "Former-agent Marques?"

"Something like that. Hey, the panel is bullet-proof and takes a special drill that your old man forgot to leave here with Carolyn." Marques's voice sounded tinny through the door.

Had she heard him right? "Carolyn May?" Rachel crinkled her nose. What in the world did the owner of Lucky Bean have to do with this?

Lilac Cottage   235

"One and the same. She has storage, plus the advantage of being located across from the police, if we have to call them in."

Maybe that was why she always wore those dark sunglasses.

The lights went out. More footfall. Conversation that they couldn't hear.

"Power is off." Agent White called out. "Agent Welling okayed a dismantle of the switches."

"Go ahead, Jack," Marques called down.

Rachel held the flashlight aloft while Jack carefully unscrewed the panel covering the toggles.

He removed the metal cover and set it aside. "Shine the light on that switch ya flipped."

She complied. Rachel held her breath. If this couldn't electronically be disengaged, by remote, then what did they do?

"Pray that I don't get electrocuted if there's any residual electricity in this panel."

"Electrocuted? Jack! Don't do it then!"

He hesitated. "Do ya realize how many people tried to keep your grandpa safe and that still didn't work?"

"I do now."

"This basement safe room has only served to trap us in."

"That's my fault. I'm sorry. I'd never forgive myself if you—"

Jack completed two swift movements. "That should do it and I'm *not* fried."

Anger mingled with relief. Cold sweat made her bangs stick to her forehead.

"Switch the electric back on!" Jack yelled toward the stairs.

Footfall sounded overhead.

The lights came on, accompanied by a slowing grating metal sound as the panel door slid back. Rachel's phone tumbled to the bottom of the stairs. It was clearly toast.

Marques and Agent White stared down at them.

"Hurry up in case that thing changes its mind and closes again," Rachel called over her shoulder as she rushed upstairs.

"That's not how it works, Rach." Jack's deadpanned words were followed by a chuckle.

The men moved aside as she reached the top. "It wasn't mice," she told them.

"Mice?" Shane frowned.

"No mice, but there may have been a squirrel down there." Jack mussed Rachel's hair, then pulled her in for a side hug.

"Hey!" she protested, but the men laughed.

Chapter Twenty-Seven

August, 2022

*S*un streamed down on Rachel's bare shoulders. Overhead, puffy cumulous clouds billowed in the azure sky. She'd taken the morning off to do some shopping in town, and Jack had given her a ride in his carriage.

He pulled over near Lucky Bean. "I accepted that offer to teach at the boat building school."

"That's great, Jack. That's what you wanted."

"Yeah." He pressed two fingers alongside his mouth.

"And I start classes in a week." She tapped on her cellphone and located the email.

"Congrats, pipsqueak."

"Really?" She made a face of disgust.

"I wish my sister was here for me to call pipsqueak."

"Aw, Jack, I'm sorry." She touched her head to his.

"I'm gonna miss you."

"I'll miss you, too."

Jack cocked his head. "The Soo isn't that far."

What was he saying? "That's true."

A couple pushing a baby carriage crossed by on the street. Would she ever be married? Have a family?

"You can come visit me, Jack."

"I'd like that."

Her face heated. They were going somewhere she wasn't sure they should be heading. Or *should they* be?

"I gotta get back to the house. I'm down a man today." He flicked her nose. "Or down a woman today."

She waved him away. "You are truly annoying."

"That's why you l—"

"Why I what?" Was he going to say love?

"Why you like me."

"Nope. It's because you're tall." An undisputed and easy fact.

"See?" He leaned in again. "You do like me."

"I'm going shopping." She got out of the carriage.

"Buy me some fudge." He cackled, just like he used to do as an annoying pre-teen, as the carriage pulled away.

"Mommy, I wants cholikts fudge," a little blond boy told his mother. He was adorable. Rachel would have bought that little cutie anything he wanted.

Conviction slammed into her so hard her breath caught. Unadulterated spoiling and buying whatever their daughter wanted. That's what had happened with Gram and Gramps. And look how Mom had turned out! With her father working all the time as a judge, they'd tried to make up for it by overspending on her.

Rachel bent her head.

A niggling in her heart made her pray, *I forgive you, Mom.* But it didn't mean she had to be caught up in her mother's toxic behavior. She opened her eyes as a carriage full of tourists rolled past. Forgiveness wasn't for the person you forgave. It was for yourself. To let it go. To get right with God.

What about the murderer? Whoa, where had that thought come from?

That head of steam she'd built up lately had been caused by the stress over that criminal. She'd have to work on that. But with God's help, forgiveness would come.

Drays and carriages rolled past as she headed toward Little Luxuries. As usual, there were bike riders who probably should have been on foot coming far too close to the horses.

As she neared the carriage tour rides, she had to scrunch against the adjacent building while passing those waiting to board the trams pulled by horses. Once she got past, the walkway cleared and she moved faster.

She had the oddest sense that someone was watching her.

Suddenly, from the other side of the street, a white-haired man in shabby clothing lurched into the roadway as a carriage moved forward at the same time. The man fell and the front right horse half-reared, but harnessed to its teammate, couldn't avoid the man as it came down. The driver halted the carriage.

"Oh my gosh," someone cried out.

A woman screamed.

Blood seeped through the man's tan t-shirt.

Rachel didn't hesitate. She wasn't a fully trained nurse yet, but she could help. "Any doctors here? Someone call 911!" she shouted as she ran toward the man. People nearby took out their phones. *Dear God, don't let them be videoing this—let them be calling for help!*

The man's full white beard was soaked in blood. His hand was split in two. She thought she saw something beneath it. Dull metal. He tried to lift his head but groaned. His eyes bulged as he glared at her. The extent of his injuries made her nearly vomit. "Sir, someone should be here soon." She bent and touched his shoulder, and he closed his eyes. *Dear God, Thy will be done in this situation. Bring comfort.*

The island doctor, a man she'd seen once for an ear infection the previous summer, ran from the opposite sidewalk and toward the injured person. Rachel turned away as another woman, attired in a polo shirt and pink capris moved in.

This was what she wanted to do. Rachel wanted to help people.

"I'm an ER nurse, can I help?" She bent and took Rachel's place.

She was filled with respect and compassion for the providers who were now easing this injured man's last moments.

"Sir, can you hear me?" The nurse asked.

There was no response.

People were merging toward the main street to gawk.

The two medical professionals exchanged a knowing look. The doctor took the fallen man's pulse and shook his head. "He's gone."

Police officers ran toward them.

I couldn't help this man, but there will be others.

She crossed the street and watched for a few minutes then headed toward Market Street.

Linda Sorensen jogged toward her. "Come on, Rachel, let's get you over to the station."

Rachel followed her to the police station.

Once inside, a young sandy-haired male officer hurried down the hall toward them. "Is this Rachel Dunmara?"

"Yup." Linda nodded.

"Weren't you helping at the scene?"

"Yes. I tried to help that poor man."

"That *poor man* had a loaded pistol in his hand when he died."

She stiffened. "What? I saw something metal in his hand, but—"

"What info do you have?" Linda asked.

"Miss Dunmara was right across the street from the guy. Apparently, he saw her and tried to cross."

"To kill her?" Linda's light eyes widened.

"That's what you usually do with a gun." The officer sounded like Jack.

Rachel needed to let Jack know she was okay. "Oh my gosh." Her grandfather's murderer could have killed her. Rachel's hands shook.

"Sit down over here and let me get you some tea." Linda put a reassuring hand on Rachel's back.

She texted Jack. *m okay m at police station*

Tears filled her eyes. Here, Jack had her back. But when she started her studies—what then?

Jack's phone rang. He pulled the rig over and took the call from Dad.

"Son, I'm with Marques. We messed up bigtime."

"That crazy old coot got to the island," Uncle Marques cut in.

His horses stomped. "Wait, what?"

A text from Rachel showed on his phone. "Why is Rachel with the cops?"

Uncle Marques uttered some profanities.

"We heard her grandfather's killer made it to the island."

"Tried to get to Rachel." Marques spat out his words.

Dear God, what would I do without Rachel? Moisture bedeviled Jack's eyes. "She'd texted that she was ok."

"We're on the mainland. We'd had a tip about him but must have missed him in passing."

"He'd been at a city pier taking pictures of West Bluff and a tourist reported him because he seemed suspicious." Marques barked a laugh. "So we got over there but in the meantime he took a ferry to the island."

"I can't believe this happened again. I let the judge down, God rest his soul."

Jack eyed the road, looking for his turnaround spot. "I'm going down to Rachel. Call me later." He ended the call. He directed the horses to move the carriage forward.

He returned to town. Tourists, drays, and the street cleaner slowed his progress. He'd never have imagined rushing to Rachel's rescue when he was a teenager.

That's a lie.

The conviction hit him hard. He'd tried to rescue the girl from the beginning. Rescue her from a mother who'd never shown up on this island again until recently.

But Rachel was a woman now, capable of taking care of herself.

I rescued you. That still small voice once again touched his heart.

Thank You, Lord, for throwing out that life raft to me.

God's people needed one another. The ultimate rescuer was God. But He'd put them on this planet to be in relationship. To help and comfort one another. He could do that for Rachel.

He passed Lucky Bean and Juan, standing outside, waved at him. Jack dipped his chin.

Slowing for a family crossing the street, Jack parked his carriage and then hurried inside.

Rachel, pale and eyes wide rose from her chair. He opened his arms and she stepped into them. He held her close, patting her silky hair.

"You're gonna be all right."

He didn't want to lose her. Didn't want her to leave.

"Jack?"

"Hmm?" He didn't release her.

"The Soo is only an hour from Hessel."

"I know."

She pulled away. "You do?"

"I've already got our visitation spots worked out."

She turned her head to the side, looking skeptical. "Visitation?"

"Yeah. I'm sure ya want to see Goldie at least twice a month."

She blushed, eliminating the pallor that had been there. "I certainly do."

"Great." He grinned.

"But you're right about something else."

"Yeah? I like being right."

"I know you do." She turned and picked up her purse from the chair. "I think you're right about the 'at least' part. Goldie would want to see me weekly, I'm sure."

"That makes you right, too." He closed one eye hard and stared with the other.

She pulled her purse strap onto her shoulder. "It will be nice seeing you, too, when I visit with Goldie."

"Of course." Jack lifted his chin. "I've already got a few places picked out that are both people and dog-friendly."

She rolled her lips together as if she was holding back a laugh.

"I bet Olivia would be glad that Goldie gets to see you still."

"I bet she is. I know I am." Rachel pointed to the door. "Can you take me to see her now? I could use a nice cuddle with her."

Jack could use a nice cuddle, too.

But with Rachel.

Dawn Charbonneau put the finishing touches on Rachel's upswept hairdo. "Looks perfect, sweety."

"Would have been better with some pink spray and fairy glitter in it," Starr groused.

Dawn playfully air-slapped at Starr. "That's more your style."

"Yup." Starr patted her turquoise, pink, and purple spiky hair.

"Don't forget these." Dawn's daughter, Jaycie, handed Rachel a pair of long glittering crystal earrings. Jaycie and her husband, Parker, had returned home for a visit after she'd suffered a miscarriage. Rachel donned the earrings.

"And this cuff bracelet." Dawn retrieved it from the bed and placed it on Rachel's wrist. "You'll be the most beautiful gal there, tonight."

Jaycie and Parker weren't attending and her parents, Dawn and Jim, weren't either, in support of their daughter.

"Rachel, did you know that Jack is named after my grandfather and great-grandfather?" Jaycie slacked her hip."

Dawn's blue eyes lit up. "My father and grandfather—the original Jack Wellings, were wonderful men."

"But my Grandpa Jack Welling, Jr., didn't have any sons. So Jack got to steal the name." Jaycie's lips formed a perfect pout.

"Hey, the whole family was good with that, and we were honored when my uncle named his son after our illustrious Jack Wellings."

"We had our Olympic gold medal winner and Word War One aviator hero, Jack Welling, Sr., and our Word War Two Silver Star recipient, Jack Welling, Jr., —both Mackinac Island boys." Jaycie raised her hand, as if to make a point.

Dawn wiped a tear from her eye.

"Hey, if you and Jack have children, you could keep the name going." Jaycie looked serious.

Horrified that Dawn's daughter would even suggest such a thing, Rachel stared at her.

Then Jaycie and Dawn burst out laughing.

"He's my boss." Rachel protested.

"Not anymore. You're done working for him." Dawn raised her arms in a circle. "And you're about to start your nurse's training."

"We're just friends." She chewed her lower lip.

"Uh huh." Jaycie lifted her left hand and pointed at her wedding ring. "Parker and I were just friends, too."

Rachel wasn't touching that statement with a ten-foot pole.

"Come look at yourself." Starr pulled Rachel over to the full-length mirror.

The lilac gown was perfection and her hair had never looked so beautiful. "It's not me." Tears threatened.

"Oh, yes, my dear, it's all you!" Dawn leaned her head against Rachel's shoulder and Jaycie moved in and adjusted the neckline.

"Yuppers, that's Miss Rachel Dunmara of Mackinac Island." Starr clapped her hands. "Mayor Doud will write all about you in her upcoming newspaper column."

"Wow, you sound pretty sure about that," Jaycie's voice held humor. She'd only met Starr that day and by the strange faces she'd been making at some of Starr's comments, Jaycie wasn't quite sure what to make of the barista.

"Oh, I am certain." Starr quirked her eyebrows.

"I feel like a fairy godmother." Dawn waved her hand in the air, as if holding a wand. "Bibiddy-bobbedy-boop! Is that how it goes?"

They all laughed.

"So does that mean Jack is Rachel's Prince Charming? I recently read that Cinder'sElla story." Starr waggled her fingers.

Jayce made a face of disbelief. "You never read Cinderella before?"

Rachel, who had a pretty good idea of where Starr came from, waggled her hands back at the barrista. "You didn't grow up around here, did you, Starr? But in a galaxy far, far, away?"

Dawn shook her head. "Now you're making her sound like a Jedi or something from *Star Wars*."

"Yup, I'm something like that." Starr framed her gamin face with her hands.

"All right, enough of that—give us a spin around, Girly." Dawn made a motion for Rachel to turn as she and the others stepped back.

Slowly, Rachel rotated in a tight circle.

Starr clutched her hands to her chest and sighed. "It's so romantic."

All three women gawked at her.

The barista raised her arms up into a circle. "Tonight's the night her Prince Charming will realize she didn't just crunch numbers for him and harass subcontractors into doing their jobs."

Dawn chuckled and then Jaycie hooted as Rachel sighed.

"Starr, I'm doing Jack a favor by accompanying him to this fundraiser." Rachel flipped her hands to palms up. "This is not a romantic date."

"You keep tellin' yourself that," Dawn mumbled.

The front door opened, then slammed closed.

"Hey! You up there?" Jack hollered.

"Yeah, and there's your Prince Charming screeching like a creature from a different book genre," Rachel tapped her bare foot. "Definitely not romantic." But very Jack-like.

"Be patient!" Dawn called out, then turned toward the women. "I'm going down to rein in that big galoot." She left the room.

"You sure you're up to doing this, Rachel?" Jack yelled.

Jaycie scowled and went to the hallway. "She's not deaf and you're a little late, Jack Welling, to be asking that question!"

"It's time." Star pretended to sprinkle something on Rachel. "It's not really fairy dust, but it's the next best thing."

"What's that?" Rachel patted her hair, feeling the stiff hairspray Dawn had used on the chignon.

"Prayers."

"Thanks." She blew out a breath and grabbed her beaded satin strappy shoes.

"Really, if you don't feel up to it, after all you've been through this week, let's just stay home and make s'mores!" Jack had lowered his volume a little, but he was still loud.

"Did you just say *home*?" Jaycie's teasing tone left no doubt what she thought about Jack's proclamation. Rachel needed to get out of there before these ladies had her married off to him.

"Coming!" Rachel called out. High heels in one hand and her gown pulled out to the side, she held the banister rail with the other hand. If Gram were there, she'd have said Rachel, 'looked like a million bucks'. *Oh, Gram I mess you so much.*

As she descended the stairs, she caught a glimpse of Jack, attired in a close-fitting deep blue suit. He looked so handsome that Rachel blinked a few times.

Had his draw dropped open? Yes, it had. For once, Jack seemed speechless.

Dawn moved alongside him. She pointed up at Rachel. "Now that's what you call a bombshell."

Jack didn't move.

Dawn poked him. "Too bad she's just doing you a favor and isn't your date."

"You know, Rachel," Jaycie called from behind Rachel. "He looks pretty decent in a suit. If Jack ever does ask you out on a date, you might want to consider it."

Jack's lips twitched. Rachel could tell he was resisting the urge to sigh. Funny the things she understood about him now, after spending so much time with him this summer.

Soft footsteps sounded behind her. Starr took Rachel's arm and gently pulled her down the steps. "I'll get pictures of you in this, for Cassie Browne. She's going to feature you on her website."

Rachel swiveled to face Starr. "How do you know Cassie?"

Starr fluttered her free hand. "Well, duh, we're Insta friends. And I asked."

"Insta?" Dawn cringed. "What's that?"

"Instagram, Mom. And I didn't realize this was one of her gowns. Wow. No wonder it's so gorgeous."

"Yup, Rachel worked for her and her mom in Chicago, before Sandi Browne retired." Starr led Rachel forward.

"I don't care who made it." Jack held his hand out to Rachel. "You look spectacular."

She squeezed his fingers. "I know and everyone there is going to be jealous of you." She said that just to tweak Jack and it got the desired response. His face began to redden.

Starr pulled out her phone and snapped a picture. "Oh, you can't make faces like that tonight, Jack, because it makes you look. . ."

"Like a loon?" Rachel raised her eyebrows and peered at the image on Starr's phone.

"A loon?" He was definitely sounding more like himself, with that irritation in his voice.

She locked gazes with him. "A very handsome loon." She pushed back a lock of his hair, that had fallen forward.

"Oooh, that's a good shot. It looks like you love him."

Both Rachel and Jack swiveled to glare at Starr.

The barista shrugged. "Just sayin'. Anyway I gotta go and get ready to meet Carter and get these pictures tonight."

"You're going with Carter?"

"Yuppers. His former fiancé, Abbi-Renae, who apparently thinks she still is his girlfriend, plans to show up there tonight. So I'm gonna be there for him."

"No way. Is she really?" Rachel couldn't believe it.

"His grandmother told me she's been texting him images of possible wedding invitations. Kareen and Gianni are worried this gal is off her rocker." Dawn shook her head.

The front door swung open and Carter, attired in khakis and a polo shirt strode in. "Starr, Abbi-Renae is here."

Starr joined him. "No worries. Let's get you home and dressed and I'll change and then we'll manage this whole situation. First, though, tell Rachel how beautiful she looks." She pointed toward Rachel.

Suddenly, she felt shy.

"Wow, I should make you come down to my Senior Formal at UVA and make all the other guys there green with envy."

Rachel turned and elbowed Jack. "See? What'd I tell you?"

"Let me get Rachel out of here before her head is so swelled up that she won't fit through the front door." Jack placed a broad hand on her shoulder. "Your carriage awaits, milady."

"Is it a pumpkin with mice?" Starr opened the front door and motioned for Carter to follow.

"Not that I know of," Jack shrugged, "but I did pay a driver for tonight. It's possible he's actually a mouse in his off-hours."

"Don't encourage her in that line of thought," Rachel whispered as they stepped onto the front porch.

"All right. But it's fun." He quirked his eyebrows.

Carter dipped his chin. "We'll see you at the Grand, later."

"Can we borrow the carriage?" Starr pointed to the street. "Otherwise we might be really late."

That was a big ask. But. . . "I don't mind walking." Rachel squeezed Jack's arm. "Do you?"

"Oh, we'll drop you off first. Right now." Starr smiled beneficently.

"Mighty nice of you, Miss Bourne." Jack closed his eyes tightly, as if he was in pain. Which maybe he was, but not the physical kind. After all, he'd kept the heavy sarcasm out of his comment, which had to have hurt him.

"Thanks." Starr ran down toward the carriage.

Jack opened his eyes. "Aunt Andrette said that Starr was the most peculiar worker she's ever had."

"Wait till Andrette meets Abbi-Renae and she'll see that Starr has competition for that title." Carter pulled at his collar. "So I wonder what that says about me."

"No comment," Jack and Rachel said, in unison.

"You two." Carter shook his head then waved over his shoulder as he jogged off. "See ya!"

"I put odds that those two will leave without us at two to one." Jack inclined his head toward the carriage, as the two of them moved down the sidewalk."

"All right. What are we wagering?"

A devilish grin stole over his handsome face. "That you'll let me take you out on some non-formal events while you're at school."

"I thought we already agreed to that."

"Yeah," he stretched the word out. There was an unspoken *but* there.

"Are you talking about those meetups being," dare she say it, "dates?"

The carriage pulled away from the curb, Starr waving energetically at them, and Carter looking down at his cell phone.

Jack chuckled. "At least I won."

"But what did you win?" She poked his shoulder.

"I guess you'll just have to figure it out."

Epilogue

The Villages, Florida
November 2022

*G*randma?" Carter's trembling voice on the phone made Kareen's hand's shake.

She set her hot mint tea down on the coffee table. "Carter? What's wrong." The boy hadn't called her since he'd left for Charlottesville in August, and he'd not taken her calls. Although he'd initially been okay with learning the truth about Hampy not being his biological grandfather, he'd walled himself off from her as had Hamp. She'd had a lot of crying episodes over that loss of contact.

Gianni muted the television show they were watching.

"There's a situation here," Carter said in a low halting voice. She could barely hear him.

Oh Lord, send help. "What's going on?"

"We're not sure. We got a text."

She put the phone on speaker mode, and Gianni set his drink down. "About what?"

"A shooting on campus."

"Oh no!"

"UVA sent a message all in caps: RUN, HIDE, FIGHT."

She sucked in a breath.

Gianni covered her hand with his.

"Grandma, I love you and I'm sorry I've been a jerk about everything."

Gianni leaned in. "Carter, this is Grandpa Gianni."

"Hi, Grandpa Gianni."

"Are you someplace safe?" A furrow formed in her husband's brow.

"We took shelter in the basement at the music building. A guy had a key, and we ran here. There's a bunch of us."

"Have you heard anything more?" Kareen managed to ask and reached for a tissue.

"We heard a lot of sirens at first."

Gianni grabbed his own phone and began searching for something.

"What about now? Any noise?" *Dear Lord, stop any killers out there.*

"Nothing. And we don't see anything in our news feed to tell us what's going on."

Gianni rose and pointed to his phone. He mouthed, "Calling Charlottesville police."

"Gianni is calling someone to see what he can find out."

"Grandma, I'm scared."

She exhaled a breath. She needed to be strong.

Had he called Maria and Hamp? Oh no, they were enroute to Florida to visit Maria's daughter at her new home. "Listen, I'll be praying for you. You keep praying, too." Her faith had gotten stronger, despite her son and grandson "ghosting" her as Rachel called it. At least Parker still kept in touch, calling her weekly from Europe. They were pregnant, again, with Jaycie in the first trimester.

"What if they—"

"Don't! Don't go there, Carter. I'm going to text Rachel and have her call on her Prayer Warriors."

"That would be good. Gosh, I feel guilty about how jealous I've been that she's a real Parker and I'm not."

"You are a real Parker. Your grandpa is still your Parker grandpa, and he loved you to pieces."

Carter sniffed.

"And Rachel has become like another family member."

"Kinda like a sister-aunt."

"More sisterly age."

"Yeah."

"She and I have gotten to be pals. I've told her a lot about Hampy. And I encouraged her to let me be like a second grandmother to her. She said yes."

"Cool. So yeah, like a sis. Always wanted one." In the background, people were talking, some crying.

God be with these young people. Find the killer now! Tears pricked her eyes.

"Grandma, I'm sorry for everything I've done. Really sorry."

What had her sweet grandson done? He was the straight arrow in their misfit family. "What do you mean?"

"Like how I cut you and Gianni, Grandpa Gianni, out of my life."

Zuzu looked up, then lowered her head.

Lilac Cottage   249

"It's all right. Maybe we could fly up for Christmas." She bit her lower lip, anticipating. Could there be reconciliation? Would her grandson get out of this situation in one piece?

"Dad asked Grandpa Wayne to come. He's flying in on a private plane."

So, Hamp had forgiven Wayne—but not Kareen?

"Grandma, you should come, too."

"If your dad says it's okay," she rushed to tell him. She switched the TV to the news. "I'm looking to see if there's any info on the television." She checked all the major news channels. *Nothing.*

"Nothing showing on my phone. One of the girls here has her charger, so as long as I have service I can talk. Mom and Dad didn't pick up."

"Probably because they are driving. I'm glad you called me."

"If I get out of here alive, I want to come see you for Thanksgiving."

"Really?"

"Yeah. And I may start talking to my old girlfriend, again. She's stopped stalking me now that she has a job."

Kareen kept her grandson talking about his former girlfriend. She even got a few laughs out of him.

Gianni strolled in, talking on his phone. "Thanks Mike, I really appreciate it." He ended the call.

Carter sniffed. "Did Grandpa Gianni find out anything?"

"Hey there, Carter," he drawled. "Three killed, two shot. My source says the chatter indicates likely limited situation and the perp is being pursued by a multitude of agencies."

"What's likely limited mean?"

Gianni rocked on his heels. "Doesn't appear random. Happened after a school outing. This is a tragedy. However, my sources say the student body at large should be okay and there is a campus-wide search in case the suspect was stupid enough to hide on campus."

"So can I go back to my room?"

"No!" Gianni and Kareen both yelled.

"Son, stay where you are in lockdown. Don't make yourself a target in case this perp is still there. Be safe."

"But in all likelihood, honey, this killer isn't going to storm across campus?" Kareen asked her husband.

"Let's hope not. Less probability of it given the situation—but stay put. You got snacks?"

Carter barked a laugh. "You're asking me if I have snacks? You must not be too worried."

Gianni and Kareen exchanged a knowing glance, and she shook her head. He was going to be all right. She quickly texted Rachel a prayer request.

"On it," Rachel texted back.

"Rachel has her prayer warriors on alert for you and everyone at UVA."

"Thanks, Grandma and Grandpa Gianni. If I can get Dad and Maria to come with me for Thanksgiving, I will."

"That would be lovely. But if they don't, we're still okay."

"Good. Oh, Dad's texting me now."

"Call us anytime tonight. We'll be up."

"Love you."

"Love you, too."

"This is lookin' to be a right long and hard night, Baby Doll." Gianni sat beside her and kissed her.

They sat in their loveseat, holding hands as rain outside made pattering sounds on the windows.

Her phone pinged.

Maria n Dad say come for xmas

Kareen blinked back tears as she raised the phone so her husband could read.

"Not so long and hard a night after all," Gianni drawled, as he pulled her close.

"Are we really doing this?" Rachel placed the tiny nurse ornament, a gift from Jack, on the Lilac Cottage Christmas tree. *May this be the first of many Christmases spent here.*

Goldie looked up at her, from where she lay on a thick wool rug, then laid her head down again.

"If you mean Christmas on the island—then yes." Jack plugged the new multi-colored LED lights in and stood back.

"That looks so pretty." Rachel stepped back and admired the fresh fir tree they'd trimmed with the few ornaments they each owned. "I still can't believe my grandparents' belongings in Chicago are gone."

Jack gave her a quick hug. "Hey, it was very merciful of you to allow your mom to stay in that high-rise even after the judge ruled that she had no right to remain."

A curt laugh burst out of her. "I'd never have imagined she'd torch the place."

"Yeah, she literally burned her bridges with you, didn't she?"

"Maybe I'm not surprised."

"Has the insurance company determined if the kitchen fire was accidental or deliberate?"

Rachel shrugged. "They're still working on that."

"So, she might still be charged with arson?"

"Apparently so." The sound of the crackling fire in the fireplace suddenly seemed ominous rather than comforting. "We better keep an eye on those logs, so we don't burn *this* place down."

"It'll be fine. I'll keep watch." Jack sat on the antique settee, looking far too big to be comfortable there.

"Wasn't that fun earlier, riding over on the ferry with Kareen and Gianni Franchetti onboard, too?"

"It was until they asked us to help get their huge stash of gifts over to the carriage." He shook his head.

"There weren't too many dock porters around were there?"

"It all worked out."

"Wasn't it weird what Kareen said about Carter seeing Juan Pablo and Starr working at a pop-up coffee place on the UVA campus after the tragedy?"

"Maybe they go where their ministry takes them—like they told Carter."

"Maybe." Or was there something more to those two, like she thought?

"Kareen and Gianni sure plan to spoil people this year."

Rachel pointed to a small box under the tree. "It was super sweet that they even had a gift for me."

"I have gifts for you, too." He arched an eyebrow.

"You better, because I got you something, too." It was a silly engineering mug she hoped he'd get a kick out of, and she'd placed two tickets inside for a Lake Superior State hockey game.

"I bet my gift is better." He laughed.

"Bet it isn't." Their visits often ended up like this, with them playfully arguing over who had done what thing better.

"We should get this place fixed up like we did next door. I could help this summer."

Rachel's talk with her nursing dean had her dreaming all kinds of plans she'd shared with Jack. "That would be super."

"You better let Maria know, because her grandsons are bugging her about coming back when school lets out."

"Can you believe they're related to me?"

"Yeah. And they're good workers."

"As are all the medical professionals I've met." She chewed her lower lip.

Jack gestured for her to sit beside him. "You're really gonna open this place up, aren't you?"

Warmth, and not just from the fire, coursed through her. If someone could sense God's approval on a plan, then maybe this sensation was affirmation. "Yes. Definitely."

"That's great. I think the nurses, doctors, and other medical staff would love to take a retreat here at Lilac Cottage."

"We could clear out that safe room in the basement and create some storage and maybe a mini-auditorium for continuing education training on the retreat."

Jack shook his head. "Nah. Let them just relax. Those folks have earned it. Between the pandemic, the triple curse of RSV, flu, and another variant of Covid—they just need some good old R&R."

"Maybe you're right." She poked his arm. "Hey, I got all A's in my classes."

"Of course, you did." He winked at her. "I'm proud of you."

"Thank you." She had another year and a half of coursework to do. "The dean took me aside and encouraged me to consider medical management, rather than direct care. But that usually means another advanced degree, and I'm not so sure about that." She'd be over thirty by the time she was done.

A log shifted in the fireplace and they both startled. Goldie jumped up and then slumped at Rachel's feet.

Jack tapped his foot. "You were great with keeping track of everything last summer. When I saw that list of linens, towels and all that stuff and the vendors and cost comparisons and shipping time it reminded me of looking at a spreadsheet of ship parts. Takes a certain type of person to keep track of the details."

She patted Goldie's soft head. "When I had a heart-to-heart with the dean, I explained about all the court and legal stuff, plus all the financial things in the estate, and the donations and whatnot that I'd helped Gram manage over the years. She said I had a gift. I never thought of managing all that stuff as any kind of gift. More like a responsibility I did out of love for my grandmother." But what she wanted to do now was out of love for the Lord and to extend kindness to her fellow healthcare providers.

"Sounds like your dean is correct."

Jack's phone pinged. "Mom and Dad are getting on the ferry."

"Super." She raised her hands overhead. "This is my first Christmas on the island. I can't wait to attend the tree lighting."

"We've come up a few times. Seems a little strange to not be staying at our place, though."

"I'm so glad Maria and her family agreed to extend your family's lease. That's wonderful."

"Works for everybody for right now. Maria and Hamp have their money tied up in hotels and didn't want the responsibility of care for the place. Plus, what would happen if they did want to sell it?"

"I know it's disappointing that the asset has been taken out of your family."

He shrugged. "I know. I've had some time to process that now." A muscle in Jack's jaw jumped.

She playfully elbowed him, hoping to distract him. "On a different note, how did your students do?"

Jack stretched and placed his flannel-covered arm behind her on the settee. "They're awesome. I love those guys and gals."

"You were really good with our work crew last summer, too."

"Yeah. It's been making me want my own family sometime soon."

A frisson of something coursed down Rachel's spine. She and Jack had visited each other every other weekend during the fall semester. They'd never actually called it dating. They'd never even kissed. Yet here they were, spending Christmas together, and he was talking about wanting children. "I think you'd have to first find someone you truly love, Jack."

He dropped his arm to her shoulder and pulled her closer. "After Mei and what she did, I didn't think I could trust anyone again. I'd like to think I can always trust you, Squirt."

She swallowed hard and looked up into his searching eyes. "Yes. You—"

She didn't get to finish the thought, as Jack leaned in and pressed a firm kiss to her lips. She blinked in surprise.

Jack pressed his forehead against hers. "Pretty sure my dad would see what's going on between us, even if we don't admit it."

Rachel pulled back. "I haven't admitted to anything," she teased.

He compressed his lips. "You let me kiss you."

"Did I?" She wanted another of those.

"Yup."

Rachel leaned in and grasped the front of Jack's warm shirt. She pulled him close and kissed him like she'd imagined all these months. When she released him, a slow grin spread across his face.

Goldie looked up at them.

"I think you *like* kissing me, Rachel."

She definitely did. "Maybe. Maybe not. Maybe I'm just pretending." She pressed one finger into her cheek.

Jack stood. "I need to get the carriage ready to get my folks. While I'm gone, you can decide if you want more kisses from me in the future."

She affected a look of nonchalance, but her heart beat like crazy. "I'll make some cocoa for everyone while you're gone. Not, you, though, Goldie." She patted the dog's back.

Jack retrieved his parka from the coat rack.

When he turned around, Rachel cocked her head. "I have your answer, by the way."

Jack pulled his thermal gloves on. "And what is it?"

"You'll have to guess." She shimmied her shoulders.

"I think either you'll be the death of me, or you'll keep me on my toes."

"That's exactly right. I know you love being right, Jack."

"I do." He flexed his shoulders.

"I do, too."

He pulled his knit cap on. "I predict you'll be saying those words after graduation. But in front of a pastor."

"I don't know." She made a goofy face. "Depends on whether you will keep bringing Goldie with us on our future dates."

He arched a brow at her. "Oh yeah?"

Goldie wagged her tail and moved closer.

Jack extended his arms to Rachel.

She slipped into his embrace.

She was home. *Really home.* At Lilac Cottage.

The End

Author's Notes

The owner of Lucky Bean, Carolyn May, unlike her fictional character, actually is on-site much of the high season, running her shop—not a manager. She, like the fictional manager in this book, has been acknowledged in media for her contributions as an entrepreneurial woman. Lucky Bean is an amazing shop. If you get to the island, be sure to stop by there! Carolyn gave me permission to use the Lucky Bean name in this novel.

Linda Sorensen really is one of the founders of the Addicted to Mackinac Island Facebook group. She also has been a Mackinac Island Police Department administrator for several summers, including 2022. And she's got a beautiful soft voice, like her character in this story! I'm blessed to call her friend.

John Hubel is also a founder and administrator of the Addicted to Mackinac Island Facebook group. When this group was in its origins and I joined after my novel, *My Heart Belongs on Mackinac Island* released, we had a couple thousand members. Now as of 2023, there are over 47,000! John truly is a professional locksmith, as portrayed in this story, with a large clientele list on the island.

As in my novel, *Butterfly Cottage*, the Mackinaw City Bakery, where my characters love to get their baked goods, is a real place. Like Lucky Bean, it's addictive, welcoming, and consistently amazing! Trenary Toast is a real thing. Like Jack, I am not a fan, but tons of people love this stuff which originated in Michigan's Upper Peninsula. I'm not judging you if you enjoy it, though.

There's really a Pastor Dave. That's Pastor David Wallis of Church of the Straits in Mackinaw City. Of course, this thread in the story is fictional.

Lake Superior State University, my alma mater, does indeed have a stellar nursing program and LSSU is located in Sault Ste. Marie, Michigan. Thank you to the nursing department for answering my questions about my fictional nursing candidate, Rachel!

There is a real house that inspired Rachel's family's cottage, located on West Bluff on Mackinac Island, as well as another that inspired Jack's. They are both beautiful. Check out my Facebook author page and Pinterest accounts for images.

USMMA or the United State Merchant Marine Academy is a real institution. My husband graduated from USMMA with an engineering degree, like Jack. Candidates must receive recommendation letters from either their state representatives or senators to be considered and admitted. Fictional Jack would indeed have to be commissioned with the US Navy Reserves, like my hubs was, after graduation or fulfill the obligation in another manner.

On a sadder note, our world has changed in the past few years. From horrific worldwide pandemic to the War in Ukraine, is there anyone whose life has not been touched by "life as we know it"? You'll find this novel touches on a few of these topics. I like to think those hard topics are more like a dollop rather than even a sixteenth of a cup of ingredients for this story. If I wrote a story that included the full emotional impact of these hardships, it might be too hard to bear—being so fresh. My heroine, Rachel, has lost her beloved grandmother during the time of Covid. But Rachel has lost almost everything—like some others in our world.

In 2022, many things I referenced in the novel were true, including the Star Line ferry becoming stranded in icy conditions in the Straits of Mackinac, on April 5th. Over 144 people were rescued. Easter was late in 2022, happening on April 17th. Other actualities: some of the weather, Ukraine's ongoing war, Covid variants continuing, and difficulty in finding workers. In fact, in June, before my husband and I left for the Straits of Mackinac for a month's visit, our family all had Covid and it wasn't the first time we'd had it, either.

During the previous year, in 2021, the Omicron variant predominated and we lost many older adults. At the same time, Mackinac Island had more visitors than ever! Part of this was due to people not being able to travel to Canada or abroad. So, people took their vacations closer to home or at least within the USA. By 2022 that did calm down and island tourist traffic reverted to close to pre-pandemic levels.

During the time I wrote this novel, I had Coronavirus, an optic nerve bleed, Norovirus, flu and sinusitis with asthma flare, a suspected heart attack that wasn't (it was from my Rheumatoid Autoimmune Disease), a root canal and a crown, nearly choked to death but my hubs did Heimlich and saved me, plus some other health issues. Whew! But God is good, and He brought me through. I'm praying that my readers will be blessed by this story and these troubles have only been the devil coming against my writing ministry. If you are someone who is blessed by this Christian fiction story, I would love to hear from you, and how the Lord used this story to help you on your own faith journey. Those are my favorite stories to read!

Acknowledgements

Father God, You know I couldn't do anything without You especially after all the many illnesses while writing this novel. Thank you to Clark Pagels, my son—especially for brainstorming with me, and my husband, Jeff, for his support. Much appreciation to my critique partner, Kathleen L. Maher, for her early input. Thank you to Pegg Thomas for her editorial work shaping this manuscript up.

My amazing Beta readers: Tina St. Clair Rice and Gail Mundy—thank you for your thorough work, Melissa Henderson, Beverly Duell-Moore and Paula Shreckhise—great catches. Thank you also to my Advance Readers: Diana Flowers, Linda Sorensen, Teresa Mathews (especially for the late corrections and all your help!), Andrette Brown Herron, Robin Bunting, Anne Rightler, Melissa Main, Sherry Moe, Evelyn Foreman, Sonja Nishimoto, and Rebecca Tellez. Thank you to Early Readers: Wilani Wahl, Betti Mace, Connie Porter Saunders, and Linda Matson Thomas. Much gratitude to authors Melissa Main and Kay Moser who advance read the manuscript for endorsement.

Much appreciation to Tamara Tomac for feedback and Mary Jane Barnwell and for their support for my books set on Mackinac Island—always a blessing.

Merci to Carolyn May for allowing the use of her name and of her business's name and use as a fictional setting. My friend, Dr. Mary Svendsen, really is a licensed clinical psychologist and we previously shared an office in North Charleston. She sure keeps busy as a fictional therapist doing online appointments with my characters who are her clients!

I borrowed a number of other friends' and family member's names. Kareen is my cousin's first name. Kareen Williams Davis is the matriarch of our Williams' branch of the family. Sandi Browne is my cousin as is her daughter, Cassie Browne. Cassie actually does have her own design business, Sunflower Ally, which you can find on Facebook. Colton Byrnes is my son-in-law, not a landscaper and HGTV show star, and Cassandra is my daughter. I think they'll be happy to be together in this book—unlike in *Behind Love's Wall*!

Joy Ellis is not a bank manager, but my friend here in Virginia and a reader/reviewer/blogger. Andrette Brown Herron is a reader/reviewer and my Facebook friend. Juan Pablo is named for the child, now a young man, who I sponsored in Colombia, through Compassion International.

Kudos to the Addicted to Mackinac Island Facebook group which is a great place to hang out and learn more about the island! Thank you to the administrators Linda Sorensen and John Hubel, too, for their hard work. Thanks also to Linda Sorensen for letting me borrow her name and include her character in this book, and for becoming my dear friend. John Hubel for his advice about locks on Mackinac Island historic cottages.

Thank you to the Avid Christian Fiction Readers Facebook group for your support, especially author and administrator, Martha Artyomenko, who does so much for the Christian Fiction community.

Bio

Carrie Fancett Pagels, Ph.D., is the multi-award-winning author of over twenty-five Christian fiction books, including ECPA and Amazon bestsellers. Twenty-five years as a psychologist didn't "cure" her overactive imagination! Born a Yooper, she loves to spend part of her summers at the Straits of Mackinac, where many of her novels are set!

Social Media: Be sure to check out Carrie's Pinterest pages, with images associated with her books—including this one! You can also find Carrie online on her Facebook author page, Twitter, goodreads, Instagram, Bookbub, LinkedIn, and on her Amazon author page. Carrie also has videos on Youtube of her reading sections of some of her books. You can also contact Carrie on her Contact page on her website www.CarrieFancettPagels.com.

Mackinac Cottages Series – Book 1

Selah Awards Winner Second Place in Women's Fiction
Life-changing journeys begin when three generations of women unexpectedly spend a summer at the family's Straits of Mackinac cottage. Blurb: Three generations of women unexpectedly head out to the family's cottage at the Straits of Mackinac for a small-town Michigan summer together. Jaycie begins an archeology internship on Mackinac Island. Her mother, Tamara, takes a break from teaching kindergarteners. And her grandmother, Dawn, struggles with a decision to sell her successful travel agency and possibly retire. Each has her own journey to pursue during this short respite time from "normal" life. One of them has a secret that will change all of their lives. Can she make this one special summer to remember or will all be devastated? Faith for family and friends will be tested, with some finally able to put the past behind them and begin anew. (Set in 2018, pre-Pandemic.)

Associated Novel

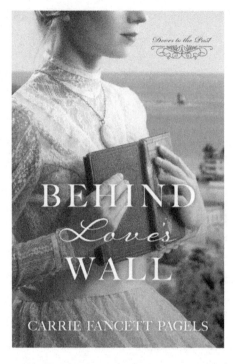

Behind Love's Wall novel (Barbour, November 2021, Oasis Audio, 2023) is part of Barbour Publishing's Doors to the Past Series but is also an associated story for the Mackinac Cottages series.

In the 2020 part of the novel, modern-day characters include some from the Mackinac Cottages Series Book 1 - *Butterfly Cottage* and Book 2 - *Lilac Cottage*.

**If you enjoyed this novel,
a review is always
very much appreciated!!!**

Made in United States
Orlando, FL
01 August 2023

35634294R00153